Ray Crowther was born in London and now
He read Cybernetics and Mathematics at Rea
variety of systems development positions in England and Germany
starting his own company, which specializes in human resources software.
The company continues to thrive although Ray has reduced his involvement
to concentrate on his writing.

The Nearest FarAway Place is his first novel and the second, *Panglossian,*
will be published at the end of 2001.

He connects the achievements in his life to running - running a successful
company; running around after his two daughters; and running the London
Marathon.

He lists his interests as armchair support of most sports, rallying, jogging
(when most of his fiction ideas evolve), personal computing, the Internet and
intellectual games.

The Nearest FarAway Place

Ray Crowther

Published by Panglossian Books

The Nearest FarAway Place

Published by Panglossian Books

ISBN: 0-9541110-0-1

Cover photographs by Ray Crowther
Cover Design by Peter Rymill

Printed and bound by Antony Rowe Limited, Eastbourne

Panglossian Books
Ivydene
Ulting Road
Hatfield Peverel
Essex CM3 2LU
England

ACKNOWLEDGEMENTS

To my proofreaders: Christine Grover, Caroline Crowther, Rebecca Crowther, Robin Hernaman, Diane Hernaman, Sue Potter, Nigel Derbyshire, Cathy Logan, Dave Keable, Steve Tumbridge, Angela Tumbridge, Pam Rymill, Sue Laver and Tony Cook.

To those people who inspired the characters: Chris Towers, Don Grünbaum, Tony Cook, Peter Hayes, Angela Tumbridge and other nameless individuals.

To Pete Rymill for cover artwork. To Emma Jay for being blonde.

To Chris Towers for Fridays.

To my daughters: Caroline and Rebecca; and Mum and Dad, for their support and enthusiasm.

To Christine for her tolerance and patience while this novel was being written.

To those who helped with research, including Mike Dunion and Sandra Stops.

To all the John Smiths, David Browns and Michael Williams in the world, with the hope that quoting their name here will entice them to buy a copy of the book.

For the original Sarah

Part One

New Beginning

Chapter 1

Friday, March 5, 1999 – 4:45 p.m.

Carl Denham did not like travelling on the underground during the rush hour. The proximity of sweaty bodies pinned his arms to his sides, which bothered his back and untaxed brain. At that moment, having over two million pounds in his pocket was little compensation.

He tried to focus on his future wealth and plans, but his mind was swamped by thoughts of his current physical and mental distress.

Two million pounds ...

It was a mystery why standing for more than five minutes gave him so much lower back pain. Fast walking and running were fine, but being upright and stationary, or shuffling along in a pedestrian queue, promoted the suffering. There was nothing physically wrong with his back according to the three osteopaths he had consulted. They all agreed as if in collusion that age – hell, he was only thirty-three - and being predominantly deskbound was the source of his trouble. Back stretching exercises were the suggested cure, and heavy or awkward lifting was to be avoided. This advice he had heeded. But the dissuasion against the spinal stress of his beloved jogging he had ignored. Jogging provided the buzz to unwind from his mental exertions.

...The huge sum meant little to him; freedom from his workaholic life was the attraction ...

His sedentary and envious friends often asked him why he started jogging. It was a story he could relate with vigour and pride. He had always liked sport at school - in small doses. Gifted with strong legs, he had acquired a reputation for sprinting and kicking a ball very hard. Anything that required stamina, like cross-country running, he avoided. So, football initially became his favoured sport. His nomination as a centre forward came from bursts of pace and shooting power rather than his work rate or ball skill. At his school, Wednesday afternoon sport was regarded as curricular rather than particular, overseen rather than coached, thus his football abilities never developed beyond running faster and kicking harder. It was running that he enjoyed most, and after proving his speed by sprinting at County level, he had drifted into an athletic vacuum for about ten years. Yet, despite the lack of exercise, he had not vegetated. The calorie-burning effort of directing a company and a careful diet had ensured that his 1.82 metres height and stable 76 kilos weight – or six feet and twelve stone in old money – had kept him acceptably proportioned.

...Freedom to discover the reason for his underlying sadness that had prevailed for the last ten years ...

In a cavalier moment about five years ago, he had been invited to join his business partner Mike Stanford and wife Lisa at a family fun day organized by Lisa's employer. When it came to the male guests' hundred-metre dash, Carl could not resist the temptation to revive the former glories of his sprinting past. He was leading at fifty metres when his unpractised hamstring gave up and brought about a spectacular head over heels accident. After four weeks of limping during the healing process, he vowed that he would never succumb to such embarrassment again, and a course of regular (leg) exercise was self-imposed. He had played squash occasionally in recent years, but long working hours, a shortage of playing partners and an even greater shortage of cash (thanks mostly to his ex-wife) had led him to embark on a more economic and less fastidious form of sport - jogging. He well remembered the early days of distance progression. A quarter of a mile and he was shattered. Then a half a mile, and one month after his jogging debut he broke through the mile barrier. From then on, it became easier, enjoyable and ultimately addictive. Two London Marathons and a handful of other long distance events had been his peak. Now, a gap of more than a few days without pounding the local roads and parks would make him tetchy and dejected, and that was how he felt now.

...A distant event that had eventually driven him to a preoccupation with work to the exclusion of other things ...

The extraordinary work pressure of recent weeks – even by his standards - had played havoc with his physical fix schedule. Jogging tonight was going to be a problem too if the back pain persisted and the developing headache took hold. The latter was almost certainly a delayed reaction to the champagne and red wine he had recently drunk at the celebration lunch at the solicitor's offices of Grant, Hernaman & Morris in Kensington. He doubted that Mike would suffer the same alcohol induced distress – he never did. Mike was still there, and might be for a while yet, despite Carl's subtle efforts to drag him away to the surprise party that Lisa had organized for him this evening. Once Mike was in a celebratory mood, it would take more than hints from his co-director to abandon his enthusiasm.

...Why, after all this time, had his thoughts returned to the source of his melancholy? ...

Marble Arch station - he could tolerate the physical pains for the remaining eight stops to Liverpool Street if he could concentrate his mind on something instead of standing there imitating a vertical sardine. In the briefcase precariously balanced between his black shoes he had an Internet commerce tome, which he was eager to read. He made a habit of always carrying absorbing reading material in case there was ever the danger of being caught, like now, in a noetic limbo. Since he started MicaCom Software he had always been forearmed with technical literature for those situations that stifled the mind: a dentist's waiting room; the queue to a supermarket checkout; being stuck in a traffic jam; waiting for a train to arrive – all these periods of potential dead time had to be exploited to the full.

...Of course, the takeover of his company had been the catalyst to unearth the images of the past ...

Attempting to extricate his book now would undoubtedly be a hazardous exercise. The inkling of a smile touched his face as he imagined bending down to his briefcase and causing a passenger domino effect of flailing arms and legs through the railway carriage. Even if he could gain his prize without inflicting injuries on his fellow passengers, his restricted movement would never have allowed him to turn the pages. He smiled again as he thought of inventing a page-turner that could be nose-operated. Anyway, he rapidly dismissed any thoughts of implementing his reading plan in such a confined, noisy environment. He preferred solitude, quiet and avoidance of prying eyes when ingesting technical information.

...Without the preoccupation of work to distract him, it was inevitable that Sarah would consume his thoughts again ...

His eyes moved through the carriage looking for something else to occupy his mind. Physiognomy was not satisfying and he knew every station on the Central line from West Ruislip to Epping without having to study the eye-level map. Usually he avoided the adverts, although he spotted something that could occupy a few moments - *If you can solve this puzzle within 30 seconds, you could become a member of Mensa*. The problem held an attraction, but there was a déjà vu feeling about it that seemed connected to his plans for the future. He had done this puzzle before and without studying the question fully, he immediately knew the answer. So much for keeping his mind active.

...Where was she? What was she doing? Why had she rejected him? ...

With a minor bodily reorganisation and some evil glances from his immediate co-travellers, he reached into the inside pocket of his suit jacket and fingered the (reward) culmination of his focused efforts of the last ten years. A slim plain white envelope containing a few legally phrased pages and a banker's cheque for a seven-figure sum dated next Friday. He had an urge to examine the small paper rectangle that could confirm his sudden and unexpected wealth. Instead, with now seven stations to his destination, and so many inquisitive travellers close by, he chose to reflect on the defining events of the previous eight weeks.

Chapter 2

Friday, January 8, 1999 – 11:00 a.m.

'You're not going to believe who just phoned me,' Mike called out, as he noticed Carl shuffling wearily towards his office at eleven o'clock. Mike followed him.

Carl dropped his briefcase, sat down at his desk and took a swig from the mug of strong tea he had just made. He did not like being confronted with surprises first thing in his morning, Mike should have known better. Over the last ten years Mike had got to know his quirks backwards, forwards, inside, outside more than anyone; disturbing him before he had finished his first brew of the day was punishable by death, or worse, like suffering a feisty Technical Director for the rest of the day. The always impeccably dressed, early rising, Managing Director of MicaCom stood hesitantly in the doorway; he must have suddenly realized this was usually a bad time. Mike was the same age – give or take a month; bespectacled; slightly shorter but heavier – a likely by-product of an obsessive love of beer; and his hair a lighter brown. There was inherent trust between them and a mutual respect that had evolved in their working lives together. In business there were no secrets, though Carl had an historical personal confidence that he would share with Mike when the time was right; and he was convinced that Mike had at least one mysterious amourette that he was vague about.

Through bleary blue eyes he said, 'Sorry Mike, what did you say?'

Mike obviously thought that because his partner had spoken it was an invitation to cross the threshold. 'You're not going to believe who just phoned me,' Mike repeated.

'Susan, asking you for a date?' He had a cheeky grin on his face, and was referring to yesterday's news that one of their ex-engineers had recently had a sex change.

'Now don't start that again,' Mike said with a touch of embarrassment and annoyance at the same time. He pulled up a chair and sat down.

'Hold on. It was a joke. I meant sissy Mark - now Susan, not your secret telephone lover,' Carl qualified.

'Oh no, George Fellgate, the Chairman and Managing Director of BinaryByte Software. You remember. We met him at the Internet Commerce seminar before Christmas,' Mike said, clearly glad to get off the Susan subject.

'The grey-haired bloke, who spent all lunch time pumping us about how the business was doing?' Carl asked, now more concerned with logging into his computer.

'Yes. George said then that we ought to get together sometime and talk about how we could help each other in the future. Well, he's invited us over for the day next Thursday,' Mike said excitedly.

'Us? I don't want to share a meal with that poser. He pissed me off by going on and on about the new Ferrari he had just bought.' Cars were a source of negative status to Carl. He did little travelling, and was content with his reliable, six-year-old BMW 316. 'I'm sure his biased idea of helping each other is to find out why Protean always seems to beat his MBridge product whenever we are in competition on a deal.'

'He as good as admitted that he was worried about the attraction of our current product. But he was more concerned with the release of Protean V,' Mike said.

'What? You told him about Protean V?' Carl gasped, giving Mike his full attention now that his computer was waiting for instructions.

'No, of course not. He already knew.' Mike said calmly. 'There are very few secrets in our industry. Anyway, our marketing and sales departments are bound to have leaked a few tit-bits to potential customers to try to psyche out the opposition. It's obviously got back to him and had the desired effect.'

'I guessed that, but even our staff don't know the details yet - only you, me and some of the trusted programmers,' Carl argued.

'I'm sure he doesn't know the *details*, but he certainly wants to know, and is willing to pay for the privilege. That's why he wants you to meet his technical staff.'

'Pay? You mean a take-over – buy us out?'

'Well his actual words were "If you can't beat them, buy them", in that patronizing voice of his.'

'And you entertained that?'

'Why not? What have we got to lose? We said two years ago that when Protean V was launched there would never be a better time to cash in on our success, become rich and do all the things we haven't had time to do over the last ten years.' Mike leaned across the desk in a gesture of enthusiasm.

Carl had had similar discussions with Mike before. In the last year there had been several tentative approaches from commercial predators and Mike had enthusiastically greeted them; to-date none had come to anything. Mike had always been cute in dealing with these situations; he knew what MicaCom was worth to the nearest pound but was always trying to wring out a few extra pence worth from a buyer. Secretly Carl thought that like himself, Mike did not really want to sell the company, yet. This time however, he seemed a bit more passionate than usual.

'If he's serious and not just spying us out. In any case we won't ship Protean V for another two months yet. Wouldn't it be better to wait a year until the revenue from it makes us irresistible to purchase?'

'Maybe, but George seems to be in a great hurry to try to conclude a deal. That gives us a psychological advantage when it comes to price. Besides, we're already on a high even without Protean V. We have record sales, more profit than we know what to do with, and we've had some great press feature articles recently about our products and us. I'm getting bored and want a crack at something else. And I think it's time that you sought the peace of mind you've been promising yourself. You deserve a break. Bloody hell, you need a break. Take a look at yourself. I suppose you were up half the night again, testing and re-testing your latest Protean baby. The product's fucking brilliant. It's ready, now. Let it go. You're too much of a perfectionist. Christ, we're paying the technical staff a fortune in salaries, let them get their hands dirty for once.'

'It's being a perfectionist that's got us where we are today.' Carl said, looking hurt by Mike's lecture.

'OK, I'm sorry. Without your money and foresight when we started this business and the hours you've put in God knows what I would have been doing today. But what do you have to show for it? A failed marriage. You're a good-looking guy with no social or sex life, and you've wrapped yourself up in your work - just work, all because of something that happened years ago – the *only thing* you've never been able to confide in me. Sure, I've reaped the benefits of your solitude and efforts, but you never wanted it any other way. You've dedicated yourself to MicaCom for so long now that I think you're scared to face life outside. Believe me, I have a good feeling about selling out now, and I know we won't regret it.'

'All right, arrange the meeting,' Carl replied reluctantly, eager to get off the subject. He had discovered a few teething problems with Protean V in the early hours of the morning and was impatient to kick the arses of the responsible programmers.

Mike looked at Carl suspiciously. 'We have to be in accord on this, you don't sound too enamoured with the idea.'

'You know I'm not at my best after an all night Protean session. I suppose there's no harm in going through the motions with BinaryByte. Let's see what happens,' Carl said.

The response seemed to satisfy Mike who had an unusual bounce in his stride as he left Carl's office.

Carl reached for his tea and cursed that it had cooled already. He would make a fresh mug soon and then vent his pent-up frustration on the programmers that had dared to taint his software creation with some bugs. First, he accessed his e-mail and was hit with a flood of messages from the software team. Plenty of technical problems to take his mind off the recent conversation, he thought, but the conversation with Mike nagged at him. Perhaps Mike was right; maybe it was time to get out. Time to get a life – or revisit an earlier one. He had sheltered himself in MicaCom for too long.

He knew how Mike would cope with wealth and unemployment. Ever since he had told Mike about his year in the States before starting MicaCom, Mike had held a long ambition to spend months touring America. He would use the trip to re-charge his enthusiasm, identify an evolving business opportunity, and then import the idea into the U.K. He was a great believer that all worthwhile endeavours started on the other side of the Atlantic. Mike, with his entrepreneurial instinct, would invest his MicaCom proceeds in the new venture and undoubtedly make a fortune all over again.

For Carl, it was not so straightforward. He knew that with freedom he would set out on a mission that would have a high emotional risk associated with it. Needing to express outcomes mathematically, he rated the odds of his success with a probability of about 0.01 - a one in a hundred chance. Success or failure, eventually he would need to exercise his mind in a gainful way. The likely proceeds from the sale of MicaCom - after tax, even with a generous offer from BinaryByte, would not last him for the rest of his life. His state of mind after his mission would dictate exactly what he attempted.

A new e-mail popped-up on Carl's screen and disturbed his thoughts.

```
BinaryByte meeting next Thursday morning at their HQ in
Cambridge. Wear a suit!
```

He was more annoyed with Mike's habit of sending him e-mails from his office next door – echoing his practice of putting everything in writing - rather than the content of the message. His reference to a suit made fun of the fact that he and his technical staff usually dressed in jeans and T-shirts, much to the irritation of the rest of the company. There was a harmony between him and Mike about office conduct and practices, but this issue had been a major source of disagreement between them a few years ago. Over a period of time it had been proven, to Mike's satisfaction, that the freakier a programmer looked and behaved, the better he would perform his duties. However, when it came to meetings with customers and people he needed to impress, he kow-towed to expected business conduct. He made a mental note to retrieve his little used suit from the back of his wardrobe and drop it into the dry cleaners.

* * *

Carl and Mike rose at seven o'clock for an early breakfast and another rehearsal of their stance at the BinaryByte meeting three hours away.

Despite the short distance from Chelmsford to Cambridge, they had driven up the night before in Mike's Porsche Coupé and had stayed at the University Arms Hotel in the city centre, so that they would be fresh for the day. Eager to impress the audience that would await them, Mike had insisted on using his silver, top-of-the-range prestige car rather than Carl's "clapped-out shopping car", as he called it.

Mike had been uncontrollably busy during the previous week talking to the company accountants and solicitors. He had been going through the financial motions of valuing MicaCom's business and preparing various draft contracts and agreements to secure their future. It was clear to Carl that Mike's original conversation with George Fellgate must have had some depth to it that Mike was keeping to himself.

They had spent the previous evening reminiscing about the early days of the company as though their disassociation from it was a foregone conclusion. He had not seen Mike so pumped up for a long time. Mike loved negotiating and he was word and number perfect about what would undoubtedly be the biggest deal he had ever made.

Carl on the contrary was depressed for two reasons. First, he had been reflecting on the last time that he had been in Cambridge – eleven years ago, and was finding it difficult to shut out the events of that distant time; second, was his concern for the future of his software efforts. He had brought the latest version of Protean with him on a CD, but privately wanted to avoid having to show it to anyone, let alone a competitor. Protean was like a son he had never had and he was a doting father. He likened the coming meeting to an encounter with social services who were about to examine his parenthood with a view to snatching away his offspring for a more deserving family.

In the hotel lounge after breakfast, this analogy was still playing through his mind.

'We have to be positive about the meeting today,' Mike said.

He knew Mike had wanted to say *you* rather than we, he had obviously detected his downbeat attitude towards the event.

'I know,' he said, 'It's just that it seems a bit one-sided. We have to reveal everything about our company and products, and if we don't conclude a deal, BinaryByte will have some valuable commercial information to use against us.'

'We *will* strike a deal. George Fellgate is hungrier than ever to acquire MicaCom. And we'll get a good price. You knock them out with Protean V and leave the finances to me.'

'I still don't understand why George is *so* keen. It weakens his position. Have you carried out a company search on BinaryByte recently?' Carl asked.

'Yes. According to their last published accounts, they're financially strong; cash rich with no bank loans. Our accountants did some backdoor investigation too and they came out clean. Don't worry.'

There were plenty of empty places as Mike gently manoeuvred his Porsche to be as close as possible to the main entrance of the BinaryByte offices on the Cambridge Science Park. The freezing weather and the fall of snow overnight had left the car park in a dangerous and slippery state.

'Nice offices,' Carl said, surveying the modern two-storey building. 'How many employees do they have?'

'As of two weeks ago, fifty-five. Forty of them are permanently based here - the remainder are out-workers in various parts of the UK.'

'I'm impressed with your knowledge. You have done your homework. There aren't many cars here though.'

Safely parked, Mike switched off the engine. 'There are three reasons for that. First, there is a regular bus service to the Science Park and BinaryByte is a *Green* company. It financially encourages its staff to use public transport rather than private cars. Second, they run a flexitime scheme. The core part of the day when the employees need to be present is 10:30 to 16:00. And lastly, I should think today's weather has played a part too.'

'Anyone would think we are trying to take-over BinaryByte with the level of detail you've gone into.'

'Well, the major objective is to get a decent price for MicaCom. But I do have a conscience regarding how it might affect our own employees. We'll have to announce the news to them as soon as we have agreed terms and they are bound to ask a lot of questions. We should be in a position to be able to answer most of them. No doubt BinaryByte will want to impose its own culture on the staff they inherit.'

They stepped out of the car and tiptoed through some slush until they got to the snow-cleared entrance. Mike was carrying a heavy black leather briefcase stuffed with paperwork. By contrast, Carl ported a slim folder containing three CDs and a few sheets of paper. As they approached the glass fronted doors they automatically separated and striding towards them with his hand outstretched was George Fellgate. Two other men held back and looked on apprehensively.

'I saw you arrive. Good to see you both again. Sorry about the weather. Welcome to BinaryByte, Carl,' George said as he beelined towards Carl and shook his hand.

Carl was taken aback. He had only met George once before and that was briefly during a buffet lunch at a seminar - yet he greeted him like an old friend. Carl would have expected him to acknowledge Mike first, particularly as he knew they had spoken frequently during the last week. Perhaps this was a form of political politeness. George only looked vaguely familiar. Carl certainly would not have recognized him again without an introduction. He was older than he remembered, probably late-fifties. Tall, slim and upright, he wore a light brown suit, which co-ordinated well with the colour of his remaining hair. His friendly face belied the true age portrayed by his creased features.

George then received Mike and introduced him and Carl to his retinue. Tony Cookson, a technical guru who was to oversee the assessment of Protean and Pete Hayden who, if all went to plan, was George's nominee to manage the MicaCom subsidiary. Both were clothed in similar navy blue suits but there the similarity ended. Pete was tall and slim. He had a wide smile on a smooth, symmetrical, ruddy face. The pinkness extended into a bald crown sandwiched between curtains of black hair. With appropriate attire, Carl considered he could pass comfortably as a vicar.

Tony was the antithesis of Pete. He was short and stocky. His hair was black too but there were no signs of alopecia. The most striking feature was his face – craggy, uneven, unsmiling with a flat nose. He appeared more like a boxer than a software wizard.

George, with Pete in tow, whisked Mike away to his office, promising to meet up with Tony and Carl later for lunch. Tony escorted Carl to a separate meeting room, so that he could prepare a PC for a demonstration of Protean to the senior development staff.

The lunch reunion never took place due to everyone's concentration on their respective meetings, so secretaries were despatched to fetch sandwiches and soft drinks.

Eventually at four o'clock Tony and Carl made their way to George's office where the other gathering seemed to have concluded.

'We were wondering if you'd finished,' George said. 'What do you think of Protean V Tony?'

'It has a few rough edges in my opinion, and is a bit lacking in comparison to MBridge, but nothing we can't correct and improve on,' Tony replied.

Everyone glared at Tony. George and Pete for lack of diplomacy, Mike and Carl for disbelief in what he had said.

Pete could not resist a jibe. 'Just because MBridge is on version ten doesn't mean that it is twice as good as Protean. More likely that you've taken twice as long to get MBridge working properly.'

The room was quiet for a few moments, and then, as the red-faced Tony was about to respond, George recovered the situation. 'Well, we seem to have the basis of an agreement,' he said glancing at Mike. 'We need to exchange our respective understandings of the details and then leave it to the legal boys to draw up the contracts.'

Carl looked at Mike for reassurance and thought he caught the inkling of smile aimed his way.

'Mike would like to head back south now that it's snowing again, so I think we'll call it a day.'

Handshakes were exchanged and George motioned for his BinaryByte colleagues to leave too. Tony in particular was purposely holding back. As Pete was about to close the door after him, George called out.

'Carl, can I have a quick word?' The exodus paused and started to do a U-turn until George added, 'In Private. 'I won't keep him long,' he said for Mike's benefit.

Bemused, Carl followed George back into his office and sat down in one of the red leather chairs that circled an antique-looking coffee table.

'Have you thought what you will do after MicaCom?' George asked.

'I'm not sure I can answer that without knowing the details of your discussion with Mike,' Carl replied wondering if he was about to be offered a job at BinaryByte.

'I'm sorry; I wasn't trying to compromise you. Assume that on acquisition you no longer have anything to do with Protean, MicaCom and BinaryByte, and have sufficient money to never *have to* work again.'

Carl wasn't sure whether George was trying to bait him in some way. Although the question seemed innocuous enough, anything he might say could perhaps jeopardize what Mike had negotiated. He decided to play a stalling game. 'I need to know why you are asking such a question in private.'

'I understand this is awkward and please believe me I'm not trying to trap you. All I can say is that one of my investors has an interest in your well-being post-MicaCom.'

Carl was still uncomfortable with the question and had no intention of telling him the truth. That might beg more questions, which he certainly did not want to answer. And who was this mysterious investor? He settled on another stall. 'I presume you can't tell me who this investor might be?'

'Unfortunately, no. I've been asked to withhold their identity,' George said.

'And can you tell me why they are interested in my welfare?'

'I really don't know. That part is a mystery to me too.'

'Does my answer influence your purchasing arrangements of MicaCom?'

'No. Not at all.'

'Actually, I can't provide you with a definitive answer. I'll invest the majority of my proceeds from the MicaCom sale. Take a long break like Mike and dwell on what to do next. I'll probably visit my parents in America.'

'OK, thanks for that. No doubt the anonymous person will reveal themselves and their reasons to you in due course.'

'I hope so. I don't like mysteries when they involve me. I've suffered from them in the past,' Carl reflected.

They said their goodbyes again and Carl joined Mike who was waiting in the reception area.

'What was that all about?' Mike asked.

'Let's get on our way and then we can swap stories,' Carl answered.

They walked carefully to the car. It felt bitterly cold and the car park surface was glassy. They headed west on the A14, preferring the main roads rather than going through the City Centre with the adverse weather conditions. With the heater on full blast, they were soon comfortably cocooned in the Porsche.

Mike was smirking when he started his debriefing. 'The deal is very simple. BinaryByte have offered to purchase MicaCom outright with a clean break from existing shareholders. In other words, you and I sell our shares and resign from MicaCom one week after the sale. There will be no retention of our services beyond that final week – we disappear and have nothing to do with MicaCom or BinaryByte ever again. Tony and Pete will take over the running of MicaCom in that last week during which we must be available at their beck and call to answer any final questions about the company. I should receive a formal Letter of Intent confirming the details tomorrow.

'The target date for signing of contracts is Friday, March 5. In exchange for our signatures, one week resignation letters and a signed covenant that we will not join or start a similar company in the next two years, we will be given a banker's draft, encashable on March 12.'

Carl had sat patiently storing the details but could not contain himself any longer with the ultimate question. 'How much?'

Mike was enjoying himself extending the tension a little longer. 'I need to supply some further documents yet about contracted customers and next week we will be descended upon by a team of accountants for the due diligence process. Subject to no adverse findings, the value of the banker's drafts will be …' Mike paused for effect just as he joined the queue to get on to the M11. He continued, 'Shit, I thought we would avoid traffic coming this way,' and looked exasperated at the volume of cars in front of him.

'Will be?' Carl prompted.

'Sorry, lost my thread for a moment. What was I talking about?' Mike said but his previously serious face dissolved in a bout of laughter.

'You teasing bastard. For Christ's sake put me out of my misery,' Carl squealed.

'£2,100,000,' Mike said.

Carl was quiet for a moment. He implicitly trusted Mike's judgement when it came to company finances, but the figure he had heard was not just disappointing, it was daylight robbery. Surely MicaCom was worth more than that – perhaps somewhere between 2.5 and 3 million.

Mike guessed what was going through Carl's mind, then added 'Each,' and he laughed again.

'Each?' Carl exclaimed.

'Each,' Mike confirmed. 'Until the taxman takes his slice you're going to be a millionaire twice over.'

'But … that's … fucking incredible. Whose wife have you got to sleep with to get that?'

'Just my own, no strings attached.'

'I thought you said you would go in high at 3.5 million?'

'I did, but I tried a bluff. I said that we wanted some BinaryByte equity and a service contract for two years.'

'That was a risk. We agreed we only wanted to have a clean break.'

'I know, but I calculated that the equity request would be a stumbling block which would have to be compensated by a higher price. It was, but the idea of a service contract was the frightener. A key issue from George's viewpoint was that we had no further involvement with MicaCom. We eventually agreed that no equity and no service contracts was worth one million pounds on top of the negotiated price of 3.2 million.'

'So say it to me again, slowly. What will the figures on my cheque show?'

'2-1-0-0-0-0-0'

'Can they afford that much?'

'BinaryByte has cash, the shareholders are putting in some money and a modest, secured bank loan will cover it.'

'Shareholders? Didn't you say that George and his wife own all the shares?'

'He was a bit vague about that. The company records show that G and S Fellgate own fifty percent of the shares each. He hinted that after the purchase of MicaCom he would begin preparations for a stock market listing, his co-owner's shares, presumably held by his wife Samantha, would be sold on the open market. What do we care how he funds the purchase so long as we get what he's promised. Now tell me about your private audience with George.'

Carl recited the conversation he had had with George.

'The mysterious investor must be linked to what I said about Samantha selling her shares. Who are you cosseted by that would consider investing in BinaryByte?'

'I've absolutely no idea. My parents are the only people that come to mind who would want to monitor my welfare. I ruled them out because I haven't told them yet about selling MicaCom, and they know nothing about the software industry.'

'Well you must have a secret, rich admirer somewhere on the planet. When you find him or her perhaps you could introduce me?'

Carl dwelt again on this enigma – briefly. His thoughts kept returning to, not the massive wealth he would acquire on March 12, but the fact that in five weeks he would be relieved of any company responsibilities and a week later he would be free. Free, possibly, to unlock his long-standing, deep-rooted unhappiness. As tempting as it was to start his search immediately, he owed it to himself to give Protean his best shot in the remaining time, so that he would feel proud with the legacy he would leave behind. He could be patient for six more weeks after waiting eleven years.

'How did you get on with Tony?' Mike said, intruding on Carl's thoughts.

'That guy is a total arsehole. The rest of the audience were polite, complimentary and asked constructive questions. I obviously didn't give too much away at this stage, but I had some useful discussions with the development staff. They are quite a friendly bunch and for programmers they are quite normal. Reading between the lines, I think they have a low opinion of Tony too. Tony spent the whole day nit-picking faults with Protean and pissing off everyone. A couple of times I had to hold myself back from hitting the bastard. It was a depressing reality to know that he will be looking after the development of Protean in the future.'

'So what do you want - two million or Protean?'

'Freedom above all, which sadly means no Protean and the two million might come in handy.'

* * *

As expected, February was a hectic month for Carl and Mike, albeit in different ways.

Carl immersed himself even deeper into the subtleties of Protean. He tuned the product to perfection and made some minor changes based upon the positive feedback from the BinaryByte development staff. His driving force was to finally spawn a product that would leave him intellectually satisfied. A product that was so perfect, at least in his eyes, that the usurpers from BinaryByte would be loath to change it, so that the legacy of Carl Denham lived beyond his departure for as long as possible. With his new life pending, he also wanted to ensure that his post-MicaCom mind was unencumbered with thoughts of refinements to Protean that he never had time to finish.

For Mike the month had comprised figures with accountants and contracts with solicitors - during work, and organizing an extensive tour of North America - during play. It had been a long held ambition to fly to New York, hire a campervan and, via a meandering route spanning from the east coast to the west coast, eventually arrive in San Francisco before flying home. He hoped that after three months of avant-garde culture he would be motivated and stimulated to reap new pastures in the British business community.

In the second week of February the take-over was announced to the staff – it had to be, because rumours had begun to spread. Despite assurances from Mike and Carl that the acquisition was a positive way forward for Protean and MicaCom, the employees were split about their employment security. The programmers, customer services staff and salesmen thought they would be indispensable, but the marketing and admin staff felt vulnerable. It was impossible for the existing directors to speculate about any rationalisation plans that BinaryByte might have and the more insecure workers began to seek alternative employers.

By the end of the month, the details of the transfer to BinaryByte had been formalized, verified and all loopholes sealed – on March 5, Mike and Carl would relinquish control of MicaCom forever.

Chapter 3

Friday, March 5, 1999 – 5:15 p.m.

Liverpool Street Station - at last. *Time to stretch my legs and ease my back*, thought Carl, as he quickly threaded his way through the throng of commuters, all probably heading for the same eastbound main line train.

Sure enough, a stream of briefcase-clutching suits was descending upon the 17:30 departure to Ipswich, which would deposit him at Chelmsford. At least he had purchased a first-class ticket that morning in anticipation of a homeward crush. He chose a carriage half way along the train and was grateful his foresight had worked - plenty of spare seats available, and settled in one by a window. His painful back almost uttered words of relief.

Opposite was a distinguished bespectacled grey man. Grey hair, suit, tie and shoes. Carl guessed, about fifty. The man was engrossed in a journal resting on his rectangular, not grey, but black briefcase and shaking his head in dismay as he made notes in the margin.

Carl balanced his briefcase on his knee, extracted his prize *Techniques of Internet Commerce*, turned to his bookmarked page and let his brain take over.

He was vaguely aware of someone taking the seat next to the grey man and then heard a voice calling his name.

'Hello. Carl isn't it? What brought you to the Smoke?'

Damn, I've just got to a good bit, he thought. The voice was unfamiliar. So was the face when he looked up.

The arrivee detected his uncertainty and said 'Chris Farley … Mike's neighbour.'

Technically, neighbour was correct. He lived about a quarter of a mile from Mike, but Mike's house was out in the sticks, surrounded by a huge garden then farmland as far as the eye could see. A golfing partner too.

'Oh, hi. Just a bit of business in town,' Carl said, not particularly wanting to air the details of the day in public.

'How about that boss of yours; making a killing selling his company? Have you still got a job? Will you be at the celebration tonight?' Chris said very loudly. The eyes of fellow passengers looked towards Carl for his reply.

He remembered he had met Chris last July when Mike had organized a party for Lisa's thirtieth birthday - quite a grand affair with a marquee in the garden. Chris was a know-all, but knows nothing kind of guy, and at the party Carl had had the misfortune to choose to engage him in conversation on the subjects of computers and motor racing. For all Chris knew, Windows were to let the light in and Formula 1 was a hairspray, and he was apparently an *executive* in international banking. Chris had assumed that he was one of Mike's employees. Carl saw no reason to enlighten him.

'No and No,' Carl said bluntly.

Chris was clearly embarrassed and looked relieved when someone else that he knew took the seat opposite him.

Carl went back to his book. He was getting into it now. It was a subject that interested him enormously, but one that had no practical use at MicaCom. Some time in the future he might want to get his hands dirty again and what he was reading now could fit the bill. He leaned back in his seat to digest the information he had just scanned. It was then that he noticed the grey man was looking at him. He caught his eye.

'You know about that stuff, do you?' he said nodding to the book in front of Carl.

'A little, but I'll be an expert by the end of the journey.' Carl joked.

'I wish I could. I'm the proverbial old dog. Maurice Patient's my name.'

'Pleased to meet you. Carl Denham.'

They shook hands awkwardly across the aisle. Carl did not usually make friendships so easily, but he was immediately comfortable with Maurice.

'You have an interest in Internet commerce?' Carl asked.

'Technically no, but I do have a project that could benefit from it,' Maurice said.

For the rest of the journey Carl and Maurice were deep in conversation, exchanging backgrounds and ideas. They were discussing some commercially sensitive material so kept their voices low, much to the displeasure of the nosy Farley. Carl was disappointed when he reached his destination since Maurice was onward bound to Ipswich, so they simply exchanged phone numbers with vague promises to call each other.

It was a fifteen-minute walk to the MicaCom office - about a mile at Carl's back-pain-preventative pace, but when he arrived, he decided to not go in, just collect his car. The final Protean modifications were complete – it was just paperwork now and that could wait until Monday. At half past six, there were still lights on in the office and other cars parked, but for once he felt no guilt about leaving his employees - or rather BinaryByte's employees, unsupervised in their subordinate efforts. He was sure they would manage without him.

Friday evenings were usually spent carrying out an audit on the development statistics at the office. It was a quiet time to check the week's progress on various project tasks, without being interrupted by the steady stream of in-house e-mails from the systems team. Friday night was deemed "P" night by the technical nerds of MicaCom and they were well departed by six o'clock. He recalled that the sequence went - piss-up, pull, pussy, poke, piss-off, pizza. Only once had he been tempted to join them and, from the little he remembered, he had invented a new "P" - pass-out, after only two hours of the piss-up stage. Nowadays he still sampled their mad ways, but only those that took place on office premises. Even then, he drew a limit at the smoking drugs. An occasional cigarette yes; but never the material that smelt like burning cat litter.

At his flat Carl could almost feel the gasp from the interior as he entered at such an early hour. He had owned the flat for nine years. Five minutes by car or twenty-five on foot from the office, it suited him well - small and in a reasonably quiet and accessible part of Springfield, an eastern district of Chelmsford. Springfield was a sprawling add-on to the town comprising a mixture of terraced, semi-detached and detached housing estates plus a scattering of two and three story apartment blocks. He had purchased a ground floor one bedroom flat in one of the latter, after he had donated his bungalow to his ex-wife.

At the time of purchase, with MicaCom just a year old and a divorce that consumed what little assets or money he had, Carl had struggled to put together a deposit for the property. A few years later, when MicaCom could afford to pay him a reasonable wage, he briefly thought about moving to a property more in keeping with his director status. In fact, Mike almost insisted on it (probably to relieve the guilt he felt for the huge house that he lived in), but Carl resisted the pressure. Moving house was stressful and time-consuming, besides he had everything he wanted for a modest bachelor life. It was the bachelor life he did not want – he wanted Sarah.

He was recalling the history of his flat as he slumped into an armchair after his milestone day and stimulating journey from Liverpool Street. He associated his flat strongly with MicaCom; it was merely an extension to his work office. He had probably spent as many hours here designing and building Protean as he had in Chelmsford. Now that MicaCom was no more, and he had an unlimited amount of money - at least as far as buying an ample property for two was concerned, it was time to think about moving on.

Tomorrow he would start that exercise. Tidy the flat first and then begin planning the mission that he should have persisted with eleven years ago.

Tonight, he just wanted to chill out. His lingering head and backache still conspired to hinder his jogging obsession. He would take a pill or two; divest himself of his unfamiliar suit; shower; prepare and consume a quick and simple meal; then for a change bury himself in some literary trivia. There was a stack of unread novels at his bedside, he would select one and disappear into an artificial world of fantasy - though he had a feeling that it would not be too long before he entered a fantasy world of his own.

Chapter 4

Saturday, March 6, 1999 – 9:00 a.m.

Carl had not spent his usual Saturday in the office working on Protean; it was not his to worry about anymore. Instead, after breakfast, he had started some long overdue spring-cleaning of his flat. It had seemed a compulsive thing to do, as though he had guests arriving or was embarking on a long journey - neither of which was true.

Cleaning a bedroom, kitchen, lounge and a bathroom would not have been a time-consuming task, but he kept getting sidetracked every time he came across an item of MicaCom memorabilia. The carbonised invoice book used in the company's first year; some photographs of himself and Mike on their first day in business together; several copies of the company accounts and numerous disks, tapes and CDs containing various archived versions of their early software products. Some of these things he was obliged to hand over to BinaryByte as part of the sale of MicaCom, so he had reluctantly and discourteously stacked them in an old printer box, ready to take to the office next week.

He had busied himself with this exercise for several hours but knew he could not put off the inevitable. He opened the lower drawer of his filing cabinet where he kept his personal records. Skipping past dividers labelled bank statements; savings accounts; mortgage; household bills and miscellaneous receipts; he rested at what appeared to be an empty file. Reaching in he knew he would find a single white envelope. He opened it and stared at a photograph he had not looked at for ten years, then moved towards a window to view it in the best possible light. He had taken it himself with a cheap disposable camera, and as photographs go it would not have won any competitions. But this was currently his most precious possession in the world; even more valuable to him than the contents of a very similar envelope he had been given yesterday at the solicitors.

The composition was simple. In the background, there were a few small trees and bushes blending into barely discernible marshlands, and the side of a stone building. He remembered it had been a warm September day, breezy, with a cloudless blue sky, although the brightness of the day and the limitations of the camera had rendered the sky a light grey. Slightly left of centre there was a twenty-year-old girl. The perspective showed that she was running towards the camera, playfully objecting to being photographed. She was wearing an oversized navy blue jumper and his University scarf that she had claimed as her own, arguing it suited her better than her own white and green variety. Not pictured, but he recalled she wore faded light blue jeans that day, and as usual her feet were unencumbered of shoes and socks. Her shoulder length blonde hair was scarcely disturbed by the breeze and one small gold earring reflected the bright light; but it was the spellbinding smile that made the photograph a masterpiece in his eyes. It was the only photograph he had left of Sarah; Janice had forced him to destroy the rest.

The photograph had been taken at the remotest and most tranquil place they could find within an hour's distance of Sarah's mother's house in Ilford. By chance, he had a car for that memorable weekend. He had had to visit a customer in Peterborough on the Friday and had used the Ford Sierra of his boss at Oxitel for the trip. Fortunately his boss was abroad on business and would not need the car until Monday, so he obtained permission to use it for a couple of days. It had been a small detour to collect Sarah from Cambridge on his way back from Peterborough. Best of all it avoided him or Sarah having to use trains to spend their weekend together. He had purchased the Ordnance Survey maps covering the Essex coast and with Sarah had spent part of Friday evening choosing where they would spend their Saturday. They had fun making a list of criteria for their idyllic trip and came up with a shortlist of locations. Eventually they had arrived at the place in the photograph.

This photograph was the only item he could produce as evidence of Sarah ever existing. The huge bundle of letters he had saved mysteriously went missing some time during his short marriage. Janice was obviously the perpetrator but he never accused her since at the time he was doing his utmost to forget about Sarah. How he wished now that he could read those letters again, if only to convince himself that there was more substance to his sorrow than a single photograph and fading memories. He went to his jacket and put the photograph in his wallet. He was thinking of the scarf when the phone rang. It was Mike.

'How did your celebration go?' Carl asked.

'Which one?' Mike laughed.

'Well, the BinaryByte one for a start.'

'You know, socially the BinaryByte guys are backward. All they wanted to do was talk about MicaCom. I tried desperately to lighten the conversation, but they were so guarded about their interests in life. George was a bit more forthcoming, but seemed obsessively interested in what we would be doing in seven days time. I got a bit uneasy about that, made my excuses and left for home,' Mike said.

It was not like Mike to miss out on some partying. 'He's probably worried we'll start all over again and begin nicking his customers when our restraint of trade document runs out in two years time,' Carl said.

'No, I don't think so. He now knows I'm taking a long holiday first, and even I don't know what you're going to do. Have you decided yet?' Mike had frequently asked him the same question over the last few weeks. Deep down Carl always knew the answer. It was only now that he was beginning to feel he could be more open with his intentions.

'Funny you should ask that. I've spent the morning tidying my flat and gathering together some nostalgia for my adventure.'

'Adventure? So, are you about to reveal all?' Mike prompted.

'Not just yet, there are still a few details - well in fact all details to resolve, but at least I've started on the plan. I'll tell you next week. What other celebrations did you have?' Carl asked innocently.

'Changing the subject again? Well, I went home, and Lisa immediately whisked me off to the golf club.'

Mike went on to describe the surprise party that had been organized for him. Carl knew about the party because Lisa had invited him and sworn him to secrecy. Lisa and Carl both knew he would not go, since Carl had always felt uncomfortable playing gooseberry to the superficially happy, affluent couples that Mike associated with, but Lisa had to go through the motions anyway. She also appreciated it was because of Carl's efforts that financially she could now hold court with the cream of the neighbourhood.

Carl became irritated with the call and after a few obviously disinterested acknowledgements to Mike's seemingly endless stories from the golf club; Mike got the message and made excuses to curtail the call.

The scarf.

He still had his University scarf that Sarah had left in the car on their last full weekend together. It was special because for years it had retained the scent of Sarah, a subtle blend of her natural fragrance and the lightest of perfumes that she wore. He had not worn it since. Instead, it was stored safely and obviously in a clear plastic bag on its own shelf in his wardrobe. As he opened the bag he realized the scarf was put there as a subconscious daily reminder of that magic past. He took the scarf and brushed it against his face. The scent had almost certainly receded by now, but his brain still reminded him of the intoxicating effect it used to have on him.

He suddenly felt foolish and, as Mike had predicted, scared. Foolish: because he was clinging to a past life, which he could probably never revisit. Scared: because for the first time in ten years, he had no way of controlling the outcome of his endeavours. What would really be achieved from seeing Sarah again? Their parting had been quite final as far as Sarah was concerned. She could be anywhere. If he did find her she could be infirm, happily married or even dead. And if none of these, would he merely open old wounds and slowly bleed to death as he had done since she spurned him? He could cope without Sarah's love, but his driving force was to discover the reason for the sudden rejection. Surely it was best to exorcise the bad times and just remember the affection and loving he had experienced. On the contrary, he was shortly to become a free man. No money worries, no responsibilities, no commitments but also no future, no focus, no contentment. If he did not try to find Sarah, then it would plague him for the rest of his life. Besides it would give him some sense of ambition, treat it as an adventure. Adventure: that was the way he had described it to Mike, and that's how he would deal with it.

He put the scarf back.

So where would he start? The most obvious source was her mother. Prior to going to Cambridge, Sarah had lived with her mother and older sister in Ilford, less than twenty miles away. Talking to her mother might bring a barrage of abuse, but one way or the other it might yield something of Sarah's whereabouts or status. He went to his computer to consult his electronic address book.

He had got used to the permanent hum of his computer - somehow it was comforting. He never switched it off because he was always frustrated how long it took to go through its start-up procedure. He just tapped the space bar on the keyboard and immediately his monitor sprang to life and demanded his password. Soon he had the required telephone number and was composing in his head what he might say to Sarah's mother when the phone rang again.

'Oh, you still live there then,' said a voice sarcastically, after he had recited the number.

'Hello Janice, what do you want?' he replied, predicting that this was not a call enquiring after his welfare.

'I thought you might have moved to some bloody great mansion somewhere and got your butler to take your calls, now that you can afford it.'

'What are you on about Janice, I'm really quite busy at the moment,' he said, knowing that as usual with Janice this was going to end up in a sparring contest.

'Well, a little bird told me that you've had a bit of a windfall, and I know that it always weighed on your conscience how you treated me. So … I just wondered whether you were feeling in the mood to atone some more for your past sins – financially that is.'

That was just typical of Janice he thought - blunt and as mercenary as ever. When they had divorced, he had given Janice his bungalow and a voluntary monthly allowance for five years, while she remained unmarried. They had started with solicitors, but negotiations had dragged on and the fees mounted up, so he had agreed to a more than generous full and final settlement; quite probably a lot more generous that even the solicitors would have concluded. He had forecast that it would not be too long before Janice found someone else, though presumably to spite him, she had skilfully avoided marriage as she went from lover to lover so that he continued to fund the allowance.

'And who might that little bird be spreading rumours?' he queried.

'Don't try to con me Carl. Paul told me all about the announcement of a take-over by BinaryByte. He reckons you're going to net at least £500,000 from the sale,' Janice lashed out.

'Ah, so Paul Westdene is your spy in my camp. Funny, I always thought he might be the sort of guy who would hang out with unscrupulous tarts,' he reacted in an unaccustomed fashion that could only be brought on by talking to Janice. He then added, 'And it's none of your fucking business anyway, I stopped being your sponsor five years ago. Isn't Brian giving you enough?'

'My dear, Brian is no more, but at least he could perform in bed, which is something you could never manage.'

He silently accepted his phrasing could have been better; he had been referring to money not sex, and this had been typically twisted to refer to their grounds for divorce. So now Brian had been kicked out, and he pitied Paul if he was the latest incumbent.

'Well? Are you going to help me out or are you planning to leave your fortune to that long lost bimbo of yours?' Janice said, continuing her venomous attack.

'I'll …', *fucking kill you, you bitch* immediately came to his mind, but he quickly found reserves of composure that he did not believe he had, '… call you', he eventually stuttered and put the phone down.

Now his passivity deserted him and he began to shake with anger. He thumped his fist on the desk and instantly regretted his action as the pain flowed up his fingers. Shaking his hand he went to the kitchen and opened the drawer where he stored his emergency cigarettes; he lit one and slumped against the sink. Except for an occasional lapse, when he was consumed with a technical problem at work, he had given up smoking, but given the tirade of abuse he had just experienced, it seemed the natural, albeit unhealthy thing to do to calm his nerves.

No longer possessing an ashtray, he spent the next five minutes trying to clear his thoughts and flicking his cigarette ash into the sink. He opened the kitchen window to disperse the smell and, with a light head from the effects of the nicotine, returned to the living room to dial the number for Sarah's mother. The ringing tone gave him satisfaction that it was still a valid number, but a minute later with no answer he replaced the receiver and turned to his computer.

Searching for Sarah on the Internet was worth a shot, he thought. They had both studied Computer Science at University, so if Sarah was single and employed somewhere in the World, there was a good chance that evidence of her might be on the Internet. He hardly watched television, but recalled a programme a few months ago, where two separated brothers had been reconciled by accidentally making contact with each other via the Internet. It seemed a bit of an unlikely event at the time because the family name of the brothers was Brown, and just how many people in the world had a surname of Brown? Here he had an advantage; he needed to search for a surname of Zurek, surely there could not be too many people with such a name.

He used the Internet everyday at work for electronic mail, and to keep in touch with technological and commercial developments that might affect MicaCom's products. However, he had never used it to try to locate a person. He reached for his mouse and clicked an icon on his screen, which dialled his modem. A minute later, he was connected to the Internet.

He initiated a people search first - a scan through various UK directories that listed names and addresses of individuals. He entered just the surname of Zurek, ignoring prompts for unknown details such as town or postcode. Ten seconds later a list of six names and addresses appeared. The last five were all names similar to Zurek, such as Zorek and Zurik, but the first was Zurek - Audrey Zurek, listed with Sarah's mother's address and the telephone number he had just dialled.

Next to try were the databases that stored electronic mail addresses. This would not be so easy, since there were several independent sources. If Sarah had an e-mail address, she would have had to have voluntarily registered it, or have sent a message to one of the thousands of discussion forums. It took five minutes, via half a dozen reputable sites, to discover that there were no Zurek entries.

Before moving on, and with the conversation with Janice still gnawing away in his head, he briefly considered trying to find an e-mail address for Janice Harding, his ex-wife's maiden name, so that he could send her a message with all the pent-up abuse he had withheld on the telephone. But common sense got the better of him, and she was too dumb anyway to operate a computer let alone have an e-mail address.

Finally, he navigated to an Internet site that would probe all the publicly available information pages. The site would submit his query to a number of search engines, which would trawl through literally billions of words and millions of entries. If the name of Zurek was contained in any document, the search engines were bound to find it. Not wanting to restrict the search in any way, he just entered Zurek as a keyword, and leant back in his chair waiting for the results. Less than a minute later, he was informed that a list of 243 references had been found.

Each entry in the list showed the title of the document containing the reference and the first few lines of the text. There was obviously a U.S.A based company called Metallica Industries Incorporated, which had a division called Zurek Metals. The first few pages of references all mentioned the name specifically. He clicked on one of the links and spent a few minutes browsing around the Zurek Metals pages looking for a family connection. All he gathered was that if he ever wanted aluminium framing for industrial racking systems then he knew that Metallica Industries or its UK controlled company Zurek plc would be the place to go. The remaining entries did not have Zurek in their title so he had to visit each link and conduct a manual search on each target page.

He found a few Zureks on pages published by organizations in America. Pamela Zurek seemed to be winning school swimming contests, John Zurek was looking for a job, Janet Zurek produced a weekly newsletter on cross-stitching and most unbelievably, Pieter Zurek was a lecturer in the sex life of fleas. That is the trouble with the Internet he thought, sometimes there is just too much information.

He began studying the site names of the links looking for any references to the UK. The first one he found was the "Portsmouth Reformation Programme". Hosted by Portsmouth City Council, the pages detailed the progress of a government-funded scheme to revive the various inner city districts of Portsmouth. Training grants, rebuilding, creation of new businesses and jobs were all part of this ambitious five-year project. Bored with the content, he read quickly looking for the name Zurek. Supposedly a *page* of information, the facts and figures went on and on until he finally came to the end and saw a list of project contacts *Technical Support: Sarah Zurek (s.zurek@portsmouth.gov.uk)*

'Bloody hell,' he said out aloud - he had found her. It had to be her. He checked the date that the page was last changed. Two weeks ago – so it was not old information he was reading. He then checked the next few links in case he found another Sarah Zurek – there were none, so he went back to the Portsmouth page to check that he had not made a mistake. No, there it was. Sarah was in Portsmouth.

Immediately he picked up the phone and dialled Directory Enquiries. There were no Zureks listed in the Portsmouth area. Not surprising he thought, otherwise he would have found it earlier. He could ring the Portsmouth City Council offices on Monday morning, but was afraid she would not speak to him. Anyway, he wanted to *see* her, so he would drive to Portsmouth now and wait outside the council offices. No that was impossible; he had to be at MicaCom next week. God, he was being stupid. He had no guarantee this really was his Sarah. Perhaps he had better be more rational about this. Send her an e-mail first and see how she replied, that is what he would do. There was no point in saying what was really going through his mind, so he kept the message short and despatched it.

He was feeling hungry now but decided to defer his main meal until the evening. Shopping for the coming week was next on his agenda – a task he deplored but was an unfortunate necessity. He had read that within the next few months his local supermarket would be offering an Internet ordering service. Click on what you want and the goods are delivered to your door the next day - now that was making the best use of the Internet, other than looking for lost girlfriends. In the meantime, he would still have to shop manually, but he had his weekly visit down to a fine art. The record time for a round trip from leaving his front door to returning with all his purchases safely stored was one hour twelve minutes. Perhaps he would try to better that today. He seldom varied his weekly shopping list, so he knew exactly where to find what he needed by rack and aisle number. Over the years he had perfected an optimal route through the store and had even identified which checkout girls provided him with the quickest exit. Today he was a bit behind schedule, since he had noted that the least busy shopping time on a Saturday was between half past twelve and half past one. As long as the supermarket had not relocated any of his purchases, as they had done before - to his great annoyance, he could still be a record breaker. He went to get his jacket, checked his watch and set off.

He never really stood a chance. There were temporary roadworks en-route, the supermarket was busier than normal, but the greatest disturbance was the daydreaming about Sarah. Browsing the shelves of food, he kept trying to recall what she liked to eat and he imagined preparing the ultimate meal for her when he brought her back to his flat.

When he had arrived home and unpacked his shopping, he did not even bother to look at his watch. It must have been two hours since he had set out, and he did not want to have the knowledge that this weekly ritual had absorbed so much precious time. Then again, what did it matter? He had nothing specific to do this weekend, except to watch the Australian Grand Prix on TV and read the *Sunday Times*, including all of its supplements. It was a perplexing realisation that without MicaCom to drive him, he would need to reorganise his life to make best use of his spare time. If only he could guarantee that Sarah would see him, the problem would be solved. He would have eleven years of catching up to occupy his mind.

The phone rang for the third time that day. This time it was Don Travis; an old school friend that by chance had also become a MicaCom customer. He had not seen for him for a while, but had kept in contact periodically by e-mail.

'Don, how's life?' Carl asked.

'Pretty good. I've a favour to ask.'

'Go ahead. I have time these days to grant favours.'

'Are you staying up tonight to watch the Grand Prix live?'

Since their schooldays, he and Don had been avid motor sport fans. They had acted as marshals at race meetings and had competed together a few times on club motor rallies. In recent years, because of their respective business commitments they had had to content themselves with being just armchair enthusiasts of, in particular, the Formula 1 World Championship. The first round of the 1999 series was being shown live from Australia on TV at two o'clock in the morning.

'I'm not sure. I was keeping my options open. I may watch the repeat at eleven o'clock. Why?' Carl asked.

'Ah, that's why I'm ringing. I'm going to miss the live broadcast unless you can help your old mate out.'

'How come?'

'One of our money-burning customers has an urgent problem with some surveillance equipment we've installed. I'm about to drive to Exeter to fix it. It should only take about an hour to solve. I'm unlikely to get home in time to watch the start, but I could get to Chelmsford.'

'I thought you had staff to do that sort of thing.'

'I do, but the stand-by engineer has gone sick, and I can't afford to let this customer down. They spend a lot of money with us.'

'I'm not trying to put you off, but won't you be knackered by the time you get here. Wouldn't it be better to watch the re-run?'

'Are you kidding? Only wimps watch re-runs. True aficionados have to watch it live.'

'OK then. I'll put some beers in the fridge. I'll see you when I see you.'

Despite his concern about how to spend his time, after Don's call the remainder of the afternoon and evening flew by.

An hour and half was healthily spent with a ten-mile jog and a shower.

Boiled pasta with a mix-in sauce provided the main course of his evening meal, since even he could manage that. While he ate, he caught up with the day's events on Ceefax since he had missed the early evening news and sports results. He was astonished that the football team he supported was still on a roll and had won 3-0, and in rugby, relieved that England had beaten Ireland and amazed that Wales had pipped France in Paris by a single point.

There was little to do regarding his weekly practice of settling bills and organizing household paperwork, so he immersed himself in some financial magazines he had bought the day before at Liverpool Street station. Each purported to advise how to invest the huge sum of money that would be available to him next week. Though it was an important consideration, he quickly became bored with the myriad of options available, and with a full stomach and tired legs fell asleep, and dreamed.

When he awoke just after ten o'clock, it was dark and he was troubled in body and mind. His body ached from the awkwardness of his position in the armchair and his mind was disturbed from the dream - more a nightmare, as he had driven aimlessly around Portsmouth trying to find Sarah's workplace. He made himself more comfortable. The darkness and the low hum from the computer were strangely soothing, as he gradually became more conscious of his surroundings. Five minutes later, he rose refreshed from the armchair, switched on a light and sat in front of his computer.

Sarah was still dominating his thoughts and suddenly he wondered if she worked on Saturdays. If she did, it was possible that she might have replied to his earlier e-mail. Full of expectation he connected to the Internet and watched transfixed as several messages appeared in this mailbox. There was nothing from Sarah. At least his e-mail to her had not bounced - a term used to describe an undeliverable message, so he would have to wait patiently for her reply on Monday. There was however the weekly news message from his parents in San Francisco. It was his mother's turn to act as scribe and, as usual, her main theme was gossip about friends, neighbours and social events, which contrasted with his father's habit of concentrating on business and political affairs. He decided to respond now with the same theme but was stuck for any gossip to relay to his mother, so he kept to trivia like the weather and Don's pending visit. It was too premature to reveal anything about his reunion with Sarah. He hoped that in two weeks time he would have a happy story to tell.

To kill the few hours before the Grand Prix and Don's arrival, he resolved to continue his spring-cleaning exercise, this time on the contents of his computer. There were plenty of MicaCom redundant files, documents and e-mails occupying storage space - it was time they were confined to the electronic trashcan.

Chapter 5

Sunday, March 7, 1999 – 1:50 a.m.

Don had timed his arrival to perfection. At ten minutes to two, the doorbell rang and Carl handed him a can of cold lager as he stepped over the threshold.

'Now that's what I call a welcome,' Don said as he took an immediate swig. He looked over his shoulder and then left to right.

'Are you expecting someone?' Carl asked.

'I hope not. I had to rush a bit through the town. I spotted a custard sandwich at a set of traffic lights. I thought it might have followed me.'

'Custard sandwich?' Carl asked, knowing it had to be one of Don's strange euphemisms.

'Police car, white, with a yellow waistband,' Don explained. Satisfied all was quiet outside he closed the front door. 'I'm dying for a piss. Where's the bog?' he then added. Carl pointed him in the direction of the bathroom.

Carl noted that Don had not really changed since their schooldays together. Don was about the same height as him, but broader and stronger. In schoolboy fights, where Carl used his legs - to run for it, Don would stand his ground and inflict his upper body strength on his opponents. To them it was always a shock because, despite Don's muscular build, he had a kindly, rounded, almost effeminate face. As soon as he acquired facial hair, he concealed his visage behind a short black beard and bushy eyebrows.

It was no surprise that on leaving school with few qualifications, Don had first taken on a number of physical occupations progressing from bouncer to labourer to security guard. It was an ignominious start for someone who was intellectually sharp, but who could not be bothered with the discipline of examinations to prove it. Don had become fascinated with the subject of security, initially of people and latterly of property.

First he started a strong man employment agency renting out his recruits for roles as bouncers, security personnel and bodyguards. Then, because of his interest in electronics, cameras and video equipment, he began to sell and install alarm and surveillance systems. Some of his early contracts were covert and probably illegal, and he never talked openly about them. From the stories he had to tell about the scrapes he and his personnel had got into, it was clear that there must have been occasions when the law of the land was a barrier to his objectives. Now, under the formal banner of Travis Security Limited, activities were supposedly strictly above board.

Returning from the bathroom, Don slumped in a chair in front of the television just as the programme was starting. Social chit-chat had come to an end, their interchanges now totally devoted to the outcome of the race.

Rival allegiances immediately became apparent with Don supporting Johnny Herbert of the Stewart team and Carl, Damon Hill from the Jordan team. Don was distraught when his favourite driver's car caught fire before he had started. All rivalry was dismissed however, when Hill was nudged off the circuit on the third bend of the first lap. Thereafter, they settled back to enjoy the drama that usually ensued with the first round of the Championship. Don soon depleted Carl's limited stock of beer and they were on their third coffee when Eddie Irvine in a Ferrari crossed the finishing line as the unexpected winner.

'I would have been really pissed off if I'd missed that,' Don said with a slur and a yawn, and then jokingly added, 'Now I'm going to crash out – just like Damon Hill.'

'Is Wendy expecting you home?' Carl asked, looking at his watch. It was a quarter past four.

'No. I said I would sleep over. That's OK presumably?'

'Yes, of course. Do you want me to wake you by any particular time?'

Don was already stretching out on the settee. 'I'm due home at two for lunch, so I need to leave here by one-thirty. If I'm still comatose at one o'clock, give me a shake.' He closed his eyes and within seconds, his heavy breathing suggested he was already asleep.

Carl and Don had risen about eleven o'clock and were standing in the kitchen having a late breakfast. Carl had recently finished telling him about the MicaCom sale and his plan to reunite with Sarah.

'We all fancied Sarah you know, and were green as snot when you scored,' Don said as he bit into his fourth slice of toast. Don was referring to the time at school when Carl had first dated Sarah. 'She was the best looking girl in the school – at least nine hundred millihelens.'

'Now you've really lost me. Millihelens?' Carl gasped.

'Blimey – I always thought you were an educated bloke. Greek mythological Helen of Troy - the most beautiful woman in the world. Her face launched a thousand ships. 'So, all women are ranked in thousandths of a Helen. It's a more grown-up scale than the score out of ten we used at school.' Don explained.

'You really amaze me at times. You must have learnt to read since the school days.'

Don aimed a mock punch at Carl's stomach and the ensuing *fou rire* caused Don to dribble toast fragments into his beard.

'Anyway, you all thought Sarah was stuck-up and a swat,' Carl remarked.

'She was, and we used to joke about you two banging away reading each other extracts from a Physics textbook. Secretly we were jealous as hell.'

'You can be a crude bastard at times, but I'll let you into a little secret. I didn't sleep with her until two years later.'

'What? No Dover for two years? You're having me on.'

'Dover?'

'Dover – Leg over,' explained Don as he dunked toast into his mug of tea.

'It wasn't that kind of arrangement to begin with. We started out as study partners. Then became pen pals when I went to University. We didn't openly fall in love until the summer of '85.'

'And I always thought that Universities were the biggest knocking shops around. That's the only regret I had about dropping out of school, I missed humping all that educated college crumpet. Didn't you brandish your intromittent organ at the girls in Warwick?'

'Where did you pick up a phrase like intromittent organ?'

'Impressed eh? I came across it in a posh sex book. I do wish authors would stick to words everyone can understand like cock or prick. Anyway, answer the question.'

'Yes, there were a couple of other girls I was intimate with.'

'Just a couple? You mean I paid income tax so that you could only hump two girls. Well, that wasn't a very good investment on my part.'

'Sorry to disappoint you, but I only humped one of them.'

'My God, Carl, it's about time you experienced a bit more of the world. You're thirty-three years old and have only had two women?'

'Three, if you include Janice.'

'Oh. I never liked that bitch. Always looked a bit shifty to me.'

'You can join my Janice the Judas club then.'

'Explain.'

'Another time perhaps. I'd rather not talk about her while I'm on a high about Sarah.'

'I'm sorry Carl, going on about humping like that. I know how you feel about Sarah. You've never really wanted anyone else, have you?'

'No. Crazy in your world I suppose?'

'No, not at all. I couldn't survive without Wendy these days. It's just that, well, I had to sample a lot more dishes before I found one that I wanted to eat over and over again. I probably suffered more indigestion than you did.'

Carl laughed. For Don that was an amazing piece of wisdom.

'Anyway,' Don continued, 'I think it's about time I left you to carry on planning how to spend your millions. Thanks for the hospitality. Come up and see Wendy and me in your chauffeur-driven Rolls if you get the opportunity. Considering the good times we had at school, we ought to see more of each other.'

Don took a last drink of tea, also swallowing the bits of sodden toast that were floating on the top.

'When I've put this Sarah obsession to bed, I'll call you,' Carl said and they laughed at the topical pun.

They went to the front door and Don paused, examining the lock.

'Dead easy to break into your flat with a lock like that – it's useless, and that's my floccinaucinihilipilification for the day.'

'Your what?'

'Floccinaucinihilipilification – it's my word of the week. I'll leave you to look it up when I've gone. Seriously though, I can do you a good deal on some state-of-the-art Japanese infrared security. Works just like a car remote locking unit. Very secure.'

'No thanks. I think I'll give that a miss. One of the first items on my millionaire's shopping list is to buy a house for Sarah and me.'

'I do hope you get back with Sarah, but take it easy if you don't. Don't forget to call.'

The rest of the day passed uneventfully; no telephone calls; no visitors; no work; just a trip to the newsagent and an uninterrupted digestion of national and world events from the Sunday papers. It was a pleasant calm before the stormy five days ahead; days as a mere employee of the company he founded ten years ago because of Sarah.

Chapter 6

Monday, March 8, 1999 – 8:00 a.m.

My last week at MicaCom thought Carl, as he entered the MicaCom building at eight o'clock on Monday morning. He could not recall the last occasion that he had arrived before anyone else – it was at least two hours prior to his average start time; even Mike was not here yet and he was a notoriously early starter.

He reasoned that his appearance at such an unnatural hour was because he had not laboured through the night working on Protean. Perhaps now he had a different sense of responsibility; after all, today he was just a short-term employee rather than a Director with unspecified privileges, like coming in late. Of course, contractually, he had to be here this week to help with any remaining arrangements for transferring the business to the purchasers. The seconded management from BinaryByte would be arriving this morning to formally take over the reins. The staff had already met their new bosses since they had been making a nuisance of themselves in recent weeks, by listing, labelling and documenting every inorganic item in the building. Maybe he had made this awakening effort to impress them? Not!

He climbed the stairs to the first floor and paused outside his office. Correction, he thought, *was* his office. Already he felt as though he was intruding as he entered. Usually he would go straight to his computer and study his e-mail messages, but today that would be up to Tony Cookson - the acting Technical Officer, as he was called, to deal with that. He went to the window and opened it. A ritual originally adopted when he still smoked and the whole building was declared a no-smoking zone. He had rebelled against his own rules by continuing to smoke – another Director privilege. He sat in the executive chair and surveyed the desk. The in-tray was overflowing with a week's worth of free computer magazines he had been too busy to read. He still wanted to keep up with events in the computer world, so he took out a memo pad from the desk drawer and wrote a note to Denise, the receptionist, to get them redirected to his home. He had just finished when a light started flashing on his telephone, and he heard a ringing on Mike's telephone from the next office. The light indicated it was Mike's direct line. Someone else is starting work early he thought. The call would eventually get diverted to the Mike's voice mail, but on impulse he pressed a button on his own phone and intercepted the call.

'Good Morning. This is MicaCom, how may I help you?' using, perhaps for the last time, the company standard phrase for answering outside calls.

There was a short silence, then a pleasant female voice said, 'Oh, can I speak to Mr. Stanford please?'

'I'm sorry Mr. Stanford hasn't arrived yet. Can I take a message for him?'

Another short silence, then in an obviously stressed voice, 'Um … no … could you tell him Susan called. I'll call back later.' Before he had a chance to acknowledge, she hung up.

The subject of the mysterious Susan had been a joke between him and Mike for ages. Carl could not remember when the enigma had first started, but it was probably six years or more. Several times when he had been talking to Mike in his office, a direct call had come through on his phone, and a flushed-face Mike had always used a hushed "speaking-to-Susan" voice. The first time that Carl had experienced this strange behaviour he had merely avoided Mike's embarrassed look. Subsequently he had attempted to make a joke of it, and Mike had responded similarly, but to this day had never offered an explanation. It was unlike Mike to be evasive about any subject, private or otherwise, and Carl's unspoken, uncorroborated but unlikely conclusion was that a romantic entanglement was in progress. If that were true, then his wife Lisa did not outwardly know about it, Mike and Lisa always appeared to be a natural and happy couple.

He began searching drawers and cupboards looking for personal items to take with him and around eight-thirty heard voices downstairs, and the click of mugs from the staff kitchen immediately below him, as some of the employees prepared their coffee fix to start the day. A few minutes later Mike appeared in the doorway.

'Bloody Hell, who kicked you out of bed this morning?' Mike said with a look of disbelief on his face.

'Well, you're late and I'm early, the world certainly *is* changing. Actually, I went to bed at eleven o'clock last night - probably the earliest this decade, and then couldn't recover from the shock when I woke up at six. What's your excuse?'

'I wanted to call in at the Travel Agents on my way to work to pick up my Concorde tickets to New York. Have to get my priorities right now that I'm a man of leisure', Mike replied, changing to a posh voice to emphasize his new status. 'And have you got your *adventure* all sorted out?' he continued in a sarcastic tone.

'Funny you should ask that, yes, I have a few ideas.'

'Then don't forget what I said last week, make sure you share them with me before you disappear.'

'OK, but I can't see that it matters too much, you will be in America and the insurance policies have been cancelled,' Carl joked. He was referring to insurance policies that they had had on each other's lives. If one of them died in MicaCom's service, it would have left the live Director sufficient funds to purchase the other's shareholding in the company.

'Ah, but it does, because I have a big surprise for you.'

'You've bought me a new BMW?'

'No, better than that, you'll see. So when are you going to tell me about your plans?'

'There's not too many plans to reveal at the moment, but I think the time is right that I told you a little, no a big, story about my life before MicaCom.'

'All right, I'm all ears,' Mike said, making himself comfortable in the chair opposite Carl.

'No, later. It might take a couple of hours, and Tony and Pete will be here at ten o'clock. I've thought of a few development issues that Tony ought to know about while they're still fresh in my mind.'

'Lunchtime then? I know, let's go to the Black Bull pub in Blackmore, where we had our first MicaCom meeting.'

'The venue's fine, but can we leave it until say, Wednesday. I should be in a position to round off the story better by then.'

'OK, after ten years another couple of days won't matter.'

'Good, and by the way you had a call from Susan half an hour ago.' Carl teased.

'You *spoke* to Susan? What did she say?' Mike asked nervously.

'Don't worry, I didn't ask her any leading questions. Your secret's safe with me. She'll call you later, but she did sound a bit stressed out.'

'Oh, and one more thing, you're reviewing the staff list with Pete this morning aren't you?'

'Don't remind me', Mike said.

'I want one last favour, can you make sure Paul Westdene ends up on the casualty list?'

'Why? What have you suddenly got against Paul? I thought he was one of your star programmers.'

'Yes, he's pretty good, but he's also been rumbled as providing company information to the enemy.'

'You mean he's been giving away our secrets to BinaryByte.'

'No. *My enemy*, Janice. It explains how she came to know quite a few things about me, which she shouldn't have.'

'Well, well, sneaky cow. Is she sleeping with him?'

'Probably, because she's given Brian the elbow.'

'I'll see what I can do, but it'll have to be Pete's final decision.'

* * *

Mike went back to his ex-office to await the arrival of Pete Hayden, the recently appointed General Manager of BinaryByte's new MicaCom division. He had agreed to help him with the unenviable task of identifying which of the current MicaCom employees could be laid off. Most of the admin staff would probably go, but he would have a hard time convincing Pete that Paul Westdene, one of the key people on the Protean project, should be dismissed.

However, that was not his major concern just now, Susan was. He knew why she had called, but it was rather unfortunate that she had spoken to Carl. He could not call her back since he had never known her phone number despite asking for it on numerous occasions. Still, tomorrow or Wednesday, he should be able to come clean with her - at last, and the deceitful burden he had carried for many years could be finally relinquished.

* * *

As usual, Sarah had arrived at work at nine o'clock but four hours later this was the first time that she had sat down at her desk.

As chief trouble-shooter of problems with the council computers, she was constantly in demand. As often happened, before she took her coat off the phone was ringing with the first plea for assistance from someone who could not fire up his or her computer after the weekend break. Today it seemed everyone had a problem.

She had joined the council eight years ago as a junior trainee in the systems department. Her first task had been to help install and configure new computers. She did that efficiently and accurately, and soon demonstrated an aptitude for solving software and hardware problems. As a result, she was now the most senior computer engineer in the council that was still involved in doing, rather then planning. Promotion had been offered several times in the last two years, but she did not want to become a paper pusher or draw attention to herself, so she had politely declined.

She was thirty-one years old, medium height, slim with short blonde hair, and still considered herself attractive to the opposite sex. Because of her roving portfolio at the council, she was well known and well liked among the conscientious staff. Her arrival in an office was a sure sign that an ailing computer was about to be given a new lease of life. This exposure and good service meant she had acquired plenty of suitors, and she had occasionally stepped out as a couple with some of the male colleagues she had regular contact with, but that was as far as she went. She had been advised to not get regularly involved with anyone and that did not bother her. She valued her freedom more than a steady relationship - the last one, many years ago, still pained her when she chose to think about it.

There was a small envelope symbol flashing on her computer screen indicating there were e-mail messages waiting. No doubt other computer users with problems, but less severe so that e-mail notification would suffice she thought. A list appeared when she opened her mailbox by clicking the envelope with her mouse. Looking at the subject line of the messages most were titled "Support Request", the standard heading from users in trouble. Others were internal messages from colleagues except for one that stood out amongst the rest "Sarah, is that really you?" She opened the message and read the brief contents.

`Can I see you? Love Carl Denham.`

At first, she thought it was a joke or a misdirected message. Then she remembered and a cold shiver went down her spine. She looked around fearful that someone might be looking over her shoulder; she made a note of the message and the source address, and then deleted it from the system. It was lunchtime and the small office she shared with two other engineers was empty, including the glass cubicle that was normally occupied by her boss. She reached into her briefcase and searched for an anonymous piece of paper with a telephone number written on it. The number was not to be called except in dire emergencies, but since this was the first time her existence had been compromised, she viewed that this was one of those urgent occasions. She had never called the eight-year-old number before and prayed that it was still valid. Keeping a watchful eye, she went to the glass room and closed the door. Last year she had helped the council install a telephone logging system and she certainly did not want her contact's phone number to be recorded against her extension. She nervously picked up the receiver and dialled the number.

'Manor Park Bicycles,' said the answering male voice.

Right place, the distinctive accent suggested the right person.

'Ivan?' she asked.

'It might be. Who's that?' he said.

'Ivan, it's me, Sarah, Sarah Zurek,' she said. There was silence from the other end, so she added, '1991, Warsaw,' for clarification.

'What the hell are you doing calling me after all this time? I hope you've a good reason,' Ivan said agitatedly.

'I may have a problem, a serious problem. I've just had an e-mail from Carl Denham,' Sarah said, whispering now that she had seen someone enter the outer office.

'Big deal. Who's Carl Denham?'

'Cast your mind back. Carl Denham was Sarah's boyfriend. Don't you remember the letters you gave me with the rest of Sarah's documents? You said I had to read them for some background.'

The line went quiet again; Ivan was presumably testing his memory, thought Sarah.

'How did he know where you were?'

'I've absolutely no idea. I've always been very careful to make sure my name didn't get publicly listed anywhere.'

'No, you must be mistaken. Somebody is playing a joke on you,' Ivan said unconvincingly.

'That may be, but if *anyone* knows the connection between Sarah and Carl Denham that could mean big trouble. You said Sarah was dead.'

'Well ... Yes.'

'Then why would Carl Denham be trying to contact her? Surely he must know she's dead.'

'It's certainly odd. Perhaps he's gone crazy. I don't know. Anyway how do you know the message is from *the* Carl Denham?' Ivan asked.

'I'm not stupid you know. The message was quite clear. It said, "Can I see you? Love Carl Denham." It came from an e-mail address of *cd2@micacom.co.uk* and how many Carl Denhams are there out there who know a Sarah Zurek. Is that specific enough for you?' Sarah screamed back now that the office was empty again.

'Keep your voice down. I'll sort it out.'

'What do you mean, "Sort it out"? What are you going to do? What am *I* supposed to do?'

'Don't do anything. Don't reply to the message, yet.'

'And if he phones?'

'Avoid the call if you can, or explain that he must have made a mistake, you're not the Sarah he thinks you are.'

'I hope you are taking this seriously. We both stand to lose if I'm found out.'

'I'll never lose as long as you keep your mouth shut,' Ivan threatened. 'Do you understand Sarah?'

'Yes,' Sarah mumbled.

'I'm not hearing you loud and clear,' Ivan prompted.

'Yes,' she replied more convincingly.

'Tell me the e-mail address again?'

'cd2@micacom.co.uk'

'I'll do some digging around and ring you tonight. Remind me of your home telephone number.'

She did, replaced the receiver and hurried back to her own desk – deep in thought.

* * *

Ivan slumped back in his chair. Of all the people he had processed in the last twelve years, Sarah Zurek was the last person he had wanted to hear from.

He went to the unused fireplace in his study and prised loose the false wooden cover to reveal his safe. He spun the combination lock a few times and the solid door clicked open. Reaching inside he extracted a file labelled 1991 and took it to his desk. He soon found the slim folder for Sarah Zurek and read through quickly to remind himself of background details.

Natasha Minski – that was Sarah's original name. There had been nothing unusual about the circumstances of her arrival. The extent of the documentation supplied for her and the unfortunate coincidence with an event in 1988 he had remembered without looking at his records. The bundle of letters had been a bonus in substantiating Sarah's existence. He read the simple notes he had made at the time - *Ten love letters (passionate), written by Carl Denham (boyfriend) from November 1987 to February 1988*. Sarah was right; Carl Denham was the old boyfriend. He did recall glancing through the letters and had formed the opinion that the couple had been quite inseparable. Perhaps this guy had had a mental relapse about his loss many years later? It could be a problem or nothing to worry about. Whatever, he could not ignore what had happened; if the connection with 1988 surfaced he, and a Polish colleague of his, might be in serious trouble.

* * *

Carl had been frustrated by his afternoon with Tony Cookson. Tony was a very bright software engineer but taking him through the Protean systems documentation had been a laborious process. He picked things up quickly, but wanted to go over the information in the finest detail since he was the designated person to understand every aspect of Protean, so that BinaryByte's acquisition realized its full commercial potential. Carl wondered if Protean V would ever come to market, because Tony was already proposing changes to the product that would surely delay its launch by several months. Why should he worry, he had to keep reminding himself. Just nod in the right places and perhaps he could go home to read the reply from Sarah.

Sarah's response had been on his mind all day. Several times he had been tempted to logon to his, or rather, Tony's computer and access the messages on his private e-mail account, but the opportunity never arose thanks to Tony wanting his undivided attention. It came as a great relief when, at almost eight o'clock that evening, Tony admitted that his brain had enough for the day and he was going back to his hotel for dinner. Tony tentatively suggested that he could join him, but it was probably a comfort to them both when he declined - they had spent quite enough time together that day already.

He was hungry too, but when he got home, food had been relegated on his priority list. He went straight to his computer and accessed his e-mail messages.

He was absorbed as he watched the counter that showed the number of new messages click from zero to four. Two were newsletters he had subscribed to for details on potential investments in start-up companies. One from a friend who had emigrated to South Africa and the last from a MicaCom employee who was asking to be considered for employment if Carl started a new company; but there was nothing from Sarah.

With a sigh, he considered the possible reasons why. She could be on holiday; out of her office on business; too busy to reply or as a worst case, ignoring him. He could not come to terms with the latter, perhaps the message had got lost? That was quite unlikely, the Internet was not perfect but it was probably more reliable than the postal service, and if the message could not be delivered he would have received an automatic response to that effect. Despondent, but pragmatic he sent another message, with a little more urgency this time, and then set about a new evening routine of jogging (it was too late for the dark country lanes, he would have to pound the street lit pavements instead), eating, *not* working and sleeping.

* * *

The Carl Denham e-mail had been on Sarah's mind all day. It was now nine o'clock and she had been sitting by the telephone all evening trying unsuccessfully to concentrate on the book in front of her. Nonetheless, she was startled when the phone finally rang.

'Sarah?'

'Ivan, have you found out something?'

'Yes, I have actually. My son is a bit of a computer freak and he has been searching the Internet for me. Carl Denham is one of two owning directors at a company called MicaCom Software. They write communications programs, are based in Chelmsford and were formed in 1989. His e-mail address is officially listed as *cd@micacom.co.uk*. My son reckons he may perhaps be using the handle of "cd2" for his private as opposed to company e-mail.'

'It must be the same person. I've read through the letters again tonight and Carl Denham was obviously a software expert. He obtained a degree in Computer Science, but in the letters he mentions working at a company called Oxitel.'

'That *was* a while ago. He must have started his own company. And I think I know how he got hold of your e-mail address. My son also did a search for the name Sarah Zurek on the Internet and he found it on a list of Portsmouth City Council staff e-mail addresses.'

'But that should only be a private list for staff members.'

'That may be, but it's accessible to the whole world at the moment. I suggest you get somebody to change it.'

'I will, but what shall I do about the e-mail?'

'My best advice is to ignore it for now, but contact me again if you hear anymore.'

Chapter 7

Tuesday, March 9, 1999 – 7:30 a.m.

Seven thirty in the morning. In eight years of working at the council it was the earliest Sarah had ever been in the office; and in the eight years since she came from Poland it was the most insecure she had ever felt. Overnight she had deliberated upon the significance of the e-mail from Carl Denham. No matter what approach she took to analysing the event, it filled her with fear. Despite reporting the problem to Ivan she was not satisfied that he had treated it seriously enough. The induction to England had not prepared her for this type of situation. Her life in Portsmouth had not been exciting, but it had at least been stable. She had followed all the rules and advice originally given to her by Ivan and everything had gone surprisingly smoothly. She had a satisfying and reasonably paid job; a number of (not too close) friends; and a comfortable roof over her head; she could not say she was deliriously happy, but happy enough. Now there was a threat and no one would be able to convince her otherwise.

Last night she had re-read the Carl Denham letters. Not that she had to, because she had become intimately aware of their contents over the years. Though the letters only reported one person's view of a love story, it was clear to her that the romance was deep and enduring. She had fantasized that the letters had been written to her, and during times of sadness they had strangely given her comfort. The letters were still an enigma to her, not the contents, but their source. A false passport, false birth certificate, false exam certificates, all these were easily manufactured, but authentic love letters were a different matter. Ivan had been appropriately vague about how he acquired them. But the most worrying aspect portrayed in the letters was the sorrow Carl Denham would feel if and when he discovered that his Sarah was dead, because it was evident, even from a single e-mail that he did not know. It was her objective to ensure that her connection with these facts - remote as it was, was never discovered.

She had switched on her computer as soon as she had arrived this morning and now she was staring at her electronic desktop. Little icons scattered here and there, one of them labelled "Mail". If she clicked it, a program would be launched which would extract the e-mails addressed to her that were currently stored on a central computer. Normally it was the first thing she did each morning, never worrying what news or pleas for help it might bring. Today, she somehow knew there would be another e-mail from Carl Denham, which was why she was here so early. It would require immediate attention and perhaps another call to Ivan, because despite her lack of confidence in his concern for her well being, she could think of no other course of action. She clicked "Mail" and closed her eyes, then opened them slowly.

Please Sarah, if it is you, at least let me know you are well.

Love Carl Denham.

She did not use English swear words as a rule, but they were so expressive and "Shit" came immediately to mind, so she said it guiltily to the empty room. Carl Denham was persistent, but that was to be expected. Without any inhibitions this time, she went to her boss's phone and called Ivan.

'This had better be important at this time of the morning,' Ivan said without finding out who was calling.

'Ivan, sorry, it's Sarah. I've had another e-mail from Carl Denham.'

'Shit. What did he say this time?'

Well at least she was not the only Pole who favoured English profanities. She quoted the short message to him.

'If he is that desperate I am surprised he hasn't tried to phone you. Perhaps that's his next move. I think you had better reply to his message and say he must have made a mistake. Hopefully that will be the end of it.'

'I hope so too. At least my name and e-mail are not accessible on the Internet anymore. I told my boss that I was getting strange e-mails from outside the council and he went to see the technician who maintains our public Internet pages. Apparently there was an incorrect security rating on the staff address book and it's been corrected now.'

'That's good. Send your reply to Carl Denham and don't call me again. OK?' Ivan said finally and cut the line.

Sarah thought long and hard about her reply to Carl. It would have to be short, polite and unambiguous. She tried to put herself in the position of a genuinely mistaken addressee. Eventually she just composed a single sentence and sent her message, but she still feared the Carl Denham saga was not over yet. Now her immediate worry was Ivan's attitude. He was supposed to provide assistance in times of need, yet he seemed unnerved by her latest call.

There were two possible explanations, both of which were disquieting. It could be that the backup service she expected was no longer available - so that if there were any repercussions from her dialogue with her "ex-boyfriend" she would have to face them alone. Alternatively, Ivan was worried too and had shown his tension by being short with her. Either way she would probably need to be here early tomorrow morning to undoubtedly intercept another overnight message from Carl Denham. His last message was sent the previous evening; he must be communicating from home.

* * *

It was an uncustomary feeling for Carl when he arrived home that evening, much more than glad or pleased, closer to ecstatic or euphoric. It had been a bitch of a day - the chief bitch being Tony Cookson. What a sarcastic, unctuous, disdainful, pathetic, et cetera creature he was. All day he had suffered his company; Tony dishing out commands; do this; do that; fetch this; fetch that; all menial tasks that were not even worthy of a junior clerk, let alone an ex-Director of MicaCom. He had bitten his tongue so many times today it was a wonder he had not choked on his own blood.

He was not enjoying his last MicaCom week at all; being subservient to an egotistical maniac was not his idea of fun. He could not react adversely and thus endanger his end-of-the-week fat cheque, and Tony was using that to his selfish advantage.

Still, now he was home, eager to engage the next phase of his Sarah reconciliation. He was nervous, his stomach said so, as he sat in front of his computer and guided his e-mail program into action. Somehow, he just knew there would be a reply from Sarah. He was not one for praying, but he said a little prayer as he saw the incoming e-mail list appear on his screen. One ... two ... three ... four ... five ... there it was, a message titled "Sarah, is that really you?" from s.zurek@portsmouth.gov.uk. He manoeuvred his mouse pointer until it hovered over the title, took a deep breath, uttered another plea and clicked.

```
I'm sorry Mr. Denham you must be mistaken; I'm not the Sarah
you are looking for.
```

He stared in disbelief at the sentence. In that moment, his dream of seeing Sarah again had been shattered. Surely that could not be, just after he had built up his hopes. It was unbelievable that this was not his Sarah Zurek. It had to be her way of saying that she did not want to see him. But she had phrased it formally. "Mr. Denham" she had written. Did that mean that he really was unknown to her, or was she doing her best to put him off? "I'm not the Sarah you are looking for." Perhaps there was a hidden meaning there. Was she implying that she had changed from the Sarah he loved so much? It did not matter how she had changed he would still love her. Or would he? Supposing she had aged horribly or her golden hair had gone prematurely grey? She could be disfigured, married but still using her maiden name or currently in love with someone else. Could he come to terms with such eventualities? Being honest with himself, he did not know for certain. His memories were of happy times. Was he just being foolish with false hopes? It had to be her. Whatever the situation with Sarah he could not give up now. He would not be able to rest until he had pursued all possibilities of seeing Sarah again.

More likely, she was testing his resolve. It could be that she would only declare herself to him if he persevered. A telephone call would perhaps be more revealing. He was sure he could still recognize her voice and that would prove it was his Sarah. He would not have to engage her in conversation – he was still afraid of a remote rejection – just hear her voice and then put the telephone down. He promised himself he would do that as a last resort. Now that he had her attention, he would send one more message to see what her reaction would be. He typed what he considered a suitably innocent request that would keep the dialogue going and despatched it to Portsmouth.

Chapter 8

Wednesday, March 10, 1999 – 7:00 a.m.

Sarah had not slept well - still attempting to understand the significance or forecast the outcome of Carl Denham's e-mails. She hoped, but doubted, that her latest response had stalled or dismissed the potential discovery of her usurpation of Sarah Zurek's identity, so again she rose early, anxious to get to work.

She skipped both breakfast and making her packed lunch, dressed in the first item of work clothes that she found in her wardrobe and didn't bother with make-up - all to expedite her departure for the short walk to the Civic Centre.

Missing breakfast was precautionary. Her stomach expected a bowl of muesli and a cup of tea, but the nervous flutters told her it was best avoided for now. Making her own lunch was a means of saving a small amount of money - today she would have to dine in the slightly more expensive subsidized council canteen. She knew the random wardrobe selection would be acceptable. The choice was limited, but her matching skirts and jackets were good quality and bought to last; all she had to add was a clean white blouse to the red separates that she had chanced upon. As for make-up, the lightest amount of lipstick and blusher that she used would not be missed. Her complexion was smooth and unmarked, and she used make-up merely as conformance to a female prerogative.

She put on her fawn coat, picked up her briefcase, and exited her apartment block. It was a cool morning, with an overcast, albeit not rain-threatening, sky and she hurried north towards the City Centre.

At her desk, she waited impatiently while her computer started up and downloaded her e-mail messages. There was only one, another from Carl Denham.

Thank you for your reply. Excuse me bothering you again, but Zurek is such a rare name, I was wondering if you had any other relatives with the name of Sarah, or perhaps had ever come across the name in some other context. I would be most grateful if you could help.

She studied the text looking for hints of suspicion. It seemed a genuinely polite acceptance of her previous reply. A "Sorry, can't help" kind of reply would hopefully terminate the exchange so that she could return to her secure, albeit uninteresting, life. Confidently she composed the words, despatched the message and then set about her daily objective of keeping the council computer users happy.

* * *

Later than arranged, Mike met Carl in the MicaCom car park and they travelled the five miles in Carl's old BMW to Blackmore. Mike explained to Carl that he had been delayed, trying again to convince Pete Hayden about Paul Westdene's termination of employment. Paul's personnel file, which was the only reference point that Pete had, was full of glowing testimonies from Carl of his excellent work for MicaCom, so he had had to invent a few rumours about his background. It had been a tough job, but he thought he had won through in the end. He did owe Carl quite a few favours, so he desperately hoped he could deliver on this one. Pete had then suggested lunch together, and Mike had to risk the sealing of the Paul issue, by declining in favour of what should be a fascinating and revealing lunch with Carl.

'Do you remember when we first came here?' Mike said to get the conversation going after ordering a couple of pints of lager.

'Of course, it's where we had our inaugural MicaCom meeting ten years ago. A lot of significant events happened before that day and some after too, particularly during the first MicaCom year,' Carl replied looking in a reflective and melancholy mood.

'I thought our vow was never to have any secrets from each other?'

'MicaCom secrets, yes. What I'm going to tell you is of a personal nature, although the facts did significantly affect the progress of MicaCom.' Carl said. 'It could have all been so different,' he added.

'Do you have some regrets about MicaCom then?' Mike said, relieved that Carl was obviously going to keep his promise about his undisclosed past.

'No, I suppose not. At the time of the meeting here, MicaCom was really the only way forward for me. I conned you, you know. I had no way of knowing that we would end up running a successful company.'

'It takes two though. I wanted something different too. You clearly had the talent and the ideas, but what persuaded me was your almost demonic determination to work and work until we succeeded. You were clearly a man possessed by something from the past. I suppose, selfishly, I never wanted to ask what it was, in case it affected our relationship. Anyway your plans sounded a lot more exciting that anything I was doing at Oxitel.'

'But it was a big risk for you surely?' Carl asked.

'Not really. I was young enough not to worry. If it had all gone wrong, I could have soon got a job somewhere else. I didn't then have any commitments, and you funded the initial operation. I must confess I just came along for the ride initially, but I wouldn't want to go through those first few nervous months again.'

'Well, I couldn't have done it without you. You've helped keep me sane all these years.'

'So what happened?' Mike asked, his impatience showing.

'The story is a Comedy of Errors, with Janice as the worst supporting actress and Sarah as the leading lady.'

'I guessed Janice was involved somewhere, but who's Sarah?' Mike said, sliding forward on his chair.

'All will be revealed in due course. Do you want the short version starting in 1988 or the long version from 1983?'

'I'm in no rush to continue my audience with Pete. The pub is open all afternoon, so go for the long version, but tell it as though you were telling a stranger. I'm interested to know the story, particularly the MicaCom part, from your unbiased perspective.'

Mike leant forward and felt like a child about to be told a bedtime story. Carl must have recognized his excitement, as he began with a childish introduction. 'Once upon a time there was a sixth form schoolboy, who was bright but lazy and about to change his life forever ....'

Part Two

Carl's Story

Chapter 9

1983 - 1984

I didn't mind travelling on the underground. Any mode of transport wasn't a waste of time to me so long as I had my transistor radio in my anorak pocket with a connection to an ear piece so that I didn't disturb my fellow passengers - I was usually thoughtful like that.

I was in a good frame of mind for two reasons. First, the DJ on the reception-disadvantaged radio had just launched a "Rave from the Grave" Beach Boys track, Good Vibrations – my favourite group and almost my favourite song. Second, and more importantly, within the last hour I thought I had made one of the most important, albeit surprising, decisions of my life. I treated the former as a good omen for the latter; all I had to do now was pass my A-levels. I wished then that I had worked harder to make my passage to University a foregone conclusion. I was quite good at Mathematics, but my efforts at Chemistry and Physics were distinctly marginal.

It was early October 1983, and I was returning with some of my classmates from an open day at Imperial College. There, not only had I been mesmerized with the equipment and facilities that they had, but the lifestyle being portrayed by the undergraduates that I had spoken to, seemed so foreign to my own rather sheltered existence. I wanted some of the action.

My school had arranged the trip, which alone was quite amazing. Firstly, the school was situated in Leytonstone - not exactly the most affluent area of London, and it had one of the worst academic records possible. Until a year earlier, the school hadn't even had its own sixth form; if any of the pupils had thoughts of doing A-levels after their GCEs, they had to transfer to another school or college. Only a few pupils had ever done that, because GCE results had never been good enough; and I'd never heard of anybody going to University. Secondly, the school had actually managed to organize a trip, but the incentive for this had come mostly from pupil power rather than the school's concern for the academic progression of its students. However, the pupil power had been more motivated by having a paid day trip to London rather than any serious interest in viewing a potential University to attend. I had thought the same way when we set out that morning, but now that had all changed.

I really was interested in bettering myself by obtaining a University degree. I knew I had the capacity and talent to really understand my study subjects. The problem was that the group I hung out with was a bad influence. We had a lot of fun together, just too much fun. Doing homework never got off the bottom rung of our agenda. I remember I had got caught out once when I handed in a completed assignment to the one of the teachers, who then broadcast in front of my mates, just how flabbergasted he was. I suffered a week's worth of ribbing and ostracism for that.

I looked around the crowded and heaving carriage from my seat by a door. When my friends and I had boarded the half-empty train, we'd rushed pushing and shouting to ensure we got seats together. Now we were being looked down upon disapprovingly by our standing elders on their way home from work. I spotted an elderly woman about two bodies from me and with my sudden new outlook on life, rose from my seat, shuffled awkwardly so that no one else could occupy the seat, and gestured to the old lady to take my place. She looked wary at first and then astonished as she realized my intentions. But nowhere near as astonished as my schoolmates, who also pulled faces suggesting I was a wimp. I avoided their looks and silent taunts and became attracted to an advert for Mensa. *If you can solve this puzzle within 30 seconds, you could become a member of Mensa.* I took on the mathematical challenge and within less than half the target time had the answer. There, I was good at maths; I just needed to apply my mind to this and the other subjects, which were on my scholastic schedule.

I would have to spend less time - considerably less time, on the frivolous activities that were conceived to avoid studies outside of school hours. The few home distractions such as television, listening to pop music and reading cheap novels would have to go. More difficult would be the evening and weekend outings with my friends. This had become a frequent occurrence since two of my closest friends, Don and Alan, had recently passed their driving tests and had almost unlimited access to their family cars. Cinema, discos, pubs, even just driving around aimlessly were all more appealing activities than striving for recognition in our exams next May.

None of my friends had any real ambition. Their final two years at school were more an avoidance of having to work for a living, rather than any real need to add to their qualifications. Don would probably fare quite well, he had a sharp brain and, coupled with his streetwise attitudes, he would certainly survive and probably excel in the outside world, even without a batch of exam certificates. The rest I feared would be satisfied with menial desk jobs or manual work.

There were no outstanding performers in my school year, but there was one in the year below me. Sarah Zurek was the school swot. She had passed ten subjects last year at GCE, all with high grades. This was easily a school record, and whenever the teachers wanted to lecture about performance and academic achievement, Sarah was always quoted as the model pupil. Although she was modest about her feats and an extremely likeable person, she was treated as a misfit. What made matters worse, was that in the eyes of me and my friends she was the most stunningly beautiful girl we had encountered. With long blonde hair, bright blue eyes, a 16-year-old school girl figure that was clearly going to mature into a goddess shape, and above all a smile that could melt ice at a hundred paces.

Sarah's existence had been enigma to us. Beauty and brains in our limited world did not make sense. So while every post-puberty male in the school fancied her, none could face the ultimate embarrassment of being associated with such a *savante* – as the French teacher referred to her. Female pupils also kept their distance in case they caught her intellectual virus, so Sarah had become somewhat of a wallflower when it came to social events.

Coincidentally, she was studying the same science subjects as me, which was a rarity for the girls in the school who seemed to prefer the more artistic disciplines of languages and literature. I had not displayed any specific courage in getting to know Sarah, but our paths had crossed on a number of occasions. Several of the Physics and Chemistry laboratory lessons were shared between the two senior years in the school. I'd even sought her help in a few Chemistry experiments, when she had finished her work and was obviously frustrated at the inactivity while her fellow students played catch up.

By now I had made up my mind, I would ask Sarah for some help. Sure I fancied her as much as any of my friends, but my motivation was strictly on a professional, not sexual basis – well, initially anyway. The problem was, did I have the guts to actually raise the subject, and then could I convince her that my interest was mental not physical. Probably not I thought, but it was an admirable idea.

The school group changed trains at Liverpool Street station to join the Central Line to complete their journey back to Leytonstone. The two teachers who had accompanied us escorted us back to school and, with only twenty minutes left of the academic day, we were given permission to go home early.

As it was Friday, my friends were eager to arrange their weekend activities. They certainly had no thoughts of discussing the trip we had just been on.

'How about going to the cinema tonight?' Don said. 'They're showing Octopussy at the Odeon this week, and after, we can hang around outside the Palais dance hall and go talent spotting.'

'Yeah,' Alan and Dave replied in unison. 'You coming Carl?' Don asked.

This was my first test of the promise I had made to myself on the train.

'Um ... well actually ... I was thinking of doing something else tonight.' In fact I was thinking of doing something right now like waiting outside school for Sarah to emerge.

'Like what?' Alan said, and before I could reply he added, 'I have my dad's car tonight and can pick you up on the way there.'

'I thought I would write up my Chemistry experiment from yesterday.' I answered unconvincingly.

'It looks like today's visit has had some influence on our Carl, but it'll soon wear off. I'll pick you up anyway. We'll meet at Don's at seven thirty so I'll see you about seven o'clock,' Alan said to me, as he strolled off on his short walk home.

Dave departed too, heading back to the station, but Don looked at his watch and said 'My brother should be picking me up in ten minutes,' referring to his usual method of getting home after school. 'Aren't you going now?'

I considered making idle conversation to while away the time. It was possible that Don could have been picked up by the time that Sarah came out of school. I was worried however that I might reveal my true intentions in front of Don. Don would then spy on me while I sought out Sarah, and I really couldn't stand the humiliation if my plan went wrong.

'Yes, I'm off now too, see you later,' I reluctantly answered.

I set out on my own walk home. My grand scheme had fallen at the first hurdle. I metaphorically kicked myself for not being open with Don. He, of all my friends, would surely have sympathized with my idea. It was too late now, and all the way home I could think of nothing else but finding a private way of contacting Sarah.

By the time I was home in Wanstead, I had a possible solution. After debriefing on the day to my mother, I found the regional telephone directory and soon found what had to be Sarah's telephone number. There was only one Zurek listed, an Audrey in Ilford, and presumably her mother. I would wait until my mother was busy in the kitchen and then I would call - but the opportunity never arose. Tea was served, then my father arrived and wanted to chat, and finally there was a telephone call for my mother, which lasted until Alan arrived to collect me.

We met up at Don's home and walked the half-mile to the cinema. Everyone was in high spirits with the weekend to look forward to, except for me, who had other things on his mind.

The film was a popular choice and we had to queue for twenty minutes, so my friends seized the opportunity to quiz me about my melancholy.

'So what's up Carl?' Don lead; always being the one to ignore any shades of diplomacy in situations like this.

I had guessed that this interrogation was coming, and knew that my friends would not give up until they had got satisfaction. To give the honest answer would have invited ridicule, so I had already decided to make fun of the situation.

'Actually, I have a sexual problem,' I replied quietly and offering the most serious look I could manage.

Predictably and without compassion Don, Dave and Alan erupted into fits of laughter. It took at least another half-minute before anyone could compose themselves and then Dave threw back, 'What, you've been wanking again and it's dropped off?'

This time they laughed so long and so loud that several people in the queue looked as though they were on the verge of calling the police or an ambulance. This was not developing the way I had intended as I felt my cheeks reddening in response.

'No, you daft buggers. I have a crush on a girl at school and I want to ask her out.'

'Well, what's the problem then? Oh no, it's not Beth is it? Everybody's had her,' Alan joked.

In fact, I thought Beth was a nice girl and that probably nobody had had her, least of all my friends. I was sure they were still virgins like me, otherwise I would have had all the intimate details by now.

'No, it's Sarah, Sarah Zurek.'

'No chance there, mate. That snooty bitch just makes love to books,' Dave said caustically. To Dave, anyone who did not react to his acerbic wit was a snooty bitch, I mused.

'Look, I'm dead serious. In fact I'm going to ask her out tonight,' I countered, and then realized too late that I had just dug a big hole for myself.

'Go on then, we'll keep your place in the queue,' Alan challenged.

Just then, the queue began to move and fortunately for me, their attention focused on stopping anyone jumping in front of us. Once inside however, the dares continued until the main feature had started.

I had a difficult time concentrating on the film and sensed that the derision and teasing would continue later. About twenty minutes into the film I took a deep breath and announced that I had to pop out for a minute. I guessed my friends would think that I had gone to the toilet and if I lost my resolve that was probably what I would do.

I headed towards the double doors and emerged into the cinema foyer. To my left was the Gents; to my right was a public telephone. I went to the telephone, picked up the receiver, squeezed coins into the slot and dialled the number I had memorised earlier. My heart was trying to break through my chest when the ringing stopped.

'Hello, who is it?' said a young female voice, but it didn't sound like Sarah.

'Oh, hello, can I speak to Sarah please?'

'Hang on.' I heard an argument in the background with one voice chastising another because she had not asked for the name of the caller.

'Hello?'

'Hi Sarah. Sorry for ringing you so late, this is Carl Denham.'

It was only half past eight, but for the moment, I could think of nothing else to say. There was a pause and I assumed she was trying to work out who I was.

'From school,' I added quickly.

'Yes, I know, how's the Chemistry going?'

Relieved that she remembered me and had perfectly set the subject for the conversation, I replied, 'Goodness, you must be a mind reader. That's exactly why I called. Are you ... busy ... tomorrow night?' I asked, now full of confidence.

'Yes, I am actually ...' and for an instant I was crushed, '... but I'm only babysitting. Do you want to study with me?'

'Well yes, that was the general idea.'

'I need to check with the parents, but I'm sure it would be OK. Do you know St. Luke's Road in Ilford?'

'No, but I can find it.'

'OK, it's number 76, next door to a newsagent. My babysitting starts at eight o'clock. Give me half an hour to get the little ones settled. So, can you get there for, say, eight thirty?'

'Yes, no problem.'

'All right, I'll see you tomorrow night. Don't forget your exercise books. Bye,' and Sarah hung up.

I put the receiver down, said a loud 'Yes' and thrust my fists in the air in a triumphant gesture. My mouth was dry and my heart was still pounding furiously, but I'd done it, I'd actually done it. I had got a date with Sarah. Well not a date in the strictest sense, but I would not tell my friends that. God, everyone would be green with envy. Now I really did have to go to the toilet. While there, I took a drink of water and splashed some on my face.

A few minutes later having stumbled through the darkness of the theatre, I took my seat again next to my friends.

'Bloody hell ...' Don whispered, '... that was a long piss.'

'Yes ...' I said with a wide grin that could not be seen in gloom, '... and I think I've solved my sexual problem too.'

By seven o'clock the following morning, I was washed, dressed, breakfasted and had several Chemistry books spread across the desk in my bedroom. It was a shock to my parents, an enigma to myself and would have brought mockery if my friends could see me. I'd only gone to bed five hours ago.

Except for my telephone call it had been a normal Friday night. Cinema, pub and back to Don's to chat about all the usual things in which we had a joint interest: football, motor racing, pop music, television, pranks at school and girls. The previous night it had been the latter which had dominated our conversation.

Following my *conquest* (as it became known) with Sarah, a contest had taken place where girls at school had been scored out of ten. It wasn't scientific in any way, except that a decimal point was allowed in the ratings to ensure there were no ties. No separate points for dress sense, brains or character, just a straight scale for "fanciability", although by Alan's voting it was viewed he was awarding points solely for the size of breasts.

Collectively we had drawn up a list of nominees from all the girls we could recall at school. Don, with his ever-present meticulous organization, had drawn a scoring table on a lined writing pad. After heated debates that went on into the early hours, Carol Sellars had emerged as the winner. Sarah had ranked a lowly fifth, despite scoring a maximum from me. I was suspicious about the results. Based upon previous scoreless surveys she had been a clear number one. I speculated that now she was *out of circulation* - a term that had been coined by Dave, and perhaps some envy, my mates had purposely scored her low. That didn't bother me, what did however, was Don threatening to post the results on the school sports notice board.

Fortunately, we had nothing specifically organized for Saturday, so I was not subjected to scorn about my own plans to cram as much scientific knowledge in my head during the day. I wanted to make sure that intellectually I would be able to hold my own, *or hers*, the next evening.

As it turned out, that evocative beginning was quite benign. It was obvious within about five minutes that our evening would be strictly educational – in the scholastic sense. Time was spent identifying each other's subject weaknesses – I had plenty, Sarah had none, then choosing study topics to review or practice. Objectively I was satisfied and for now could wish for no more.

The babysitting "dates" became a regular occurrence. Sarah was brilliant with children; whenever they required attention, they always took precedence. She had the knack of soothing their worries and getting them back to sleep as quickly and gently as possible. I was jealous of the kisses and cuddles that the infants received and I was no help to begin with, but Sarah soon educated me in her minding techniques. I never made the grade in singing lullabies or changing nappies, but I became expert at reading bedtime stories. Sarah's babysitting fame spread far and wide – well, to at least a five mile radius, so once I had passed my driving test and convinced my parents I really only wanted to use their car to go babysitting, I was able to assist with transport for the remote duties.

Love didn't blossom *between* us, but *I* was totally smitten. Babysitting priorities were always children first and studying second – there was no third. Bodily contact was strictly forbidden. The regular Saturday night and often weekday sittings were the hardest times of my life – literally. Keeping my priapism at bay for hours on end, at least once, and sometimes three times a week became a physical endurance that could only be relieved by shameful visits to the bathroom. Sarah noticed my discomfort on many occasions when I was caught organizing the contents of my trousers to a more peaceful position. Her response was always to tap my embarrassment playfully with a ruler and say, *'There will be time enough for that later'*. That was encouraging; I just wished that later would become sooner.

But I was sure that she had affection for me, she showed it in other ways. Some parents didn't like the idea of Sarah bringing male company to her babysitting appointments; but because of the demands on her, she could choose which duties she accepted, and soon only took on those where I could join her.

Some of the teachers at our school also engaged her, but my arrival at their homes usually brought dismay and comment that *brainy Sarah* should not associate with *dropout Carl*. She hated such criticism, and thereafter was always too busy to accept teacher engagements. Also, because of the money that she earned, she insisted on taking me out on the infrequent days and evenings when no one required her services. Cinemas, bowling alleys, fast-food cafés and the library were her popular choices - she wasn't a great fan of pubs, discos or nightclubs. On these occasions, physical contact *was* permitted, and I became an expert in the Victorian skill of handholding.

Naturally, I wasn't able to conceal my scarcity from my schoolmates. We still went out together if I wasn't committed to *babystudying*, as they called it, but I avoided sorties where the prime intention was to "pull birds". As far as they were concerned, I had "pulled" already. I suffered numerous questions and sexual innuendoes about what "it" was like with Sarah; they just didn't seem to understand that someone could have such a close relationship without bringing sex into it somewhere – neither could I!

After three months of my private tuition, mock exams arrived in January. I felt I'd made real progress, but promptly received a nasty shock when I failed all the exams; not by much, though I began to question my abilities. The teachers assured me that just failing was good. There were still four months to the proper exams and we hadn't yet covered all the course material. I still had doubts because my objective had changed. No longer were the studies a means of getting to University, they had become an excuse to be with Sarah.

Then one night Sarah presented me with a dilemma when were talking about Universities. It transpired it was her ambition to obtain a science degree at Cambridge University. It hadn't hit me until then. If all went well, next year I would go to University but Sarah would still be at school. Then there would be two years of University overlap and during Sarah's final degree year, I would have already graduated and presumably be working. That would mean we would apart for *four* years. I could minimise the separation by aiming to go Cambridge too, but the challenge would be enormous, I would need top grades in all my subjects to stand any chance. Supposing I did get there, maybe Sarah wouldn't. With her brain metaphorically the size of the planet, that possibility would be remote, but nothing was certain. I'd just had the first panic attack of my life. Sarah seemed unconcerned by my problem. We could still see each other occasionally she said; talk on the phone; write letters - after all, it wasn't as though we were married. And she was right of course. We were good friends and study partners, so far nothing else. Yet, I loved *her* and I wanted to tell her. Perhaps if I made such a declaration I would get some commitment from her, but I was worried that such a move might place undue pressure on our relationship. I could end up losing her *and* jeopardizing my academic ambitions. She must have recognized my predicament because she touched my hand and stared at me with her big blue eyes and said proverbially: *'Everything comes to him who waits'*.

The exams came and went in June; then it was the agonizing wait for the results in August. I got a holiday job mowing gravesides at the local cemetery. Sarah went with her sister Marion and mother to Poland for a month; a holiday combined with a visit to their estranged father and husband. When they returned, Sarah took on some paid clerical work at a local solicitor, and I set out for a two-week tour of Scotland with Dave Starry in his rusting, but fortunately reliable Ford Escort. These events conspired to keep Sarah and I apart, and I dropped into an emotional vacuum for two months.

On August 23rd, 1984 the exam results envelope arrived. I didn't open it but phoned Sarah; it was the excuse I needed - Could we meet? She seemed genuinely excited by the prospect. Was it the teacher excited for her student or the girlfriend for her boyfriend? In front of her I opened the envelope slowly and withdrew the piece of paper slowly to reveal the grades ... A ... A ...B ... B. They were good, but not good enough. Goodbye Cambridge, hello ... Warwick - as it was to be.

Chapter 10

1984 - 1988

The first year at Warwick flew by. Everything was new. The freedom, the social life, the parties, the bars, all served as distractions from the innermost thought of my mind. Sarah was still in my head; after all, she had got me to University in the first place. I phoned her once a week and to begin with, wrote every few days. I always signed my letters "Love Carl" and she signed her weekly letter "Love Sarah", but there were no declarations of love in the body of the letters. I wanted to pour out my heart but feared that this would somehow show a weakness or compromise the relationship. We were acting just like inseparable brother and sister.

My letter frequency began to tail off, as I became more involved in the aspects of University life. Then one Sunday morning I awoke naked in bed with a fellow, female student. I didn't remember what had happened during the night, though *fuck all* according to my erudite bed-partner. There had been a party to celebrate a rare event like someone attending a lecture, and a so-so brunette had tagged on to me. When the cheap (subsequently discovered to mean, contaminated) beer had run out, she – I don't recall her name, had escorted my drunken body back to my room, presumably with procreative intentions. Her wish hadn't been granted courtesy of my need to sleep off a thumping head, but her reapplication in the morning was successful to the verge of penetration. Whereupon a sudden urge to go to the bathroom brought forth a shrivelling of the penis, and a rising of the previous night's fermented barley into the sink and surrounding porcelain. I failed to reawaken the lust of my hastily departing Jane Doe and virginity stayed with me for another week.

Sunday afternoons were the designated times to call Sarah. She was an excitable girl on the telephone, usually dominating the conversation with her own news, but at least I was often left with plenty to mention in my letters. Strangely during the phone call after the "gag shag" – as my friends called it, Sarah for once had little to report, so I related the tale of the party from the night before. At first, I held back with the intimate part, unwilling to taint the relationship I wanted to have with Sarah. But then with a rush of hung-over bravado or pent up guilt, I revealed the details. She calmly chastised me about the revelation, and I was relieved that she had appeared, apparently, so understanding. But by Wednesday morning, I had the first inkling that my confession had backfired when no letter appeared.

Regularly in the post, I had a letter from Sarah; she would write it on Sunday night, despatch it by first-class post on the way to school on Monday and it usually arrived on Tuesday morning - though never later than Wednesday. I phoned her on Wednesday evening, and Thursday and Friday, but according to her mother or sister, she was out babysitting. The messages I left to call me went unanswered and still there was no letter. Did I already have a relationship with Sarah where the brink of infidelity would cause her to reject me? If so, why had we always been so arm's length about our affair, never daring to declare true affections to each other? I felt confused and uncertain.

By Saturday I had drifted into a kind of void, so when another "cheap-beer" party was offered, I was eager to attend in order to drown my sorrows. This time I erred on the side of caution and chose vodka as my numbing fluid. It was a different crowd of revellers, so I hoped I wouldn't bump into Jane Doe - and indeed didn't, but I did meet a pretty, shy, geography student called Susan. Somehow, we discovered that we were both born under the Zodiac sign of Virgo, and by drunken word association established how appropriate that was considering our respective virginal states. We were both embarrassed by our condition and clinically decided to remedy the situation. The sex was clinical too - no whispered words, no foreplay, and no promises to meet again. She was in my room for less than ten minutes. We were both so polite and grateful to each other for the experience shared, it had been like a visit to the doctors. I was proud that, at last, I had broken my duck, and my friends were too. They would remind me throughout the rest of my University life of the night of "Wham, bam, thank you ma'am".

Sarah did speak to me on Sunday afternoon when I called. It was an awkward conversation. Yes, she had been avoiding me; yes, she was upset by what I had confessed last Sunday; yes, I was sorry it had happened; yes, perhaps we ought to cool it for a bit; yes, we would still be good friends; yes, perhaps we could review the situation in two months time, once she had finished her 'A' level exams. I didn't then disclose that the previous night I had strayed even further from the confines of our unwritten understanding - but did that evening in a letter. I threw caution to the wind; now I added to my confessional, kept using the word clinical to disguise my sin and finally I poured out my heart. It was my first attempt at romantic prose and I rewrote the letter many times attempting to communicate my true feelings to her; I posted it on Monday morning and waited for a response.

I was still waiting on Saturday morning, so I wrote another letter – still no reply. Then I wrote every day for eight weeks. The letters always had the same theme; I was sorry for what had happened; I was thinking of her constantly; she was not to dwell on the matter and affect her studies, because all she needed to know was that I loved her and always would.

By the end of June, I believed I was a master writer of billets-doux, and flirted with the idea of swapping my computing degree course for one in romantic literature. At the end of term, my parents collected me from Warwick and as soon as we reached home, I borrowed the car and headed to Sarah's home in Ilford. Her mother said she was working in the public library. A put off I thought; exams were finished, but aware of Sarah's conscientiousness I concluded she had probably already begun studying for her degree.

As I walked the half-mile to the local library, I began to have doubts about my mission. Were the halcyon days of our friendship over? I was only 19; Sarah was 18; we were still teenagers for Christ's sake. What had we experienced of life and other relationships? Sarah was my first *love*, or was it teenage hormones sending false signals to my brain. And was Sarah, or had Sarah ever been, in love with me? She had never said the magic words. Had my sexual infidelity, or rather *inopportune carnal discovery*, really upset her? Wasn't that an indication of love? Well bugger it, I thought. All this theorizing and soul searching was getting me nowhere. I loved Sarah and I wanted her love back - that is why I was here.

I found her sitting alone at a table behind the Foreign Language shelves. She didn't look up, so I watched her for a few minutes. She was wearing a two-tone blue dress with red piping at the short sleeves and neck. Her hair was longer than I remembered, and she kept brushing it from her cheeks and tucking it behind her ears. The teenage hormones were working overtime; I had that slightly nervous, heart pounding, dry mouthed, inner warm feeling that I recognized as love. It certainly wasn't sexual desire in its carnal sense - no twitches down below; I just wanted to be with her, talk to her, hold her in my arms. I went to the shelves immediately behind her and pretended to select a book; she was a metre from me and I swear I could detect her scent. I tried to see what she was reading so absorbedly, but I just saw text – no diagrams or pictures to give me a clue. I could reach out and stroke her hair if I wanted to, yet I held back in case it alarmed her. I chose words instead and leant towards her.

'I love you, Sarah Zurek,' I said quietly, 'Don't ever forget that.'

She raised her head from the book suddenly, and then slowly rotated to look up at me - her cheeks were flushed. I panicked a little; her face was expressionless so I couldn't tell the reason for the glow. She rose leisurely from the chair and stared at me with her bright blue eyes. I thought I caught the beginning of a smile, but before I was certain she put her arms around my waist and rested her head on my chest. *Then* I stroked her hair and I heard her cry for the first time. She sobbed for a minute and raised her head; there were still rivulets of tears, which conflicted with the sparkling smile she wore; at last she spoke the words I was desperate to hear. '*Je t'aimerai toujours*, Carl Denham.' The language was a surprise – now I knew the book she was studying. And then another first - we kissed, oblivious of the inquisitive faces around us.

We walked back to her home, I was invited in (yes, yet another first) and her mother was clearly flustered by the arrival of a boyfriend of Sarah's, much to my jealous relief. The matriarchal response was to serve tea and cakes, and eye me surreptitiously. There was an awkward silence for a while, and then Sarah drew a deep breath and said:

'Mother, I know this will come as a shock ...' (her mother's mouth gaped open) '... and I know that you'll lecture me later that it can't be true ...' (eyes on stalks, expecting the worst) '... but Carl and I ...' (now looking at me with daggers drawn) '... are in love with each other ...' (incredulity arriving) '... and will be forever,' (total disbelief)

Total disbelief from me too - not the facts, but that Sarah had spoken so openly and determinedly.

I was invited for dinner and to accompany Sarah for the babysitting assignment she had that evening. Marion arrived home from work and Sarah whisked her away upstairs, to tell her, I found out later, about the *entente cordiale* that had been declared between us - a phrase adopted by my now French-speaking Sarah. I felt under scrutiny during dinner with the elder females asking searching, but disguised questions about my intentions and prospects, and it was a relief to eventually be alone with Sarah at 69 Congress Road. I remember the address well, because it was the location (with an apt name) where Sarah and I first made love, although the number – *soixante-neuf* as Sarah would call it, was not significant. Sarah's babysitting rules still applied; the children were top priority, but for once there was no second priority to study, and we were blessed with a single child to tend, who was asleep when we arrived, and stayed safely asleep until we left. In between, on a sofa, and later on a sheepskin rug, we consummated our *amour*.

We were sensible with our relationship for the remainder of the summer, carefully balancing the time we spent with each other, and friends and family. We always endeavoured to be together on babysitting trips and took sexual liberties when the prime duty allowed.

Good news came at the end of August, when, as expected, Sarah scored straight A's in her science exams, so she was set to be Cambridge bound in October. By virtue of Sarah's sitting income, in September, we spent a weekend in a hotel in Cambridge with the view to become familiar with the city, but instead became intimately familiar with the hotel bedroom; justifying that Sarah would have plenty of exploration time once term had started.

The next two years were routine by comparison. Term time we were busy with our studies and University life, although some weekends I hitchhiked from Warwick to Cambridge. During the holidays, we were mostly together. Having made our commitments, we were content to get the most from University, academically and socially; there was no discussion about the future. We worked hard and played hard, and there were never any doubts about being faithful to each other.

May 1987 was a tough month. It was exam time for finals and the days merged into nights with my head buried in books and study notes. An added complication was that Sarah had planned to go to Poland for her sister

Marion's wedding, and she wanted me to accompany her so that I could meet her father. I couldn't afford the time or the money, and she was obviously disappointed but realistic about the situation. It was the second time that I had declined a trip to Poland - the previous year I had had similar reasons to miss her father's re-marriage.

The hard work paid off. I graduated with a first class honours degree at the end of June.

I had been looking forward to spending the summer with Sarah. The round of interviews for a job had been and gone, and I had fortunately received a number of offers. However, by stalling a possible start date to be with Sarah, the best positions were withdrawn. Then Sarah announced that she would be staying on in Cambridge for July and August. She had the chance to do some innovative research work with her Professor, and after that she had acquired a placement at a local electronics company, which was going to pay handsomely for her efforts. It was difficult to be angry, since it was an excellent opportunity for her. I re-started the job hunt and eventually secured a position at a small, but growing software company in Brentwood, albeit at a lower salary than I had hoped.

I started at Oxitel Limited in August. The discipline of nine to five working was a shock to be begin with, particularly when the norm became nine to nine, such were the demands on my and everyone else's time, from the Directors down to the secretaries. I enjoyed it though. I was happy to spend the evenings working rather than moping around at home. I'd fitted in well and the prospects were good.

At last, in September, Sarah took her summer break. We wanted to have a modest holiday together, but it was now my turn to scupper the plans. My new job was as demanding as ever, weekend working was common. I was well regarded and rewarded with a substantial pay rise, and with the overtime, I felt I was on a ladder to success. It was Sarah's turn to understand and she contented herself with her studies. We did manage to spend a few days together before Sarah's final year at Cambridge and we talked about love, the future and our respective involvement in software developments. We were both full of ideas for innovative products and vowed that eventually we would pool them and make ourselves into millionaires. One day in particular was spent at a remote part of the Essex coast. Of all the days that we were together, it was the most memorable. It was where we committed to each other that we wanted to be together for the rest of our lives.

I had only been at Oxitel for three months when my father's mother died. She had lived alone in a small bungalow in Ongar since her husband died five years earlier. My parents owned their own house and lived comfortably, so my grandmother had said that she would leave the bungalow to me. Her Will confirmed that and added a bonus of £12,000 in cash much to my amazement.

It had always been my intention to move out from my parents as soon as I could afford to. Not that I had problems with my parents, quite the contrary, but every young man likes his space and independence and I was no exception. As it turned out, my father had the opportunity of getting a transfer to work in California. Therefore, with me employed and now a property owner, I encouraged my parents to take the plunge and go west, promising them I would visit as soon as I could afford the time. Surprisingly, they did not need encouragement. I had forgotten they had both been flower children, so San Francisco was still a Mecca to them, even 20 years later.

I transferred my modest possessions from Wanstead to Ongar using the second hand Ford Fiesta that I had bought out of my inheritance money. The bungalow became public knowledge, but the money windfall I kept secret, even from Sarah, for the time being. I decided to lock the money away in a one year Building Society bond and would plan its disbursement with Sarah when she graduated.

December was frantic and Oxitel began recruiting additional staff. My boss acquired a secretary to deal with the administration and documentation workload that was becoming an increasing burden in our developments. Janice Harding got the job. She was only nineteen, slim, pretty, with masses of curly reddish-brown hair. She wasn't that bright, having flunked at school at 16, but she was an expert with a word processor and efficient secretarially. Her most well defined trait was persistence. Once she had her mind on a task she wouldn't let go. That was an admirable characteristic at work, but when she actually asked me out and I refused, I became a challenge and obsession to her. I resisted her advances and ignored her sexual innuendoes, but I began to have an aversion for going to work, in fear of what her latest ploy might be. Secretly I was attracted to her too, but only physically, and I confess there were times when I felt like yielding to her constant flirting, if only as a means to disappoint her in some way. It was a genuine relief when Sarah came home for the Christmas break.

I spent Christmas with Sarah and her mother. I considered visiting my parents in the States, but Sarah was missing her mother, and I was missing Sarah, so the decision was easy.

Just before Christmas, Sarah and I had the most severe test so far of our *affaire de coeur*. I'd gone to the Oxitel Xmas party and little did I know what raucous affairs they were. I got very drunk, and recalled little of the proceedings. I was unceremoniously dumped on the doorstep of Sarah's mother's house in a dishevelled, drunken state, with lipstick on my face and stinking of beer and perfume. Her mother was prudish, and this was the first time she had witnessed any loutish behaviour from me. I know that behind my back she tried to persuade Sarah to send me on my way, but after a short period of uncertainty, Sarah's allegiance was restored. She moved in with me at Ongar for the two weeks before she went back to Cambridge, much against her mother's Victorian principles.

After Sarah had returned to Cambridge in January 1988, I settled back into the development bedlam at Oxitel. For a month, life was good, but busy and I began to enjoy work again – even Janice seemed to have given upon on her quest, then on February 11th my world started to fall apart.

Chapter 11

Thursday, February 11, 1988 – 10:00 a.m.

I was reviewing some software code with my boss Steve Masterson, when Janice interrupted us.

'You have a call on your phone from Kate,' Janice said, seemingly enjoying the embarrassment this would cause me.

Kate? Kate who? I thought. 'I'll have to call back, I'm rather busy right now,' I said, feeling, but not seeing, the glare that Steve was giving me.

'She said it was *very* urgent.'

I looked pleadingly at Steve, who said, 'Go on, take the call, but please try to keep your private life out of the office.'

I nodded my appreciation and went to my desk aware that the only Kate I knew was one of Sarah's housemates in Cambridge.

'Kate? What's wrong?' There had to be something wrong for Kate to ring me.

'Carl, you must come to Cambridge, Sarah's been taken to hospital.'

'Oh Christ, what's happened?'

'She's had some kind of breakdown. I was in the kitchen when I heard her screaming and sobbing. I rushed into her room and she was going crazy and smashing things. I tried to calm her down, but she hit out at me. I just couldn't do anything. She carried on like this for a few minutes. Then she seemed to have difficulty catching a breath and collapsed on the floor clutching her chest. I called an ambulance and tried to revive her. She came round and then started going crazy again. It took both of the ambulance crew to hold her down and sedate her before she hurt herself. They've only just left.'

Kate was in tears now. The situation had obviously upset her considerably. I wasn't feeling too good either.

'Kate, please calm down. Do you know what brought this on?' I said.

'I've no idea. She was OK last night, but I hadn't seen her this morning until I went into her room.'

'Where have they taken her?'

'They've gone to Addenbrooke's hospital. Do you know where that is?'

'Yes, I pass near it on the way to you. Look, I'm leaving now, but it will take me an hour and a half's drive - I should arrive about eleven thirty. Could you meet me there?'

'Yes, OK. I was going there as soon as I reached you anyway.'

The journey to Cambridge was uneventful except for the furious activity going on in my mind. Steve had been distinctly unimpressed with my sudden departure even when I had told him the reason. Thankfully, Janice had made herself scarce when I was leaving, the last thing I needed was any sexual innuendo from her. My primary concern though was Sarah. Last weekend she had been more subdued than normal, but I attributed this to the fact that her final exams were now only two months away. As usual, she was pushing herself hard, too hard I viewed, and I was always fearful that the tiniest upset could have an adverse affect.

Deep in thought, a couple of times I recklessly lost my concentration and narrowly avoided accidents. However, once I was on the M11 heading North, I focused hard on my driving and went as fast as my Ford Fiesta would take me.

I arrived at the hospital entrance ten minutes inside my predicted time, and then promptly lost my advantage trying to find a parking place in the sprawling campus of the hospital. I went through the main doors and stopped to look for a reception desk through the blur of hospital activity confronting me. As I strode towards a likely looking information point, I heard my name being called. It was Kate.

'How is she?' I asked.

'They don't know yet. She's still sedated. They'll carry out some tests when she comes round. She's in a private room just outside ward C2, I'll take you to her, but there's something I need to ask you before we go.'

'Yes?'

'When did you last speak to Sarah?'

'Not since I left her on Sunday night, four days ago. You know that Sarah made the rules. No phone calls during the week except on Friday night to confirm the weekend arrangements. It's so I don't distract her from her studies.'

'It's just that, she ... well ... she seemed a bit upset with you.'

'What, just now?'

'No, when she was screaming at the house. I don't remember her exact words, but she kept shouting your name and something like *How could you do this to me?*'

'Are you sure, Kate? Really, we haven't made contact since last Sunday, and everything was fine then.'

'Yes, I'm sure. She was mumbling similar things in her sleep when I first arrived here, so something must be wrong. Be careful when you see her.'

'Before I forget, have you phoned her mother?'

'No, I haven't. I don't have her number.'

'OK, let me see Sarah first, then I'll make the call.'

Kate led me towards ward C2. At first, the duty nurse was reluctant to let me see Sarah because the administrating doctor, Dr. Phipps, had advised that she needed undisturbed rest and no visitors. After an emotional pleading, the nurse eventually acquiesced and granted me a few minutes, as long as I was quiet.

Looking at Sarah, I thought she looked at complete peace with the world. Except for the sterile location, and intravenous drip into her arm, it could have been a scene after we had spent a night together. I wanted to stroke her hair and kiss her cheek as I had always done to wake her, but the watchful eyes of the nurse inhibited me. I felt a sense of guilt too. Was there anything I had said or done to bring this about? I looked at the nurse trying to cast an expression of *Can I touch her*, but she merely ushered me out of the room with a beckoning finger. That was the last time I saw Sarah.

'She's still asleep,' I said to Kate. 'You may as well go back to the house. Do you want a lift?'

'Actually I'm due at a lecture soon, but I don't really feel up to it. I'll keep you company if you like. Perhaps we could get a cup of coffee somewhere?'

I established from the nurse that Sarah had been tranquillized, and would probably be asleep for at least the next two hours, so there was plenty of time for a drink and something to eat too. She gave us directions to the coffee shop in the main concourse.

On the way, I stopped by a pay phone to call Sarah's mother, but there was no answer.

Kate and I had several cups of coffee while we waited, but neither of us had any stomach for food. We chatted about all kinds of things to try to take our minds off our concern for Sarah, but she kept coming back into the conversation. I ascertained from Kate that between weekends Sarah was totally focused on her studies. Only very occasionally did she join her housemates for any of the frequent pub visits, parties or society meetings that were the hub of University life. Even then, she never stayed out late. Her reasoning was that Monday to Friday was for studies, and Saturday and Sunday for me, so she had to squeeze seven days of work into five. This worried me because I knew from my own experience that the social life at University was an essential ingredient for character development. Kate assured me however, that despite her obsession with work, Sarah was the happiest and most well adjusted person she had ever come across. Everybody liked her.

Referring to Sarah's outburst, I asked Kate if Sarah had dealings with any other male students, particularly ones called Carl. Kate confirmed that she did have other boy*friends*, but she could not recall another "Carl". The two hours quickly passed interrupted only by my unsuccessful attempts to ring Sarah's mother.

We returned to the ward and were advised that she had woken disorientated, and Dr. Phipps was with her conducting some tests. The nurse explained that these would be at least an electrocardiogram and blood tests to identify if there were any physical abnormalities. She asked us to wait because the doctor might need to ask us some questions.

The doctor quizzed us on Sarah's physical and emotional background, and as far as Kate and I knew, Sarah had never suffered such major infirmities. His preliminary diagnosis, based upon Sarah's lethargy and temporary amnesia, was that she had been exposed to a traumatic incident. If we became aware of the cause, we were to notify Dr. Phipps immediately, since it could dictate the remedial therapy. Nervously Kate had felt obliged to tell the doctor regarding Sarah's rantings about me, but of course I could not enlighten him in any way. Nonetheless, his parting instruction was that I was not to attempt any communication with her without his authority.

'Shall I take you go back to the house now? I'll then come back here to see if there is anything I can do,' I said to Kate.

'Will you be OK on your own? How long will you stay?'

'Until I can talk to Sarah, assuming I'm allowed to.'

'Look, take me back to the house, I'll tidy Sarah's room, and then you can come back later and stay the night.'

It seemed the best solution to kill some time, so we set out for the short journey to the North side of Cambridge. We took the ring road to the West, which ran parallel to the River Cam. On the way, I was reminded of the beauty of the City, the colleges and their striking architecture, and the abundance of open spaces. Given the choice I would have studied for my degree in Cambridge, but my grades had fallen short of the necessary standard. Sarah and I used to joke about that. I playfully suggested that her tutoring of me was simply not good enough and she argued I should have met up with her earlier.

I also envied the house that Kate and Sarah shared with three other girls. Situated in St. Johns Road it was an old terraced house with a black and white façade and large bay windows. It looked small and insignificant from the outside, but the inside was bright, clean and spacious; better than any choices I had at Warwick. Less than a minute from the house was the grassed expanse of Jesus Green that Sarah and I had walked during the weekends that I visited her.

When I got back to the hospital, there was no change in Sarah's condition, so I telephoned Sarah's mother again and this time she was home. She was already aware of the sad news from Kate, since by chance she had just tried to telephone Sarah at the house. Our conversation was strained. Despite the vigil I intended to keep by Sarah's side until her mother came tomorrow, she was stony towards me, but at the time I ascribed this to the shock of her daughter's situation.

The vigil wasn't to be. When I consulted the ward sister, she asked me to leave and return the next morning. I insisted that I was quite prepared to sit it out, but she resisted more forcefully, arguing that it was in my own and Sarah's best interests if I got a good night's sleep.

I called the office to say that I wouldn't be in until Monday, and made my way back to Sarah's house. I had to ring the bell several times before Kate came to answer the door. She stood in the doorway as though she was greeting a stranger.

'I'm sorry Carl; there's been a development. You can't stay here after all,' she said.

I was rather taken aback by her change in attitude. The friendly Kate I had transported just an hour ago was now treating me like a cold-calling double-glazing salesman.

'What sort of development?' I replied in a tone half way between anger and disappointment. Kate looked embarrassed and chose to study her feet.

'Is it something to do with Sarah's mother?' I suggested.

Kate appeared to gain in confidence. 'Look Carl. Don't play the innocent with me. Just go away. You're not wanted here,' she said and quickly shut the door before I could react.

I banged on the door in frustration rattling the glass panel, and rang the bell dementedly. With no response I shouted through the letterbox, 'Kate. What's going on? I don't understand.'

Beyond the letterbox I saw Caroline, one of the other resident students peering nervously down the corridor. 'If you don't leave I'll have to call the police,' she said.

A similar exchange continued for a few minutes and short of breaking down the door, I wasn't going to make any progress, so I sat in the car trying to unravel the puzzle presented to me. I had to be at fault somewhere; I was the common denominator in the odd behaviour of Sarah, her mother and now Kate. My mind again went back to recent events but there was nothing that could possibly have caused such a bizarre set of reactions. I resigned myself to bedding down somewhere locally for the night, and eventually spent a disturbed, mind-racking but otherwise uneventful evening in a cheap hotel I found on Chesterton Road.

I was ill equipped for an overnight stay: no change of clothes, razor or toothbrush, so the following morning was an inauspicious start to the day, which was compounded by heavy rain. I paid the modest bill - which befitted a hotel without a restaurant, private facilities or other creature comforts, and left before suffering what would certainly be an inadequate and unwanted breakfast.

I was pestering the staff of ward C2 by half past seven. Their resolve of the previous day was undaunted though, even with a change of personnel. It seemed I was a marked man. I would have to wait until Dr. Phipps came on duty at nine o'clock.

There was no point brooding over my dilemma anymore – I'd had my fill of that in the hotel room - so I visited the small shop adjacent to the main reception and returned with a bundle of newspapers and magazines.

When he arrived, Dr. Phipps was made aware of my presence, acknowledged it and then disappeared towards Sarah's room. It was twenty minutes before he came back.

He was studying a clipboard when he approached, 'Hello again. Mr. Denham?'

I nodded.

'I'm sorry to keep you waiting. Miss Zurek is comfortable. Unfortunately that's all I can tell you at the moment since you are not immediate family. I believe Mrs. Zurek will be here later this morning and I'll be giving her a full briefing. It has to be her decision whether she provides you with further information,' Dr. Phipps said rather formally.

'You don't understand doctor. Sarah and I have been together for over four years now. We are practically ... engaged.' I said pleadingly.

Dr. Phipps held out his hands as if in submission. 'I'm afraid we are dealing with hospital rules regarding provision of patient details. I hope you won't have to wait too long until Mrs. Zurek arrives,' he replied.

His pragmatic approach didn't fool me. I was certain he could have been more accommodating. There was surely some other force at work.

In my opinion, two hours, was too long. Time enough for two newspapers, three crosswords, a computer magazine, and a triple check of the number of carpet tiles in the waiting area.

I didn't recognize Audrey at first. The dark brown raincoat complete with hood concealed her shape and facial features. With her haste to the reception desk and vigorous shaking of surface raindrops on the carpet, she didn't notice me either.

With the mention of Zurek, removal of the brown camouflage and a cascade of faded blonde hair I rose from my seat to greet Audrey. The reception nurse must have whispered something because Audrey turned to face me.

'I don't think there's any point in you staying. Sarah won't see you,' she said. The tone of her voice was disapproving, but the scowl on her face was the most alarming feature.

'I think that ought to be Sarah's decision don't you?' I said. I had raised my voice because I was getting rather fed-up with everyone coming down on me for no apparent reason. 'Have you spoken to her?'

'No, but the doctor has discerned from Sarah's mutterings that you are the likely cause of her distress.'

'That can't be true. There must be some mistake.' I was getting angrier and louder. I noticed the reception nurse signalling to someone with her hand.

'I think you will find that Kate can verify the story.'

'Kate? What has ...' I was interrupted by Dr. Phipps stepping in front of me.

'Is there a problem here?' he said.

'Damn right. Is it true that I can't see Sarah?'

Dr. Phipps moved to look questioningly at Audrey. She responded with a despairing nod.

'We believe that would be in Sarah's best interest.' Dr. Phipps said.

I looked at Audrey with a view to reminding her of the bond that Sarah and I had, but she averted her eyes. I looked at Dr. Phipps for support, but his expression was neutral. I turned around and left the hospital.

When, three weeks later, Steve said, 'Let's go to my office, Carl,' I recognized the request had a finality about it. It was ten o'clock and I had only just arrived at work, but that wasn't the problem.

With the relentless pressure of work on me and the rest of the development staff, we had formed a protest group complaining about working conditions. If we were going to sell our souls to Oxitel, we wanted the most up-to-date computers, large monitors, cigarette breaks and above all, flexible working hours. We negotiated a simple scheme. Any start and finish time each day, including Saturdays and Sundays, and subtract an hour for breaks. Add up the net hours worked in a week; the first forty were at normal time, the residual at double time. Amazingly, the scheme had been accepted without a complaint from the management.

My problem had been achieving thirty hours in a week, let alone forty. I typically arrived at ten and usually gave up before four, Mondays to Fridays. Attempting to concentrate for periods longer than that was becoming increasingly difficult. My body was in Chelmsford but my mind was in Cambridge. Sure, I was only paid for the hours worked, but my productivity was poor. Oxitel had become dependent on me for some important projects and these were seriously behind schedule.

I was also reprimanded daily about the duration and manner of my personal telephone calls. I had tried all kinds of deception with the hospital staff to try to speak to Sarah, but I never managed to penetrate the Carl Denham barrier that had been erected.

Calls to Sarah's house to get information from Kate brought abuse from whoever answered.

Sarah's mother consistently put the phone down every time I spoke. Eventually I received a letter from her solicitor threatening a restraining order unless I desisted in my attempts to contact Sarah.

Janice had made matters worse. She recognized my insecurity and her insensitive flirting had continued unabated.

Steve came straight to the point, 'We're going to have to lay you off.' He genuinely looked sad. 'I know you've been through a bad patch over the last few weeks, but *Time is a physician that heals every grief* doesn't seem to apply to you,' he said.

I presumed the quotation was supposed to give credence to his pronouncement. In fact, it just wound me up, so I said nothing.

Feeling awkward Steve continued, 'We'll give you a good technical reference if you want one.'

I noted the specificity of technical, rather than work or general.

'When do you want me to leave?' I asked.

'Brief me where you are on your projects and then you can go. We've paid you to the end of the month of course,' he said and gave me an envelope which I presumed contained my P45 and final cheque.

It only took fifteen minutes to conduct the briefing. I could have spent hours but I think Steve was under some pressure from his boss to get rid of me as quickly as possible.

The goodbyes didn't take too long. My immediate colleagues had little to say. I think they knew what was going to happen; they might have even engineered the dismissal. I had not exactly been a joy to work with in recent weeks and my lack of effort would have affected their own targets. They promised to keep in touch but secretly we knew that would not be the case.

Janice was red-eyed about the event; she had wanted to make arrangements about continuing to see me but I managed to slip out of the room while she was using the telephone.

My final goodbye was to Mike Stanford in the marketing department. I met Mike shortly after he had joined Oxitel two months previously. Coincidentally he had graduated from Warwick University at the same time as me, albeit in Economics, but until Oxitel, we had never met. We got on well together and always had a lot to talk about, particularly since he was responsible for the marketing plans for the products on which I was working. My departure was a surprise to him and this time the promise to keep in touch was one I hoped would be honoured.

The sacking was so inevitable that I had already begun to make plans for my future. My car was up for sale and I had made enquiries about renting out my bungalow. I had a list of travel companies that could offer cheap and short notice flights to the States and I had intimated to my parents that I might see them soon. By the following Friday I was in San Francisco.

I never told my parents the truth about Sarah. Instead, I simply said that we had mutually decided to go our own ways. The lie had the desired effect and Sarah was not mentioned again. I was questioned about my blatantly obvious melancholy for a while, but I concealed this first as jet lag, then homesickness and finally American cultural shock until my underlying sadness became a way of life.

I qualified the reasons for going to California as wanting to experience the technological centre of the world and to see my parents, both of which were true. The dominant reason, to get away from things that reminded me of Sarah, I somehow forgot to mention.

I had no idea how long I would stay in San Francisco. Money was not a problem as long as I had enough for a return air ticket - if indeed I wanted to return. Mum and Dad were naturally happy to have me there; adding another person to their large house in Oakland was not a space or financial burden. They had already decided, and had made the necessary moves, to resettle in San Francisco, so it was understandable that they tried to convince me to do the same. I resisted the pressure though - I wanted to keep my options open.

I spent the first month absorbing myself in the culture. I became an expert on the geography of the city. I walked everywhere and visited every monument, museum and tourist attraction that existed. My favourite place was the waterfront and pier areas. I was content to while away time watching the comings and goings of the visitors and ferries, and drinking coffee at one of the many cafés.

Sarah was constantly in my mind. I lost count of the number of times that I swear my heart stopped when I thought I had spied a Sarah look-alike. I considered writing to her and telephoning her, but felt I would not be able to cope with any more written or verbal rejections. It was like waiting for an illness to subside. Everyday I took the medicine in the form of isolation and gradually the pain subsided. By the end of April 1988, I was ready to face the world again.

I did not have a work permit, so, officially, I could not take a job. I became desperate to get involved in some technical challenge that would distract me from my Cambridge memories. By fortune, my father had friends who had friends who had contacts, and a telephone call to my professor at Warwick University also brought forth a list of intermediaries. Soon afterwards, I was intellectually employed, or rather used, on short-term assignments in a succession of software-based companies in the Bay area. I was of novelty value because I was English and free, although sometimes I was paid a few dollars out of petty cash.

The experience and knowledge I obtained on these assignments was invaluable. Using this and some ideas I had once discussed with Sarah, I began to formulate an innovative telecommunications software application. In my spare time – using the PC that my parents had purchased for me (as probably another incentive to settle in San Francisco) – I began to document my thoughts and write some code. Nine months into my exile I had a working prototype.

From my arrival in the States, Mike and I kept our promises and communicated with each other mostly by letter and occasionally by telephone. Mike was the only regular contact I had with my past in England.

An unfortunate event happened during one of our telephone calls – Janice arrived to speak to Mike and eavesdropped on his side of the conversation. She quickly grasped that he was speaking to me and asked if she could speak too. Luckily I overheard the request and made an excuse to finish the call before she came on the line. That evening I called Mike at home and briefed him about the trouble I'd had with Janice at Oxitel, but it was too late, the damage had already been done.

Although Mike refused to divulge my whereabouts to Janice, she started to pass him messages and then letters to be forwarded to me. Dutifully, because he was that kind of person, Mike honoured the arrangement. Without fail, every week, I then received a letter from Janice enclosed in an envelope addressed by Mike. About one in four of the deliveries also had a letter from Mike. Then Janice stopped supplying letters to Mike and I began to receive them directly from her. Mike swore that he never passed on my address and I believed him. He and I concluded that Janice had secretly searched his briefcase and either noted the address from an incoming or outgoing letter, or had referenced his address book. There was no proof, but thereafter Mike was wary of Janice and avoided her as much as possible.

Her letters to me always expressed the same sentiment, only the order of the words and sentences changed. She loved me, missed me, and wanted to marry me and have my babies. I stopped reading them after the first half dozen or so and, recognizing her distinctive handwriting on the envelopes, dropped them in the trash as soon as they arrived. I never replied but did sympathise with her obsession. The strength of her apparent love for me was the same as mine for Sarah. I began to feel sorry for her, a feeling that would eventually backfire on me.

In early January 1989, Mike telephoned me about the Oxitel Christmas party. It had been its usual manic affair. The highlight of the evening had been an inebriated Janice seizing the disk jockey's microphone, whereupon she announced to the audience that Carl Denham was coming back to England soon and that they were to be married. The gathered staff had collectively sniggered at this outrageous proclamation until she provided evidence in the form of a single-diamond engagement ring. Mike was also fooled by this fabrication and it took more than I thought was necessary to convince him that the story was total rubbish. At least the engagement was, because strangely I was thinking seriously about returning to the U.K. - it depended upon Mike's reaction to the proposal I had for him.

I hadn't previously told Mike about my private software project. He listened patiently while I enthused about the product I'd christened Protean and the ambitions I had for it.

Mike was quiet for a moment and I eagerly awaited his response.

'It won't sell,' he said eventually. 'It's too visionary. There might be a market for it in the States, but you seem to forget that us limeys are a bit technologically challenged.'

'Then join me in San Francisco,' I said undeterred.

'How do I fit into this project exactly?' he asked.

'I'll develop the product and I want you to market and sell it.'

'You're crazy. I don't know anything about the software market there.'

'You'll soon pick it up. Anyway, all you have to do is make a big noise. People listen over here.'

'I thought you had your heart set on coming back to England, rather than me coming to the States.' Mike was obviously thinking about the idea.

'That's my preference. However, if I can't make megabucks in England then it will have to be gigabucks here.'

'It could be megabucks if you were willing to adapt the product to something more in tune with the European requirements.'

'Adapt? What have you in mind?'

'Well, I don't like the name much. What's a Protean anyway?'

'It's used in the adjectival form not as a noun. It describes the mythological sea-god Proteus, who could take, or exist in, many forms. I thought that summed up the versatility of the product quite well.'

Having overcome that first barrier with Mike, he then went on to propose some commercial and product ideas. The longer we debated the issues, the more excited Mike became. We were both mentally exhausted when Mike ended the call. He had made the call to me from Oxitel and told me later, that when his boss discovered he had been on the telephone to the States for three hours on private business, he had received a written warning about his conduct. He didn't care though because he had already made up his mind that he was leaving Oxitel.

Chapter 12

Saturday, February 11, 1989 – 6:00 a.m.

I returned to England early on the morning of Saturday, February 11, 1989. The previous month had been a busy one. I felt obliged to complete some work I had been doing for Digital Micronics Inc., even though I had only been paid in kind rather than dollars. It was hard preparing my parents for my imminent departure. They had got used to having me around, but the promise that I would see them at least once a year thereafter was sincere and honoured. In fact, I next saw them ten months later when they came to my wedding. Finally, via the estate agents, I had to give notice to the tenants in my bungalow so that I had somewhere to live and use as a base for what was to emerge as MicaCom Software Limited.

On the flight back, it briefly registered that it was the one-year anniversary of the last time that I had seen Sarah. She was still in my head, but I'd now learnt to control the times when I allowed my thoughts to be overtaken with her memory.

Mike collected me from Heathrow airport and was preaching the benefits of freedom. The day before had been his last at Oxitel. Despite his enthusiasm for my project, it hadn't been an easy decision to leave paid employment. The Oxitel directors had worked hard to convince him to stay, with promises of a substantial pay-rise and additional perks. With their efforts to retain his services and his determination to refute them, it boded well for our coming partnership together. He had kept his detail plans secret and had merely stated that he was going to help an old colleague in a new venture. This concealment had been my idea, not that I minded Oxitel in general knowing about Mike's future, but I was keen that the information was kept from Janice. I should have known better. That girl had an uncanny knack of finding out things, the proof being the "Welcome Home" present from her that he presented to me at the airport. The gift was a book of an *Anthology of English Love Poems*.

The first meeting of MicaCom took place later that day. My biological clock was still confused, and the bungalow was in a frightful state of disrepair, courtesy of its temporary occupants and lack of diligence from the estate agents, so we adjourned to the Black Bull pub in Blackmore - one of Mike's favourite haunts.

Mike had been busy organizing the formation of the company while I served notice on my exile. He had agonized about a name for the company and had toyed with unused ones like MicaSoft (too similar to a growing Corporation called Microsoft), CamiSoft (sounded like a manufacturer of knickers) and FormicaSoft (a possible trademark problem). He ultimately favoured MicaCom, because it was Mike and Carl's Communication software company and had the best ring to it. He had been worried that the choice had implied seniority of Mi(ke) over Ca(rl). It didn't bother me though - I liked the catchy name too; besides, it was too late, a small stock of company stationery and business cards with the MicaCom name had already been printed. It was fortunate that I had recruited Mike's commercial brain for this venture. If I'd been on my own, I'm sure I would have chosen an emotionally stupid and commercially vacant name like SarahSoft.

Mike had been meticulous too in the checklist of decisions and purchases we had to make. I had already agreed to my £10,000 of residual inheritance to fund the initial months of the company. The computer equipment was the biggest expense, but we also needed some office essentials like a filing cabinet and a photocopier. Although Mike had already cultivated some useful contacts and potential customers for Protean, we had no idea when it would start generating income, so my *Carl and Sarah future* savings would also have to be the source of day to day living expenses. Proper office premises were out of the question for the time being, so my bungalow was to be the base for our operations. Mike had two more weeks of rental left on the house he shared with three other people in Billericay, after that, to save money he was to move in with me.

MicaCom was truly on its way. My real plan was going to work. MicaCom and Protean weren't directly about making money and creating job satisfaction, they were merely the means by which I could irrevocably purge the pain of being without Sarah.

Sadly, something else contributed to my purging of Sarah – my Nemesis, Janice. It was the day after the inaugural meeting of MicaCom at about nine o'clock in the evening. Mike had just left. We had begun the day cleaning and airing the bungalow and then worked on our respective MicaCom tasks for twelve hours non-stop. All I wanted to do was put on a Beach Boy's album and crash out in an armchair, but the doorbell rang. I first assumed Mike had forgotten something, but then remembered I had given him a key earlier in the day. I opened the front door, hoping it would be a minor intrusion on the solace I'd planned.

'Hello, Carl. Can I come in?' Janice said casually, obviously not troubled by the expression of panic that must have drifted across my face.

The answer I wanted to give never came. I was probably too shocked and too tired to put up a fight, and simply held the door ajar for her to enter. She turned to the road and waved. I heard a car with its engine running pull away and watched it disappear into the distance.

'Who was that?' I said, stuck for something more critical or constructive.

'My friend Lucy,' Janice said.

An observer would not have believed that it had been a year since we'd seen each other and that I had ignored forty or more letters Janice had sent to me.

Janice walked in, took off her coat and tossed it on a chair. She wore a cream knitted top and a short tan skirt, which left little to the imagination as she settled on the settee. She did look good.

'Can I get you a coffee?' I said. I remained standing.

'No thanks. I'll come straight to the point.' She usually did. 'I've missed you desperately. I was so sad that you never replied to my letters, but I knew you would come back to me eventually.'

'But I haven't come back *to you*, Janice. I've just come back. I've started ...' I managed to say before she interrupted.

'I've been faithful to you. I've turned down so many men, that everyone thinks I'm a lesbian. It's because I love you. I don't want anyone else. I know what you are going to say, you are still in love with Sarah. But that's over now Carl. You have to start again, and I want to be part of your life.'

'Janice, I'm sorry. I have started again. Mike and I have gone into business together, but I'm not ready for a relationship yet. I do still love Sarah and I'll never forget her.'

Janice stood and walked towards me. 'I know Sarah will always be your first choice ...' she said, stopping close to me and staring at me with the bright brown eyes that she had.

I shuffled backwards a little.

'... and I know I'll have to come to terms with that,' she continued, closing the gap between us. 'I've always known that I'm your second choice, and it's time that you acknowledged that fact.'

I edged away again, but she kept with up me and put her hands on my hips. My arms hung loose at my side.

'Janice, please. This isn't going to work. I don't want it to work.'

'It will, if you give it a chance.' She took my arms and positioned them around her waist. She drew me towards her so that our bodies touched, then went on tiptoe so our lips were close.

I've relived and regretted that moment many times. To this day, I can't remember what on earth was going through my mind. Being celibate for a year was obviously a factor and my Trans-Atlantic tiredness had weakened my resistance. Her sweet breath and gentle panting were arousing as she brushed her lips against mine.

I realised later that her actions were a deliberate ploy. She just stayed like that with our lips barely touching. She was waiting for me to sanction the intimacy by making the first move. I was mesmerized like a rabbit in headlights. Eventually she would slip away when her tipped-toes weakened. I was tense with the efforts of the day. I needed to unwind. My arms slipped down to her bottom and I pressed just enough so that our lips connected. She closed her eyes and still waited, but I couldn't. I leaned forward and felt the full moist passion of the kiss. My tongue explored her teeth and she parted her mouth slightly so that our tongues met. The embrace evolved and lingered. Janice must have detected the hardening in my trousers and drew me closer to feel the effect she was having on me. Finally, her toes gave way and she broke the union.

'Oh Carl, I've waited for so long for that second kiss,' she said, beginning to undo the buttons on my shirt.

I must have looked puzzled because she added, 'Don't you remember the first at the Oxitel Christmas party two years ago?'

I didn't, nor much else about that drunken night.

This evening I was sober and the following three hours of lovemaking were the most disordered my brain had ever been. At the time, it was an enthusiasm born of frustration; on reflection, it was a madness that only Janice could engender.

Eager to start work, Mike let himself in at eight o'clock the following morning. He was surprised not to find me already labouring on my PC and assumed I had slept late. He went to the kitchen and noisily began to make tea, hoping it would wake me. It had the desired effect; a minute later, I emerged from the bedroom in just a dressing gown. I must have looked guilty, tired or both.

'What happened to you?'

'Is there such a thing as male rape?' I asked.

'You mean a guy raping another guy?'

'No. A man raped by a woman.'

'Not that I've heard of, but there's a first for everything.'

'Then call the *Guinness Book of Records*,' I said, trying to make fun of a situation that I knew was going to cause trouble.

Mike looked at me as though I was crazy, but his expression changed to disbelief when he heard a voice he knew call from the bedroom.

'Carl. I can't find my bra.'

I backtracked to the bedroom and closed the door after me.

'Ah, found it. Can you run me to work, I'm going to be late?' Janice said. She stood naked in front me and was hooking her brassiere.

'I don't have a car yet. I'll have to call you a cab.'

'That will take too long. Perhaps I'll call in sick, then we could spend the day together ...' Janice said, unfastening her brassiere again and letting it fall to the floor, ' ... in bed.'

There wasn't anything further from my mind. 'No. Mike's just arrived. I'll get him to take you.'

I hastened back to Mike. He was sitting in the kitchen drinking his tea. He didn't look too pleased.

'I'll explain later, but I need a *big* favour,' I said. Mike just stared back. 'Could you take Janice to work? Otherwise we'll be stuck with her all day.'

Mike appeared hurt and let down, like a child that had a promise of a McDonald's visit withdrawn. I worried that I may have just lost a good friend. He replied with an unconvincing: 'OK'.

I pulled up a chair at the kitchen table, sat down and poured myself some tea. We sat in silence until Janice came bouncing into the kitchen.

'Hello, Mike. I'm ready,' she said.

Agonizingly later, I looked at my watch. It had been three hours since Mike had departed with Janice on a round trip that should not have taken more than an hour, even through the rush hour traffic of Chelmsford. I had speculated numerous theories of why Mike hadn't returned yet. The best candidate was that he was holed up somewhere considering the worth of his future with a Machiavellian partner. Christ, what a mess, I thought. Day two of MicaCom and we were already facing our first crisis.

I had been sitting at the computer for most of the time, but all I'd achieved was a single paragraph of Protean documentation. I couldn't get out of my head what a fool I'd been. After all I had said to Mike about Janice, at our first renewed encounter I'd been seduced by her, but *it takes two to tango*. I could have stopped it. I should have stopped it. Was the onerous guilt I felt related to Sarah or Mike? It wasn't as if I'd actually been unfaithful to Sarah, except in the confinement of my obsessive thoughts of the past. No, it was Mike's trust I had betrayed. The key problem was to understand my true feelings for Janice, and I needed to resolve this before Mike came back.

I genuinely liked Janice, but the constant pressure of her past attentions had turned me against her. If it hadn't been for Sarah, would I have fallen for Janice? Possibly. Now I was about to face a period of uncertainty in my life. Would Protean have the success I had planned for it? I couldn't do it on my own – I needed Mike's marketing flair. If I spurned Janice, would she make my life a misery with her well-practiced persistence? If I courted Janice, would her passion be tempered? Moreover, would she give me emotional, maybe financial, support during the growing pains of MicaCom? My first love was Sarah; my second was now MicaCom. On balance, perhaps it was time I made Janice third and began to use her to further my ambitions for MicaCom.

After another hour, I decided to try to ring Mike at home. There was no answer but as I re-cradled the receiver, his car pulled into the drive.

It took an hour to clear the air. I had never told Mike about Sarah and didn't then. It seemed a bit pointless declaring the history and sincerity of my lost love when I was about to announce the start of a new relationship. His major concern, of course, was the adverse influence that Janice might have on me, and therefore MicaCom. I argued, and convinced Mike - though not myself - that I had finally realized that "I needed the love of a good woman", to provide some stability in my life. I couldn't believe I'd used such an inane cliché, though it was subtle since Mike had met someone called Lisa, and it was clear to me from Mike's frequent mention of her, that she would become his good woman, sooner rather than later.

We celebrated the resolution of our short-term problem with a couple of cans of beer and then resumed the MicaCom plan as though nothing had happened.

The first MicaCom month was probably the most intense period of work I had ever experienced, worse than the peak times at Oxitel. So feverish, that I swear there were some days when I didn't think of Sarah. The working day became so long that Mike was often too tired to drive home. Within a week, he had accelerated his departure from Billericay and moved into the bungalow. That suited me fine because it acted as a deterrent to excessive visits from Janice. I kept the liaisons with her to no more than twice a week. She usually stayed on Saturday nights and one other night during the week. We rarely went out. I was often too busy and certainly reluctant to use the MicaCom reserve funds for social spending. Surprisingly, Janice accepted the situation. Having won my unwilling affection, for a while she became a different person, understanding, thoughtful and not too much trouble. Unfortunately, her reformation stopped short when it came to my financial aid - directly anyway. She set about a miserly campaign to save money for our wedding. Not that we'd discussed such an event, she just assumed it would happen.

Luckily for MicaCom, Mike's relationship with Lisa flourished. Lisa Rollinson was a poorly paid nurse but her income was generously supplemented by the wealth of her parents. Lisa was a social junkie who needed a regular fix of parties, cinema and theatre trips, and outings. Initially Mike was hesitant in accommodating Lisa's extrovert demands since this was contrary to the MicaCom founders' culture of "all work, no play and no pay". One day Mike presented his emotional dilemma to me, Lisa would dump him unless he acceded to her socialite wishes. The complication was quickly solved. Whilst I wanted to be manic about my endeavours for MicaCom, it wasn't a problem for Mike to widen his social exposure. I allayed his guilt by suggesting it might prove beneficial to mix with the wealthy contacts of the Rollinson family, and he should treat it as part of the job. It turned out to be a fortuitous concession.

By June 1989, I had gone as far as I could with the Protean project. The software was functional, visually pleasing, easy to use, debugged and fully documented. It now needed paying customers and commercial use, before the sequel and add-ons could be considered. This milestone coincided with a grand affair at the Rollinson mansion to celebrate the marriage of Lisa's elder sister. Janice and I were but two of the hundred or more prominent guests that attended this ostentatious event in the Essex countryside. I'd become tired of Janice's constant allusions to the joy of marriage, so after the wedding breakfast I searched for Mike's more edifying company. I found him with an audience of three outwardly upright men, engrossed in Mike's delivery. I hovered in the vicinity hoping to be invited to join the assemblage, but Mike's attention never diverted from his avid listeners. It wasn't until the newly married couple was about to leave for their honeymoon, that Mike emerged from his meeting and led me to a white table-clothed trestle table in the now vacant marquee.

'Sit down and prepare yourself for some good news,' he said.

'You've got the first order for Protean,' I guessed.

'You were eavesdropping? No ...', Mike paused teasingly. '... I have two.'

'Two! From the guys you were speaking to?'

'Yep. The distinguished looking grey-haired man is Gerard Henson, a golfing friend of old man Rollinson. He is the Finance Director of Sencad Holdings. The other two are Manufacturing Managers of Sencad sites in Thetford and Kings Lynn. Protean is perfect for their operations. I'm to confirm the prices and installation dates on Monday. We should have the written order from Gerard by Wednesday. You're going to install on Thursday and Friday.'

'How much did you charge?'

'The order's worth £4,000 plus fees for installation and training, and an annual maintenance fee of £750.'

'Bloody hell. That's a fortune. And you did that all by yourself?'

'Not totally. I've had to forsake some ... freedom ... for it. I had a good word put in by my future father-in-law.'

'Father-in-law?'

'Yes. Lisa and I got engaged today.'

I took the news as an ultimate sacrifice from Mike. He'd not mentioned this intention before so I chose to believe that it was a spur of the moment decision fuelled by the prospect of MicaCom's first sale. With no ring yet to confirm the coming union, it gave credence to my supposition. Mike was clearly overjoyed by the day's events, so I never bothered to enquire whether his decision was born of love of MicaCom or Lisa.

The software installations went well and Gerard, no doubt with some persuasion from Ken - Lisa's father, began to broadcast what a sound investment he had made. From that point MicaCom went from strength to strength.

I estimated that about twenty percent of Mike's time was immediately diverted to his marriage plans now that MicaCom had some security and guaranteed income. It didn't bother my ambitions for MicaCom, but the constant theme of marriage in the air had Janice putting similar pressures on me. Mike and Lisa had set their happy day for September 16th. A short engagement, but Mike was the director of *a company that was going places*, according to the influential Ken, so why wait? I sarcastically assumed there was some tax avoidance scheme in place by marrying off his two daughters in the same fiscal year.

For a time, Janice and Lisa started to play games about a double wedding, but I already had my excuses prepared. Mike and I couldn't be away on our honeymoons at the same time, no matter how short. *We* were MicaCom and could not afford to neglect the company during such a crucial period. Furthermore, we now needed premises beyond the confines of my bungalow's lounge, and extra staff to handle the growth in accounting, secretarial, sales, support and technical challenges that had come from our success. Somebody in authority had to be present to deal with these matters, which would reach their zenith during September. I carefully concealed the fact that I had instigated these events to coincide with Mike's marital vacation, and therefore to forestall my own.

As October began, Mike and Lisa were experiencing domestic bliss in their new house in Brentwood (courtesy of the Rollinsons), having returned from their two-week honeymoon in the Virgin Islands (also courtesy of the Rollinsons). Mike was back at work in the first proper MicaCom office – three rooms rented in an unusually ugly concrete block in Chelmsford. The four additional employees were wondering if they had made the right decision to join a company where the standard working day lasted typically 12 hours. Janice had volunteered to leave her secure, well-paid job at Oxitel, to join our workaholic ranks, but with little effort, I persuaded her that it was not a good idea.

It was around this time that Janice must have started to feel insecure about the somewhat too laid-back relationship I had engineered. I had never recovered from the guilt that I felt from the sexual encounter we had in February. I had skilfully avoided sexual intercourse since then, with a stock set of excuses built upon work pressures, lack of opportunity and a renewed Christian need to wait until we were married. Amazingly, Janice had been tolerant of these deceptions, until one night in early October, when a shared bottle of wine, a lecture from Janice on womanly needs and a bucketful of tears led to a second, reluctant, consummation of our relationship.

Four weeks later, Janice told me a visit to the doctors had confirmed she was pregnant. She swore me to secrecy, moved into my bungalow and made haste with her mother - who I had only just met, to prepare for the wedding.

The pregnancy was a big surprise to me. I had incorrectly assumed it was normal that all girls took precautions. I suppose with my Sarah-influenced disinterest in sex - I had never thought to ask Janice if she was normal. She was overjoyed with the news. So, with a hidden sense of foreboding and a visible display of responsibility, I mentally prepared myself for the lifestyle changes that were coming.

Janice took a week's holiday before the wedding day, and on the Tuesday, I received a pleading call from her to come home from work because she was unwell. When I arrived, she was in bed sobbing. She said she had been sick, feverish and had lost the baby. Stunned, I consoled her as best I could and asked her mother to come round. I wanted to call the doctor, but she insisted that physically she was intact and just needed rest and her mother's administration. I suggested that we postponed the wedding until she had fully recovered, but she was adamant that she would soon be better.

The wedding went ahead as planned on Saturday, December 9th, 1989. It was a low-key, registry office ceremony with 40 guests (including my parents who had flown over from America) and a buffet reception in the village hall.

Despite the realisation that the marriage was not necessary now, I shared the grief that had befallen us a few days earlier, and vowed I would do everything to make Janice happy. Unprompted, I even approached the subject of making love on our wedding night, but understandably I thought, Janice preferred to wait a few days until she had "healed". Sunday was our honeymoon and we spent a quiet day in Hatfield Forest with a picnic and wading through a fresh fall of snow. I had promised that we would take a long break the following spring, when I forecast that MicaCom duties would be less demanding. I went back to work on Monday morning.

I'd always keep reasonably fit with squash in Oxitel days, but while in the States had adopted its exercise culture of jogging. Even with the demands of MicaCom, I had kept up the regime, but in recent weeks had developed a sore Achilles tendon. With rest and TLC it hadn't improved, so I had arranged a doctor's visit on Monday afternoon. The cure was more rest and special stretching exercises. In passing, since I had the same doctor as Janice, I mentioned the sad news of her miscarriage. He looked puzzled and went to a filing cabinet of patient notes. He returned and stated that there must have been a mistake – he hadn't consulted with Janice for over two years, and by the way, she really ought to make an appointment to see him, she had never completed her course of psychotherapy at the hospital. The doctor was reluctant to elaborate on this revelation; he thought it best for Janice to explain to me directly.

I never said anything to Janice about her treatment, and I assumed that she must have changed her doctor without telling me. She was still upset about the baby and had my full sympathy. I wasn't suspicious at first. Then two facts a few days later brought Janice's deception to the surface.

For a change, I had arrived home early in the evening intent on carrying out some domestic filing and bill paying. Since Janice had moved into the bungalow, the household paperwork had been piled high in a box awaiting transfer to an organized filing cabinet. Amongst the pile of Janice's documents was her medical card, dated just a few months earlier, which confirmed she had the same doctor as me. I looked across the lounge at Janice who was watching the closing scenes of a film on television. Had she spun me a yarn about the pregnancy? At times, I'd thought she'd been suffering from monomania with me as the subject of her paranoia. If that were true, could it have made her invent a baby to make me marry her? There was something I could check which might conceivably damn or exonerate her.

I kept busy with the filing until Janice started to get ready for bed. She had a ritual of undressing in the bedroom, strolling around naked while she chose her clothes for the following day, donning her dressing gown and then going to the bathroom. She always carried a small blue make-up bag, which she transferred from handbag to handbag.

I waited until she had gone to the bathroom and locked the door behind her; we had no bodily inhibitions between us except for this nightly sacrament. I went quickly to the bathroom door and knocked, pleading a sudden stomach ache and a desperate need to use the toilet before she started her ablutions. She emerged, voiced a minor complaint and went to the bedroom. When I saw the object of my attention, I locked the door and began my inspection. A chill went through me as I found a card of birth control pills in the small blue bag. She hadn't taken today's – the Wednesday pill was still inside its plastic bubble, but there were fourteen vacant bubbles immediately before it, spanning the day when she allegedly had had her miscarriage.

I didn't share the marital bed that night. Instead, I worked on some modifications to Protean II until the early hours, and then slept on the settee. It was the best way I knew to control the disillusionment and anger that I felt. I knew then that it was over between us.

By design, I stayed late at the office every night after that discovery, unable to face the Gorgon that Janice had become in my eyes. Typically, I would return home past midnight and slip into bed beside her and I'd fantasise that it was Sarah next to me. Strangely, I wanted the comfort of a woman next to me to relieve the loneliness that I was experiencing, safe that it was dark and I wouldn't have to look at her. Now that she was *healed*, and undeterred by the hour, Janice would often attempt to arouse me. She never succeeded and I knew it wouldn't be long before my chastity and apathy towards her, sparked a theatrical reaction from the ever patient Janice. The charade lasted for a month. Then one night as I came home around two o'clock in the morning she was sitting in a chair facing the front door. For someone who rarely stayed awake beyond midnight, it was obvious she was about to embark on the confrontation I was expecting.

'I rang the office, but there was no answer. Where have you been?' Janice asked. There was no anger in her voice, just a subdued resignation.

I *had* been at the office and the phone had been ringing just before I left, but it was time to bring the relationship to an end.

'With my girlfriend,' I said casually.

'Boyfriend more like,' she replied, now with venom. 'Women obviously don't turn you on anymore.'

An over generalisation, of course, it was just one woman in particular. Then she revealed her outstanding psychiatric needs by going completely berserk and throwing every movable object in my direction. I went back to the office with a gash on my forehead, innumerable bruises and a bloodstained shirt.

I guess you know the rest Mike. I stayed with you for a couple of months, bought a flat in Springfield, and struggled via solicitors until Janice and I were finally divorced in March 1991.

Part Three

Search

Chapter 13

Wednesday, March 10, 1999 – 3:00 p.m.

Throughout the story, Carl noticed that Mike's expression and body language displayed various extremes. He could not determine whether it was Mike's interest in the story or his steady intake of alcohol. At the start, Mike had been quite chatty and asked many questions about his life at school and university, oddly about whether he had ever seen "Wham bam" Susan again. They joked and made comparisons between his fidelity and Mike's infidelity in their adolescent relationships.

As the facts about Sarah's breakdown were revealed, Mike appeared to portray varying expressions of sympathy, unease, shock and strangely, guilt. Mike said little during this expose, except to ask about likely reasons for Sarah acting the way that she did. There, Carl had little to add to his tale.

Reflection on the time at Oxitel unearthed many forgotten anecdotes, particularly the extent to which Janice pursued Carl's attention. He joined in with Mike's laughter as Mike related the gossip and innuendo that enriched the lives of the Oxitel staff while Carl was in the States. One especially loud outburst brought glares from other patrons who were obviously unused to noise in this sleepy country pub. To control themselves they both had to take a toilet break before Carl had continued the story.

Mike had many questions about his experiences of California during his exile, since this would be a major element of Mike's three-month tour of North America.

Carl's recollection of the early days of MicaCom tallied almost perfectly with Mike's. The revelations about Janice came as a shock to Mike, and he had obviously wanted to ask questions, but Carl had ploughed on regardless.

At three hours, Carl knew he had achieved a personal record for delivering any monologue; even the Protean IV launch meeting to the systems staff a few years earlier had only taken him two hours.

They were the only two patrons left in the pub now. The barman appeared to have nodded off behind the bar.

'That's it. Since the divorce there's been nothing to add to the Sarah story until recently,' he said, downing a large swig of beer to refresh his dry mouth.

'Wow, that's a story and a half. It explains quite a few things over the years. Your tone when talking about my relationship with Lisa suggested that it pissed you off.'

'Yes, I was jealous at the time. Not because you married into money, rather that you were so bloody happy together. Over nine years later you're still with Lisa and even happier. That's rare these days and I'm more jealous.'

Mike smiled. Carl assumed with his achievement, not because he was pleased that Carl was jealous.

'The bit about Janice's pregnancy blackmail is incredible. Why didn't you tell me at the time? She got great mileage broadcasting that the reason for the divorce was your total lack of performance in bed.'

'I think I was too embarrassed by the whole affair. First, I was drawn into an unwanted relationship because she caught me at a vulnerable time. Then, for the sake of MicaCom, I thought it would be easier to play along rather then resist her advances. Finally, I was conned into a marriage I didn't want. I felt stupid.'

'But if you'd revealed the true reason for the marriage and the divorce, you wouldn't have lost your bungalow and you could've saved yourself a small fortune in maintenance payments. Plus you would have achieved a moral victory over her.'

'I know. In hindsight, perhaps I should have been more open and forceful. At the time I just wanted Janice out of my life, so I could bury myself in MicaCom. It didn't completely work though. Janice continues to be a pain in the arse even now.'

'Does she know that you found out about her false pregnancy?'

'I don't think so. I certainly never mentioned it. If I had, she would have found some twisted way of turning my embarrassment to her advantage.'

'So now you're going to look for Sarah. Why have you left it so long?'

'MicaCom got in the way. I made it get in the way. It was the ultimate antidote. It did make me forget her, consciously. Sub-consciously, she's always been inside me. When we started the negotiations with BinaryByte, I did some heavy thinking about what I would do post-MicaCom. There is really only one thing I want do, find Sarah.'

'That's her real name is it, Sarah?'

'That's a strange question to ask, why should I try to disguise her name?'

'Oh, no reason. You just don't look like a … *Sarah Person.*'

'Even stranger. What *do* I look like, a *Susan Person*? Perhaps you have a secret to tell me?'

'No. I don't think Susan's relevant anymore.'

'Anymore? You're talking in riddles today Mike. Have you had too much to drink?'

'Probably, but I think I could do with another. My round I think.' Mike hurried towards the bar for two more pints. The barman almost fell of his stool at the sudden revival in customer interest.

Carl considered the last exchange, but before he could form an opinion of Mike's incoherence, he staggered back, spilt some beer on the table and quickly asked with an audible slur, 'So what will you do if you can't find Sarah?'

'I've already found her.'

'What? When did you do that?'

'Over the last few days. I found her via the Internet. We've been sending each other e-mails.'

'Well I'll be buggered. Where is she? When are you seeing her? Bloody hell, you kept that quiet.'

'Slow down. It's no big deal. I'm cool about it. She's working in Portsmouth, but I don't think she wants to see me. Don't worry; I'm not going to do anything stupid. After all this time it's probably a bit of a shock that I've suddenly turned up. I'm trying to be realistic and at least satisfy myself that she's alive and well. I will go to see her, if only to find out the reason why she rejected me.'

'And then what?'

'If it's a fairy tale ending, we'll fall in love again and live happily ever after. If not, a visit to my parents in San Francisco is long overdue. I still have a few contacts there - perhaps I'll find something that will keep me busy. That reminds me. Do you still intend visiting my parents on your trip?'

'Yes, of course. The itinerary is still a bit vague, but I plan to be in California around the end of May. I'll ring them when I know for certain.'

'There's a good chance I might see you there. Assuming the fairies don't come up trumps. Perhaps we ought to be getting back now. You're clearly in no fit state to drive and I'm over the legal limit. I'll call Jacqui and get her to come out with someone to take us back to the office,' Carl said and disappeared to the pub entrance to use the public telephone.

'Hey Mike, cheer up, you're looking distinctly depressed,' Carl joked when he returned. 'Jacqui and Naomi will be here in about 20 minutes to take us back to our new bosses. Let's talk about something a bit more cheerful. Tell me about your trip to America.'

Mike seemed glad for the change of subject, and visibly lifted himself out of his despondency as he described his provisional itinerary from Saturday morning. His travelogue did not last the distance, and there were a few minutes of awkward silence before Jacqui and Naomi walked into the bar.

'Look Carl, I don't want to go back yet. I haven't got anything special to do this afternoon, I think I'll get something to eat and call a cab later,' Mike said.

'Is he OK?' Naomi whispered to Carl. And then louder, trying to lighten the subdued atmosphere she added, 'He looks as though he's bet his millions on a horse and it's come in last.'

Mike managed a weak smile as though he was trying to express a *Don't worry about me* response, but Naomi was not convinced.

'I'll tell you what,' Naomi said turning to Jacqui, 'you take Carl back in his car. I'll have a quick drink with Mike and we'll catch up with you later.'

Carl looked knowingly at Naomi. If anyone could lift Mike out of his sudden malaise it would be Naomi, so he quickly seconded the proposal and headed towards the exit with Jacqui before Mike could argue.

* * *

On the journey back to the office, Carl had wanted to think about Mike's odd reaction to his story. However, the company gossip, Jacqui, wanted to take the opportunity to bring him up to date on the sordid goings on at MicaCom. He had no option but to listen and gasp and groan at the appropriate places. It always amazed him that if everything Jacqui said was to be believed, then MicaCom would be a classic subject for a television soap opera. A was screwing B, who really loved C, but C was a lesbian who had just slept with D, but don't tell E because he would be jealous and so it went on in the most glorious uninhibited detail. If he still owned the company, he would have asked Naomi to investigate; not whether the stories were true, rather to find out how much time wasting resulted from this accumulation of knowledge. Jacqui would really be in heaven once the BinaryByte staff were established at the office; she would have a whole new set of sexual scandals to invent.

As he passed through reception, Denise – the main receptionist, called to him, 'Have you seen Mike? There's been a very persistent woman called Susan ringing for him …'

Mike never did tell him about Susan he thought. He noticed that Jacqui was one step behind him listening intently and was probably storing this little gem away in her MicaCom peccadillo book.

'... and then she asked to speak to you if he wasn't around,' Denise finished.

Well that will certainly warrant a new chapter for Jacqui, he speculated *Troilism amongst the ex-MicaCom directors.*

'Are you sure she asked for me?'

'Yes, I've written down the number for you,' and she passed him a sticky yellow note.

He took it looking puzzled, observed that Jacqui looked puzzled too, then put the note in his jacket pocket and continued to his office.

As he entered, Tony Cookson was putting his coat on.

'Good Lunch?' Tony asked, presumably referring sarcastically to the time he had been away.

'All for your benefit,' he replied whilst conjuring up an answer for the next question.

'How so?'

'I've been reviewing the handover with Mike to ensure that we've covered everything to make life as easy as possible for you and Pete when we have gone,' Carl lied calmly with a poker face.

'Yeah, very good, pull the other one. I can't believe you have a conscience anymore with a few million quid in your pocket. And Mike's still at the pub is he, doing a private review?'

Carl knew the rules. If someone was trying to bait you, stem the anger by counting to ten before replying. He only got as far as three.

'Now look you stuck-up little shit, this may not be my company anymore, but I'm proud of what I've created here. So, yes, I do have a conscience because I would be pretty pissed off if a tosser like you fucked up all my good work. So is there something you would like to go through?'

Tony took a step backwards, but his voice was calm. 'No, I have to get back to Cambridge tonight, I have a meeting with George first thing in the morning.'

To tell him I took a long lunch break no doubt you raging sycophant, he thought, but said, 'You're not here tomorrow then?'

'Yes, but not until the afternoon.'

'What about the project plans for the next release of Protean? I thought you wanted to go through those today.'

'Well, it's a bit late now, isn't it?' Tony said patronizingly. 'Anyway I studied them while you were out. I don't agree with them but I do understand them, so there's nothing I need to ask you about.'

Carl clenched his fists. Tony took another step back.

'That was the last item on our agenda for the week, so you don't need me anymore?'

'Correct, that's it. You're finished here Carl. You can go and spend your millions now,' Tony said, nervously gathering some papers from the desk and stuffing them quickly in his briefcase.

Carl began his count again. Only two this time.

'That's official is it? There's nothing else you need from me. I really don't have to listen to the crap that comes out of your mouth ever again.'

'You're a bit slow on the uptake in your old age Carl. Look at my lips F-I-N-I-S-H-E-D finished. I'll ask George to send you a confirmation fax tomorrow. Don't forget to leave your office keys on my desk when you go,' Tony concluded as he rapidly disappeared down the corridor almost knocking Jacqui over as she came out of Mike's office.

Carl's immediate thought was to chase after him and give him the bloody nose he had wanted to at their first meeting. Fuck, he had to do something violent to release the enormous tension that was building up inside his body.

He turned to the desk and launched himself at his relief valve. Grabbing it by the throat he squeezed until he imagined his Tony substitute gurgling into submission. Not satisfied, he twisted Tony's right arm through 360 degrees and tugged it as far as it would go behind his back and across his throat. Now holding Tony with one hand, he used the other to attack his legs. First, he seized the left member and wound it twice at the knee before stretching it and stuffing the foot into the mouth. For the right leg, he wound that in the opposite direction and extended it via Tony's groin to meet with the grossly disfigured right arm. For the remaining arm, he twisted it round and round until it started to show signs of being severed at the shoulder. As a final act of wanton bodily destruction, he hurled Tony towards the gap in the door. But the mid-air decompression of misshapen rubberized limbs interfered with his aim and a hopelessly contorted Tony bounced off the doorframe and landed at his feet. He viewed this as a last desperate plea for mercy from Tony, but Carl was not feeling in a forgiving mood, so a well-aimed heel towards Tony's neck and the full weight of his body brought ultimate satisfaction as Tony's head parted from his torso.

Carl's programmers at the last office Christmas party had presented him with the bendy figure of Bill Gates. They had joked that he could "Beat the shit out of Bill Gates" instead of them whenever something failed in the Protean software. He felt justified the toy had served its purpose well since Tony Cookson was probably going to be the biggest failure in Protean. Carl picked up the remains of Tony alias Bill, and tossed them into the metal rubbish bin by his desk.

Immediate tension dissipated, he sat in his old chair and let his eyes wander round his room. He remembered choosing the wallpaper depicting blue sky and wispy clouds in 1995 to match the standard background of Windows, a peaceful contrast to the psychedelic colour extravaganza in the "asylum" – the office where the programmers worked. The wall to his right now just contained a single picture hook where there used to be a photograph of him crossing the finish line on the London Marathon. In front of him, two visitors' chairs, then wall-to-wall bookcases containing technical books and magazines. He moved one of the chairs adjacent to the open window to his left and sat down. He looked out beyond the small courtyard below, to the distant parkland, letting the incoming cool air blow over his face. He remained there for ten minutes burning images and memories of MicaCom into his mind – it was probably the last time he would be here. He now regretted that Mike had talked him into selling out so early. There were still exciting developments to pursue with Protean and he feared that under Tony Cookson's direction they would never see the light of day. Should he care? If Tony screwed up, BinaryByte would still have access to MicaCom's impressive list of customers and could *upgrade* them eventually with its own inferior MBridge product.

What was he thinking? It was not Mike's fault. The offer from BinaryByte was *too good* to refuse. Either Mike had underestimated MicaCom's value or maybe George Fellgate had some private knowledge that had influenced his inflated bid. But personally he had not traded MicaCom for money; his trade was for freedom to kick-start his life – the life he hoped to rediscover with Sarah.

* * *

Mike was definitely light-headed, confused and troubled. He had drunk four pints of beer. Normally his body could cope with that, but with his absorption in Carl's story, they had not got around to ordering food, and this contributed to his alcoholic haze. His confusion and troubles arose from what he was going to say to Susan; she was sure to telephone him this afternoon. He had promised her that today would be the best time for him to reveal his own secret to Carl, but that had all changed with the story he had just heard. Instead of losing Carl as his closest friend, he was now going to ruin the position of trust he had secured with Susan for the last eight years.

He looked at Naomi. She had always been regarded as the backbone of MicaCom and had joined during its formative years to look after the modest accounting requirements for the business. In later years she had built her own accounts department and was now looking after all personnel issues for the company. Her biggest asset was that she was regarded as the *mum* for MicaCom – if anyone had problems she was always the first port of call. Her age of fifty years, portly size and permanent smile helped this image. The company programmers, who all seemed to be Star Trek fans, had lovingly called her Di, likening her to Diana Troy, the counsellor of the Starship Enterprise, and the nickname had stuck. He had often benefited from her kindness and words of wisdom in a crisis.

'Anybody in? I'd like an orange juice please,' Naomi said, waving her hand in front of Mike's face.

'Oh shit, I'm sorry Di,' Mike said. He went to the bar and returned with her drink and another pint for himself.

'Is that really going to help?'

'What, the beer? Sure, I'm OK.'

'Now look, I'm not a mind reader, but it's pretty obvious to me and anyone within a million miles of here, that something's up. You know I'm a good listener. Is it to do with the BinaryByte take-over?'

He was feeling particularly vulnerable. He had always been very positive with Naomi; he had had to be because she had been his subordinate. Her role was different now and he felt the need to share his problem with someone. Like opening a floodgate, he immediately began to unburden himself.

'Around the time you joined MicaCom - eight years ago, I had a call from someone called Susan. She said she was an old girlfriend of Carl and wanted to contact him again. I asked the obvious question of why she hadn't contacted him directly, and her excuse was that she had hurt him terribly some years ago and only wanted to speak to him if he was unattached, unhappy or in trouble.

'She knew Carl had started a new life without her and she didn't want to interfere, particularly when I told her he was married. Although she couldn't do anything for him then, she wanted me to promise her, that if ever Carl had any kind of problem, or got into difficulty with anything, I was to let her know. I wasn't to tell anybody, least of all Carl, about the arrangement.

'Well you can imagine how I felt about this. I'd never kept anything secret from Carl. Our whole foundation was based upon total trust and openness. I found it very difficult to agree to her idea, but she was extremely insistent. Eventually I yielded in order to get rid of her, thinking that maybe she was some sort of crank, especially as she wouldn't tell me her surname, where she lived, or give me a phone number where I could reach her. She said she would call me instead on a regular basis.

'It was eerie because she knew a lot about the company and had taken me into her confidence assuming Carl and I were very close, and I would always be in a position to keep an eye on him.

'What she didn't know then, and I had no intention of telling her, was at that very time Carl was going through a major crisis. He was separated from Janice and still trying to come to terms with his mistake of marrying her. Plus,

MicaCom was going through a tough time too. We were close to having a major breakthrough with one of our early products, which would have secured the company's future for the next few years, and Carl's effort was central to achieve that. His problems with Janice were seriously affecting his work and there was no way I could have had added to his problems by introducing the subject of Susan.

'We were very short of cash for a while, because suddenly Carl, who had been funding the company until then, gave up just about all his possessions to Janice. Once the divorce was settled, Carl quickly got back into gear, finished the project, and we've been growing like crazy ever since.

'I said nothing about this to Susan. I'm sure it would have been a big relief to her had she known about Carl splitting from Janice, but I couldn't take the risk. I wanted Carl to be completely focused on MicaCom.

'Susan kept her promise and began phoning me at about monthly intervals. To begin with, we were formal with our conversations, but as time went on, we became good friends. I hated lying to her though. She caught me out once when she found out that Carl and Janice were divorced, and asked why I hadn't told her. I said that Carl wasn't upset or troubled by it and had started going out with someone else. I kept this story line going for ages, making up a succession of female partners for Carl, always saying he was keeping well and was happy. I kept lying to Susan because I didn't want Carl to have any interruptions in his efforts to make us both wealthy. I assumed for a long time that Carl didn't want to get involved with anyone after his bad experience with Janice, but it was deeper rooted than that. I eventually guessed that there was perhaps something in his more distant past, like Susan, that was the cause.

'Anyway, after the deal with BinaryByte had been confirmed, I decided that I would come clean with Carl. Just as well, because strangely Susan knew about BinaryByte and had suggested that the time was right for Carl to know. I convinced myself it was best not to tell him until this week; get the hand-over completed first. The real reason was that I couldn't face Carl's reaction until we were about to go our separate paths. He would be destroyed when he knew how I had deceived him for the last eight years.'

Mike paused for a long swig from his beer, and Naomi took the opportunity to butt in.

'What I don't understand is ...' Naomi said before Mike put his hand up to stop her.

'I'm sure you have many questions Di, but I haven't completed the story yet. There's an even nastier twist,' Mike continued wiping some froth from his mouth.

'Carl and I have been talking about our respective plans for life after MicaCom. He kept mentioning about the *adventure* he was going to embark on. I suppose I was so wrapped up with the Susan episode that I assumed that he was going to try to start over with Susan. So whilst I was worried about Carl's response to keeping Susan from him, I thought telling him that she was well and anxious to see him would mollify the revelation. That all changed about an hour ago.'

He then went on to relate an abbreviated version of Carl's story. At the end Naomi was eager to add her contribution.

'I can't really see how the Sarah story changes the situation. It's obvious that Sarah and Susan is the same person,' she said.

'I thought that at first, but there are distinct differences between the two storylines.'

'First, why would Sarah be calling herself Susan? If I'd told Carl about Susan he'd think I was joking. It's Sarah that he wants to be with.

'Second, he said that having contacted Sarah, she's shown great reluctance to see him, whereas Susan is desperate to make contact.

'Lastly, Sarah is working in Portsmouth. I don't know for sure, but in my many conversations with Susan I've formed the impression that she doesn't work and she's living not far from here.'

'Didn't Carl mention anything about a Susan? Perhaps that was the reason he and Janice got divorced,' Naomi asked.

'Not significantly. He did tell me why they got divorced and it wasn't because of another woman. To my knowledge there hasn't been anyone since. Carl flirts with the female staff, other than that I believe he leads a monk's existence. The question is what do I do now? Say nothing to Carl about Susan? In theory I then won't risk falling out with him. If I tell him, and he looks blank, where will that get me? It's very confusing.

'The problem I'm left with is Susan. She's probably rung me this afternoon demanding to know what's going on. I don't know what I'm going to say to her.'

'You said that Susan seemed to know a lot about you, Carl's status and the company. How do you explain that?' Naomi asked.

'I'm not sure I can. Though Carl said on Monday that Paul Westdene had been feeding Janice with information.'

'What sort of information?'

'Apparently, Janice has some facts about the amount of money we've got for selling MicaCom and she's started pestering Carl for a cut. She's admitted that Paul, the current man in her life has provided the details.'

'So you think Paul is a mole for Susan too.'

'No, I don't think so. That doesn't stack up. Janice is a bitch, but Susan comes across as being quite the opposite. It must be someone else.'

Naomi touched Mike's hand. 'I know it's an old cliché, but honesty is the best policy, but in being honest you can be kind rather than brutal. Choose your words carefully, but you should tell Susan and Carl the truth. You can't let this go. When you set out to America, you'll want a clean conscience. Sleep on it and tell them tomorrow.'

'You've never given me any bad advice before Di and I'm sure you don't want to spoil your record now. That's what I'll do.'

'Do you have to go back to the office this afternoon? It's late, perhaps I'll just take you home.'

On the drive back home Mike began to feel better. The alcohol's effects were subsiding and he began to frame in his mind how he would deal with tomorrow. He would be open with Carl and Susan, but above all he was keen to know just how Susan fit into the equation. Having acceded to Susan's wishes for so long, he thought it was time he got to the bottom of this puzzle.

Naomi pulled up outside Mike's house. 'You know there is a funny side to this situation.'

'Being?'

'I've thought for a long time that you were having an affair with someone called Susan, because I've spoken to her quite a few times.'

'You have?'

'Yes. Don't you remember? Before we changed the telephone system a couple of years ago so that the key people had their own direct dial numbers, calls used to go through the main switchboard. If you were ever out of the office and reception thought that there was an important call for you, they used to route them to me. I remember her calls well. She was always pleasant but guarded on the phone, and would never leave a message. I'm afraid I assumed she was your mistress.'

'Funny that, Carl thought the same thing too.'

* * *

Carl dumped the cardboard box containing the personal effects retrieved from work in the hall and immediately went to sit at his computer. He went through the Internet connection routine and downloaded his e-mails. As he confidently expected, there was a reply from Sarah. She was still playing games with him:

```
Again I can't help you Mr. Denham. Sadly, I have no living
relatives, nor am I aware of anyone else with the same surname.
I wish you success with your search.
```

It did not matter – he had already resolved that he would go to Portsmouth tomorrow, whatever excuses Sarah had concocted this time. He thought for a moment about sending Sarah an e-mail to announce his arrival - not a good idea. She might invent some contrivance to avoid him and he knew, he just knew, that when they saw each other again, the eleven-year-old flame would be rekindled. He smiled, he ought to warn the Portsmouth fire brigade, there was about to be a spontaneous conflagration in the City.

He disconnected from the Internet and considered ringing Mike to tell him about the showdown with Tony. He doubted Mike had gone back to the office. Mike was probably a bit hung over after the liquid lunch and sleeping it off – he would call him from Portsmouth tomorrow and tell him the good news about Sarah.

Two hours later, after a jog, shower and a microwaved meal-in-a-packet, and wanting some distraction from the excitement coming tomorrow, he sat again at his computer. It had been a while since he used the computer for leisure and digging around the disk he found a compendium of card games of patience to distract him.

Studying the card layout in his first game, his attention was drawn to the background wallpaper on the screen. It was a surrealistic image of a water scene comprising swirling blue shapes. The picture had been given to him by one of the MicaCom programmers who created the graphics for Protean. It had remained unchanged on his screen for several years and Carl had a sudden desire to replace it with a new picture.

He went to his jacket and took out the remaining photograph of Sarah from his wallet. He placed it in the scanner next to his computer and ran the program to convert the photo from the chemical image to its electronic form. Then he loaded the resultant image into a picture-editing program that would allow him to clean up the original imperfections and those that had appeared through the ageing process. First he cropped the picture to match the aspect ratio of his screen, ensuring that Sarah was the centre of the composition. Next he spent ages removing the odd blemishes with a re-touching tool and finally brightened some of the colours, particularly the sky, changing it from grey to the turquoise that he remembered.

The colour of Sarah's hair was perfect and needed no enhancement. The Greeks had a word to describe it, *Xanthous*, which suggested not only blondeness but also yellow, gold-yellow, touched by light.

He saved his efforts, configured his masterpiece to be his new screen wallpaper and sat back in awe of the girl before him. He checked the small clock on the screen - it was late. He wanted to make an early start in the morning. He looked at the picture again.

'Goodnight Sarah,' he said, 'I'll see you tomorrow.'

Chapter 14

Thursday, March 11, 1999 – 6:00 a.m.

The alarm clock eventually rang at six o'clock much to Carl's relief. He was sure he had been waiting for it for the last two hours, his impatience fed by his excitement to embrace the first day of his new life. The time lying there had been profitably spent. He had rehearsed what he would say to Sarah; anticipated every possible reply and refusal; worked out in detail how he would deal with each situation and resolved how to react to the knowledge of why she had rejected him.

He washed and then dressed quickly in the clothes he had selected the night before. Casual was best, and he had chosen a pale blue shirt and black denim trousers.

Dry toast was all he could manage to eat, despite the nervous rumblings in his stomach. A cup of tea, cleaning of teeth, packing of toothbrush and a few spare clothes in his overnight bag and he was ready.

He stepped out into cool, dry spring morning twenty minutes after rising. It was cloudy, but with no hint of rain. He hoped this was early enough to avoid the traffic on the M25.

His trusty old BMW was waiting for him. Previously owned by MicaCom he had insisted that part of his severance deal was to take the car with him complete with insurance and breakdown cover for one year. Although he could soon afford any car he wanted, his driving ambitions were modest. He did not want to be bothered with choosing something new or different, the red BMW suited him fine.

The run from Chelmsford to Brentwood on the A12 was busy, but painless, as were the first few miles on the M25. Then the traffic increased, went slower and then finally stopped a few miles short of the Dartford Crossing. He cursed his inadequate timing plan, turned the radio on for some background music, and went stop, start for the next thirty minutes, for no apparent reason other than volume of traffic.

Having crossed the Thames, he managed to keep a steady, near legal pace until Leatherhead when there was another frustrating bumper-to-bumper spell. Clear of that, the M3 turn-off was a welcome sight and the rest of the journey via the M3, Fleet Services for fuel, M27 and M275 passed quickly and trouble-free.

He arrived on the outskirts of Portsmouth around nine-thirty and kept watch for road signs pointing towards Portsmouth and Southsea station or the Civic Offices. Studying a town map last night in an old AA road atlas, he had noticed that both of these sites were specifically highlighted near the centre of the city. Sarah's workplace, the Civic Centre, he had assumed would be nearby. Initially he followed signs for the City Centre, and then at a roundabout near the Tricorn shopping centre he spotted the direction signs he was seeking. Shortly after, he saw the station and turned right into the historically named, but seemingly misplaced, Isambard Brunel Road. Facing him then was the square where the Civic Offices were located. There was no obvious on-road parking place available so he headed for the car park signposted at the back of the station in Greetham Street. Spaces were aplenty there and no wonder he thought at the price they were charging. At the Pay and Display machine, not knowing quite how long he would need to be parked he opted for more than two hours and paid his £4. With increasing excitement (or was it trepidation?), he crossed back over Isambard Brunel Road and aimed for the Civic Offices.

* * *

Mike arrived at MicaCom later than he wanted to that morning. With his car left at the office and his wife needing to run some early morning errands, she eventually deposited him at the main door shortly before ten o'clock. He was eager to make his peace with Carl and Susan, but his malaise of yesterday returned when he noticed that Carl's car was not in its usual parking place.

'Heard anything from Carl?' Mike asked Jacqui who was using the photocopier.

Jacqui looked puzzled and shrugged her shoulders, 'Best check with Naomi,' she replied, apparently not wanting to be drawn into conversation.

Mike found Naomi talking quietly to Pete Hayden in her office. 'Something up?' he asked innocently looking at Naomi then Pete.

'Will you tell him or shall I?' said Pete rhetorically, leaving the room immediately.

'What's going on?' Mike asked.

'Apparently when Carl arrived back here yesterday he had a flaming row with Tony Cookson, then said goodbye to everyone saying that he'd now finished at MicaCom.'

106

'What? He can't do that; we're both contracted to see the week out here. Who told you that?'

'Pete did. Tony rang him last night.'

'I don't believe it. Where's Tony?'

'He went to Cambridge last night after the row to have a meeting with George Fellgate early this morning. He's due back here at lunchtime.'

'Have you tried to get Carl?'

'Yes, but there's no answer from home and as usual there's no service to his mobile.'

'Oh, shit. I bet he's left for Portsmouth already. I can't believe he would have gone off just like that. He knows the conditions of transfer. If we breach contract, BinaryByte has the right to cancel their payment to us and renegotiate the deal.'

'Haven't you been paid already?'

'Yes and no. I have the banker's draft in my pocket, but it can't be cashed until tomorrow.

'Is there something I can do?'

'Yes, you remember yesterday when I told you that Carl had found Sarah working in Portsmouth?'

'Yes.'

'He said he'd found her name on the Internet. Could you get someone to carry out a search for *Sarah Zurek in Portsmouth*? Try Grahame in Marketing, he uses the Internet a lot.'

'I'll do it for you.'

'I didn't know you were an Internet expert.'

'I wouldn't say I'm an expert, but I've used search engines many times to look for supplier information'

Pete appeared at the door. 'There's a Susan on your direct line. Says it's urgent.'

Mike looked at Naomi in desperation. 'You speak to Susan. At least get that problem out of the way. Leave the search to me. I'll find Sarah.'

Pete had raised his eyebrows in bewilderment and was about to speak.

'Please, don't say anything,' Mike said with a resigned look on his face, 'You'd never begin to understand. I need to take this call in private, could you make yourself scarce for ten minutes?' Without waiting for an answer Mike strode down the corridor stepped into his ex-office and shut the door.

* * *

Carl passed under a walkway and then left into the large open City Square. A fingerpost told him what the various buildings were bordering the Square. To his right was the impressive looking Guildhall with grey stone steps leading to its pillared entranceway. Facing him were the Norrish Central Library and some University of Portsmouth buildings. To his left and also above and behind him were the Civic Offices, a modern monolith of about five stories with a smoked glass façade. The main entrance was reached by a wide staircase of bricked steps guarded at the centre by a monument of Queen Victoria. Two sets of automatic sliding doors welcomed his arrival between which a small dog was tethered and whining for its owner, much to the distress of some emerging patrons. Immediately facing him was the reception desk with a very large, rather obvious Ask Here for Help sign. Two receptionists amidst piles of paperwork were dealing with a small queue of enquirers. According to arrowed signs corridors to the left and right led to various council departments the most prominently displayed one being Cash Payments. Strategically placed around the reception work area were a number of modern PCs, large diameter screens and laser printers. From this Carl assumed the council had a generous IT budget and in his previous life he would have had no hesitation in presenting his business card for an audience with the IT manager in order to interest him in MicaCom's products. Today, however, he had other things on his mind. The receptionists were dealing with their customers courteously but pedantically. Help was being administered on planning applications, job interviews and complaints about refuse collection. It was another five minutes before it was his turn to be attended to by the younger, bespectacled clerk.

'Good Morning, I'd like to see Sarah Zurek please,' he said.

'Your name is?' asked the young woman.

'Carl Denham.'

'And do you have an appointment Mr. Denham?'

'I'm afraid not, but it is a rather important matter.'

'So, could you tell me the nature of your business?'

'Please, could you just ring Sarah and tell her I am here. I'm sure she will want to see me.'

'I'll try her phone,' said the receptionist, looking through a list and punching four numbers on the telephone keypad.

'I'm sorry, but there's no answer. I'll leave a message on her pager to call reception. Take a seat Mr. Denham and I'll tell you when she calls back.'

He was directed to a seating area to the left of reception where a few other people were waiting. Literature racks encircled the area, advertising the tourist sites and attractions in and around Portsmouth. He selected a few to browse and began his wait. He looked up expectantly every time he heard a telephone ring hopeful that he would be summoned. He was nervous. All his worries about the welfare and status of Sarah were returning the longer he waited. Twenty minutes later he went back to reception to check if Sarah had rung. She had, but it could be another half an hour because she was very busy.

Was that another put off, he wondered? Sarah had always been very conscientious in her work so there was a plausible reason. What was another half an hour after eleven years? He did wish he had brought something more interesting to occupy his mind like a newspaper or magazine instead of being forced to eavesdrop on the domestic problems being discussed around him and by new arrivals at reception.

A steady procession of council staff kept appearing, calling out someone's name and then disappearing with their acquisition in tow down one of the corridors.

He studied each arrival hoping to spot Sarah.

* * *

Mike realized that he had no option but to be honest with Susan, took a deep breath and picked up the receiver from the desk.

'Hello, Susan.'

'Mike, have you been avoiding me? I tried to reach you several times yesterday. I even left a message for Carl. Have you told him yet?'

'When did you leave a message for Carl? What did it say?'

'Well, it wasn't a message as such. Just asking him to call me. It was at about three o'clock.'

'Did he call you?'

'No, of course not, that's why I'm ringing now.'

'Susan, I'm sorry, but Carl vanished before I had a chance to speak to him.'

'What do you mean vanished? That sounds pretty final.'

'Apparently he stormed out of the office yesterday after a row with one the new bosses here and hasn't turned up this morning. He's causing me a big problem right now.'

'Where's he gone? Perhaps he's at home. Have you tried friends or parents?'

'I wish I could tell you under better circumstances. I think he's gone to Portsmouth. It's a long story, which I'll tell you sometime, but he's gone to visit an old girl friend who's working there. If I don't find him quickly we both stand to lose a substantial amount of the proceeds from the sale of MicaCom. Perhaps you'll give me your telephone number now. I promise to call you when all this has blown over.'

'Who's he gone to see in Portsmouth?'

'Somebody called Sarah Zurek.'

There was an eerie silence from Susan's end of the line before she spoke again.

'How could you let me down on this Mike? You knew it was important to me.'

'I know, but give me your number, and really, you'll be the first person I'll call when I've located Carl.'

After the call Mike stood looking out of the window feeling depressed with guilt. Eight years he'd carried out this charade with Susan and at the final hurdle he'd screwed up. Maybe Carl's disappearance and the possible resultant financial consequences would be his punishment for procrastination of the reunion of Carl and Susan. He hoped that at least Carl would find his fairy tale ending in Portsmouth; it would then be just him and Susan who would be the losers. Still deep in thought it took a few moments before Mike realized the phone was ringing. He picked it up hoping it was news from Naomi.

'I have George Fellgate on the phone for you,' Naomi said.

Shit thought Mike; here comes my comeuppance.

'Hello, George, do you know what happened yesterday?'

'Yes, Tony told me about it this morning. It seems you might have a problem.'

'I'm aware of that. Can I hear your, or rather, Tony's side of the story?'

'It appears to be fairly straightforward. Tony was asking Carl some routine questions about the Protean project plan. Carl refused to answer, went into rage, threatened Tony physically and then stormed out saying he was finished with MicaCom. As a consequence I've advised the bank to put a hold on the banker's drafts.'

'Now don't be hasty George. I'm certain there must be a misunderstanding here. That doesn't sound like Carl at all. Is Tony sure about the facts?'

'Absolutely. Are you suggesting that Tony's been lying?'

'No, of course not. It's just that … well … there's no reason that Carl would jeopardise the deal now.'

'Well, he has, so you had better do something about it - quickly. I'm coming over to MicaCom tomorrow. I suggest that you and Carl be there for a final debriefing. I'll then reconsider the hold on the money, if I get satisfaction. If not, I'll have to invoke the penalty clauses,' George threatened.

Mike tried to make light of the matter. 'Don't worry George. I'm on Carl's trail as we speak. I'm confident the situation will be resolved very soon.'

But as he put the receiver down Mike knew he had lied. He wasn't confident at all. If Carl's adventure were successful, the last thing on his mind would be what might be happening at MicaCom. Carl would only find out there was a problem when he tried to pay in his BinaryByte cheque – then it would be too late. Mike tried to recall the text of the penalty clauses. He and the company solicitors hadn't paid much attention to them at the time since they doubted they would be needed. He did remember the clauses were severe, wiping a large percentage off the negotiated price. It was obviously in George's best interest if Carl had gone missing. A ridiculous notion then entered Mike's head – perhaps BinaryByte had engineered the situation?

* * *

The promised thirty minutes had elapsed and it was now almost eleven o'clock, Carl was ready for another visit to reception when he noticed an extremely attractive woman appear from a corridor and head towards reception. She had short blonde hair swept tight behind her ears and was wearing a white blouse, beige suit and brown low-heeled shoes. She walked with an air of authority and confidence. At reception, she seemed to be idly chatting with the receptionist who then pointed a finger in his direction. The blonde woman nodded to the receptionist and then started to walk towards him. Carl's first thought was that this was Sarah's boss or a colleague sent to provide an excuse for Sarah's absence.

'Mr. Denham?'

'Yes.'

'Perhaps now you can now see the mistake you have made …' and when he looked bewildered, continued '… I'm Sarah Zurek'.

Shocked, he stuttered, 'B-b-but you can't be. Is this some kind of joke?'

'Mr. Denham I had already informed you that I am not the person you are looking for. I'm sorry you've had a wasted journey,' Sarah replied, abruptly turning and walking down the corridor to his left.

'No, please wait.' he called after her, conscious that his voice was loud as all the mundane conversations around him stopped to listen to this more interesting exchange.

She looked back and he rose from his seat to catch up with her.

'Please, at least spare me just a few minutes of your time. Is there somewhere more private we could talk?'

'Look, I'm really busy and don't see what purpose it would serve,' she answered angrily.

'Really, just five minutes. Please,' he implored.

'OK, but no more than five minutes. I'll check if there is an empty office available somewhere'.

Carl suddenly felt foolish. Why didn't he accept what he had read in the e-mails? Normally he would never have pursued such an obvious fool's errand, but love is blind, and his own eyes were clouded in his search for Sarah – the real Sarah. His only possibility left now was to telephone Sarah's mother. He should have done that in the first place. Now that he was here, he might as well try to salvage some information. It did strike him as odd, that this Sarah was unnaturally rattled by his presence.

Sarah came back and led him to a door labelled Environmental Research, which opened to an unoccupied room containing a trestle table, four chairs and not much else. Intending to keep the meeting short Sarah remained standing while Carl pulled a chair to one side of the table and sat down. His eyes met hers and with a shrug of her shoulders, she did the same.

'I really am sorry to bother you and I apologize for arriving unannounced. I was convinced you were the Sarah I was looking for and that the e-mail replies had been designed to put me off. Zurek is such a rare name that I'd built up my hopes you were her, so it's come as a bit of an anti-climax. You even look like her a bit and are about the same age.' Carl paused briefly in case she was going to offer a figure, but Sarah just stared back at him.

'I just wanted to ask you if perhaps you have other relatives that might be able to help me.'

'I've already answered that question. Don't you think I would know if there was another Sarah Zurek in my family?'

He had not noticed up to now, but this ersatz Sarah had a slight accent. Not British, foreign, Eastern European perhaps.

'Yes of course, but I was thinking of something else. Perhaps your father or mother might have come across someone with the name Zurek, even though they are not related. It's a coincidence that wouldn't be forgotten.'

'No, I don't think so –' she said pausing as if she were composing an acceptable answer, '- both my father and mother are dead, and I don't have any other close relatives.'

'Oh, I'm sorry, but you do have *other* relatives with the name Zurek?'

'Yes, probably, but I've lost contact with any of them that still exist.'

'Is there a reason for that?'

'Not particularly, but it's none of your business anyway. Let me ask you a question. Doesn't your Sarah have any family you could contact?'

'I believe her mother is still alive, but I haven't contacted her yet. That was to be my next step.'

'If you'd listened to me in the first place there wouldn't have needed to be a next step.'

'Point taken,' he said.

'Why is this Sarah so important to you?'

'I'm trying to find her because we were in love and something unexplained happened which caused her to turn me away. I'm trying to find out the reason and hoping we can get back together again.'

'After all these years … maybe she doesn't want to see you again'.

Carl noticed that Sarah had hesitated in mid-sentence. It could have been for effect, but the look on her face said otherwise. He replied quickly, hoping she had not detected his perception.

'That's the risk I may have to face'.

Carl stood to indicate that he had finished his interrogation and offered his hand.

'Thank you for listening to me. If you do by chance come across any information that might help me, you know my e-mail address. Thanks again.'

Sarah stood too and shook his hand.

'I doubt it. Goodbye Mr. Denham'

He watched as she opened a door into a large, busy open-planned office and closed it after her. If her hair was longer, if she had walked with a less sensual gait, and most importantly, if she proved she could smile, she could have passed for his Sarah given the time since he had last seen her.

Chapter 15

Thursday, March 11, 1999 – 11:15 a.m.

'I've drawn a blank,' Naomi said as Mike entered her office, 'I've found plenty of Zurek references, but no matches with Sarah or Portsmouth.'

'You must have missed something. I'm sure Carl said he'd found a reference to her on the Internet. No disrespect Naomi, but get Grahame to carry out a separate search. Perhaps he knows a few backdoors that you haven't discovered yet.'

'It's already in hand. Grahame should be doing it right now. I'll let you know immediately if he finds something. How did it go with Susan?'

'Not at all well. I do feel bad about this. I've strung her along for so long now and on the day she should be reunited with Carl, I've had to tell her that he's probably gone to meet a completely different girlfriend. It's no wonder that she slammed the phone down on me.'

'And with George?'

'He's pissed with me too. Making threats about penalty clauses. Could you get the company solicitors on the phone? I need to know where I stand if we can't find Carl. Keep trying Carl's home and mobile phone.'

* * *

Carl headed towards the main doors unsure of what to do next. He needed to think events through.

A milky sun had arrived when he got outside; just warm enough to be comfortable. Immediately in front of the Civic Centre were several long back-to-back bench seats made of stone. He chose an unoccupied one facing the Guildhall Square and sat down.

After all these years nagged in his mind like a piece of meat stuck in a tooth. He mentally replayed the content of the brief e-mails and their short conversation, trying to identify words that had been written or said which

114

implied the time span of his separation from Sarah - there were none. So, why had she used that phrase? Perhaps she had guessed that his search had been a long one. Maybe she had read an aged look in his face. Then why did she hesitate after she had said it? The slight pause was clear to both of them. Possibly, she had detected that she had made an assumption and was expecting him to confirm or deny her suggestion. If she had made a slip, it implied that she knew something about her namesake. They could be related; their physical similarities might stem from a bloodline connection. She may be protecting the existence of perhaps a cousin with the same name. The only way he could think of resolving his suspicions was to confront her again.

It was now just after midday. The wispy clouds had suddenly cleared leaving the sun to oversee a perfect spring day. If he went back into the building and asked to speak to Sarah again his request would undoubtedly be refused. There was a chance that she might emerge into the bright daylight for a lunch break. Sarah had however seemed to be a tough, career-minded character and probably worked during her break. Only by looking over his right shoulder could he see the main entrance of the Civic Centre, so to get a clearer view he moved to sit and face the building. The benches were a popular lunchtime venue. Already a number of likely staff members had emerged from their workplace and sat down with packed lunches to take advantage of the fine weather. It exacerbated his own need for food. He had decided to sit it out, when he noticed a woman exit the Centre and search for somewhere to sit. She headed in his direction aiming for one of the few remaining seating places. As she got closer there was a brief moment of recognition and then she lowered herself a foot from him.

'Hello again, isn't it a lovely day?' said the receptionist.

'Yes, it's quite warm now,' he said trying to be attentive, yet fixated on the sliding doors.

'You had your chat with Sarah then. She didn't seem too pleased to see you. Sarah's a nice girl; I hope there's nothing wrong. She's been a good friend to me.'

All these sentences were phrased as questions rather than statements. Carefully avoiding a direct response he said 'You know Sarah quite well then?'

'Oh yes, we joined the council around the same time. We were on the same induction course together.'

'That was a long time ago,' he said gambling on her answer.

'Goodness, yes. 1991 I think,' she said reaching into a lunch bag and extracting a sandwich.

'Strange, I don't recall her mentioning you.'

'She must have done, I'm Veronica, Vi.'

'Ah, of course. I didn't link you with the receptionist job.'

'That's because I'm actually in the same department as Sarah. I do all the systems accounting, but I started in reception and help out there occasionally when they are short staffed.'

He took his eyes off the door and looked longingly at the sandwich as Vi took a bite. If he was careful maybe he could keep this conversation going and glean some more information about Sarah without having to confront her again.

'I'm sorry, would you like a sandwich? They're cheese and tomato.'

'Actually, I am quite hungry. Can you spare one?'

'Of course, help yourself.'

He took one and while savouring his first mouthful, concentrated on what his next exploratory question could be.

'I'm a bit worried about Sarah. I bumped into a mutual friend of ours recently and she thought that Sarah was having some work or family problems,' he offered, hoping that Vi's loose tongue might continue its revelations.

'Well I wouldn't call them problems. She has turned down a promotion a few times, but wasn't unhappy about it – but the bosses were though. I think they liked the idea of a Cambridge student running the IT department. As for family, I don't think she's seen her mother or sister for years, not surprising considering the way they treated her.'

'She never mentioned the promotion to me.' True he thought, nor anything else for that matter.

'You know Sarah, never likes to be in the limelight. She thought that it would draw too much attention to herself. She prefers a quiet life. Anyway, why are you sitting here?'

'Oh, I have a long journey back home and I thought I would soak up some sunshine before I left. I suppose I ought to be off soon to avoid the traffic. Goodbye and thanks again for the sandwich.' He thought Vi might be becoming suspicious about his questioning and he wasn't sure he could keep talking about someone he hadn't met before today. He stood up and left quickly in the direction of the library before Vi engaged him again.

Carl considered how fortunate he had been in his conversation with Vi. Somehow he had obtained plenty of answers and given none; but the answers had demanded more questions that were too risky to pose. Sarah had been in Portsmouth for eight years, three years less than the last time he had seen his own Sarah, who had also been at Cambridge University. Vi mentioned a mother and sister, which contradicted Sarah's own conversation with him. Mother and sister were the only relations of his Sarah he had ever met. There were too many coincidences. What the hell was going on here?

At the library he was directed to the reference area where he first examined the stack of local Portsmouth and district telephone directories. As he had discovered before there were no entries for Zurek. No phone or ex-directory? The latter would go with her apparent need for anonymity. More promising had to be the area electoral register. By law all UK residents had to provide residence information for voting purposes in local, National and EC elections and he needed her address for the plan he had in mind. He had to request the register at the information desk and the librarian presented him with a small flat book containing a cross reference between street name and polling district, and a huge bound book of over a thousand pages listing all eligible voters.

His immediate problem was that the listings were in address order within districts, split into three columns per page. After checking with a librarian that there was no alternative listing, or other method to find the address he was looking for, he resigned himself to the only option. Searching for the name Zurek would be a laborious task, he was at least grateful it wasn't Brown or Smith.

* * *

Mike was sitting in Tony's née Carl's office after Pete had reclaimed his office following Mike's phone calls. Irrespective of the problem with Carl, he had hated this week, being office-less and treated as a mere employee. With his newly acquired wealth - if it actually materialized - he vowed that in any future career, he would have to be in charge of his own destiny. Having tasted the power of self-determination he could not go back to taking orders from someone else. Currently he was annotating some sales analysis figures that Pete had wanted his comment on. It was a menial task, one that Pete should have delegated elsewhere, but Pete obviously wanted to make a demeaning point by the exercise. Mike knew better than to rebel like Carl, the solicitors had told him to hold station, be subservient to BinaryByte's wishes and above all, get Carl's arse back to Chelmsford. The bottom line was that if Carl wasn't back by tomorrow the sale proceeds would be diminished by fifty percent. Over two million pounds down the toilet – which would teach him not to mess about with Carl's private life. One consolation was that Pete had told him a few minutes ago that Paul Westdene no longer worked at MicaCom. The dismissal had apparently not been easy, Paul requiring physical ejection from the building. If Carl returned, that was one piece, in fact the only piece, of good news he could give him.

Mike looked up as the door opened.

'What are *you* doing in my office?' Tony said in an unfriendly tone.

The likely conspirator had returned thought Mike. He had been waiting for this moment. 'Your boss's suggestion, not mine,' Mike countered, knowing it would torment Tony.

'Pete's not my boss, but I'm yours, so find somewhere else to work. Actually, I'm surprised you are still here. I would have thought you might have run away to join your errant partner,' Tony said disrespectfully.

Mike stayed calm. 'I'm glad you brought that subject up. Perhaps you could tell me *exactly* what happened between you and Carl yesterday afternoon?'

'That's none of your business. George knows all the details.'

'Oh, but it is very much my business. Because if there's been any improbity on your part, my solicitors have advised that it would be regarded as conspiracy to defraud.'

'Don't be ridiculous. It's my word against Carl's, and Carl is not exactly in a position to defend himself.'

* * *

After two hours of mundane searching, Carl had drawn a blank and took a break to visit the Crow's Nest tea and coffee lounge on the third floor. He ordered a mug of tea and a slice of fruitcake and took his snack to the balcony that overlooked Guildhall Square. There he partially satisfied his stomach and dwelt on his lack of success. He should have found Sarah listed unless perhaps she lived outside of the sprawling Portsmouth catchment area. Or he'd missed it somewhere despite being meticulous about his inspection. Then again, if Sarah were attempting to hide her existence, keeping her name from the electoral register would have been essential, albeit not risky. He decided to have one more flick through the electoral tome and if he were unsuccessful then an alternative strategy would be required.

Half an hour later he left the library despondent after another session of failed Zurek spotting, but now more resolved than ever to get to the bottom of the mystery. Back at the station car park, he sat in his car and studied his city map looking for a hotel. None were marked so he chose to drive a mile south to find somewhere in the open spaces of Southsea Common. Within ten minutes he was close to the passenger hovercraft terminal to the Isle of Wight and noticed a Post House hotel that would suit his needs.

At the hotel reception, he requested a room for the night. *I will have to check sir, we are very busy at moment* was the reply he always seemed to receive, followed by *You are in luck we have one room left*. He didn't believe a word of it. He was sure that was a stock answer always given to unannounced arrivals to make them feel privileged and grateful.

The room was modern with the usual comforts like telephone, television, chilled mini-bar and most importantly, self-brewing facilities. His first tasks were to brew hot water for coffee and help himself to an extortionately priced chocolate snack from the mini-bar. While waiting for the kettle, he stretched out on the bed, ate his confectionery and composed how he would convince Don to help him with his plan.

Chocolate finished and coffee cooling in the cup, and eager to make progress, he reached for the phone and dialled the MicaCom office.

'Good Afternoon. This is MicaCom, how may I help you?'

'Hello, Jacqui. It's Carl.'

'Carl. Where are you? Everybody's going crazy here wanting to speak to you.'

'What do you mean, everybody? I've only been gone half a day.'

'I'll have to put you through to Mike, he wants to speak to you urgently.'

'Hold on Jacqui. You must do something for me first. Access the customer file for Travis Security, go to the contacts list, and tell me the private number for Don Travis.'

'I'll put you through to Mike first, and then he can transfer you back to me.'

'NO Jacqui. Do it now will you. I'll speak to Mike afterwards.'

'OK, OK, there's no need to shout.'

She read out the number. 'I'll transfer you...' Jacqui said as Carl pressed the disconnect button.

He immediately dialled the number for Don.

'Don? Carl Denham.'

'Gosh, speaking to you twice in the same week. Must be a record.'

'Don, I have a big problem and I need your professional help. Your *old* professional help.'

'Sorry, I'm not quite with you.'

'Are you free tomorrow?'

'Well, I have nothing planned that can't wait for a day.'

'Can you get to Portsmouth, by, say, seven o'clock tomorrow morning.'

'Portsmouth? Seven o'clock? Are you crazy? What's happened?'

'I can't go into it now. Trust me. It's *very* important. Bring your tools with you.'

'Now I really ...'

Carl interrupted, 'It's to do with Sarah.'

'You've found her?'

'Not exactly. But I've maybe found someone who's impersonating her. I want you to break into her home.'

'Jesus, Carl. I don't do that sort of stuff anymore.'

'All right then. It doesn't have to be you, but presumably you still have some *contacts*?'

'There might be one or two people I could reach, though I doubt I could get them with such short notice.'

'No. It has to be tomorrow. I'd feel happier if you could do it.'

'Look, there's no way I could get up early enough in the morning. How 'bout if I set out this afternoon?'

'That's perfect. I knew you wouldn't let me down. Come to the Post House hotel. When you come off the M275 follow the signs for the hovercraft terminal on Southsea Common. The hotel is in Pembroke Road. You can't miss it. What time will you be here?'

'It's three-thirty now. I'll need to pack a bag, get some implements. I'll pop home now and make my excuses to Wendy. I should be there about … seven o'clock.'

'I'll book a room in your name. I may not be here when you arrive. Just hang about in your room. Thanks again Don. I'll see you later.'

That was a lot easier than expected, thought Carl. He didn't know whether all aspects of Don's business were straight these days, but he hoped that Don would rise to the challenge. Once a rogue always a rogue.

For Don to do his job, he would first have to find out where Sarah lived. He wished now he had taken the risk and attempted to get the information from Veronica. He had two remaining possibilities, both of them were going to be difficult to execute.

He picked up the phone for the third time and punched the numbers for the Civic Centre.

'Portsmouth Civic Offices, can I help you?'

'Hello. Could you put me through to reception please?'

'Just a moment please,' a click and a ringing tone then a different voice, 'Reception.'

'Could I speak to Veronica please?'

'No, I'm sorry, Veronica's not here now. She's gone back to her own department. Do you want me to transfer you?'

'No, that's OK. You might be able to help me. I'm Don Travis representing Overland Transport Services. Overland were due to deliver an urgent private parcel to a Miss Sarah Zurek this afternoon, but unfortunately the delivery van has broken down. We have arranged alternative transport but may be a bit late. Could you tell me what time Sarah Zurek leaves for home?'

'Well I can't answer personally for Sarah, but the normal finishing time here is five o'clock.'

'Oh dear. I'm not sure we could get there by then. Six o'clock is the earliest we could make it. Could you give me her home address instead?'

'I'm sorry sir, I'm not allowed to give out that information. I'll put you through to Sarah so that you can make ...' He never heard the rest of the sentence; he had replaced the receiver. Plan A had failed, but at least he now knew what time Sarah might be leaving work.

With some time to kill Carl briefly considered calling MicaCom. He wondered what all the fuss could be about. Whatever it was, they could stuff it, he didn't work there anymore and that was official. Maybe Mike wanted to speak to him personally, so with the risk of getting trapped he tried his direct line. It was engaged. Fate presumably was dictating that his current task was more important.

* * *

Jacqui found Mike sitting at a spare desk in the Sales office. 'Mike, I've just had a call from Carl,' Jacqui said, knowing she was about to get some verbal abuse.

'Bloody hell Jacqui I asked you to put him through to me if he called. What did he want?' Mike yelled in disbelief.

'I tried honestly, but he cut me off as soon as I gave him the information that he wanted.'

'What was that?'

'He wanted the private number for Don Travis at Travis Security.'

'Did he say why?'

'No, but he seemed in a hurry. Here's the number, I thought you would want it.' Jacqui said, and passed a note to Mike.

Why would Carl want to speak to Don Travis, Mike silently asked himself. He immediately called the number but there was no answer. He called Jacqui to get the Travis Security switchboard number. Dialled it, and was put through to Don's Secretary who informed him that Don had recently left for the day, and no she would not supply his mobile or home phone number. The best Mike could achieve was a promise that she would pass on his urgent request.

Twenty minutes later having heard nothing, he dialled Travis Security again. Don's wife had been contacted and had advised that Don had had to go to Portsmouth on an urgent personal matter.

Frustrated he went to see Naomi and told her about Don Travis.

'That seems to confirm that Carl is in Portsmouth, but what Don Travis has to do with it heavens knows. I want you to phone every hotel in the

Portsmouth area. Ask whether a Carl Denham or Don Travis is registered. Come to find me if you get any news.'

* * *

Carl unpacked the modest collection of clothes and toiletries from his bag. He ought to change to minimize the chance of being recognized. By luck, he had brought along a pair of blue jeans, and with the anorak in his car it would be the best disguise he could manage. He also pocketed his mobile phone, charged and packed the night before. He sometimes carried it when he travelled any distance, for emergency outgoing use only. Only a few close confidants had the number and he always kept it switched off – he hated being disturbed.

Back in the hotel reception, he went through the expected exchange to book a room for Don. A different reception person this time, a young lady who had obviously been on the same customer relations course, and after receiving the customary *very busy* and *one room left*, he secured the room next to his own. He picked up a spare copy of *The Daily Telegraph* and asked for the most detailed map of Portsmouth that also illustrated public transport routes. He was provided with a photocopied map of the city centre and a bus route leaflet that he had originally browsed at the Civic Centre. He sat in the lounge area for a while studying the map in ever increasing circles from the Civic Centre, attempting to familiarize himself with the surrounding roads. Satisfied he went to his car, donned his anorak and set off for the city centre.

* * *

At the fifth attempt on her hotel phone round Naomi had struck lucky and relayed the information to Mike.

'Mike, both Carl and Don Travis are booked into the Post House in Portsmouth. Carl has just left the hotel, destination unknown. Don Travis hasn't arrived yet but is due at about seven o'clock. I've left urgent messages for either of them to call you. I've given your private and mobile numbers.'

Chapter 16

Thursday, March 11, 1999 – 4:30 p.m.

By four-thirty, Carl was parked in a small Permit Holders Only parking area between the Guildhall and a war memorial. It was as close as he could get his car to the Civic Centre and still keep the entrance in view. There was plenty of room and this late in the day he was prepared to take the risk of having his car "booked" to secure the advantage of a quick getaway if needed.

He had no idea whether Sarah travelled to work by foot, public transport or car. Whichever way there was a good chance that she would come out of the main entrance. He had not noticed any other entrances or exits, but he would need to check before choosing his vantage point. He stuffed his mobile phone and newspaper in his anorak pockets, immobilized his car and walked across the square.

Circumambulating the Civic Centre he discovered the building was T-shaped with a footbridge crossing over Isambard Brunel road to join to another office complex. Whilst there were several other doorways, none appeared to be regularly used exits since they were either locked or obstructed by office furniture or equipment.

The most worrying find was a sign for an underground **Civic Offices Private Car Park** at the rear of the building. There was no obvious pedestrian entry, so access was presumably from inside the Civic Centre. If Sarah had a car and was authorized to use the car park, it would be impossible to observe employees leaving the main entrance and the car park at the same time. He decided to gamble on watching the main entrance. If he was wrong then the plan surrounding his summoning of Don to join him in Portsmouth was going to be a complete waste of time.

He tracked back to the front of the building. The stone seats immediately outside the Civic Centre were uncomfortably close to the entrance. They would provide a perfect observation point for identifying Sarah leaving work, but to ensure she didn't see him, it was best to conduct his spying operation from a greater distance. Instead, Carl chose a place at the top of the steps leading from the Square. Here there was a balcony area that also had stone seating along its two edges. It was about fifty metres from the entrance. Close enough to study people leaving the Centre, but not too close that he might be recognized. Carl sat down and extracted the newspaper from his inside pocket. He folded it into quarter size and with one eye on the crossword on the back page and the other trained on the entrance, he began his stakeout and considered his plan.

Tracking someone on foot was not something he had done before. Keeping a safe but close distance would be difficult. If she went home by public transport, in joining her on the same bus for example, he would certainly be spotted. Plus, for all he knew, she might not go straight home, could exit the building by a back door, or disappear by car. He wished Don were here; he was bound to have more experience in surveillance techniques.

A few minutes before five o'clock, the daily staff exodus began. For the next twenty minutes, there was a hive of pedestrian activity. Carl found it difficult to be one hundred percent vigilant such were the number of people in motion. His eyes darted this way and that seeking out in order of preference, females, with short blonde hair and beige suit, the suit being the least significant in case a coat covered it. The majority of those exiting turned right, possibly heading towards the railway station. Several times he rose quickly with an adrenaline rush having spied likely candidates, but on closer inspection none were Sarah. By five-thirty, with now only a trickle of homeward bound staff, he was becoming increasingly sceptical about his scheme, when he noticed Veronica emerge. She turned right. Perhaps Sarah and Veronica's department had had an after-hours meeting that had just broken up? Ten minutes later he assumed his hopeful guess has been wrong when no one else came out. It was now relatively quiet and relying on his ears to alert him of further movement, he focused his attention on the crossword. One of the clues was strangely ominous: *Uses a clot to mix-up no-hoper (4,5)*. He penned in the answer *Lost Cause*.

Just after six o'clock a burly looking uniformed guard appeared at the entrance doors. He was busy around the doors for a while and then returned inside the building. Six o'clock must be curfew time for the council. There were now a few lights on in the building, so there were still presumably some staff at work. Shortly after another wave of employees began to emerge, each one having to wait for the guard to unlock the door and release them as if in prison. No doubt the security man had ushered people home so that he could settle in or lock up for the night.

Then he saw her. She was wearing an unbuttoned fawn coat over the beige suit and carrying a tan briefcase, but it was the sexy walk that convinced him that he had encountered his target. She exchanged a few words with the guard, maybe even smiled, and then set off right at a brisk pace. He waited to ensure she did not show any sign of turning back, tossed the unfinished crossword into a nearby waste bin, then set off in pursuit. She reached the main road and turned right again, away from the station. Fortunately the traffic was heavy, helping to mask any noise that might carry from his footsteps. Offices lined the road, so there were several entranceways that he could slip into if Sarah looked back. He slowed as she neared a bus shelter, but she took no interest in it, much to his relief. No car, no train, no bus, perhaps she was walking home, affording him the best chance of keeping with her. Two hundred metres later they approach a busy T-junction navigated by a roundabout with a dual carriageway in each direction. A sign showed this was Winston Churchill Avenue. Sarah went right.

To the right was a Police Station and Magistrates Courts and for a brief moment he considered proclaiming his suspicions to the duty officer, but they were still suspicions only; he would need a lot more evidence before he could seek the support of the local constabulary. Another hundred metres further on there was a pedestrian underpass and Sarah chose the downward steps to disappear below ground. He held back fearful that the narrow confines of the stone tunnel would amplify his presence. The underpass was simply a means of safely crossing the busy road. On the other side Sarah would either go left or right. He waited until he could see which way she chose and jogged through the tunnel and up the steps until he had re-established a safe distance. She was maintaining a good pace, and probably worked out, or was maybe a jogger, he thought. At the first turning she took a left into Middle Street, passing an art college.

The street began with an open grass area on the left and small business workshops on the right, and then narrowed into a mixture of terraced houses of varying shapes and sizes. In convoy they continued along Middle Street for about four minutes until it met the turning into Yorke Street. Sarah looked benignly his way, then crossed the road and continued right. The architecture changed style now, houses being replaced with larger shoebox-shaped four storey buildings - probably flats. Carl confirmed this when he noticed shared entranceways and names like Drake Court and Francis Court. Another hundred metres and Sarah turned right through a gap in some railings, took the path across a lawn, and disappeared through the entrance to Maynard Court 1-16. A prominent sign on the lawn just beyond the railings stated City of Portsmouth Housing Department. Parking Spaces Reserved. He ducked into a sheltered area opposite where there were a few trees and a line of six terraced garages that provided some cover for his observation. Though he had seen Sarah enter the building the distance had prevented him seeing her further progress. Did she turn left or right, or go up? With dusk approaching some of the windows were lit, but the lighting had not changed within a few minutes of Sarah's arrival. If the flats were symmetrical, eight either side of the central entrance, four up and four down, four front and four back, it indicated that maybe Sarah occupied a rear flat. He continued watching for a few minutes longer and then thought he ought to move on. Despite his cover, hanging around for more than a few minutes in a quiet residential area was sure to alert someone, so he began to backtrack along his original route.

When he got to the start of Middle Street, he checked his watch – ten minutes to seven, took out his mobile phone, powered it on and called his hotel.

'Post House Hotel.'

'Hello, this is Carl Denham; I'm in room 217. Could you tell me if Don Travis has checked in yet?'

After a short silence, 'No Mr. Denham. Not yet, but both of you have received urgent messages to call Mike Stanford. Do you want the numbers?'

Something pretty serious must be going on if Mike had managed to track him down to his hotel in Portsmouth he thought, but it would have to wait.

'Not just now. I'll get them later. I noticed that you had a display case containing jewellery for sale in your reception area?'

'Yes, that's right.'

'Then could I ask you to do me a big, strange favour?'

'Do you want me to get something for you?'

'Yes, could you get, say a necklace for me, put it in a gift box then put that in a much larger box, about shoebox size. Pack it with newspaper perhaps to stop the gift box rattling about. Then wrap the larger box in plain brown paper.'

'Well, I'll see what I can do. Any particular type of necklace and how much do you want to spend?'

'No problem with price. £20 or £30 maybe? I know this rather an odd request, but it is important. I'd be most grateful for your help. When Mr. Travis arrives, give him the parcel and ask him to call me on my mobile.' He gave her the number. 'Charge any costs to my room account. Oh, and could you obtain a plain greetings card and give that to Mr. Travis too?'

'I'll do my best. Supposing I choose the wrong necklace or card?'

'Please, don't worry. It's always the thought that counts with a gift. You have the telephone number?'

The receptionist read back the number; he thanked her again, and promised her a big tip for her troubles. This time he left his phone switched on and for once was impatient to receive a call.

By the time Don did call back, Carl had returned twice to Yorke Street to become familiar with the territory. He plucked up the courage to go to the entrance to Maynard Court hopeful that there was perhaps a list of residents inside the hallway, or named mailboxes but there were none. He did however confirm his suspicion of the layout of the flats. There were thoroughfares for pedestrians that connected each block of flats. One of them went to the rear of Maynard Court and he discovered that it was merely surrounded by a lawn containing a few stepping-stones. It gave him some time to spy on the rear of the building and although some rooms were lit with no curtains drawn, he failed to recognize Sarah from the people he saw.

When the phone rang it took him by surprise. It had been so long since he had taken an incoming call that the tinny tune of *Frère Jacques* emanating from his inside pocket disturbed his thoughts and the surrounding peace. By now he was back at the confluence of Middle and Yorke Street and continued walking towards the main road as he pressed the answer button on the telephone keypad.

'Don? You're a bit late.'

'Sorry mate, I had a last minute bit of domestic rescheduling to do with Wendy and then there was an accident just after the Dartford Crossing. When I got here there was also an urgent message for me to ring your partner. This is getting to be a bit like a spy movie. Where the hell are you?'

'Don't worry about ringing Mike. I'll explain more when you get here, just listen for now. Get a map or instructions at reception of how to get to Middle Street – it's not far from the hotel, a turning off the Winston Churchill Avenue. Also collect a brown paper parcel, which is waiting for you. Have you any security clothing with you?'

'I already have the parcel and a card, and I have the standard company uniform in my kit.'

'OK. Put the uniform on, and then get here as quickly as possible. I'll be on the left-hand side of the road as you turn into Middle Street. What car are you in?'

'I'll be in my silver Audi A4. How far is it from here?'

'No more than five minutes away.'

'I need to change so should be there in about fifteen.'

'Just get here as soon as possible,' Carl concluded and powered off the phone.

It was seven-thirty and dark when Don pulled up at the kerb.

'Hey, you look smart,' Carl said referring to Don's navy blue uniform with white piping.

'Now don't take the piss, just tell me what's going on.'

In two minutes Carl summarized what had happened so far that day. Don was silent throughout, looking thoughtful and dreading what was to be requested of him guessed Carl.

When Carl had finished, Don said 'OK, I think I've worked out what you want. I'm to deliver the parcel to find out exactly where this bogus Sarah lives.'

'Almost right,' Carl replied. 'This is exactly what I want you to do,' and then continued to explain in detail the role Don was to play. Don protested and made excuses, but Carl knew he was just going through the motions; he would not let him down.

Don parked his car at the beginning of Yorke Street and Carl watched from the passenger seat as Don went through the entrance to Maynard Court clutching the parcel. Carl had written Sarah's name and address on the parcel and purposely omitted the unknown flat number. On the card he had written a short teasing message and tucked it in the box with the necklace after carefully unsealing and resealing the securing tape.

In the entrance hall Don surveyed the layout. There were two front doors each to his right and left and a stairway facing him. Numbers 1 and 2 at the front of the building, 3 and 4 to the rear. Randomly he went right. The flooring and walls showed signs of ageing presumably none of the occupants claiming responsibility for the upkeep. Don could hear at least two varieties of music coming from the flats – soundproof walls were clearly not of prime concern to the builders of this apparently down market accommodation. Each door had a spy hole but only one - number 4 - had a bell push. He decided to try that first.

A slim, smartly dressed man in his late twenties opened the door. Well-spoken he said 'Good evening, how can I help you?'

Don looked over the man's shoulder and was surprised what he saw. In contrast to the run-down exterior, he noticed a palatial looking room; brightly lit with modern leather and chrome furniture, and a scattering of white shaggy sheepskin mats.

In his most formal voice Don answered 'Good evening, sir. I wonder if you can help me. I need to deliver an urgent parcel to a Sarah Zurek, who I believe lives in this block, but unfortunately I don't know which flat. Would you possibly know the number?'

'I'm not sure I can help you. I've only been here for three weeks and I haven't really got to know anyone yet. What does she look like?'

'I'm told she is about 30, short blonde hair, slim, well-dressed,' Don said, not concerned with the flaw that a deliveryman would hardly have a physical description of his recipient.

'That might fit someone I've seen going upstairs a few times. Other than that I've no idea.'

Don thanked him, turned and noticed that the door opposite was open ajar, held by a security chain, with a frail looking lady staring at him through the gap.

'You'll be wanting the snotty foreigner upstairs in number 7,' she said unprompted.

'Oh, you know her do you?'

'Nah, I've never spoken to her, but she's been here a long while. I'll give her the parcel if you like.'

'No, I need to deliver it personally. Thank you for the information,' Don said, eager to continue his mission.

Back at the entrance hall Don strode up the stairs now nervous of the next part of his performance. Carl had briefed him thoroughly on what to do, and the knowledge that he may be helping to uncover a conspiracy overcame his apprehension as he approached the door to number 7. His subsequent job of breaking into Sarah's flat would be more difficult by being on an upper floor. The only practical way in would be the front door. He listened carefully for activity at the other flats, studied the lock to number 7 then pressed the doorbell.

Don heard footsteps approach the front door then there was a pause. He felt self-conscious assuming he was being sized up through the spy hole. A female voice behind the door shouted 'Who is it?'

'Overland Transport. Package for Sarah Zurek,' he shouted back, using the identity chosen by Carl that afternoon in case his call to the council offices had been passed on.

'Give me a minute,' the voice replied.

When she opened the door the reason for the delay was obvious. The woman wore a dressing gown and a towel wrapped around her head like a turban. Clearly Don had disturbed her bath, shower or hair washing, but it did provide him with the essential information that his target was probably alone in the flat.

'This is a strange time to deliver a package,' Sarah said.

'I'm sorry to disturb you but I was told that this was an urgent delivery that had to be with you today.'

'I'm not expecting anything. Are you from the company that called my office this afternoon? How did you know my home address?'

Don shrugged his shoulders trying to underscore his reply. 'I don't know anything about that Miss; I was just told to deliver this parcel to this address. And I was to verify that it was only given to a "Sarah Zurek". Can you do that for me? I'd really like to get home now.'

'Yes, well I *am* Sarah Zurek. Have you something for me to sign?'

'No Miss. I was asked to check any kind of document with your name on it.'

'This is crazy,' Sarah said, but Don gave her his best *It's more than my job's worth* look, so she continued, 'OK, just a moment,' and she went to a handbag lying on a table close to the front door. She rummaged around and finally extracted a credit card size security badge and showed it to him. The Portsmouth Council Systems Department had issued the badge, which showed a photograph, name and signature - all accredited to a Sarah Zurek.

'Thank you Miss,' Don said. 'Here's your parcel. I'm sorry to have bothered you so late. Goodnight.'

Don strolled away from the door, but hastened his pace when he reached the top of the stairs, and was almost running by the time he got back to the car.

'Jesus, that was scary. Mission accomplished,' Don said as he climbed into the driver's seat and immediately started the engine. 'Let's get out of here.'

* * *

Sarah went into the living room and sat down on the settee with the parcel on her lap. It was light and she could hear a rustling inside like popcorn. She tore away the brown paper wrapping to reveal a plain white box. She undid the flaps and saw a card lying on top of little pieces of white polystyrene as packing material. The card contained a short message **Thanks, Carl**. She pushed her hand inside and fished out a small scarlet-coloured velvet-covered box. Inside that there was an elegant neck chain of knotted gold.

She went back to the bathroom to finish drying her hair; her thoughts now occupied with one more unusual event from the day. Carl Denham turning up unannounced was bad enough, but an unexplained parcel delivered to her private address was a more serious matter. She would have to ring Ivan soon to relate what had happened; these latest happenings would reveal whether he would provide her with support or leave her to face any consequences alone.

Normally she was so cautious about the things that she did and said, but Carl Denham's appearance had rattled her usual calm state. She believed she had conducted herself like a true case of mistaken identity, except maybe for the small slip she had made during their brief conversation. Surely it was a reasonable assumption to make that several years had elapsed since Carl had seen Sarah?

The chance encounter between Carl and Veronica had been unfortunate. Veronica was a trustworthy friend; she had said that it was just a casual chat, although she did refer to him as *dishy*, and Sarah hoped that this did not mean Veronica had been too free with information. He was on his way home though and had obviously arranged for the gift to be sent to her. Was it a love token? (sadly probably not); genuine thanks? (possibly); an apology for inconveniencing her? (the most likely) or a trap (what sort of trap?) The biggest mystery was how he or the courier had acquired her home address. Jenny at reception had recounted the call from Overland Transport about the potential delivery. Despite not mentioning it to her, she must have breached council rules and told them her home address. Probably not significant, but Sarah did notice that the deliveryman had an insignia on his uniform jacket which had stated **Travis Security.**

She felt sorry for Carl; he had looked devastated when he discovered she was not his Sarah Zurek. The letters had demonstrated how in love he had been; and since she had been close to love herself once before, she could sympathize with the emotions he must have felt. His sadness had touched her deeply and although she had not shown it, she had desperately wanted to put her arms around him for comfort - she blushed at the thought. Maybe it was not the end of the story; eventually he would find out that Sarah was dead and no doubt he would return to interrogate her again.

Whatever her immediate feelings for Carl there remained the possibility of a threat to her anonymity and Ivan's illegal activities. She guessed that Ivan's reception would either be cool or angry, but thought it prudent to ring him anyway.

While she updated him with recent events, Ivan first seemed merely attentive then he became volatile as she admitted her potential mistake.

'You stupid bitch,' he said when she had finished. 'I think you've really blown it. I'm not convinced this is as innocent as you think. Denham's not stupid and he's on a mission driven by passion – he won't let this rest. I reckon the delivery to you was just a sham in order to suss out you or your flat. The letters I gave you, is there an address on them for this Denham guy?'

'Yes, I'll go to get them,' Sarah said, and disappeared to retrieve them from her underwear drawer.

'OK, it's 17 Wickham Gardens, Ongar, Essex, but the last letter is dated February 1988.'

'It's a long while ago, but at least it's something to go on. Don't do anything else until you hear from me again. Don't answer the door; only answer the phone after a coded call of three rings and don't go to bed until I've called you back later.'

Well, thought Sarah; at least I now know Ivan's true feelings about the matter; he was obviously a worried man.

Chapter 17

Thursday, March 11, 1999 – 8:30 p.m.

Don dropped Carl off to collect his car, then they returned in convoy to the hotel. Carl went to book a table in the restaurant while Don ordered two beers in the bar.

'Food in half an hour,' Carl said as he sat next to Don and took a gulp from his glass. 'Tell me exactly what happened.'

Don narrated the story just like a passage from a book. Giving every detail, verbatim dialogue, even describing the feelings and emotions he felt during his assignment.

'Was she suspicious?' Carl asked when Don had finished.

'I'm not sure. Agitated would be a better description, but I'm sure that changed when she opened the card and parcel. Do you think that was a good idea bearing in mind tomorrow's exercise?'

'I really don't know. What with my visit to her office and then a mysterious parcel, she'll hopefully be panicked into doing something rash.'

'Like what? And we're not going to be in a position to find out what she does or how she reacts.'

'But she might reveal her hand if I confront her again. It depends on what compromising evidence you can find tomorrow. How do feel about that?'

'Well, breaking in should be easy. The front door has a simple Yale lock. There's no sign of alarms or wires. The place seems pretty quiet and private. The major worry will be the other three flats in the corridor. As long as they don't get disturbed or suspicious it should be a piece of cake. What time do you want me to go drumming?'

Carl looked perplexed at Don's jargon.

'Drumming, stealing, burglary, house-breaking, thieving, pilfering …'

'Yes, OK. I get the drift. I don't know what time she'll leave for work. The safest approach is to set out early in the morning and watch her leave home.

Wait a while until all the usual comings and goings are over like postmen and then in we go.'

'We? That's not a good idea. I don't want you lumbering about the place making a mess or leaving evidence behind. Anyway, a lone uniformed man about the place might not be unusual. Two men with one dressed in civvies would be asking for trouble. I *have* done this sort of thing before. When I was out in the field before starting Travis Security I specialized in divorce cases. I often had to search mistress's premises looking for evidence of adulterous husbands' visits. This isn't so different. I know where to look and what to look for. What if I find out that her real name isn't Sarah Zurek, what are you going to do then?'

'The obvious answer is to inform the police. Maybe then I can get a lead to find out where the real Sarah is. I do still need to try Sarah's mother again, perhaps I'll try once more before we have dinner.' Carl finished his drink and jogged up the stairs to his second floor room.

* * *

Ivanhoe Gorvan was a worried man; the Carl Denham story had unnerved him. Known as Ivan, he was content with his life and business interests and wanted it to stay that way. He had been born in Lublin in Poland just after the war and had lived in England since 1984. He had a doting English wife and two bright sons aged eleven and fourteen. The legitimate business that he ran, a High Street bicycle shop in Manor Park on the East Side of London, was ageless. He had been running it since 1987 and the previous incumbent had done the same for at least ten years. There had been at least two managers before that, so he had no idea when the operation had been established. Despite always stocking the latest fashion in bicycles and no other local competition, the shop was never going to make him a wealthy man. Trade was brisk, but hardly profitable. He had once calculated that based on his estimate of true turnover, with reasonable margins and overheads, the shop would have made sufficient profit to perhaps keep him and his wife just above the local poverty level. However, other than the barest minimum of accounting records, he never had to concern himself with the finances of the shop, Gregor – his recondite Polish contact, collected his basic statistics once a week and provided him with all the necessary paperwork to satisfy any inspectors that might call. Tax returns, VAT records, annual accounts, all appeared as if by magic, and were manipulated to better reflect his more demanding lifestyle of well-fed and educated children. Bills were always paid on time, forms were completed without error, customers were treated courteously, so there were never any official visits, letters or phone calls – as far as the authorities were concerned Manor Park Bicycles were model traders in the community.

Above the shop there was ample room for him and his family, with a spare bedroom always available for his irregular, short-stay lodgers. All the transients were English-speaking, well-educated Polish illegal immigrants whose appearance had been arranged, usually with about two weeks notice via communications from Gregor. Ivan never knew nor asked their origin or how they had arrived in Manor Park, although he believed that they entered the UK via Harwich concealed in Freight vehicles. His advance information from Gregor consisted of a name, sex, age, physical description, distinguishing characteristics, a photograph and qualifications, together with a generous fee to cover Ivan's expenses. The details were then passed to several of the contacts that he had inherited when he was installed at the bicycle shop. It was up to him to negotiate fees with his contacts and he would be disappointed if he did not make at least £1,000 for processing each fugitive. By the time a transient arrived, a full set of British documents was available for them. Around a week later, after a briefing from him, a new "British" citizen was ready to face the world, often with a ready-made job to go to.

Ivan had been one of the transient arrivals in 1984. The discovery of his part in a failed bank robbery, during which a bank employee had been killed, had threatened to incarcerate him in Polish prison for the rest of his life. Oles Gomulka, who was a senior Polish Government official controlling the transient operation and a friend of his brother had, for a fee, come to his rescue. And three years later, it was Oles who had given him the privilege of running the UK operation. Ivan had attempted to pay back the favour in 1988 with the original Sarah Zurek as the target of Oles's attention. Now - eleven years later, if his theory about the bogus parcel were true, that favour had come back to haunt him and Oles and he would have to stop Carl Denham snooping around.

Ivan went to wake his eldest son.

* * *

Carl dialled the Ilford number. This time he was somewhat unprepared when the phone was picked up after the second ring.

'Hello?' said a young sounding female voice, seemingly surprised at the telephone ringing.

'Marion?' replied Carl trying to remember desperately what Sarah's sister's voice sounded like.

'No, this is April.'

'I'm sorry; perhaps I've misdialled. I was hoping to speak to Mrs. Zurek.'

'This is Audrey Zurek's home, but I'm afraid she can't come to the phone just now. Who's calling please?'

'My name is Carl Denham. I'm …' and he wondered how to introduce himself to a stranger, '… an old friend of Sarah, her daughter. Is there a more convenient time I could call?'

'I don't think so Mr. Denham, Mrs. Zurek is … rather busy,' was the cold, obstructive reply.

'And just who is April may I ask?' he questioned, attempting to sound formal in order to break down the icy barrier.

'I am Mrs. Zurek's nurse.'

'Forgive me, I wasn't aware that Mrs. Zurek was unwell. I don't want to disturb her. It's possible you might be able to help me. I'm just trying to find out how I could contact Sarah. I've not seen her for years and I have some important information for her.'

There was a pause before the reply came. 'I don't think Mrs. Zurek or I could help you with that. When did you last see Sarah?' said the nurse now speaking very quietly.

'About eleven years ago,' he said, but mystified by the change in voice level and concluding that for some reason this was concealment from Mrs. Zurek.

'I'm terribly sorry Mr. Denham, Sarah died in March 1988.'

Carl felt his throat tighten but could not swallow. He had been standing but slumped back into the chair behind him. His felt a chill in his body but his hands were moist – the telephone receiver almost slipped through his fingers. He stared at the wall not seeing his wan face and the wetness of his eyes reflected in the mirror.

'Mr. Denham? Are you there?'

'Excuse me this has come as a bit of a shock. Do you know what happened?'

'I'm afraid not. It happened a long while before I started looking after Mrs. Zurek. I am sorry to bring you bad news. Were you very close?'

'Yes. She was my …' fiancée was the unwritten word that he and Sarah might have used once, but he chose a less controversial phrase '… best friend.'

He paused a moment to reflect upon his next choice of words. 'Please, could I come to see Mrs. Zurek to express my condolences,' thinking that being truthful about wanting to learn about Sarah's final days would not be acceptable.

The nurse replied with regret in her voice. 'Really, that wouldn't be in Mrs. Zurek's best interests. Part of her on-going distress dates from the time of Sarah's death. You said *Marion* when I answered the phone. I presume you thought I was Sarah's sister. You could speak to her about what happened. I believe she was closely involved in dealing with the matter at the time. I could call her tomorrow to check whether she would see you.'

'The last I knew of Marion was that she was living in Poland?' he queried.

'Well, she was until about six years ago. She lives quite close to here now,' April answered vaguely.

'If you could give me her phone number, I'm sure Marion wouldn't object to talking to me.'

'No offence Mr. Denham, but as neither of us are direct members of the family I don't think I can do that freely. Give me your number and I'll speak to Marion in the morning. I'll call you afterwards.'

'Carl, Carl, for Christ's sake open the door. Are you in there?' Don was thumping furiously on the hotel room door.

Carl rose from the chair where he had slumped twenty minutes earlier. He glanced in the mirror, this time seeing an ashen face with red eyes. He tried to steady himself on the dressing table but his trembling hand made a barely adequate attempt at providing the purchase he needed. He stumbled towards the door with his insides churning, released the catch and took two drunken-like steps into the bathroom to his left. The bathroom was dark and his eyes were immediately grateful for the minor relief to the pounding in his forehead that the unlit environment provided. He collapsed over the wash basin and retched over and over, unaware that the largely liquid contents of his stomach missed their target and oozed slowly over the rim onto the white tiled floor under his feet.

'Bloody hell Carl, you look like a bulldog with a boil on his butt. What's brought this on?' Don said supporting Carl around the waist with his right arm fearful he was about to crash to the floor. With his left hand Don turned on the cold tap and sprayed water into Carl's face. There was a delayed reaction then Carl began to cough and splutter. He straightened, reached for a hand towel hanging next to the basin, and sat with a thump onto the toilet seat behind him.

'She's dead. Christ, she's dead. Why didn't I know?' Carl shouted, mopping the water and vomit from his face.

'Who's dead? What do you mean?' Don asked.

He stared up vacantly at Don standing over him.

'Sarah's dead, Don. I've spent the last eleven years wanting her back and all this time she's been dead. What a fucking waste of a life.'

Don wasn't sure whether Carl was referring to his own life or Sarah's, but it amounted to the same thing.

'Are you telling me you spoke to Sarah's mother and she said Sarah had copped it?'

Carl did not answer, but struggled to stand and they adjourned to the bedroom area. But for the interruption of a final retching session in the bathroom, Carl recounted his telephone call in full. They then sat in silence for a few minutes neither really knowing how to continue the conversation.

'My God, maybe it's not the right time but have you thought what this means?' Don asked eventually.

'I think we both already know the answer to that,' Carl said. 'There is a more sinister connection between the two Sarah's than we originally thought.'

'We can't make too many assumptions here. You don't know the circumstances of Sarah's death.'

'I *do* know that she died in the month I went to San Francisco. I can't help but think that the reason we split up had something to do with her death. I never did find out why she had her breakdown. Maybe it eventually led to her death. Looking at the timing it seems that the substitute Sarah appeared about two to three years after the real Sarah disappeared. You're right though, there's not necessarily any direct connection between the two events. Somebody could be creating new identities for people based upon the deaths of others. That could explain the relative anonymity that surrounds the renaissance lady. God, what a mess. What am I going to do?' Carl pleaded.

'Do you really want to pursue this anymore Carl? Isn't the shock about Sarah enough? I don't want to belittle your grief but perhaps you should move on now. Start your new life. Take a holiday. Come to stay for a while with Wendy and me. You've had eleven years of mourning already; don't prolong it anymore. Why don't we get something to eat and then just get pissed? Talk about the school days and the schemes we used to get up to.'

'It's the school days when all this started. Do you remember when I first dated Sarah? I walked out during a film at the cinema, came back beaming and you, Alan and Dave didn't believe what I'd just done. You were so jealous when you found out I was telling the truth. I then had almost five perfect years loving Sarah. Although it went wrong at the end I've relived the good times over and over again. I owe Sarah something for all that she gave me. I intend to repay that debt and find out what happened to her. I don't care how long it takes or what it costs. If you still want to help me with part of the puzzle then fine, if not I'll go it alone.'

Don tried to moderate Carl's suggestion. 'Aren't you being rather overdramatic about this. Her death could have been an illness or an accident? And if you are right with your new identity theory, that could just be an unfortunate coincidence.'

'And the *coincidences* about mother and sister, Cambridge? I don't buy it and I intend to find out what's been going on. So are you with me or not?'

'You read me wrong Carl. I was attempting to be conciliatory. I'm with you one hundred percent on this. I won't let you down.'

'Then let's eat. No, sod the food, let's just get pissed, but not too pissed – we have an early start in the morning.'

* * *

Ivan looked on in admiration as the screen in front of his fourteen-year-old son Ivan rapidly changed from page to page. Ivan had been asleep but there were no complaints, other than from his mother, when he was woken to utilize his Internet searching expertise. After a ten-minute demonstration of lightning keyboard and mouse skills he had announced confidently there was no record of a company called Overland Transport. Well, surprise surprise thought Ivan.

He then directed his son's attention to search for Travis Security. Within seconds several references were displayed. All but one referred to pages on Travis Security's own web site, which was advertising its range of security services and devices. He asked for a print of the page that contained general information about the company and photos of key personnel. The remaining reference led to the MicaCom site, a page that contained a sample list of client companies including Travis Security. So, there was a link between Denham's company MicaCom and the deliveryman from Travis Security; too much of a coincidence he concluded. Denham was up to something; there was now little doubt about that.

He asked to see the main MicaCom pages and there was a photograph and biography of Carl Denham so he got a print of that too. There was however something more interesting, an article on the take-over of MicaCom by a company called BinaryByte. A statement by the Managing Director Mike Stanford said all the things that MicaCom's clients would want to hear like "continuation of support for MicaCom's products" and "a solid foundation for the growth of the company". It didn't refer to the continued status of the existing directors, but he wondered whether Denham was now a free and wealthy man.

He led his son back to bed, promised him a new game for his computer for the help he had given him recently and then returned to his office to think things through.

He had the impression from Natasha that Denham was a rather determined character and was unlikely to abandon his mission yet, particularly if he had been sharp enough to detect the faults admitted by Natasha. However, so long as Natasha was careful in the future there was nothing that could lead Denham to discovering what had happened to the real Sarah, or his own part in her death. Nonetheless, it was still a risk he was unwilling to take alone.

Reluctantly he resolved that he would have to seek a second opinion and meet with Oles.

* * *

Mike knew he should have driven down to Portsmouth tonight. It would have at least been something positive to do instead of sitting here staring at the phone. He had telephoned the Post House numerous times and left messages for Carl or Don to call him. He had tried Carl's mobile too, but as usual that was out of service. The hotel reception had sworn that they had passed on his urgent message, so why had Carl not called? And what was Don doing with him? Fortunately Lisa was upstairs busily packing for their holiday so she was not witnessing the frustration he was going through. He had told her about Carl's disappearance, but not the financial consequences, or that her packing may be in vain, if he was not found. It was ten o'clock now. If Carl and Don had gone out for a meal or boozing surely they would be back soon. His only solution was to keep phoning and if he had not made contact by, say, four o'clock in the morning, he would have no option but to drive to Portsmouth and find out first hand what the hell was going on.

* * *

The Pig and Whistle pub in Romford was empty but for a group of old codgers playing dominos in one corner. It was a shabby establishment; the best entertainment it could offer was a grossly distorted dartboard in the public bar, which he had never seen anyone use. The tables and chairs rocked on the uneven floor and Ivan had seen a better and cheaper selection of beers and spirits in the local supermarket. When there was a race meeting at the nearby Greyhound track, the Pig and Whistle was packed to capacity before and after the event, but the rest of the time, like now, it was quiet.

Avoiding the beer and wanting to keep a clear head, Ivan was halfway through his orange juice when the creaky front door opened and Oles walked in. Anyone guessing at Oles's age from a distance would have said late twenties. His physique, height, uprightness and stride were those of an athlete. His immaculate dress sense and coiffeured hair was more in keeping with a young executive, and he looked distinctly out of place in the pub's tatty surroundings. It was only when you saw the craggy lines and the chiselled features of his face that his true age of early forties might have been revealed. At first, he appeared not to notice Ivan as he walked towards the bar. The power and authority in his voice when he ordered a scotch caused the domino players to briefly look up and then exchange whispered words. He downed the drink with one slug, ordered another and brought it to the table where Ivan was sitting.

Oles lit a cigarette and drank half his scotch before he spoke. 'What's the problem?' he said in a manner dismissive of the friendship that Ivan thought he had with him.

'It's about the favour I did for you in 1988. There's been ...' Ivan paused searching for appropriate words, '... a development.'

Ivan continued in a hushed voice. 'About three years later, I processed a transient called Natasha Minski ...'

Oles, smiling for the first time, interrupted, 'Yes, I arranged for the importing of Natasha. She was ... a close friend of mine at the Supreme Court.'

'My God, you know her. Well, this is even more unbelievable. The sets of documents for Natasha were from Sarah Zurek, your Sarah Zurek.'

Oles eyes widened and his forehead creased in apparent disbelief. Ivan waited for the outburst, but Oles responded calmly.

'And your explanation for this?'

'If you recall, I used the same contact for the hit as I do for acquiring false documents. I can only assume that after the failed murder attempt on Sarah the documents were kept and recycled later.'

'Why didn't you query this at the time?'

'I recognized the connection but thought nothing of it. All the new identities are created from people that have been dead for a few years anyway. It's a lot easier to generate documents for a real, albeit dead, person than it is to create them from scratch,' Ivan said in mitigation.

'Remember you still owe me from that bungled attempt. Actually that whole exercise turned out to be a waste of effort, I never did get the satisfaction I wanted even when she eventually ... died.'

Ivan looked at Oles in anticipation of a further explanation, but Oles continued without offering one.

'It is unfortunate that a new Sarah Zurek was created, but if anyone has a potential problem it must be Natasha. There's nothing to link you or me with Sarah's death so long as everyone is discreet?' Oles said, phrasing the question as a threat. 'Anyway, this is old news. Natasha's been here for eight years now.'

'Ah, but I haven't finished yet. There is a further complication. Part of the documentation I handed over to Natasha was a stack of letters addressed to Sarah. Whenever there is any ancillary information that will help the transient to adopt their new identity it is always provided. Included are such things as newspaper cuttings, photographs and sometimes letters. The letters were from

Sarah's boyfriend, Carl Denham. Presumably you knew this guy?' asked Ivan wondering if Denham was somehow the reason for Sarah's demise.

'I knew of him, but we'd never met.'

'Well, he's been snooping about and seems pretty determined to find out what's been going on.'

Ivan then told the story about Carl's e-mails, the visit to Natasha and the Travis Security delivery. Oles finished his scotch and started another cigarette.

'I know what you're thinking,' Ivan said, when Oles looked thoughtful. 'Why is Denham looking for Sarah and why now? His last letter to Sarah was in February 1988 just after they split up and he was very cut up about it. I presume she died in March 1988?' Again, Ivan looked to Oles for confirmation, but he just stared coldly.

'Take a look at this.' Ivan produced from his jacket pocket the pages his son had printed from the Internet.

'It says Denham was working in the States from March 1988 to February 1989. It was there apparently that he picked up his ideas that led him to form his own company, MicaCom. Maybe he wanted to get away from the memories of Sarah. So he was out of the country when Sarah died. It's quite possible that he didn't know she was dead. When he returned to England he was probably too pre-occupied with the business and had no inclination to try to get back with Sarah.'

Oles nodded.

'On the next page there is an announcement about MicaCom being sold to BinaryByte. My guess is that Denham now has time on his hands and money in the bank, so maybe he's trying to get back some of his past,' Ivan said and sat back, content with his deductions.

'But why didn't he contact Sarah's family first? He would have found out from them that she was dead and then he wouldn't have gone to Portsmouth.'

Ivan shrugged. 'You have the advantage there since I don't know anything about Sarah's family. My theory is that he conducted a search on the Internet first and came across Sarah's name. Now that he knows he has the wrong Sarah he may have contacted the family. In which case, either he has given up and gone home or he's suspicious and is going to do some digging around.'

'He'll only make progress if he can prove that Sarah is really Natasha. If he goes to the police, under pressure Natasha could implicate you and blow open the whole transient operation. If you then squealed on me ...', Oles grabbed Ivan by the wrist and squeezed hard, '... I guarantee you would be joining Sarah.'

'Y-y-you ... can trust me Oles,' Ivan stuttered.

'We first have to make sure that Natasha hasn't any evidence - like letters, linking her to Sarah. Then, we have to stop Natasha, Denham and Travis talking - *permanently.*'

'Oh no. I'm not getting involved in anything like that, once was enough for me.'

'My dear Ivan, you don't think I would entrust such a delicate matter to you again after the previous fuck up. This time I wouldn't want anything left to chance. I'll deal with it myself, but I will need some *materials*, if you understand me, tonight. And I expect you to supply them to me for free to discharge your debt. When you ring Natasha back tonight, this is what you should say ...'

Chapter 18

Friday, March 12, 1999 – 6:50 a.m.

Natasha had waited until two in the morning for Ivan's telephone call and had not slept well after the conversation. It was already bright outside and no doubt the alarm clock would soon be blasting her with news from Radio 5 at its earlier than usual time of seven o'clock. Her visitor was due in half an hour, so she wanted to make sure she was clean and decent before he arrived. Until then she would stay snug under the duvet and reflect yet again on the update she had had from Ivan.

He was obviously worried after yesterday's events and had squarely laid the blame on her. Carl Denham was perceived as a threat to her continued portrayal of Sarah Zurek and the transient processing. The reason for Carl Denham seeking Sarah seemed to have been clarified, and the delivery was clearly a reconnaissance of her and her home, based upon the information about Travis Security and Overland Transport. What would happen next was going to be explained to her by one of Ivan's henchmen before she left for work. She had not liked the sound of that. Sending someone overnight to Portsmouth smacked of an urgency and desperation that she could not comprehend.

She did not fully trust Ivan. When she came to England he was helpful and supportive; and without his induction she would never have been able to cope with her new life, but she guessed that his line of business necessitated contact with rogues and lowlife, whose tolerance of problems would be minimal. She prayed that her life and Carl Denham's were not in imminent danger. She was content with her relatively lonely existence. She had friends, not close friends, but ones she could rely on and she had great satisfaction from her work. Her protection of that was vital.

She opened her tired but sleepless eyes and cast them round her bedroom. The room was small, but cosy and colourful. The decoration was all her own work, completed during solitary evenings and weekends. In fact, she had become rather expert at all kinds of domestic maintenance, not wanting any inquisitive strangers to intrude on her seclusion. Except for a small mortgage she owned this little piece of England around her and would be sorry to have to give it up. She was sure it would not come to that if there were any justice in this world. Excluding her illegal immigration she had been an honest, hard-working citizen, contributing to the Portsmouth economy in her own small way. Her charitable work for the local church was not a means of clearing her conscience; she actually enjoyed helping people less fortunate than herself. Surely all these things would be taken into consideration if her hidden background were exposed. The more she thought about it, the more despondent she became, and when the radio alarm clock finally clicked into the news headlines, for once she welcomed its intrusion.

She threw the duvet from her naked body and switched off the alarm mode of the clock as she rose from the bed. She put on her dressing gown and then went through her early morning ritual of toilet, washing and teeth cleaning. She was sitting at her dressing table brushing her hair when the doorbell rang. Cursing the premature arrival, Natasha went to the front door.

She looked through the spy hole but all she could see was the outline of a tall man with his back to the door.

'Who's there?'

'Ivan sent me,' was the reply.

She tightened the cord on her dressing gown and opened the door. Her mouth gaped open as she thought she recognized her visitor.

'Oles?'

'*Cześć* Natasha.'

'Aren't you going to invite me in?' Oles said when she showed no sign of moving or talking.

She just held the door open, her mind too confused to say anything else. Oles strode past her, turned right into the living room and began to inspect ornaments on the sideboard under the window. He spotted a framed photograph of her with a group of children. 'What, no photographs of me then?'

'Why are you here Oles?'

'I've already said, Ivan sent me.'

'I didn't even know you were in the country.'

'Have you been trying to keep tabs on me then? I didn't think you still cared,' he said smirking.

'Mind if I smoke?' he continued and lit an unfiltered cigarette before she could answer.

'Yes, I do actually. You never used to smoke in Poland.'

He ignored her protest. 'Pressure of work these days. Have you an ashtray?' he said, blowing clouds of grey acrid smoke into the room.

She went to the kitchen and came back with a saucer as the best substitute she could find, and placed it on the coffee table in front of the settee where Oles had made himself comfortable. He patted the cushion next to him as an enticement for her to sit down. Ignoring his offer she said, 'You haven't answered my question. Why are you here?'

'I've heard you've been a silly girl, so I came to give you some advice. Any chance of some breakfast? I've been on the road for the last three hours.' He flicked his cigarette as he held it above the saucer, but the ash ended up on the table.

'I need some answers before you get anything from me.' She moved the saucer closer to him and then retreated.

'Why have you come all this way and what's your involvement with the Carl Denham problem?'

'I haven't come from Poland, if that's what you mean. I'm now a bona fide British citizen – unlike you. I've been here for several years now. I've no particular interest in Denham, but I do have an interest in Sarah Zurek.'

'Me or the dead one?' She pulled her dressing gown tighter and sat on a hard backed chair on the opposite side of the room.

'Both actually.'

Oles did not seem to want to elaborate and Natasha was feeling very vulnerable in her present state. 'I'm going to get dressed. I'll leave some breakfast things out in the kitchen for you.'

She went to the kitchen, opened a few cupboards and the fridge, and arranged food and dishes on a worktop. As she turned to leave, Oles was standing in the kitchen doorway. She moved towards him but he stayed where he was and extended his right hand to her face. Instinctively she flinched.

'I'm not going to hurt you,' he said and stroked his fingers in a caress on her cheek. With Natasha distracted he placed his left hand inside her dressing gown. 'There's no hurry to get dressed.'

Natasha stepped back, saw the bread knife she had placed on the worktop and picked it up. Brandishing it in the air she yelled 'Keep your hands off me Oles, you screwed up my life once before, I'm not going to let you do it again.'

'OK, OK, just testing the water to see how frustrated you were. When were you last satisfied by a man?'

'You sicken me Oles, now get out of my way,' she said, this time holding the knife in front of her and pointing it as though she was about to charge forward.

Oles stepped aside. Cautiously she walked past him still gripping the knife. She moved crab-like towards the bedroom never taking her eyes off him; opened the door and shut it behind her. Visibly shaking she dropped the knife and quickly grabbed an upright chair and wedged the back under the doorknob. She shivered and beads of sweat appeared on her face, not from exertion, but fright. Sitting at her dressing table, she looked at herself in the mirror for the second time that morning. The contrast from twenty minutes earlier was remarkable. Her previously sparkling eyes were now red and looked unsightly against her pale face. She drew a tissue from a box, mopped her brow and thought about Oles.

She found it hard to believe that she and Oles were once lovers. Lovers in the physical sense certainly and for a while she had loved him emotionally too. It started in Warsaw in 1989, where they both worked at the Supreme Court. She was a legal secretary, employed in the foreign affairs department and Oles was an administrative clerk with responsibilities for liaison with the *Voivodships* - the District Courts. They saw a lot of each other because Oles used her for secretly translating various documents between English and Polish. The documents were nothing to do with their respective legal occupations, but from the covert nature of the supplied papers to Natasha it was obvious that Oles was involved in an illegal emigration activity. This was clearly a profitable venture, because Oles was never short of *zloty*, and she was well rewarded for her extra-curricular efforts with gifts, money and then a loving partnership. Oles kept his private life secret and it was a year into their relationship before a friend told her that he was married. She had guessed that, but until then had chosen not to confront Oles with her suspicion. When she quizzed him about his wife, he had simply said that he had not got what he wanted from the marriage. The nights and weekends they spent together had been easily concealed, since his wife apparently had accepted his absences as part of his normal job. Natasha had persisted with the questioning about his wife and Oles had become increasingly angry, eventually hitting her as a warning to avoid the subject.

From that point the relationship deteriorated; Oles's strange ways began to frighten her and although she attempted reconciliation, she knew it was motivated by loneliness rather than love. Oles still used her for translations, but their meetings outside became less frequent. Oles's excuses majored on urgent matters related to his foreign contacts, but twice she learned via friends that he had been observed dining out with his wife. Natasha convinced herself that this was only an essential part of Oles's emigration dealings until one of their colleagues qualified as a Judge and an unusually grand departmental party was held in his honour. The upper echelons of the Supreme Court were present as well as some of the junior staff by invitation, including her. Partners were asked too and Oles took his wife. It was the first time that Natasha had seen her and she marvelled at her beauty, elegance and sociability, and wondered why Oles had ever wanted to cheat on his wife. It was obvious to Natasha that Oles had been avoiding her at the party, but she could not stop herself from graduating ever closer to his wife to eavesdrop on conversations. When she was within earshot an even greater surprise was that Oles's wife was speaking perfect English with the occasional Polish words or sentences. Everyone seemed to be using her as an opportunity to practice their English, laughter breaking out whenever someone made a mistake. She had forced eye contact with Oles and walked towards him. What happened next was still a blur to her. She remembered shouting at Oles, then hitting him and an unsavoury brawl breaking out as a result.

The following day she was summoned to a meeting with her boss as soon as she arrived at work. It came as no surprise to her that her position had become untenable and she was to leave immediately. As she was clearing her desk, Oles appeared and requested an urgent rendezvous in the café down the street. There she learned that despite Oles's protestations on her behalf (which she did not believe), she had been blacklisted for any similar position in Warsaw and was unlikely to find a job in the foreseeable future. Oles thought that she should get away from Warsaw, Poland even, and start afresh somewhere else - he could of course help with that. She knew that leaving Poland was more for Oles's benefit than her own, but she realized she had little choice in the matter. Anyway, after the emotional stress she had suffered in recent months, starting a new life appealed to her. Then came the rub, the standard relocation charge was £10,000. For that she would be given a completely new and valid identity in England, somewhere to live, and a number of interviews for appropriate jobs. Oles knew full well that she would not be able to afford the fee, but promised to make up any shortfall that she could not fund. She had eventually raised £5,000 from savings and by selling everything she owned. Two weeks later on August 6th, 1991 she said goodbye to Poland and by the end of September she had become Sarah Zurek working for Portsmouth District Council.

Reflecting she realized what she had experienced with Oles was a combination of lust, comfort and excitement, masquerading as love. The sex was a substitute for a union with someone since her parents were dead. She never wanted for anything, Oles bought whatever she needed and it was exciting that he was involved with something clandestine that was profitable, probably dangerous and stood against the establishment. She had had fun, but it was not love that she felt - now it was hate; she wondered if she would ever trust a man again.

The shaking had stopped but Natasha felt tired and apprehensive. She desperately needed a shower to freshen up, but she did not believe that Oles would leave her alone. Instead she dressed quickly, unconsciously selecting a sombre dark grey outfit, which matched her mood. She cleansed her face with some scented, moist tissue wipes and then applied a modicum of make-up. Noticing the necklace from Carl on her dressing table, she put it on, as a symbolic protest against Oles's appearance.

She picked up the bread knife and was relieved that it slipped neatly into her briefcase. Finally she returned the protective chair to its original place, took a deep breath and opened the door to the living room.

The smell of toast made her stomach growl, but food was not on her mind. Oles was tucking into a plate piled with toast and cheese.

'Ready for some advice then,' said Oles with a mouth full of toast.

Natasha ignored him and went to the kitchen; she could sacrifice food at the moment but not a shot of caffeine. She returned a few minutes later cradling a steaming mug of coffee in her hands and sat in an armchair opposite Oles.

'First I want you to take a look at these photos. Do you recognize anyone?' Oles took the printouts from a manila folder that Ivan had given him the previous night and passed them to Natasha. She put her mug down and took the two pages.

'That's Carl Denham,' she said without hesitation pointing to the MicaCom page. 'I'm not certain but this looks like the deliveryman that came last night. All men with beards look the same to me,' indicating the photo of Don Travis from Travis Security.

'As I suspected. Now I want you to give me any evidence you have regarding your past in Poland. I've checked in here and can't find anything incriminating,' Oles said waving his arm to indicate the living room.

'You've no right to go through my things.'

'Oh, but I have every right. Who set you up over here in the first place? I think you owe me Natasha.'

She just glared in reply. She wanted to get this meeting over with as quickly as possible and had no intention of saying what she really thought.

'So, get the stuff *now* and don't forget anything, particularly the Denham letters. Don't try to trick me, I'll check later when you've gone to work.'

'I'm not leaving you here when I go out.'

'Don't worry I'm not going to steal anything, not that there's anything to steal in this dump. And I promise not to go through your panty drawer; I just want to give your visitor a little surprise.'

'What visitor?'

'Are you totally stupid? Haven't you worked out yet that the parcel delivered to you last night was just a means of checking out you and your flat? I reckon there'll be visit sometime today from Denham, or more likely Travis, to have a look around.'

'But I won't be here.'

'Bloody hell you're sharp. Of course not, he's going to break-in. Your security here isn't exactly state-of-the-art.'

'And what are you going to do when he comes in?'

'I want to find out what he knows. He may need a little persuading though.'

'Oh God. This is a nightmare. You can't do things like that and certainly not in my flat.'

Oles rubbed his head as though in pain and then threw his empty plate on the coffee table; leaped from the settee and in one stride stepped around the table to bear down on her. He grabbed her by the wrist and twisted his hand forcing her to stand. Ignoring her yelps of pain he said, 'Shut up you little slut, I'm running this show and I know what's best. So get those documents, NOW, before I really lose my temper.'

Chapter 19

Friday, March 12, 1999 – 7:30 a.m.

It was another crisp, clear morning and Don had arrived in Yorke Street shortly before seven a.m. – half an hour ago, after he and Carl had checked out of the hotel. He was not sure how he had managed such an early morning start, considering the quantity of booze he had put away the night before. The throbbing pain above his eyes made him squint, his insides felt as though someone had kicked him in the stomach and he had a raging thirst. He enjoyed his beer in moderation, but had felt obliged last night to keep up with Carl's rate of consumption. From recollection, Carl was not renowned for his alcohol intake, but the sad news about Sarah had taken its toll on him, and drink and compassion from Don had been his only comforts.

Carl had rung his room at six a.m. to remind him of his morning activity, not that he needed reminding, he had thought about nothing else whilst trying to sleep last night. They had met in Carl's room fifteen minutes later and had used the self-brewing facilities to make black coffee, before reconfirming their plan of action. Reflecting on Carl's state of mind and intoxication a few hours earlier, he had acted surprisingly calm and sober. He had half hoped that after yesterday's trauma Carl would call off this morning's exercise. Don could now detect an underlying sadness in Carl but his resolve to uncover a potential conspiracy was greater then ever.

Don was sitting in his car about fifty metres beyond the entrance to Maynard Court so that when Sarah emerged she should turn left and not pass by. He had the radio tuned to Radio 4 to listen to the news but the volume was so low that the words being broadcast were more a companion that an enlightenment.

He had dressed in his security uniform again believing this was the most creditable attire for flat breaking. This time though, he had removed the Travis Security badge; he wanted to look official, but be anonymous. Concealed in his pockets were his mobile phone, various keys and oddly shaped pieces of metal and wire. He pretended to be dozing in the car thinking this would be the most natural state to draw least attention to himself.

Since his surveillance began there had been some activity already as, through slit eyes, he observed the early starters and those with longer journeys depart for their working day. There had been only one arrival. A strangely out-of-place Mercedes Coupe had cruised up and down the road a few times before parking in a reserved place. A slickly dressed man of about forty had alighted, gone into Maynard Court and not re-appeared.

At eight-fifteen he became more attentive, as the comings and goings of the working day reached their morning peak. It was another fifteen minutes before he saw Sarah, recognizing her initially by the tan briefcase that Carl had mentioned she carried. Within a minute she was out of sight. He waited another minute in case she had forgotten something then rang Carl on his mobile phone. He answered immediately.

'She left a couple of minutes ago. All OK this end,' he said.

'OK. Good luck,' Carl replied and the connection was terminated.

Don was now eager to complete his task, but knew for safety that he should wait a while longer. He looked at his watch. He'd make his move as agreed with Carl, at nine-thirty.

* * *

Carl tucked his phone back into his inside jacket pocket. He had been pacing up, down and around Winston Churchill Avenue since seven-thirty. Now the changeling was on her way to work, time to get into position.

Unlike Don his head was clear. He had lost count of how much vodka he had drunk the previous night, but suspected it was ten shots or more. The alcohol had just numbed him rather than made him feel ill, which was just how he wanted to feel; he could not have coped with the amount of beer Don had drunk without throwing up. He had slept well except for being disturbed a few times in the early hours when he was convinced he heard the internal phone ringing buried beneath the clothes he had discarded after returning to the room.

This morning he had felt guilty about driving from the hotel to the station car park because a blood test may have told tales about how much alcohol was still in his system. However, he felt sharp and more clear-headed than he had for some time; he needed to be, to confront the bogus Sarah again. Yesterday he had been polite and humble, now he would have to play a tougher line. He knew there was still a slight possibility that this whole situation was just a horrible coincidence of names and events, nonetheless he felt he had nothing to lose. He would not; he could not be violent towards this woman; it was not in his nature. Instead he would harass and cajole her into telling him why she was masquerading as a reincarnation of his Sarah. If he were wrong, the worst that could happen would be that she would inform the police. Then he would have a real story to tell which would let him off the hook - unless of course Don messed up somehow, then he might get charged with orchestrating a burglary. He really owed Don for what he was about to do.

Carl was at the top of Middle Street and glanced at his watch – eight thirty-six. Like real secret agents he had synchronized his watch with Don at the hotel earlier that morning. He looked down the street. There was a woman carrying a briefcase walking towards him about a hundred metres away, it was Sarah. He stepped around the corner and pretended to look into a showroom for the Art College. He counted a minute and then heard footsteps pass by. He turned to his left and with half a dozen large strides was beside her.

'Hello, *Sarah?*' Carl said, intoning his voice deliberately so that it was obviously a question. An alarmed look appeared on Sarah's face but she kept walking.

'I've nothing more to say to you Mr. Denham.' She stared ahead to avoid his eyes.

'Oh, but you do, *Sarah*. I hope you don't mind me calling you that as I don't know your real name. But you can call me Carl. That *is* my real name.'

She stopped.

'Look, *Carl*, I'm not going through this again. I'm not the person you are looking for and, if you keep pestering me like this, I shall have to inform the police.'

This time she did look at him and Carl noticed that her eyes were red, as though she'd been crying.

They carried on walking down the ramp into the underpass to cross the main road.

'OK, *Sarah*,' Carl shouted, knowing his voice would echo intimidatingly around the concrete corridor of the tunnel, 'The local police station is at the next corner, we'll call in and tell them what our respective problems are. *After all these years* they might be interested in what I have to say.'

Hearing those words Sarah checked her stride briefly and he knew now for certain that they were significant. They emerged on the other side of the underpass with Carl keeping pace alongside Sarah. As they neared the corner with Isambard Brunel Road, he speeded up for a moment, turned and stopped directly in front of her.

'OK. Here we are. Do you want to make a complaint first or shall I?' he said indicating the entrance to the police station.

Sarah looked at the doorway and then looked at him. His determined face looked back to indicate he was not bluffing. Her shoulders seemed to slump resignedly.

'There is a very simple explanation.'

'Tell me then.'

'Could we keep walking? I don't want to be late for work.'

He stepped aside and they carried on walking together.

'The explanation is simple, but we need to talk about the implications of what I'll tell you. Could we meet somewhere for lunch?'

'Oh no. I need answers now. It's important that I know within the next …' he looked at his watch and saw it was eight forty-one, '… forty-nine minutes.'

Sarah cast him a puzzled glance.

'Look, I simply must go into the office first. I'll make an excuse about, say, an urgent dental appointment and then I'll come straight back out. Really, I promise I won't let you down. What's going to happen in forty-nine minutes?'

'Never mind for now. I'll meet you in the Crow's Nest lounge in the library. If you're not there by ten past nine, I'll go back to the police station,' he threatened.

'I've given you my promise. You'll have to trust me.'

They walked in silence until they arrived at Guildhall Square and had climbed the steps together towards the Civic Centre. He looked at his watch again. 'I'll see you in fifteen minutes,' he said and held back to watch Sarah hurry through the main entrance.

Carl sat down on the familiar stone bench and kept his eye on the entrance for a few minutes in case Sarah doubled back, then took the short walk to the library. He arrived just as the doors were being unlocked. Taking the stairs to the third floor he entered the empty Crow's Nest. The shutters were still down over the counter, but he could hear noises behind suggesting the catering staff were present and preparing for the day's first customers. The sliding glass door to the balcony area was open so he stepped out and went to the edge to look out over the Square. He tried to guess what Sarah was about to tell him. She was clearly frightened by his threats and probably for good reason, as she seemed to have taken the place of a person who had died eleven years ago. The answers to the obvious How and Why questions were beyond him at the moment, but if she kept to her word he'd be finding out any minute now.

The noise of shutters being lifted aroused him from his thoughts and he went to the counter to get something to drink. He returned to the balcony with a mug of black coffee and gazed towards the Civic Centre. Sarah was heading towards the library. He went to the lounge door to wait for her to appear and then led her to a table on the balcony.

'Something to drink?'

'Not at the moment, thank you.'

He looked at his watch and waited while she composed herself. She then spoke quietly.

'My real name is Natasha Minski. I'm originally from Poland, but came to England in 1991 as an illegal immigrant. My new name, background and supporting documents were given to me when I arrived. Apparently identities are derived from people that have died, since they are easier to substantiate than creating new ones. It appears that coincidentally I was given the alias of the woman you were seeking. I'm sorry, but this must mean that your Sarah Zurek has been dead for over eight years.'

There was a slight reverberation in her voice – she was very nervous. He studied her while she talked and noticed she was wearing the necklace he had sent her.

'I now know that Sarah's dead. I found out last night when I tried to call her mother,' he said sadly.

'What I don't understand is why you didn't know.'

From her explanation he knew that his "adventure" was at an end. Suddenly, even to a relative stranger, he felt the need to provide his own explanation.

'Sarah was my girlfriend and in 1988 and we inexplicably split up. I went through a bad time, lost my job and decided to go abroad for a while to forget. That must be when Sarah died. When I came back, I started a new career, a new business and a new life. I purposely avoided any contact with the past and completely wrapped myself up in work, telling myself this was the best antidote to cope with my separation from Sarah. But I never forgot her; she was always in the back of my mind. I recently sold the business for a sizeable profit and suddenly thought what am I going to do with the rest of my life? But I already knew the answer. I would try to rekindle the happy past. So I set out to track Sarah down. I now realize it was rather unfortunate that I searched for her on the Internet first, and came across you. I was convinced you had to be Sarah so I stopped looking anywhere else, and on impulse decided to come to Portsmouth.'

'I'm so sorry it's turned out this way. What will you do now?'

'I'm not sure. Go back home. Visit Sarah's family. I'd still like to find out what supposedly went wrong between us all those years ago.'

'And what about me?'

'You know you look a bit like Sarah. Was that part of the matching process for new identities?'

'Yes, but what I meant was, will you be reporting me to the authorities?' whispered Sarah now that a few more people were bringing early morning snacks to the balcony.

'No. What's the point? You're clearly an innocent party as far as Sarah's concerned. There's nothing to be gained by stirring up any more trouble. If somebody else like me comes along looking for the real Sarah then you may not get off so lightly, but I should think that's fairly remote. I'll not mention this visit to anyone and I'll make sure that Don … shit, what's the time?' he looked at his watch; it was nine twenty-five. 'Excuse me, I need to make an urgent phone call.'

He took out his mobile phone and dialled Don's number. He heard it ringing then it abruptly stopped. He immediately dialled again and this time received an "Out of Service" message. Not satisfied he tried once more but he got the same answer.

'Bugger. His phone doesn't seem to be working,' he said to himself.

'Is something wrong?' Natasha asked.

'I hope not,' he said. 'Actually I've a confession to make. My friend Don is about to break into your flat to try to find out who you really are.'

'Oh no,' Natasha gasped putting her hand over her mouth. 'Is that …'

'Don't worry,' he said, interrupting her. 'He's a professional. He won't damage anything.'

'… the deliveryman? Don Travis? Have you got a car here?' Natasha exclaimed, standing up and tugging strongly at his sleeve.

'Yes, to all three questions. How do you know about Don? And what's the panic?' he said, also standing to avoid toppling off his chair.

'Quick. I'll explain on the way. I'm afraid your friend is going to have a nasty surprise.'

* * *

Don was bored; bored with the scenery and bored with sitting in the car. He had been here over two hours. He had carried out surveillance duties in the past and had not complained - it had been part of the job. But this was not his proper job now; this was a favour. A man who owned and ran his own company had no right to be bored. There had been no people or car activity now for at least ten minutes, and he was becoming increasingly uncomfortable with his seating position and his exposure. He peered through his slit eyes at the clock on the dashboard – nine-fifteen. Carl had not called and that meant he had not acquired the information he wanted from Sarah. She must be at work now and Carl had probably gone back to the hotel. Sod it - he may as well get this job over and done with.

He eased himself up in his seat and opened his eyes wide. He looked up and down the street. Two women were chatting on the pavement down the road away from Maynard Court, but other than that it was quiet. Employees were employed; the unemployed still in bed and no doubt the housewives were doing their dusting. He checked that his pockets still contained his metallic accessories; put on his thin leather gloves; smoothed down his uniform and climbed out of the car. He pushed the door gently shut to minimize noise and operated the infrared remote locking key.

Keeping a straight back and striding evenly to assume an official posture, he approached Maynard Court. He kept his ears tuned to his surroundings, attempting to pick up any noise that might indicate a problem. In the ground floor hallway he heard some faint music coming from a door on his left. He climbed the stairs as softly as possible, aided by the standard issue Travis rubber-soled walking shoes, and paused at the top - silence. He went to the door of flat seven and pressed his ear against the door - silence. He rang the doorbell, armed with an excuse should somebody open it. He waited a moment and rang again, cringing slightly at the noise in case someone from the other three flats on the floor came out to investigate. With all still quiet, he reached carefully inside a jacket pocket and withdrew a ring containing an assortment of keys, pieces of metal and wires that he had chosen after studying the front door lock the previous evening. He selected a thin, flat metal strip with a serrated edge and eased it into the lock, rocking it gently left and right. Feeling some resistance, he tried to rotate the strip delicately clockwise to avoid the fragile metal bending. A little more twisting and there was a sharp click and with some forward pressure the door swung open. He smiled to himself; it had been quite a few years since he had done this, but he was pleased he had not lost his touch. He paused and listened again. Satisfied he stepped into the flat and eased the door shut.

Facing him was a narrow corridor with four doorways on the right. The first door was shut. The second was ajar opening to a narrow kitchen. The third was also shut. The fourth led to the bedroom; he would start there. To speed his search he decided to look in obvious places first and return for a more thorough search later if he found nothing. There were not too many locations here. After five minutes he had been through every drawer and cupboard. One of the drawers in the dressing table was the most interesting. It was full of the usual documents one would expect to find in any household: bank statements, cheque book stubs, utility bills and receipts. He spent a while studying these looking for any clues or anomalies, but found nothing suspicious. He returned along the corridor to the third door. As he had guessed it was a combined bathroom and toilet; he ignored it for now, the kitchen would be more promising. Lots of cupboards to examine and he noticed a few shelves containing paperwork. There was a door ajar on the right hand side, which he presumed led to the living room. It was then that he detected the smell, cigarette smoke. As a non-smoker, his nose was sensitive to the aroma and he was momentarily puzzled since he had not labelled Sarah as a smoker. Besides, the smell was recent - very recent. He nudged the bottom of the door with his foot and as it swung open, it revealed a large man sitting on the settee facing towards the door.

'Hello, Don Travis. I've been expecting you,' Oles said.

Don was set to run back through the kitchen, when Oles lifted his right hand from his lap and aimed a handgun at him. Don recognized the gun - a Beretta .25 caliber automatic with a silencer, and the man – the Mercedes driver.

'Why don't you sit down so we can have a chat?'

Don had to consider his options quickly.

If he ran for it, would this man really try to shoot him or was he bluffing? The gun was silenced, so there would be no explosive sound to attract attention. If a bullet hit him non-fatally, would he then be killed with a second shot? If his body were left in the flat, Sarah would discover it and know the killer, since she must have let him in. Did this man care how that would incriminate Sarah?

If he stayed put, would he be killed anyway? Perhaps he could negotiate his position, get some useful information and then be sent on his way? Or, if he was bluffing, maybe he could tackle him? The man was bigger and looked stronger than him and had the advantage of a blunt instrument in his hand.

He decided on the latter strategy and walked slowly into the living room.

Oles rose from the settee, still pointing the gun at him.

'Who the fuck are you? How do you know my name?' Don said, attempting to take the initiative.

'I think I'm in the best position to be asking questions, don't you? Sit down,' Oles responded waving the gun at the chair opposite the settee.

Don was about to sit down when the mobile phone tucked into the breast pocket of his uniform began to ring. He instinctively moved his hand towards it.

'Steady now. No sudden movements,' Oles warned, raising the gun slightly in a threatening way. 'Give me the phone, slowly. If that's your fucking friend Carl Denham I want a word with him,' now beckoning with his left hand.

Afterwards Don thought that the sudden adrenaline rush that he experienced then was caused by the defamatory remark against his friend. With an unexpected surge of energy and speed he pulled the phone from his pocket, arched his arm and hurled it towards the source of abuse. So fast was his movement that he never had time to notice the surprised look on Oles's face as the phone hit him above his left ear with a sickening thud. At that moment Don was thankful that he had never bothered to upgrade his ancient, but heavy phone to one of the modern, slim, lightweight models. Not that the phone did the real damage. As Oles reflexively raised his right hand to the point of impact he pulled the gun's trigger and a sound similar to a cork being popped from a wine bottle was followed by the smashing of glass as a framed photograph exploded on the sideboard. The recoil caused Oles to lose his balance and he fell backwards hitting his head on the corner of the coffee table, which collapsed beneath him.

Don was already heading for escape when he looked back and saw the results of his well-aimed throw. He paused to survey the extent of the immobilization of his opponent. The man was not moving so he crept slowly closer. There was blood spreading across his cheek from the weeping gash above his left ear. He was still breathing evident from the small groaning emanating from his mouth. Don now moved quickly. He first located his phone. The rear compartment had smashed and the battery was missing, but he did not bother to look for it. The gun was lying next to the prostrate body. He hesitated then picked it up and tucked it in the waistband of his trousers. He carefully frisked the body - all the time keeping an eye open for any signs of recuperative movement, but he found nothing of interest. He turned his attention to the manila folder that had been resting on the settee. Opening it, he quickly inspected the contents and realized this was what he was seeking. The groaning was getting louder and he saw a hand being raised hesitantly towards the bloody source of pain. It was time to leave. He hastened to the living room door, threw it open and seconds later was bounding down the steps of the shared stairway.

When he emerged into the daylight he checked his pace, and strode swiftly, but deliberately along the path leading to the road, listening for noises of pursuit behind him. Reaching his car all his body wanted to do was slump into the seat to regain its composure, but the urge to retreat in his mind was dominant. He fired the ignition, engaged first gear and with a squeal of tyres accelerated away.

* * *

Carl and Natasha pulled out of the station car park, perspiring after their dash from the library. All Natasha had managed to say so far was that there would be someone in the flat when Don arrived.

'Who's in the flat then?' he asked, as he turned into Isambard Brunel Road.

'When I reported the details of your investigation into Sarah Zurek to my contact, he arranged for someone to visit to advise me what to do. That person arrived at my flat early this morning and turned out to be coincidentally the man who had originally arranged my entry into England. They'd cleverly seen through your plan to reconnoitre my flat and attempt a break-in. My visitor was lying in wait assuming it would take place today.'

He turned into Middle Street. 'But for what purpose? Perhaps your unsavoury friends think Don and I are investigators attempting to uncover their operation?'

'I don't think so. Last night I was shown photographs of you and Don that they had obtained from the Internet. So they know your backgrounds. Anyway, they already knew that you were Sarah's boyfriend when she died,' she said, clutching the seat as Carl swerved into Yorke Street and almost lost control of the car.

'How the hell did they know that?' he screamed bringing the car to an untidy halt close to Maynard Court.

Before Natasha had a chance to answer she had the car door open and was racing towards her flat. Carl cut the engine and followed her, not wasting time in locking the car.

At the landing to her flat, Natasha stopped when she saw that her front door was open.

Carl followed her eyes, pushed past and rushed through the door and randomly turned right into the living room. He cast his eyes quickly about looking for signs of life. 'Don. Are you here?' he called and then disappeared through the door that led to the kitchen.

'Oh my God,' Natasha said as she surveyed the damage before her in the living room. She heard Carl going through the other rooms in the flat as she moved towards the remains of her coffee table.

He returned panting. 'There's nobody here.'

Natasha bent down and wiped a finger through a dark stain on the broken surface of the table. 'There's blood here,' she said and shivered at the consequences.

Carl looked around the room. 'Look at this,' he said pointing to the shattered picture frame and a crater in the wall just above it. 'Did your friend have a gun?'

'I don't know,' she replied 'but I wouldn't be surprised if he had.'

'I'd better get to my hotel to see whether Don has returned in one piece. We'd arranged to meet there later. Before I go I want you to answer my earlier question; how your friends knew I was Sarah's boyfriend?'

'As I explained in the library, when I arrived in England I was given documents relating to Sarah Zurek. Parts of those documents were letters that you had written to Sarah.'

'Letters? What kind of letters?'

'I'm not sure what you mean. Letters. Love letters. Written to her when she was at University.'

'How did they get hold of these letters?'

'I don't know. I was told that whenever possible any supporting paperwork is passed over to the immigrant to substantiate their new identity. I was told to keep the letters as background material.'

'Show me the letters.'

'I can't. I was forced to hand them over to …', she hesitated and then continued, '… the man that was here in the flat.'

'Just who is this man you keep referring to. I want to know his name.' Carl raised his voice and grabbed Natasha's arms.

She shook her arms free. 'I can't tell you that. I think he'd hurt me if he knew I'd told you his name.'

'Well, I'm leaving now to check that Don is all right, but don't think this is the end of my investigation. You can forget what I said in the library. This whole story is more complicated that it seems. I'll have to go to the police. I can't believe that private letters from me to Sarah could come into the hands of your accomplices without some dishonesty. Can't you understand that, or are you directly involved in the conspiracy that's unfolding here? There's something more at stake than just your anonymity. The blood and bullet holes in this room bear witness to that.'

'Please Carl; I swear I know nothing else about Sarah. She'd been dead three years before I came here. I'm frightened by what's happened too. Can I come with you to the hotel?'

The tears flowing from her eyes looked genuine enough to Carl. Either she was a good actress or she really was an unwilling partner in all that had happened. He saw no harm; in fact it might be advantageous, if he kept her close by for the time being.

'OK,' he said, 'But if you're telling me the truth then I'm going to need a lot more information from you before the day's out.'

Chapter 20

Friday, March 12, 1999 – 10:00 a.m.

As Carl drove into the car park of the Post House hotel a few minutes before ten o'clock, his mobile phone started ringing. He parked quickly and pressed the answer button.

'Carl? Where are you?' said Don's troubled voice.

'Don. Are you OK? Are you hurt?' Carl asked.

'I'm fine, but you'll never believe what's just happened.'

'I've a good idea. I've just arrived at the hotel.'

'Thank God. I'm calling from the hotel lobby. I'll meet you in the lounge area.'

Carl found Don talking to one of the hotel staff, ordering tea, toast and cakes.

Don looked surprised and disapproving when he saw Sarah. 'Better make that order for three instead of two,' he said to the waitress.

Carl re-introduced Sarah as Natasha to a bemused Don and they chose a quiet corner to sit where their controversial exchanges could not be overheard. Don and Carl were like two excited children, each wanting to be first to tell their tales. Natasha, seemingly eager to help their cause, acted as arbiter and quelled the situation when their impatient voices became too loud. Carl told his and Natasha's story first. Natasha qualified any vague points, but became less helpful after suspicious glares from Don. When the story reached the part about their visit to the flat, Don only had to correct a few points in Carl's estimation of what had happened.

They interrupted their statements while their late breakfast was delivered, then a few minutes of silence passed broken only by the sound of eating and tea being poured. Don eventually posed a threatening question to Natasha.

'How did this fruitcake friend of yours with a gun get hold of the information about us?' he said pointing to the folder he had shown them earlier.

Natasha looked guiltily into her lap, so Carl answered.

'Information about me was easy, I think,' Carl said, looking at Natasha for confirmation. 'Natasha gave my name and probably my e-mail address to her contacts. Searching for that combination on the Internet would have produced a hit on MicaCom's pages. That's what's been printed out.' Natasha nodded nervously. 'I'm not sure about you though,' Carl said, looking enquiringly at Natasha.

'When Don delivered the parcel to me I noticed the Travis Security badge on your uniform,' she replied, averting the hostile looks she assumed she was still getting from Don.

'Shit. You know I worried about that at the time, but never dreamed that you would be so observant or your thug friends so resourceful. As for the photo of me on the Internet, I never did like that idea, but my business buddies said it was the right thing to do.' Don said defensively and clearly rattled that he had been detected so easily.

'You're obviously losing your touch in your old age,' Carl said with a smirk on his face.

'Now look. I did you a fucking favour this morning and almost became a stiff in the process. There's no need to take the piss,' Don answered angrily and loudly.

'Keep your voice down,' Natasha whispered.

'And I don't need this fucking foreigner telling me what to do. How can you trust this bitch after all she's put you through?' Don said, aiming his wrath at Carl.

'Don please calm down. I was only joking. If I had known what was going to happen I wouldn't have dragged you into this. And don't be too harsh on Natasha. None of this is her fault directly. She's on our side now and has promised to try to help us solve this puzzle.' Carl countered.

'Us? Us solve this puzzle? You can count me out. I think I've honoured our friendship to the limit. What do you intend doing? Tell the police and get me put in the slammer for burglary? Or are we going to hunt down Natasha's hoodlums and beat the shit out of them until we find out how they obtained the letters? I'm no coward but I'm not getting involved in any more risky business. I've a wife and kids to go home to. Why don't you let go of your past Carl? Don't fuck up your future. You're stinking rich and the way Natasha keeps looking at you, you'll soon have a woman in tow.'

Natasha flushed at Don's last statement while Carl stared incredulously at his friend. There was an uncomfortable silence while everyone absorbed the contents of Don's outburst.

Finally Carl said 'I'm sorry, Don. I don't suppose I'd appreciated what you've been through. I'm indebted to you for what you did, but if you want to head back home now, that's OK with me.'

'Not until I've finished my breakfast,' Don said, calmly picking up a slice of toast. Carl was puzzled by Don's sudden change of tone and didn't know how to continue.

'Don't worry about me. Continue your scheming. Pretend I've gone already,' Don said, realizing his continued presence was inhibiting further discussion.

Carl hoped that Don wasn't going to walk out on him. He needed a friend right now to see his plan through. If he kept talking perhaps he could revive Don's support. First he had to make sure he had all the facts to hand. He turned to Natasha.

'If I'm going to make some progress here, I need some details from you Natasha. Can you name the people who are involved in the illegal immigrant processing? Just give me some brief details that can't compromise you to begin with so we know who we are talking about,'

'OK. The man that was in my flat is called Oles. He was the one that made the arrangements for me to come to England. At the time, he was the guy that ran the transient operation - as it was called, from Poland. He told me that he's been in England now for several years, but I don't know where he lives or what he does.'

'Have you any idea why he's become involved in what's been going on?'

'No. When you started contacting me, I passed all the information on to someone called Ivan. He inducts all the transients coming to England and was the person I had to contact if there was ever an emergency. He said he was going to send someone to see me and it turned out to be Oles.'

'Is there any possible connection between Oles and Sarah Zurek?'

'I shouldn't think so. I believe the new identities are researched and prepared in England by Ivan and his contacts. When Oles made the arrangements for transients he mainly organized the transport from Poland to England. My false documents were given to me one or two weeks after I met Ivan.'

'Oles's involvement still puzzles me though. I've obtained the impression that you know, or knew, Oles quite well?'

Natasha appeared to be considering her answer.

'In Warsaw we both had Government jobs working for the Supreme Court. Because of my fluent English, Oles recruited me, unofficially, to help with some of the transient paperwork. We were close friends for a couple of years and when I became an embarrassment to him, I was more or less forced to leave Poland and ironically came out via the transient operation.'

'Was the operation Government sponsored?' Carl asked.

'I'm not sure. Oles had an official job that was nothing to do with transients, but it seemed to leave him lots of spare time and freedom to conduct his illegal activities.'

'I presume *close friends* means you were lovers?' Carl knew this question would discomfort her, but he had to know her level of involvement with Oles.

'Yes,' Natasha said quietly.

'How did you embarrass him?'

'He was married and when he started to make excuses why he couldn't see me I discovered that he was reconciling with his wife. I caused a bit of a scene at a Government function when I confronted him about it.'

'Are you still in love with him?'

'On reflection I don't think I ever loved him. I was excited by the lifestyle he gave me, but there was always an underlying evil streak in him. Now I can't bear to be near him.'

'Did Ivan know about your affair with Oles? Perhaps that's why he got him to come to see you?'

'He never mentioned it. But I suppose it's conceivable that he heard about it through the Polish grapevine.'

'That still doesn't explain why Oles should be adopting heavy tactics involving a firearm. If we were to go to the police with this information, the only certain outcome is that you would have a big problem. I not sure what the result would be, but entering the country illegally and impersonating a dead person couldn't go unpunished. The biggest mystery is how you, or rather Ivan, came into possession of my letters to Sarah. There's a missing link somewhere. From what you've told me it's obviously easy to manufacture a counterfeit set of identity papers, but to acquire an original set of letters doesn't stack up. I'm sure the police would be interested in that. Finding Oles and interrogating him might solve the mystery, particularly if they discovered he had a gun.'

'He doesn't have the gun anymore, I do.' Don said, who had seemed more interested in his breakfast rather than the immediate conversation. 'I took it as a precaution in case he chased after me with it.'

'What do you intend doing with it?' Carl inquired.

'Don't panic. I'm not going to use it on anyone except maybe you, unless you abandon this exercise.'

With Don's current mood Carl could not be sure whether he was serious or joking.

Don seemed to sense Carl's predicament and continued.

'Actually I'd planned to chuck it in a river on the way home.'

Carl thought for a moment then said 'No. Don't do that. We might need it for evidence against Oles. Are your prints on it?'

'You may think I'm losing my touch, but I'm not a complete dork. I was wearing gloves and it's now wrapped in a rag in the boot of my car. I'll give it to you before I go.'

At that moment a smartly dressed woman in a blue skirt and white blouse came to their table. Carl recognized her from the night before at the reception desk. 'Excuse me interrupting. Would I be right in saying that one of you is Carl Denham?' she said looking at Carl then Don.

'That's me,' Carl said.

'You had a visitor earlier this morning, a Mr. Stanford, at about half past seven. When I told him you and Mr. Travis had already checked out he became most distressed. Insisted that if I saw you again I was to make sure that you telephoned him immediately. He said it was vitally urgent.'

Carl looked at his watch. That was about three hours ago.

'Did he say where he was going?'

'Not exactly. He cursed about coming all this way for nothing and thought he might as well drive around Portsmouth for a while trying to find you. I'm sorry, I didn't know that you would be coming back.'

'OK. Thank you.' Carl said, waiting for the woman to leave. When she didn't he asked 'Was there something else?'

'I don't wish to be rude but he did say I was to stay with you until you called him.' said the woman hesitantly.

'You never did tell me what the problem was at the office.' Don reminded.

'I don't know either,' Carl said standing up, 'I suppose I'd better call him, but I need to go to the car to look up his mobile number. I can never remember it. I'll be back soon.'

The hotel woman eyed him suspiciously. Carl caught her look. 'You can come with me if you like,' giving her the option of honouring her pledge.

'No, that won't be necessary Sir,' she replied.

* * *

Carl reached his car and then remembered that Mike's mobile number had been left at reception earlier. They'd probably lost it by now so he searched for his Casio organizer that he used to store just telephone numbers and addresses. He found it in his travel bag, looked up the number and then decided to sit in the warm sunshine to make his call. Nearby was a patch of lawn with a couple of tree stumps made into seats. He chose one and sat down.

He could not think what could be so urgent for Mike to have travelled all the way to Portsmouth. He hoped that it was nothing that required his attention; he was beginning to enjoy his freedom, bizarre as it was at the moment. If Mike had left three hours ago and toured Portsmouth first, he must still be on his way back to Chelmsford, so he punched the digits for his mobile.

Carl had to let it ring for a while, before it was answered.

'Mike Stanford.'

'Hi Mike. What's the problem?'

'Carl? Is that you? Where the fucking hell are you?' Mike shouted, trying to raise his voice above the interference on the line.

'Sorry Mike, I missed you. I'm still in Portsmouth.'

'I'll tell you some news about Susan in a minute, but first get your arse back to MicaCom. George Fellgate's steaming about you walking out and is withholding payment to us.'

'I didn't walk out. Tony Cookson agreed that he wanted nothing more from me and there was no problem with me leaving. A fax confirming that should have arrived from George yesterday.'

'Well it didn't, and that's not the version of Tony's story according to George.'

'Tony Cookson is lying. You know I wouldn't have compromised the deal going through.'

'Look, we may get cut off in a moment; I'm at the Dartford Toll about to go through the tunnel. You *are* coming back to clear up this mess?'

'Yes, don't worry. I've a few things to sort out then I'll be on my way. I should be back about three. Now what's this about Susan? Mike? Are you still there?' The static noise indicated he was not. He was probably thirty feet under the Thames by now.

He had even less respect for Tony Cookson after what he had heard. What was the point in lying about their meeting? Perhaps he was trying to score points with George Fellgate. He could not believe George had engineered the deceit. He was a tough character but Carl believed he was an honest sort of guy.

He was puzzled why Mike should want to tell him some news about Susan, but not ask about his visit to Sarah. Surely Mike wasn't having an affair. In all the years he had known him, and the female possibilities that were available for successful businessmen, Mike had flirted, but had never strayed from his devotion to Lisa. Then again, affairs of the heart had uncharacteristic effects on people; his current situation bore witness to that. Bloody hell, Mike was going to America tomorrow; perhaps he was taking Susan with him instead of Lisa! He recalled that Denise had given *him* a telephone number for Susan, which was still in his pocket. If he were not otherwise occupied he would have called the number now out of sheer curiosity.

* * *

'What have you two been chatting about then?' Carl asked sarcastically when he returned to the lounge, knowing that the friction between Don and Natasha probably meant the last ten minutes had been silent between them.

Don ignored the remark and asked, 'Everything all right at the office?'

'Not exactly,' he said, sitting down. 'I'm on the verge of losing two million pounds unless I get back to MicaCom today.'

A surprised look appeared on Natasha's face and she opened her mouth as if to say something.

'You're kidding me.' Don said.

'I hope so,' he said, putting on his most serious face. 'There's a small contractual problem I need to resolve. The weaponry in your boot might be useful after all.'

When both Don and Natasha looked shocked at his statement he grinned and added, 'It's a nice idea, but hardly my style. I do need to get back though. I'm not sure we ...' then looking at Don and recollecting his earlier outburst he corrected himself, '... sorry *I*, can do much more down here. I can't convince myself that going to the police will help me find out what happened to Sarah. And unless I adopt some heavy and risky tactics against Ivan, and Oles, assuming I could find them, I probably won't get very far.'

'So are you going to give up?' Natasha asked with sadness in her voice.

'No, not yet. I'm hoping to see Marion, Sarah's sister. They were very close and apparently she knows the circumstances of Sarah's death. If that doesn't lead anywhere then I'll consider pursuing the more dangerous Ivan and Oles trails again.'

'What's going to happen about me?' Natasha asked.

'Well, nothing? I'm not going to involve the police, so you can get back to your normal life. I'm sure we can trust Don to keep your secret.'

Don nodded his agreement.

'Oles is bound to come back and see me though.'

Carl noticed how worried she looked.

'Just tell him that I approached you again, confessed what a mistake I'd made, and have gone back home.'

'Even I can see that's a bit naïve,' Don said. 'He's been knocked out, had his gun nicked, and some potentially incriminating letters are missing.

Remember, I've met the guy, and he isn't going to take that lot lying down. I think he's a sick puppy and he'll want his revenge.'

'I'm scared Carl. He threatened and hurt me this morning. God knows what he'll do next time.'

'Perhaps you ought to lay low for a while. Is there someone you could stay with - Veronica for example? She seemed to be a good friend of yours.'

'A friend, yes. But she's rather a gossip. I don't think I could rely on her confidentiality in a situation like this. I don't know where else I could go. I do have some overdue holiday owing to me from work though. Getting away for a couple of weeks shouldn't be a problem. Even with such short notice I could probably organize that this morning.'

'OK. We'll go back to your flat. Pack a suitcase, make the arrangements with your office and we'll get you booked into a hotel somewhere away from Portsmouth. How about Southampton? It's only a small detour on the return journey. Don could you help out here? I can't really afford any more delays, I need to make a move.'

'I suppose so,' Don said unenthusiastically.

'No. Really I can't put you to any more trouble. I'll manage with taxis and trains.'

'I've a better idea,' Don said, with a mischievous smirk. Carl regarded him suspiciously; Natasha looked hopeful. 'Why can't Natasha go back with you? You got her in this mess in the first place. There's room in your flat.'

Carl waited for the refutation from Natasha, but none was forthcoming. He frowned at Don, but his matchmaking smirk remained. He liked Natasha and did have a feeling of guilt about exposing her to the problems she faced. He would welcome some support in his endeavours, and felt she might provide it.

'OK then, if that's acceptable to Natasha,' Carl said, hoping her reticence so far would not continue.

A humble Natasha replied. 'Well it is a solution, and I would like to help you find the truth.'

'I'll take that as a yes then. So could we please leave now? It's already eleven o'clock' said Carl looking at his watch.

'I expect you'll want these,' Don said handing over the folder of letters.

Carl took them and browsed nostalgically through the contents and murmured to himself 'Poor Sarah', then the threesome stood up and headed towards the exit.

Near the lounge door Carl stopped and looked back at Natasha and Don behind him.

'There is one serious matter still to settle,' Carl said.

'What's that?' Don asked.

'Who's going to pay for the breakfast?'

Chapter 21

Friday, March 12, 1999 – 11:00 a.m.

George Fellgate yawned. 'Excuse me,' he said to his two managers, Pete Hayden and Tony Cookson. 'My early start is catching up with me'.

George had left his home in Fulbourn at five o'clock that morning. First he'd had to head out to the Essex coast as a result of a telephone call yesterday afternoon. The news he had received had certainly been a shock. Except for one point, he had already put it to the back of his mind so that he could concentrate on the business of the day.

A short while ago he had arrived at the MicaCom offices. Naomi had been waiting at the front door when he arrived and he was now sitting at a conference table in the training room. Drinking his coffee he waited patiently while opposite him Tony and Pete shuffled paperwork to present their reports. Tony was ready first and looked at George for a sign to continue. George nodded.

'I've finished the review of the current status of Protean development and I'm pleased to report that everything is in accordance with our purchase agreement. However, as you are aware, I haven't been able to complete the study of the future plans because of the disappearance of Carl Denham. I am not therefore in a position to sanction the release of the payment due to Messrs. Denham and Stanford …'

'Shut up Tony,' George said, savagely interrupting him. Tony's mouth hung open in mid-sentence.

George added, 'You're in no position to sanction anything.'

Tony tried to carry on. 'What I meant was …', but George continued speaking.

'I'm the only person who does any sanctioning around here. And following a meeting of BinaryByte's shareholders earlier this morning, there will not be a problem in releasing the money that is due to MicaCom's directors.'

'But that's ridiculous, Denham's left me, left us, in the shit about the plans for Protean. That's crucial to the acquisition,' Tony gasped.

'Actually, ten minutes ago I might have agreed with you. Have you something against Carl?'

'No,' Tony said.

George looked at him questioningly.

'Well, I don't like the guy. He thinks he knows everything,' Tony said.

'About Protean he does,' George said. 'Is that the reason you don't like him, because he'd masterminded a product so much better than any you've been able to produce? Or is it that you *have* completed your review of the plans, but don't understand them?'

'No, I ...' Tony stuttered.

'George, what's got into you? Whose side are you on?' Pete interjected.

'It's your turn to shut up now,' George said. 'Let him finish.'

'Are you questioning my honesty and ability?' Tony asked, apparently relieved to get support from Pete.

'I'll give you some facts shall I and then we'll take a vote on it? First. After you'd left Cambridge yesterday having told me about Carl's *desertion*, I was very worried about our exposure and showed a copy of the Protean future plans to our Chief Designer, Chris Finchley. After studying them for half an hour, he burst into my office positively wetting himself with enthusiasm. He couldn't wait to get his hands on the software. He thought it was the most visionary and lucid document he had ever been through. I ended up spending the rest of the day with him.'

'Yes, but he's ...'

'Second. Mike was on the phone for me when I arrived here. He is on his way back from Portsmouth. He's located Carl and spoken to him. Carl said that you had told him he wasn't required anymore and *I* would send a fax confirming that yesterday.'

'That's not quite ...'

'Third. Mike should be here soon to confirm his conversation with Carl.'

'But Mike ...'

'Fourth. Carl is also on his way here, so we should be able to get his version of events sometime this afternoon.' George paused this time to let Tony have his say before delivering the *coup de grace*.

'It'll still be Carl's word against mine, and unbelievably you seem to be siding with his story, not mine.'

'Fifth. I spoke to Jacqui in reception after I'd finished the call from Carl; she's MicaCom's resident eavesdropper. You were probably unaware that during your last meeting, or should I say argument, with Carl, she was listening outside the room. She had an uncanny recollection of who said what, word for word, and it was an exact paraphrase of what Carl had relayed. Even her rendition of your voice would have made Rory Bremner proud.'

George sat back in his chair. He knew he had just destroyed Tony's credibility and if he didn't get his resignation he would have to dismiss him. A week ago he could not have entertained this possibility, since it was fundamentally important that Protean's future development had a strong technical leadership. He had thought that Tony was the person to take that role. But George had to have ultimate trust in his senior staff and Tony had revealed a trait of his character that did not cohere with BinaryByte's culture. He was confident that Chris Finchley would make an excellent replacement.

* * *

Oles felt one of his strange head pains coming on. He already had a headache - courtesy of that bastard Travis, emanating from the cut above his left ear. At least it had stopped bleeding now and he had washed away the coagulated blood at the Motorway service area.

The *pain* was different - it came when he was angry. It welled up inside his head until he thought it would explode. It had happened many times before and only went away when he had avenged the source of his anger.

It was his own fault according to his *Mamusia*. She had explained to him many years ago that he had been a problem child, and his misbehaviour always had to be punished with a good beating. A punch to his head had usually done the trick - until the next time. He had just become, well, a bit different from other boys.

Then of course there was the *big* secret. His father had been naughty too, but he was too strong for Mamusia to use her hands, so she had used sticks and brooms on him. And once, when he was very naughty and lost his wages gambling, she had used a poker. Mamusia told everyone that he had hit *her* with a poker and had then run away. That was the secret - he and Mamusia had buried him in the field at the back of the house. Mamusia always knew what was best.

He had first started to get his head pains while he was running the transient operation in Warsaw. If any of the potential emigrants messed him about or refused to pay him the fee, the pain would start, and he would make sure they were punished like naughty boys and girls in order to make the pain go away. He did not necessarily have to punish them himself; he had lots of friends who would do it for him - for a fee. Sometimes when Mamusia got angry, he got angry too and the cause of her anger would have to be dealt with.

Today he was angry with Denham, Minski and Travis. The tell-tale tic on his right cheek was going crazy. Denham was too suspicious about Sarah and

171

his determination was getting in the way; Minski should have been punished years ago when she caused that scene in Poland; and Travis had given him a headache. He would get Minski later - she would be easy. He would screw her one last time and then she would disappear as remarkably as she had appeared. Denham and Travis would need more careful consideration. He had Denham's home address and Travis's business address, which were useful starting points. But unlike Poland he no longer had friends to call upon to administer his dirty work, this time he would have to do this himself. Not physically of course, he was going to call on Ivan first to get another gun and maybe some explosives. Meanwhile he had to concentrate hard to see through squinted eyes as he sped along the M25 in his Mercedes.

* * *

Natasha said she was nervous about going back to her flat in case Oles had returned. Carl was apprehensive too and with some friendly persuasion convinced Don to accompany them. Three of them should be able to handle the Polish brute, he hoped. Without a key or Don's skills at lock-picking Oles should not have been inside the flat, so they drove around the nearby streets a few times to make sure that his Mercedes was not parked. They still entered the flat with due caution but their fears were unwarranted.

Don went to the kitchen to make coffee. He drank his quickly and announced he was heading home. Carl promised to keep him up-to-date with his investigation and Don parted with a rude gesture and a wink to Carl when Natasha was not looking.

Natasha phoned her office at the council and by the one-sided conversation Carl heard, her employers were most understanding about the imaginary family bereavement that she had suffered, and accepted her request for a fortnight's compassionate leave. She also called Veronica, gave her the briefest of details and promised to call later with more information.

It did not take Natasha long to pack for her withdrawal, but it was a large and heavy suitcase that appeared. Carl made no remarks, but he wondered whether she was assuming that she was going to stay with him for the full two weeks. After so many years on his own, he was not sure he could cope with that.

The speed with which Natasha packed was countered with the time she took to clean up the mess of Don and Oles's encounter. Carl helped break up the ruined coffee table into disposable pieces while Natasha fussed with getting everything tidy and back into it's original location. Eventually she was satisfied, left a cancellation note for the milkman, and they were on their way back to Essex.

While negotiating the exit from Portsmouth, Natasha gave a commentary on the sights of the City like an enthusiastic tourist guide. When they reached the motorway, conversation subsided as both were absorbed in their own thoughts. Natasha finally broke the silence as they headed North on the M3.

'Are you going straight back to your office?'

'No. I'll drop you off at my flat first. The office is only about five minutes from there.'

'You're going to sort out your two million pounds?'

Carl pondered his potential wealth for a moment so hesitated in answering.

'I'm sorry, it's none of my business,' Natasha said when he did not reply.

'No, it's not that. I was just thinking what a fool I've been. Looking back, my reason to sell the company wasn't to make a lot of money - it was to give me the freedom to find Sarah. I assumed I would find her, win her back and live happily ever after. And what happens? Sarah's dead; I've no job; and if the MicaCom money was a consolation prize, I'm on the verge of chucking it all away. Today has been an enormous anti-climax.'

'What will you do once you've found out what happened to Sarah?'

'I'll probably invest my MicaCom money - what's left of it; spend some time with my parents in America; do some travelling and then maybe start a new business. Though I'm not sure where or what type of business. I still get excited about the potential of the software industry and the Internet in particular, so it wouldn't surprise me if I ended up doing something similar to MicaCom. What do you do at Portsmouth council?'

'I'm a PC support engineer. I install and maintain its hardware and software.'

'Now there's a possibility; I'll open a computer shop and you can run it for me!'

They both laughed.

'Is that really a possibility? Me running a shop for you, I mean.' Natasha said, but his reply was intercepted when a muffled *Frère Jacques* tune came from his jacket pocket. He slowed the car to fifty miles per hour, pulled into the inside lane of the motorway and took out his mobile phone.

'Carl Denham.'

'Hello, Mr. Denham, this is April Washington.'

'April, thanks for calling me. Have you spoken to Marion?'

'Yes, I have. I'm afraid she wasn't too pleased, but she did consent to see you. She said she would be at home today if you wanted to call. Here's the number ...'

Carl asked Natasha to reach into the glovebox to get a pen and paper. He noticed her hesitance as she carefully lifted out the rag-wrapped gun that Don had stored there before she noted the number that he called out. He thanked April and gave the phone to Natasha to dial Marion's number for him.

'Marion? This is Carl Denham. How are you?'

'No better for hearing from you, thank you,' Marion said hostilely. It was not what he had expected. He presumed she was angry that it had been so long since he had been in contact.

'I'm sorry Marion, I only found out about Sarah yesterday. I still can't take it in.'

'Don't you think you've done enough damage without raising this matter after all this time,' Marion continued in the same aggressive manner.

'I don't think I'm quite with you. I only wanted to find out what happened to Sarah.'

'You're unbelievable. Are you trying to tell me that for eleven years you've lived in ignorant bliss not knowing how you contributed to her suicide?'

'Suicide? How *I* contributed? What are you talking about?'

'You really don't know, do you? I don't want to talk about it on the telephone anymore. By all means come to see me. I'd personally like to burden you with your own share of suffering and guilt.'

'I'm very confused by this Marion. I'd like to clear it up as soon as possible. Can I visit you this afternoon?'

She was not happy but she agreed. Natasha acted as scribe again, this time to note the address and directions to a large house in Colchester. Fortunately he did not have to commit to a specific time, since he was unsure how long the MicaCom matter might take to resolve.

When he had finished the call he put the phone back into his pocket and said to Natasha, 'I guess you got the gist of that?'

'Sarah committed suicide?'

'Apparently so, and I'm partly to blame,' he said, feeling as though he'd woken from a bad dream. 'It stacks up with the circumstances of our parting. Her breakdown was supposedly caused by something I'd done. But to lead her to suicide doesn't make any sense. She was a highly-strung girl but she loved life. She couldn't have done anything like that. I'd like to go straight to Colchester to meet Marion. Mike should be back at the office soon, I think I'll call later to see what's happening.'

* * *

Mike joined the meeting in the training room.

'Mike, how was your round trip to Portsmouth?' George asked.

'Hi George. Hi Pete. I must be mad. Seven hours of driving already today and it's not even lunchtime yet. I am sorry about this trouble with Carl. I'd found out late yesterday that he was staying in a hotel in Portsmouth. I'd left innumerable messages for him to call. I'd even rung his room at two o'clock this morning. In desperation I set out at four o'clock to drive down there. And then I found out ...'

'Slow down Mike. It's all been sorted out. I'm sorry you've been put to all this trouble,' George said.

Mike looked at George, then Pete. 'Where's Tony?'

'Tony was the problem, not Carl. Tony has resigned. You have Jacqui to thank for rescuing the situation,' George said.

Mike looked puzzled.

'Get Naomi or Jacqui to explain it to you some time.'

'What's the situation with the Banker's drafts?' Mike asked.

'Pete and I have been through the handover requirements. They've all been satisfied so I've already notified the bank that the final settlement can be drawn any time from now. So you had better get to your bank before they close, and then you can go home and pack for your States trip.'

'Does that apply to Carl too?'

'Of course. Carl did depart before he was supposed to, but that was under instructions from Tony. So he's in the clear. He's still coming back here today though, isn't he?'

'Yes. He reckoned he'd be back by three o'clock. Presumably he doesn't have to now?'

'No, but I have an urgent message for him from Susan which I need to give him personally. I found out this morning that you know Susan quite well, and she's not particularly happy with you.'

'Susan? You know Susan?'

'Well, I should do. She owns half of BinaryByte.'

'Susan Fellgate? Your wife?'

'Good Lord, no. In fact we're not even related.'

'But I've always assumed from your company records that BinaryByte was wholly owned by you and your wife.'

'No, my wife's name is Samantha. Susan is ... Look, why don't I take you to the pub? We can celebrate your retirement and I can tell you an unbelievable story that I only heard a few hours ago.'

* * *

175

Carl took out his mobile phone and passed it to Natasha. 'Mike should be back at the office by now. Could you dial the number for me?'

Natasha keyed the number, waited for the ringing tone and passed the phone back to him.

'Good Afternoon. You've reached BinaryByte, how may I help you?' It was Jacqui's voice.

'So, they've trained you already with the new name?'

'Oh Carl, I'm sorry.'

'Nothing to be sorry about. How are the new bosses?'

'Well, Pete seems OK and George has always been sweet to me. I had a long chat with him this morning about you.'

'You did? I hope you said what a reliable guy I am.'

'Oh, more than that, I told him about your row with Tony on Wednesday. He was most impressed with all the details I gave him. Then he said he'd sack me if I were caught eavesdropping again, but he went and sacked Tony instead.'

'You heard the row?'

'I was in the next office, but you couldn't miss it.'

'You Angel. You absolute Angel. I'd give you a pay rise if I could. Why didn't you mention this before?'

'I was a bit scared to say anything on Wednesday, and then I had Thursday off to get ...', Jacqui reduced her voice to a whisper, '... my lips pierced.'

He burst out laughing. 'You're unbelievable. Am I really a free man now?'

'I think you must be.'

'I was puzzled by something you said earlier "George has always been sweet to me". Have you met him before?'

'Oh yes ... I ... used to work at BinaryByte. You knew that didn't you?'

'I suppose I did. It hadn't clicked that you might know George well.'

'Anyway, am I ever going to see you again?' Jacqui said, seeming to want to change the subject.

'Actually I was on my way to you right now, but in view of what's happened I don't suppose that's necessary now. Can I speak to Mike?'

'You've just missed him. He's gone to the pub with George to celebrate his retirement.'

'No problem. Just tell him that I called and something's cropped up which means I'll be going straight home. I'll call him tonight. My new life is getting a bit hectic already but I hope to pop in to see you sometime next week. I think I owe you a drink or three.'

'I'll look forward ...,' Jacqui started to say before she was cut off.

He stared at the blank display on the phone. 'Shit. The battery's dead.'

'Who's the *Angel* at your office?' Natasha asked.

Carl detected a hint of jealousy in her voice. 'Jacqui. She's restored my credibility and solved my problem at the office. It's a long story.'

'Well, I was hoping to call Veronica but as your phone isn't working, why don't you tell me your long story instead? It will help pass the time.'

* * *

Over lunch, George had briefed Mike regarding his background with Susan. Mike had been so staggered by the revelations that he was still trying to understand the implications when he returned to the office.

Jacqui stopped Mike in reception.

'Carl called while you were out. As everything is sorted out here and something has cropped up, he won't be coming back to the office. He said he would call you tonight.'

Mike looked at George.

'Damn, did he say where he was going Jacqui?'

'Yes. He said he was going home.'

George stepped in and took Jacqui to one side. They chatted for a while out of Mike's earshot.

George rejoined Mike. 'OK. I've sorted that out. Jacqui will call Susan and update her about Carl.'

'Jacqui will? Does Jacqui know Susan?'

'Ah. That's one part of the story I didn't get round to telling you.'

* * *

Carl carried Natasha's suitcase through the front door of his flat and dropped it on the floor in the hall.

'Welcome to your home for the next few days,' he said. Then with a straight face added, 'It's nothing special, but clean and comfortable, so I won't charge you too much rent.'

Natasha looked surprised. She obviously didn't know whether to take him seriously.

He reassured her, 'It'll be free so long as you don't break anything or have any nasty habits.'

She then saw the funny side. 'I only break hearts and eat raw carrots.'

'That's all right then,' he said, pleased that she had a sense of humour.

He gave Natasha a quick tour of the flat.

'I had better be going now. Help yourself to anything you want, food, drink, television. The only things out of bounds are my PC and underwear drawer.' He could not believe he had just said that. On the verge of finding out about Sarah's death, he was making smutty jokes with a woman that he had only known for a day. He put it down to nerves and a need to unwind before his serious interview with Marion.

She smiled and responded to his teasing. 'Only if you wear Y-fronts and not frilly knickers - like me.'

Now it really was time for him to go. He reached into his back pocket and took out two twenty-pound notes and gave them Natasha.

'Should you need anything while I'm out,' he explained. 'If you exit the flat, turn right and right again, you'll come to a small parade of shops. There's a spare front door key by the telephone.'

'What time will you be back?'

'I can't really say, five o'clock maybe.'

Chapter 22

Friday, March 12, 1999 – 3:00 p.m.

On the way to Colchester Carl tried to remember what he could about Marion. She was two years older than Sarah, so she must be thirty-four now. He'd last seen her in early 1987 during one of the weekends when he had hitchhiked from Warwick to see Sarah in Cambridge. Marion had come to tell Sarah that she was engaged to her stepbrother.

He had never met and knew little about Marion and Sarah's father – Max. Max had already abandoned Audrey - his first wife - by the time he first dated Sarah. Max went back to his parent's home country, Poland and had remarried. Max had continued to support and maintain contact with Sarah and Marion. Unlike her sister, Marion never had any academic aspirations. She had left school at eighteen and sampled several different careers without success or enthusiasm. Often with spare time on her hands, she had visited Max, mainly because he had paid the airfare. It was on one of these occasions that she had fallen for Max's new stepson. In May 1987, she married him and settled in Poland, much to the apparent disapproval of both Max and Audrey. Despite their different outlooks on life, Sarah and Marion were very close, and Sarah had willingly gone to the wedding. Sarah had wanted him to go with her, but cost and above all a clash with his University finals, had been insurmountable barriers.

He knew Colchester quite well and he soon found Marion's house in Lexden, one of the more affluent parts of town. Marion had described it as a big old detached house and it clearly stood out amongst the more modern dwellings in the road. Located on its own miniature hill, there was no obvious driveway at the front so he parked his car in the road, mildly perturbed by his BMW uncharacteristically coughing and spluttering to a halt. Access to the house, named Croftview, was by way of a gate, then a steep stone path that zigzagged through sloping manicured gardens to a solid wooden arch-shaped front door. There was no doorbell, instead he rapped hard with the solid brass ring hanging at the centre of the door and heard the knock echo inside.

Marion opened the door. He would just about have recognized her. She was tall and used to be skinny, now she would be regarded merely as slim - too slim to be a mother. Her auburn hair was still long and neat, covering more of her face than he remembered. The funereal dark brown, long-sleeved shirt and black trousers that she wore were not flattering, but she had the curves of an attractive woman.

'Hello, Carl. You're earlier than I expected,' Marion said. It was a gentler greeting than he had anticipated. 'You haven't changed much. A bit thinner than I remembered,' she continued, looking him up and down like a soldier on drill parade.

'I could say the same about you,' he replied, not being truthful, but he viewed that compliments would be a good foundation for their meeting.

'Come in. Can I get you something to drink?'

'Tea would be fine, thanks.'

They were in a wide entrance hall with dark wooden doors and beams in abundance. The whitewashed walls were adorned with original paintings, prints and brass objects. The house had an ancient feel about it, so the woodwork could be original. She led him to the end of the hall, then right into a spacious lounge. Comfort abounded here with lush carpets, rugs and body enveloping armchairs and sofas. Everything had a sense of order and tidiness about it and - there were no family portraits on display - not the kind of house occupied by a working woman with children. If the house, furniture and fittings were representative of Marion's status, she was also probably quite a wealthy woman.

While Marion disappeared to make the tea, he looked through the large patio windows that overlooked the rear garden. It was simpler than the front, comprised mostly of lawn and trees extending as far as he could see. There was a bricked drive along one edge of the garden. Parked was a metallic blue BMW saloon like his except this year's model and with a body kit to give it styling of a racing car. Beyond the car to the right there was a wooden building with windows, probably a summerhouse, which reminded him of a pavilion at a village cricket ground.

The rattle of cups on a silver tray announced Marion's return.

'You have a beautiful home,' he said, another compliment - but he meant it this time.

'Thank you. Please sit down.'

He chose an armchair and sat upright on the edge to avoid being swallowed into its soft cushioning. He tried to keep the conversation superficial.

'When did you come back to England?'

'Some time in 1993. I was homesick and Alexander managed to acquire a job here.'

Marion placed the tray on a small table and poured the tea from a china teapot into dainty china cups. As she stretched forward the cuff of her shirt rose up and he noticed what appeared to be a dark bruise on her wrist. She noticed him looking and moved away leaving his cup, milkless and only half full. She sat on the sofa opposite him and her weak smile suddenly evaporated. Her face turned to a scowl and metaphorically she grew horns before starting her onslaught.

'You bastard Carl. How you could you let Sarah down so badly? She was such a happy girl. I've never known someone so in love as her. She would have done anything for you and then you broke her heart. For what? A romp in the hay with some fucking tart? Then, when she was getting better, you disappeared and now you turn up here eleven years later playing the fucking innocent. Where the hell have you been?'

He could not believe his ears. Marion was never an angel, but the profanity came as a shock.

'Whoa, whoa. Please Marion. Let me tell my side of the story and perhaps you can fill in the gaps as I go along?' He hoped his despairing look would bring some order to her outburst. She stared at him and said nothing.

'The first I knew of Sarah's breakdown was a call from her friend Kate.' He went on to explain his first visit to the hospital and the cruel rejection he'd had from Sarah once she'd emerged from her distressed state.

'So you're claiming that you don't know what initiated the breakdown?'

Marion shook her head and as her hair lifted from her face, he was sure he noticed another bruise high on her cheek.

'I've absolutely no idea. As you will remember I was never permitted to speak to Sarah. You and your mother refused to discuss the matter with me, and the hospital staff would never connect me with Sarah when I rang. Nobody provided an explanation other than Sarah's insistence that she never wanted to see me again,' he assured.

Marion eyed him suspiciously before she continued. 'The Monday before Sarah's breakdown, Max - our father, died of a heart attack. I telephoned her from Poland with the sad news and she took it pretty badly. Although I was the daughter who paid him most attention, the bond between Sarah and father was special. Sarah was always his pride and joy. Father loved me dearly too, but he was a great believer in hard work, common sense and intelligence. I let him down on all three attributes. In particular he never approved of me marrying Alexander. Despite being his stepson he viewed him as a bit of a rogue.'

'I'm sorry. Sarah spoke little about Max. I'd never met him, and I certainly didn't know that he'd died.'

'Sarah was inconsolable. There was nothing I could do or say to help her. You were to be her salvation when you came on the following Friday night. She always longed for your weekend meetings and knew that you would help her through the trauma. She was going to ask if you would accompany her to the funeral in Poland.' Marion took a sip from her black tea.

He wanted to do the same but was engrossed by the story. 'She never rang me.'

'A letter arrived for Sarah in the post on the Thursday morning, postmarked Chelmsford. I never saw the letter, but it was apparently from your anonymous secret lover. The contents explicitly described your sexual activities with her, how you'd wined, dined and screwed her, and the plans you had for the future together. She said that you were finding it impossible to tell Sarah about the affair, so it was her duty to reveal all the facts and let Sarah make her own judgement.'

His mouth gaped in astonishment. 'But that's total and utter crap. I wasn't having an affair. Someone was playing a hoax. I can't believe that Sarah could have been taken in by such a pack of lies,' he said, standing and pacing up and down.

'Remember, Sarah was feeling very down and vulnerable about our father dying.'

'Even so, she was an intelligent girl. She would at least have confronted me with the letter.'

'Maybe, but it was the photographs that pushed her over the edge.'

'Photographs? What photographs?' he exclaimed and sat down again.

'Evidently – I never saw them, enclosed with the letter were photos of you with your lover, kissing and in a compromising position.'

'That's impossible. Who told you this story?'

'Sarah did eventually, though Kate told me first. Kate had found the letter and photographs when she was tidying-up Sarah's room after you had taken her home from the hospital.'

'So that's why Kate suddenly turned against me. Who would do such a thing? The whole thing was fabricated. It must have taken a pretty determined mind to doctor some photographs. I swear I wasn't having affair. I've never loved anyone but Sarah.'

'And you'd always been faithful to her?'

'Yes, of course.' But he could tell from Marion's disapproving look that she knew otherwise. 'Sarah told you about my Warwick confessions?'

Marion nodded.

'OK. Two small transgressions *before* Sarah and I became an item. Once I *slept* with a girl at University, but nothing happened, I was too drunk. On another occasion I … I don't know why I'm telling you this, it has nothing to do with what happened to Sarah.'

'Perhaps it does. I'm just testing how truthful you are.'

'Don't play games with me Marion. I've a clear conscience about my relationship with Sarah whether you believe me or not. It's no wonder that you put the blame on me though. Nonetheless, it still doesn't make sense that Sarah took her own life because of some bogus photographs.'

Marion looked impatient. 'I haven't finished yet. Sarah was in hospital for a month. She hardly ate or drank anything and lost a lot of weight. It was a terrible time for mother and me. Mother had to shoulder the burden of tending to Sarah for the first week, but she was distraught by Max's death too. Although they'd been divorced by then for five years, I think she still loved him. I was torn too - I wanted to see Sarah but was obliged to stay in Poland to help out with the funeral arrangements. After Max was buried, I came to stay with mother and thereafter we commuted regularly to Cambridge. We knew about your frequent phone calls and attempted visits, but since you were the cause of the original problem, the psychiatric advice was to keep you away. A week later Eliza and Alexander came to England for the reading of Max's Will. Did you know much about Max's business interests?'

'No. Is it relevant?' he asked, eager for Marion to complete the story.

'Very relevant, if you want to understand Sarah's final days. Shall I make some fresh tea? You've haven't touched yours.'

'Yes please,' he agreed, wanting a few moments for private thoughts. Max's death, a letter, photographs – if only Sarah had called him. He could have consoled her and proven that the photographs were faked, but who sent them – from Chelmsford? There were no old or rival girlfriends. Nobody he knew that would have had Sarah's address. Were there any jealous prospective boyfriends at Cambridge? If there were, how did they get photographs of him to defame? Anyone determined enough could have arranged the posting from Chelmsford.

Marion returned with fresh cups of tea, already milked and waited for him to drink this time before continuing her story.

'Max's parents came to England in 1939 following the invasion of Poland. Max was just a baby, two or three years old. They settled in the East End of London and his father, Josep, who was a skilled metalworker, worked in a factory manufacturing aircraft parts. After the war, Josep and a few of his work colleagues started a business making varieties of metal framing for the massive reconstruction projects at the time. The business grew steadily over the years and when Max was old enough to start work, Josep owned the whole of a successful and substantial company.'

'Zurek Metals?' he guessed.

'You do know,' Marion said.

'Just a little from the Internet. Carry on.'

'Once Max was experienced enough, Josep took a back seat and let Max run the company. Max was eager to impress his father and when Josep died, the year I was born, 1965, Zurek Metals was exporting all over the world. Josep left his money to his wife and the company to Max. Josep's dying wish was for Max to start a subsidiary of Zurek Metals back in his birthplace of Krakow. Max did that and also started an outlet in the USA. The one in Krakow existed just to satisfy his father's wishes, but the American one blossomed. The success meant that Sarah and I saw little of Max in our early years. The amount of time that he spent away on business was always a source of friction between mother and father, and when mother threatened him with divorce in 1983, he decided to sell the company to save his marriage. In his haste to sell the company, he realized a tidy sum, but not as much as it was really worth. But the void between Max and Audrey had grown too wide and it didn't solve the underlying problem. They divorced anyway but before Max finally gave up ownership of Zurek Metals, he negotiated to take over the running of the Polish subsidiary. Three years later he met and married Eliza. And a year after that I married Eliza's son Alexander.'

'The Will?' he prompted.

'The Will had been lodged with the same firm of solicitors in London that Max had used for Zurek Metals.'

'The contents of the Will were a huge surprise. Like his father, Max left all his ready money to his wife, excluding the proceeds of selling Zurek Metals. Eliza received around £12,000. The Zurek Metals money had been invested in a portfolio of shares and gilt-edged securities, which was to be realized on Max's death. Of that, mother and I each received five percent of the value, approximately £10,000. The balance was left to Sarah.'

'Whew, £180,000?' he calculated. 'But why so much to Sarah.'

'Give or take a few thousand, yes. Max had viewed that, as the brains of the family Sarah would invest it wisely. Eliza went crazy. She made all sorts of noises about contesting the Will. She said it wasn't legal under Polish law and so on, but she had no chance of doing anything. The Will was legal and binding, the money had been invested in the U.K. and Max's solicitors had complete control of it.'

'What happened to the money?' he asked.

Marion ignored the question and carried on.

'A month after Sarah's breakdown she discharged herself from hospital and went back to the University house. She must have been getting better because she'd realized that her finals were only two months away and was determined to tackle them. In hindsight this was probably the wrong thing to do. She was still emotionally distressed and was having great problems trying to catch up a lost month and concentrate on her studies. She hadn't forgiven you but was at least prepared to talk to you. She tried calling you at home but the phone was never answered. She called your workplace and found out that you had lost your job. I went to your house in Ongar but you weren't there. I spoke to your neighbours and work colleagues and it was rumoured you'd gone abroad. On another trip to Ongar I saw an estate agent's board had been erected at your bungalow. The agent told me that you had put the property in their hands to rent for a year, but they had no forwarding address.

'When I told Sarah that I couldn't find you it was the proverbial final straw and she became insular and depressed again. Mother and I were so worried that we tried to persuade her to be readmitted to hospital. She then accused us of trying to take the money she had inherited from Max, but *our plan* wouldn't work because she was going to give it all away.

'Undaunted we made arrangements with the hospital and several days later arrived at her house early in the morning to take her to hospital. She wasn't there and her housemates said that she'd been acting strange for a few days. We searched her room and found the suicide note.'

'God, this is like a bad dream. Where was she found?'

'She wasn't. So the police started making inquiries. They had one report that a girl had been seen in the area being attacked, but nothing came of it. They wanted to interview you and I told them about my own attempts at locating you. They established you'd left the country a week before she disappeared. Then they picked on me for a while because Sarah had made a Will leaving her estate to me.'

'That was my idea,' he said. 'I remember the University had a "Free Wills for Students" week and I encouraged her to take advantage of it. She wanted to leave everything to me but I said that wasn't appropriate until we were married. I thought you ought to be the beneficiary.'

'For a while they treated her as a missing person. But as the details of her mental state emerged and all attempts at locating her failed, they became convinced that she had indeed committed suicide. I stayed in England for another month trying to find her and then went back to Poland.'

'Three months after she disappeared, some letters from you to her were found near the River Cam, less than a quarter of mile from her house. That convinced the police that their original premise was true - she had killed herself in a state of distress at losing you. They dredged part of the river but found nothing.'

He thought about the letters. Was there a connection with the letters that Natasha had been given? And should he tell Marion about Natasha? Maybe later.

'You asked about the money. It never actually got to Sarah, to any known account anyway. The day before she disappeared she gave instructions to our solicitors to transfer the money to another account. My only hope was that she did something sensible with it. Mother and I didn't make a fuss, but Eliza did. She badgered the solicitors trying to get information from them, but they pleaded confidentiality. Then Eliza tried to get statements from the hospital that she was of unsound mind when she transferred the money. The whole thing caused a big rift between Alexander and me for a while.'

'You don't think she was forced to hand the money over to someone under duress?'

'The police did consider that, but dismissed it because of what she'd said about giving the money away and the suicide note.'

'What did the note say?'

'I don't remember exactly. It was something like "My life is over. I'm going to the nearest faraway place'

He sat bolt upright in his chair as difficult as that was. 'Say that again!'

Marion repeated the words looking at him as though he had flipped.

'She's not dead, Marion. She's not dead. Don't you understand the significance of what the note said?'

'No. Should I?'

'It wasn't a suicide note. It was a message. "The Nearest FarAway Place" is the name we gave to a place where we spent our happiest day together.' He reached into the inside pocket of his jacket and took out his wallet. He extracted a photograph, 'Look. This is a photograph I took of Sarah at *The Nearest FarAway Place*,' and passed it to Marion.

Marion took it but could not bear to look now that doubt confronted her. 'Don't be ridiculous. It's just an unfortunate coincidence. The police said it was probably a reference to the place where they assumed she had drowned herself.'

'No. Think about it. Why would she have chosen those words? It's an odd phrase for a suicide note. A body was never found. And I still can't credit Sarah with taking her own life, irrespective of her mental state.'

'Carl, stop this, it's upsetting me. You're just trying to conjure up reasons to protect your own feeling of guilt. Let me pose you some questions. Why were your letters found beside the river? Why did she dispose of all that money? If she went to this place why hasn't she contacted you … me … anybody, in the last ten years?' Marion said angrily thrusting the photograph back to him.

They were valid points he thought. Maybe in a twisted way Sarah had associated "The Nearest FarAway Place" with death. Despite that, it gave him some hope and some direction of what to do next.

'I'm sorry Marion. Even with your arguments I can't dismiss the possibility that I might be right.' He looked at the photograph. 'I'm going to this place to ask a few questions. It's the only lead I have.'

'Not only are you a bastard, you're a fool too. Where is this utopian place anyway?'

'Actually it's no more than ten miles from here, as the crow flies. The photograph was taken at St. Peter's Chapel. It's on the coast near Bradwell.'

'I still think you are crazy ... but ... just supposing you did find her. What would you do?'

'If only you knew how many times I'd asked myself that question. I don't know. I'm still in love with her. No, that's not quite right. I'm still in love with her memory. If she is alive and I find her, I'm very scared about the result. If she suffered so much mental stress she might hate me, not even remember me. She could be happily married with kids.'

'Why did you leave it so long before trying to find her?'

'That story would be longer than the one you've just told me. Briefly, I went to America for a year. Came back and started my own business. I've completely wrapped myself up in that for the last ten years, trying to purge the past. Now I'm a free man again. No business, no commitments, it was time to get on with my life again. Then I realized that life meant Sarah.'

'You know, I think I may have to change my opinion of you. From what you've said I believe the affair might have been a hoax. If it hadn't been for that, Sarah might still be alive.'

'Despite that, Sarah might still be alive,' he corrected her. 'That's still a mystery to me. You said earlier that Kate had found the accusing letters and photograph. I don't suppose you know what happened to them, or Kate Robins?'

'No. I did correspond with Kate for a while. She stayed on at Cambridge to do a post-graduate degree, but I lost touch with her when she left University.'

'One more question about Sarah's Will,' he said. 'Did you know before Sarah died that you would benefit from it?'

'Yes. I think she told me in one of her letters.'

'Did anyone else know?'

'I don't think so. I may have mentioned it to Alexander, but I can't remember.'

'I must meet Alexander one day. I presume you're still married?'

'Of course, you never did get to the wedding. Yes, we're still ... together.'

He noticed the slight hesitancy in her voice, and thought that "together" sounded less compatible than "married".

'Well, you seem to have done all right for yourselves. What does Alexander actually do?'

'He's … the UK Sales Manager … for Zurek Metals … but he had some savings from his job in Poland.'

He thought he must have asked a sensitive question. Her answer was awkward – not too sure about the job and needing to qualify their income.

'He's been away for a few days but he should be home soon,' Marion added.

Was that an invitation to stay? He looked at his watch - it was half past four. 'I'd better be going. I didn't realize it was so late. I was contemplating going to Bradwell, but I'll leave that until tomorrow. It's been a long and exceptional day. Thanks Marion. It was good to see you again after so long. I wish it could have been under better circumstances.'

They went to the front door. 'I really think you're on a wild goose chase, but if you do find out anything, good or bad, will you let me know?' Marion said.

'You'll be the first, I promise,' he said and walked back down the hill to his car. He climbed in and put the key in the ignition lock and turned. There was a click, a metallic clonk, and then nothing. He tried again. This time there was no sound at all. A third time brought the same result. 'Shit,' he said. His trusty old BMW had never let him down before and he was irked that it should happen now. He knew little about car mechanics but nonetheless went through the motions of lifting the bonnet and peering into the gloom of the engine compartment. To avoid embarrassment he looked for obvious problems and prodded a few things, but knew that he would need external help. He climbed the hill again and when Marion opened the door, he presented his dilemma and asked if he could use the phone. Fortunately MicaCom had subscribed to a "Get You Home" service for all its vehicles and he was relieved to hear that a breakdown truck could be with him in fifteen minutes. Marion offered more tea, but he declined, bid his goodbye again and went to wait in the car.

* * *

Marion was clearing away the tea things when she heard a car pull up in the rear drive. She looked out of the kitchen window – Alexander was back. She watched him for a moment unload some items from the boot and put them into the summerhouse. A few minutes later the kitchen door opened.

'Hello, Alexander. Good trip?'

'OK.'

'What was in the car?'

'Just some samples from work. Have you just had a visitor?' Alexander asked. Marion was puzzled how he knew and then she saw him looking at the two sets of crockery she was washing up.

'Yes, and a very surprising one. Carl Denham's been here.'

'Is that who I saw sitting in the red BMW at the front of the house?'

'I expect so. His car wouldn't start and he's waiting for the breakdown company to arrive. It was quite a strange meeting.'

'Interesting. Why don't you make me a cup of tea and tell me about it.'

She did tell him, except for the lie about his job. He *used* to have a job at Zurek Metals, but she had discovered that he had lost that several years ago. She did not know why and was afraid to ask. They always had plenty of money available; so these days it was best to say nothing because when she became too inquisitive he punished her.

Chapter 23

Friday, March 12, 1999 – 5:00 p.m.

Carl wanted peace and quiet to think things through but that was proving impossible because of the idle chatter coming from the truck driver. He was obviously a football fan and was seeking Carl's opinion of the current form of Ipswich Town and Manchester United, his local and favourite football teams respectively.

Incredibly the breakdown company had kept to its promise, even exceeded it, by keeping him waiting for only ten minutes. The car had sounded terminal and the expert now piloting him home along the A12 had confirmed this. There was a problem with the ignition or starter-motor that was irreparable at the roadside. He would need to get the car to the local BMW dealer himself - his driver was only obliged to transport it on the rear trailer to Carl's home address.

Against his principles he found himself thinking that he would deposit the two million pounds piece of paper in his pocket at the bank on Monday morning and then buy himself a new car. In the meantime, if he were going to conduct his search of the Bradwell area he would have to hire a car in the morning.

By the time he reached his flat in Springfield, he had been indoctrinated with the merits of the local football team, and was quite relieved to say thanks and goodbye to the breakdown man.

He looked at his broken car like an old friend. Perhaps he would get a new car eventually; in the meantime he would get his ageing transport fixed up and give it a second chance.

Carl was startled as he entered his flat. Not by the sound of the television or the smell of the cooking, it was the realization that his bachelor domain was now inhabited by a second person - moreover it was female. He first regretted allowing the intrusion to have taken place, then immediately had second thoughts. He badly needed to share his afternoon revelations with someone else, male or female.

Natasha was in the kitchen. She had changed into an unflattering pair of blue jeans and baggy brown jumper. Mysteriously she had managed to create mouth-watering smells from his limited stock of basic ingredients. He knew he would be grateful for whatever was served up; such was the hunger that suddenly revisited him. She hadn't heard him arrive with all the bubbling and hissing that was coming from boiling saucepans. Saucepans he was sure he'd never used or seen before. It briefly vexed him that a stranger could so quickly become intimate with his kitchen.

'You managed to find everything then?' he said, and then realized his unanticipated approach should have been more obvious when Natasha almost sliced her finger instead of a carrot.

'Oh, you did give me a fright. You should have banged the front door or something' she replied.

Already she was telling him what to do in his own flat.

'I'm sorry. That must have sounded a bit bossy.'

She could mind read as well as cook.

'I didn't know I owned carrots, broccoli and cauliflower,' he said while examining the contents of the saucepans.

'You didn't. I went for a walk and found the local grocers. I hope you're not a vegetarian, I also bought a steak and kidney pie, but that's out of a packet,' she explained.

'It all sounds and smells perfect to me,' he said, wondering what the cost of a permanent housekeeper might be.

He felt he was intruding in the kitchen and returned to the lounge and slumped into a soft chair.

'How was my *sister*?' she called from the kitchen and then appeared in the doorway munching a raw carrot.

'Damn. I'm sorry, that was in bad taste. It was my poor attempt at a joke. You looked a bit tense. I won't speak again until I'm spoken to,' she said and disappeared back into the kitchen.

He changed his mind again; he was beginning to feel very uncomfortable about this temporary arrangement. When he first met Natasha he had formed the impression that she was a hard, independent, formal person. Now she was the complete opposite, amiable, vulnerable and too casual.

He watched the television, not really taking much in. Cartoons with super strength robots did not inspire him. The noise of the television, the catering sounds in the kitchen, and most recently, Natasha singing to herself, was beginning to grate. He needed some air and exercise.

He went to the kitchen. 'How long to dinner?'

'I'm going as quickly as I can. Probably half an hour,' she replied.

'I'm not rushing you. Make it an hour. I'm going out for a jog.'

Natasha gave him a disapproving look – something else he could do without.

He went to the bedroom and quickly changed into his running kit. An hour would give him time for a few warm-up exercises, one of his five-mile routes and a shower before dinner. He exited to the street, started his stopwatch and set off.

The exercise was beneficial, but most of all it was a great time for some clear thinking. Previously he used his jogging time to think through software problems; now he dwelt on the events of the last few days. After ten years of frantic software development and not a lot else, the contrast over the last thirty-six hours was astonishing. Oddly he was not missing work, but as so much had happened to concentrate his mind elsewhere, it was not really a surprise. His "adventure" had lived up to its name, albeit the end result had not been what he expected or wanted. Currently there were only two remaining matters to pursue. Visit Bradwell and try to contact Kate.

Tomorrow he would go to Bradwell, although he was uncertain what he would do there. A more positive plan was of course to visit the local library and wade through the electoral register listings. But what should he look for? Zurek or maybe some unknown married name. After his futile attempt at doing the same in Portsmouth, he could not face being stuck in a library for hours. Besides, he wanted to be in Bradwell and if it was a nice day, he could revisit some of the walks he had taken with Sarah.

Contacting Kate might be more difficult. The starting point would be to speak to someone at the University. They might be able to supply him with a forwarding address. He would look at the University web pages later.

His fear was that these two avenues might lead nowhere. What then? Should he go to the police and tell them about the letters that had been passed to Natasha? That would compromise Natasha, but perhaps her employers would testify that she had been a model employee and persuade officialdom that she could stay in England unpunished. If he did nothing then he would have to get on with the rest of his life. Just what the rest of his life might be at the moment was anyone's guess.

When he arrived back at the front door of his flat, he stopped the chronometer of his watch. He was disappointed with his time for the jog; he put it down to recent lack of practice and promised to be more disciplined over the next two weeks.

As he entered the flat breathing heavily, the cooking smells were more overpowering now that his hunger had been sharpened from the exercise.

Natasha was sprawled out on the settee watching the television. She had a gruff look her face. Perhaps she had spoilt the dinner.

'You had a phone call while you were out ...', she said in a matter of fact way, '... from an angry woman.'

He looked baffled.

'A very unpleasant ex-wife called Janice. You're to call her back immediately.' Then added accusingly 'You didn't tell me you'd been married!'

Another jealous indicator. He ignored the censure, it was none of her business and he felt like saying so. Instead he simply said, 'I'm going to shower. I'll call her later.'

So, now I have two women interfering with my life he thought as the hot water played onto his invigorated body. There was already evidence of Natasha making herself at home, with strange bottles of shampoo and conditioner propped against the shower cubicle - he would have to speak his mind with Natasha. And Janice was becoming a bloody nuisance. No doubt she was still scheming to get some money from him.

Exercised, cleaned, with fresh clothes and the promise of a good meal, he was feeling good when he joined Natasha in the lounge. The dining table, which he had rarely used for meals, was adorned like a restaurant. A white tablecloth had magically appeared on which, there were two neat place settings, a vase of fresh flowers, an opened bottle of white wine, a jug of water and four glasses. He was thankful that he had no candles or candlesticks in the flat. He was about to ask if he could help, when Natasha disappeared to the kitchen and returned with two bowls of steaming soup.

'Fresh vegetable soup,' Natasha said by way of explanation. 'Be careful it's hot.'

They both sat down.

'While the soup's cooling, can I be blunt about something Natasha?'

She returned a sad look like a child about to be scolded.

'I'm very happy to let you stay here for a while, but, I'm not sure how to put this ... just back off a bit. Stop trying so hard to please me. I think I am going to be very grateful for this meal, but there was no need to go to so much trouble - we could have ordered a takeaway. I also sense that you are ... attracted to me and even after such a short time I am fond of you too; but this last week has turned my life upside down and my emotions inside out. It's as though I'm on a different planet, a parallel universe. I don't want to be fussed over right now. I have enough problems to sort out without being immersed in some kind of pseudo domestic bliss.'

Natasha was close to tears. He had been hard, too hard perhaps, but to back off now would send the wrong signals. He lowered his voice.

'If we are going to co-habit for a while, then let's keep the arrangements more formal. OK?'

Natasha looked into her soup. 'OK. It's just that … oh … it doesn't matter.'

He had an idea of what she was about to say, but decided to change the subject. 'Hey, this soup is delicious. Where did you learn to cook like this?'

'I taught myself. Cooking and decorating have been my hobbies for a few years now. They're both subjects you can practice without a partner,' she replied with a hint of innuendo.

They silently finished the remainder of the soup and a few minutes later generous helpings of steak and kidney pie, mashed potatoes and cabbage appeared. Less interesting than the soup but just as tasty he thought.

'Do you want to hear about my visit to Marion?'

'I've been burning to ask you but wasn't sure you wanted to tell me,' she said humbly.

Between mouthfuls he related as much as he could remember about his meeting with Marion and also filled in some historical gaps for Natasha's benefit. The story continued through a bottle of wine, fresh fruit salad and cream, and finished during the coffee. Throughout, Natasha seemed spellbound, too absorbed to ask a question or seek clarification, too polite to interrupt.

After, Natasha began to clear the dining table. 'So have you convinced yourself that Sarah is in Bradwell?' she asked.

'No, but it's a possibility I can't ignore.'

'Can I come with you tomorrow?'

He laughed. 'Can you picture the situation? I find Sarah and say *Oh, hello Sarah, can I introduce you to Sarah Zurek?*'

'Yes. I suppose that could be quite embarrassing.'

'I'll give you a local map. Perhaps you could take in the sights of Chelmsford. It has a good shopping area and a modern cinema complex.'

Natasha looked disappointed.

'I'll call Janice now.'

He went to the telephone while Natasha was busy with the washing up. Despite Janice's phone number having been his own number many years ago he could not bring it mind, so he dialled 1471 to get the number of the previous call. The stuttering recorded voice announced the caller was from a 01621 dialling code - the Maldon area, at 17:39. That was odd he thought, not 01277 for the Ongar area as he was expecting. The number did look familiar though.

He called to Natasha. 'I did get just one phone call, didn't I?'

'Yes,' she called back after an unnatural delay.

It was possible there could have been a second call that she had not heard particularly if she had been rattling pans in the kitchen.

He thought of pressing 3 on the telephone to dial-back the last caller, but then recalled Janice's number and dialled that instead. Janice answered.

'You called me?'

'I tried to, but some unhelpful scrubber answered the phone. Who is she?'

There was no point in reacting to her taunt, he said, 'Exactly that, a scrubber. My new cleaner.'

'At least she's not in danger of getting screwed.'

'At sixty two years old, you're probably right,' he countered.

'Liar. Anyway, I don't know what you've been up to Carl, but I've done you a big favour, so you owe me.'

Here it comes, he thought; I feel a money demand coming. 'Get to the point, Janice.'

'I had a visit this afternoon from some big bloke who said he was a friend of yours. Wanted to know where you were. When I said you hadn't lived here for years and wouldn't tell him your new address, he started to get stroppy. It was fortunate that Paul was here to get in the way otherwise I might be in hospital by now. Who was he?'

'I've no idea,' he said. 'Describe him to me.'

'Smartly dressed, tall, athletically built, late thirties, thick black hair, bit of a foreign accent. He drove off in a sporty car. Paul thinks it was a Merc. Now do you know?'

'Still no idea,' he lied. 'Have you notified the police?'

'No. He didn't actually do anything wrong and I was worried I might get you into trouble.'

'That's unusually magnanimous of you Janice. The new boyfriend having a positive effect on you?'

'Very funny. So do I get a reward or something?'

'Not a reward, but I may have a big surprise for you in the near future. I'll let you know. One final thing, when you called earlier, where did you call from?'

'From here of course. What a stupid question.'

'Yes. I've been asking a lot of stupid questions lately. Thanks for the tip off Janice. I'll be in touch.'

Natasha was still washing-up, so he joined her to dry the dishes.

'It might be best if you come with me tomorrow after all. Oles visited my ex-wife this afternoon.'

Natasha dropped a glass in the sink but it didn't break. 'How can that be?'

'That's one puzzle I *can* work out. Janice still lives in the bungalow in Ongar I used to own when I was writing to Sarah. I gave it to Janice in the divorce settlement. Oles obviously extracted the address from the letters you gave him.'

'Oh God. You know what this means?'

'I don't know what it means, but I think we may be in some danger. Fortunately Janice never gave him my new address. But Oles is a resourceful and ruthless man, it won't take him long to find out. Either Oles is a complete nutcase or we've uncovered something that threatens him in some way, something to do with Sarah Zurek. Whatever, it's best if we aren't here tomorrow. We'll book into a hotel tomorrow night, so you'll need to pack some things for at least a couple of days. I'll get you a smaller holdall.'

'Oh Carl, this is getting out of control. Why don't we just go to the police and tell them everything. Surely enough has happened already for them to take a serious interest.'

'Perhaps. Though the only positive action that they can take is to arrest you for some immigration infringement. That's got to be a last resort. Let's just avoid trouble for now rather than seek it.'

'What does Oles hope to achieve by hunting you down? What would he have done if he'd found you in Ongar?'

'If his encounter with Don is anything to go by, he would have probably shot me.'

'But he doesn't have his gun now and surely nothing can be that serious that he would kill someone?'

The kitchen chores were finished and they moved to the lounge and sat next to each other on the settee.

'You know him better than I do and said yourself he had an evil streak in him. Maybe he's killed already. He might have killed Sarah. I now reckon there are three possibilities regarding Sarah's "death". One – Everything we've heard is correct. She committed suicide while mentally disturbed, and that's probably my fault. Two – She faked her own suicide. She wanted to start a new life, maybe in the Bradwell area. Three – She was killed and it was made to look like suicide.

'You can't fault the first possibility. What I've uncovered so far sadly points to that being the most plausible outcome. The second explanation is flawed. There is no trace of her. She hasn't told her mother or sister, or tried to contact me. The third possibility has only arisen because of Oles's apparent interest in my investigation.'

'What reason would Oles have for killing her? There's no connection. In any case Oles was in Poland when she died.'

'If I knew a reason I'd have solved the mystery. But there are connections. Sarah's father was Polish. He was living in Poland when she died. You are Polish. Oles is Polish. Maybe with a warped sense of humour he arranged for you to take Sarah's identity. When did you meet Oles?'

'1989.'

'Sarah died in 1988. Do you know for a fact he was in Poland then? No, of course not.'

'And you don't know whether Sarah's mother or sister are keeping some dark secret.'

'True. That's why I want to contact Kate. She was the closest person to Sarah when she died. Which reminds me I need to look up something on the Internet.'

He went to his desk, sat down and moved the mouse to stop the screen saver.

Natasha pulled up a chair to sit next to him and noticed him staring at the photographic background on the screen. 'Is that Sarah?' she asked.

'Yes,' he said, emerging from his trance and connecting to the Internet.

'She's very beautiful. Is that the photograph you showed to Marion?'

He was embarrassed by her interest. 'Yes,' he simply said and maximized the size of his web browser to cover the background image. He connected to the Internet and navigated straight to the Cambridge University home page. It was already on his "Favourites" list in an "Academia" folder. There was no obvious link for finding ex-students so he surfed for a while until he came across a "Lost and Found" page. He pointed to a reference on the screen for Alumni Relations Office. 'That's it,' he said.

'What does Alumni mean?' she asked.

'It's a Latin word meaning previous students of a University or College,' he said. He noted the displayed contact name, Sandy Halts and the phone number. 'I expect the office will be unattended now. I'll give them a call tomorrow. Hopefully someone will be there on a Saturday morning.'

He stood up. 'I forgot to mention that the car broke down at Marion's and I had to get it transported back. I'm going to the car; I need some bits to transfer to a hire car tomorrow, but I'm uncertain what to do about the gun. I think I'll just lock it in the glovebox; I don't want to carry it around or leave it in the flat.'

'Be careful in case Oles is watching the flat.'

'No problem,' he said with a confident air and then joked, 'I'll out-jog him if I see him.'

He returned a few minutes later with a carrier bag, which contained several maps, a torch, a pair of sunglasses, a disposable camera and a few documents. Natasha was engrossed on the computer playing a game of patience.

He selected the Ordnance Survey map of the Colchester area and folded it to centre on Bradwell. He recalled doing the same many years ago when he was looking for somewhere remote to spend the day with Sarah. Using the map as a prompt, he began to trace the events of that distant day.

They had wanted a place within easy reach - to reduce travelling time; on the coast - because they both loved the sea; and, there had to be a dearth of populated places for peaceful hand-in-hand exploratory walks. Finding such a location in Essex was always going to be difficult, but the spur of land sandwiched between the estuaries of the Rivers Blackwater and Crouch had held the best possibilities for them.

Unsuccessfully they had stopped at Maylandsea and then St. Lawrence Bay, but neither offered the tranquillity they had been seeking. Maylandsea was too developed and boasted a busy marina. St. Lawrence Bay was better situated but had a party of well-behaved - though noisy children, who appeared to have settled in for the day to comb the beach for collectible stones or shells. Continuing their journey they had stopped at a pub at Bradwell Waterside for lunch; and afterwards took the old Roman road out of Bradwell village towards the furthest accessible point East. A mile later they had left the last of a few scattered bungalows behind them and half a mile further the road terminated at a piece of arbitrarily fenced ground loosely called a car park. There had been one other car parked with two elderly occupants eating sandwiches. An unmade track bordered by bushes and farmland led to the coast and a five-minute walk had brought them to the sea's edge. On their approach they had initially been disappointed when a building appeared beyond some trees. They had soon dismissed their discontent when it turned out to be an ancient, restored Saxon church; and then spent the first thirty minutes of their isolation from the world studying the history of St Peter's Chapel. Later while walking the footpaths, sea defences and beach they discovered some pre-fabricated buildings sheltered by a copse, but this apparent religious sanctuary called Othona was unoccupied.

They had said little to each other during their wanderings - they did not have to, since they were both awestruck with the perfection of their discovery. He remembered that the only disturbance to the tranquillity of their afternoon had been a man walking a dog and the passing of a speedboat; he would never forget the speedboat. They had stopped to rest on a sheltered stretch of lush grass adjacent to the beach and had lain down with Sarah's head resting in his lap. He had stroked her golden hair until they had both fallen asleep. The noise from the boat had woken them and refreshed from their siesta they had sat up, and knowingly gazed into each other's eyes. After checking that were still alone they had kissed, undressed and made love in the open air for the first time. That had been the perfect end to a perfect day. Later, in memory of the happy time they had spent there, they had christened the area "The Nearest FarAway Place".

Returning to the present day, he considered his strategy for tomorrow. If Sarah was alive, and living in the area of their adopted nirvana, there were probably no more than 100 possible dwellings within a two-mile radius of the centre of Bradwell-on-Sea. If he had to, he would conduct a house-to-house enquiry. Surely that would not be necessary? Showing his aged photograph to the residents and patrons of the local shops, pubs and churches should yield some information. If Sarah had not changed too much in appearance or character, the parochial residents would remember a stunningly beautiful blonde and vibrant woman in their midst.

An excited scream of "Yes" from Natasha stirred him from his musings and he went to see what had produced the outburst.

'That's the first time I've ever completed that game,' she explained, pointing to four neat stacks of playing cards displayed on the screen.

'Do you like computer games?' he asked.

'I don't like action games much,' she replied, 'I only like ones where you have to use your brain. I have a selection on my PC at work which I play sometimes during the lunch break.'

'Have you ever played an adventure game, where you have to direct a character to find objects and then use them in the right places to progress further? They're taxing and great fun.'

'No. I've read about them but never played.'

He began to sift through a stack of CDs piled high on a shelf near his desk. 'This is what I was looking for,' he said, showing Natasha a game called Kings Quest VI. 'I've had this for a few years now and never found time to play it.'

He loaded the game into the PC's CD drive and followed the on-screen instructions to install it. He explained the game play to Natasha and for the next three hours, with a single break for coffee, they were lost in the world of mythical kings, knights, fabulous monsters and perplexing animated puzzles, taking it in turns to control the plight of the hero with the mouse. They were comfortable with each others company; the earlier friction put to one side as they pooled their minds to win treasure and defeat monsters; relieved to relax after their day of trauma. The first yawn from Natasha signalled him to check the time. It was just past midnight and they agreed to a halt in their fantasy adventure, particularly as they had become frustrated in their search for a key to unlock the cell door of their entrapped protagonist.

'I'll get some spare sheets, blankets and pillow for you. I think you'll find the settee quite comfortable to sleep on,' he said as he headed towards his bedroom. He wondered if Natasha had wanted to complain about his chivalry. By rights he should have perhaps offered to sleep on the settee himself, but he wanted his earlier stance on conviviality, or lack of, to be clearly demonstrated.

He began an attempt to make a bed out of the linen he had produced, but Natasha ushered him away when it was obvious he was failing miserably.

For the first time since he had been in the flat he went to the front door, engaged the security lock and checked that all the windows were fastened too.

He used the bathroom while Natasha prepared her sleeping area.

"Hope you sleep OK,' he said when he had finished. 'I'm usually awake quite early. I'll try not to disturb you. I'd like to leave for Bradwell as soon as I've sorted out the hire car. So will breakfast at eight o'clock be acceptable?'

Natasha agreed.

While undressing, he thought again about the dramatic change in his life. MicaCom was no more. He had not been there for two days, but it seemed like years. A feeling of guilt arose when he remembered he should have rung Mike tonight. It was too late now - he would be in bed, and in a few hours he would be on a plane to New York. Carl was already looking forward to his return in three months time; he would have so much to tell him. He had the feeling that he would not be rendezvousing with him in California as he had suggested.

His thoughts prompted him to recharge his mobile phone. Previously just a dumb appendage it had been a major help to him over the last two days. He would use his new wealth to replace his relatively ancient analogue device with a modern digital model.

In bed, he picked up a novel he had been reading. It was a modern day romantic thriller about a man who was in love with two women, and the anguish and plots he goes through to decide who he should favour. He thought that was a bit too inappropriate at the moment, so he put it down and was asleep almost immediately.

Chapter 24

Saturday, March 13, 1999 – 7:30 a.m.

The sound of running water woke Carl about five minutes before the alarm was due. He cursed when he remembered his plan for the day. Traipsing about Bradwell in wet weather would be none too pleasant.

He got out of bed and looked out of the window. The pavement was barely damp, there was slight drizzle, then he realized that it was not a rain shower he had heard - it was the bathroom shower in the adjacent room; Natasha was already up. As he had company he slipped his dressing gown on and went to the kitchen to make tea.

He was about to pour the tea when he heard the bathroom door open. He stepped towards the lounge to ask Natasha what she wanted for breakfast and stopped at the threshold. Natasha was vigorously rubbing her hair with a towel, which he assumed, was the reason she had not heard him busy in the kitchen. She was naked, her back towards him, and like himself this was probably a normal routine when living alone. He knew he should have turned away or made a noise, but he was mesmerized by the curves of her body.

The clothes he had seen her in so far had done little justice to the shapely figure before him. She finished drying her hair and bent down to her open suitcase to retrieve some underwear. He felt his eyes grow wide and his penis stir. She straightened up, turned and caught him staring at her.

Without shock or noticeable embarrassment, she said, 'Good Morning. I didn't know you were already up.'

He was unsure what to say or do. She was too cool in her reaction; she must have known he was looking at her and was seemingly enjoying the attention she was getting. He was torn between studying her firm white breasts and the soft blonde patch between her legs. At least she was a true blonde he thought. Without hesitation, she lifted each leg in turn to put on the frilly white panties she had chosen. He was convinced she was doing it in slow motion to tease him.

'Er … toast and cereal for breakfast?' he finally managed to ask, still not averting his stare.

She bent down again, this time selecting a matching white bra. She gave him an amorous smile and agreed to the breakfast suggestion. Turning sideways to fasten the hook on her bra, he was sure her nipples were erect and looking down at the front of his dressing gown realized he had a similar engorging problem. He hoped Natasha had not noticed. Finally acknowledging the discomfort in his mind and now in his body he returned to his tea-making task.

She finished dressing and appeared close to him in the kitchen. 'Can I help you with anything?'

The problem beneath his dressing down was the honest answer but he said, 'Only to help yourself to the cereal you want. Muesli or Shredded Wheat.'

He turned to face her. Gone was the staid businesswoman he had first met on Thursday morning; before him was a reincarnated Sarah.

She was wearing a white, almost see-through, short-sleeved blouse with lace trimmings and snug black slacks. The combination emphasized the sensual shape of her body he had seen minutes earlier. Her yellow hair reflected the daylight from the kitchen window and she had applied a small amount of blusher to her cheeks. There was the hint of a mild perfume. The resemblance to his memory of Sarah was uncanny. Her hair was shorter and her features were sharper; it was as though she had tried to model herself on the screen image she had seen last night. It was no wonder he had become aroused. She noticed he was examining her.

'I chose light casual clothes as I assumed we would be trekking about a lot today. And I'm wearing comfortable flat shoes. Is that OK?' she asked.

He replied distantly, 'Fine. Good idea.'

He left her to finish making the tea and toast, and went to shower and get dressed. Normally the shower from the previous night would have sufficed, but he wanted another one now - a cold one.

By the time he had showered and dressed casually in jeans and T-shirt, he felt he had his libido under control, and joined Natasha for breakfast.

She had had muesli and toast with cheese spread, and he chose the same.

They first made small talk about breakfast preferences and then she wanted to know about his plans for the day.

'Frankly, I'm not sure. We'll head for Bradwell and make enquiries at any public places, although from memory there aren't too many.'

'Where exactly is Bradwell?' she asked.

He went to get the map and traced the journey he had made with Sarah.

'Have you got photographs you can show people? I expected your flat to have photos of Sarah on display.'

He explained what had happened to his photographs and letters, and showed Natasha the only remaining photograph that he had used for his PC wallpaper.

Now past nine o'clock, it was time for him to make some telephone calls. He first flicked through the Yellow Pages until he found the telephone number for the local BMW dealer - Beamers. He explained as best he could the problem with his car and arranged for it to be collected; it was possible they might be able to send someone today, if not he would have to wait until Monday. He would deliver the key on his way out later that morning. When he asked for a brochure and price list of new BMWs to be dropped through his letterbox at the same time, suddenly there was more interest in his problem. The dealer could not help with a hire car but they could let him have a courtesy loan car until Monday afternoon, by which time they would have collected and repaired his own car. In exchange they offered a one-year-old BMW 320, not too dissimilar to the new car he had considered buying. So there was no need to phone around for a hire car. He arranged to collect it an hour later.

Next, he telephoned a local taxi company. It was too far to walk to the dealer in Chelmsford, particularly with luggage, so he requested a cab to call at ten o'clock.

Finally, he tried the Cambridge University number that he had noted from the Internet last night. He let the telephone ring for almost a minute and was about to give up when it was answered.

'Alumni Relations Office,' said a female voice.

'Hello. Would that be Sally Halts?' he asked.

'Yes it is.'

'That's lucky. I wasn't sure whether your office would be open today. My name is Carl Denham. I'm trying to locate the whereabouts of an ex-student of the University.'

'I need to know some information about them. Can you tell me their full name, College and Year of Matriculation?' Sally asked.

He thought for a moment. 'The name is Kate Robins. I'm not sure about the college, possibly Queens'. She would have got her first degree in 1988, I think in Biology. Then I believe she stayed on for a post-graduate degree. Robins is her single name of course, I don't know if she's married now.'

'Can you bear with me a few minutes? I'm not usually here on Saturdays and my computer terminal isn't switched on,' Sally apologized.

He hung on patiently and heard a keyboard being tapped in the background.

'Hello, Mr. Denham. Yes, I believe I've found who you are looking for. The information may not be fully up-to-date since it's three years old now.'

'OK, that will do. Do you have a telephone number?'

'I'm sorry Mr. Denham I can't directly provide you with that information. The correct procedure is that I will write to the alum on your behalf passing on your contact details and say that you would like to hear from her again. The Data Protection Act prevents us from passing database information on. We have to abide strictly by these rules,' she explained.

'How long will that take?'

'Correspondence is always sent first class so the system is fast and effective. I'll write on Monday.'

'It's quite important that I speak to her soon. Would it be possible for you to phone her?'

'I can't do that, but I've just noticed that she has an e-mail address. I could try that.'

'I don't suppose you can give me that either?'

'I'm sorry. No.'

'OK, here are the details I would like you to pass on. My name is Carl Denham. I was a friend of her University colleague Sarah Zurek. I would urgently like to speak to her about Sarah's suicide. I may be travelling about over the next few days so my mobile number is …' He quoted his number.

'A suicide. Oh, how awful. I can only pass on your name and telephone number, but I'll send that straight away.'

'Could you also check whether you have any details for Sarah Zurek too? She would have graduated in Computer Science in 1988. She was at Queens' too.'

'Just a moment.'

There were more keyboard noises.

'Yes, we have her on record as dying before she completed her degree, but I could only forward a request after consulting the College about the family circumstances,' Sally said.

'There's no need. I just wanted to check that my facts were correct,' he said, then expressed his sincere thanks and finished the call.

The taxi arrived 15 minutes late.

At the BMW dealer reception he handed over the key to his car and gave instructions to where it could be collected. A smartly dressed salesman then appeared and took him to his loan black BMW. The salesman obviously knew about his intention to purchase a new car and immediately launched into his standard, well-practised sales patter. Carl indulged him for a few minutes, then during a pause in his delivery while he seemed to mentally disrobe Natasha, he took the opportunity to interrupt and say that he had an urgent appointment to attend; Natasha grinned, presumably thinking he had displayed a jealous streak.

The journey to Bradwell took about half an hour and their first stop was at a small, ramshackled petrol station and workshop on the edge of the village; it seemed the ideal place to start.

If Sarah did live alone in the area she would undoubtedly need a car for transport; he had not seen a bus since the outskirts of Maldon, and the nearest train station was five miles away in Southminster.

Despite the garage being the only such place in Bradwell, the old man in charge, who looked well past retirement age, could not help. He had lived and worked there for 40 years and maintained he could remember everyone he had served during that time.

Next was the Green Man pub at Bradwell Waterside. They arrived just as it was opening. The reaction here was the complete opposite. The barman had only been working there for two weeks; he did not live in the area and seemed to be the sort of person that would not have recognized himself in the mirror. He did say that the pub was the most popular in the village and would be teeming with customers in two hours. Looking at the extensive house menu on display that was not surprising. Therefore, rather than settle now, Carl earmarked it for a return visit later.

They drove through the high street of the main village, made a note of any public places, and then parked the car.

The centre of the village boasted just a small dual-purpose post office and general store, another pub - the Kings Head, and the parish church St. Thomas'.

The woman owning and tending the store was another long established resident, who was sure she knew everyone in the area. As a depot for retaining parcels that could not be delivered, she said she would have recalled an unusual name like Zurek. When she was shown the photograph, she remarked that it looked like the friend of her brother-in-law's niece who lived in Southend and then related what wonderful work she did as a Samaritan. He soon became bored, but frustratingly Natasha kept the conversation going until the storeowner was talked out.

The parish church was next to the store. He circled the building with Natasha looking for an open door or cleric but, unsuccessful, they crossed the road to the Kings Head.

The bartender was a young girl who did not look old enough to be working in a pub. When he started asking questions, she became nervous and scurried off to get the proprietor. He was a broad man with a bright grey beard, who was ill at ease until Carl assured him they were not from the police.

Then he took charge of the questioning, wanting to know the intimate details of why they were looking for Sarah. Carl kept the story as simple and non-controversial as possible, but vowed that in all future enquiries it would be easier to just say he was searching for his missing sister, rather that the complicated story of Sarah's true disappearance.

The proprietor could not help but pointed Carl in the direction of a table of elderly locals. It took a while to attract their attention since they were deep into discussing the merits of beers they had sampled in their accumulated lifetimes. They were sympathetic to his cause, and wanted him and his *attractive companion* to join them for a drink, but he declined when it was obvious they wanted company rather than to supply any useful information.

They went to the car to review their progress so far.

'It's not too promising, is it?' Natasha said.

'I'm sorry to say we've barely started. This must be extremely boring for you.'

'Not really. It makes a pleasant change to fixing computers and software all day. Where are we going next?'

He pulled out his Ordnance Survey map and studied the Bradwell area again.

'There's one more pub marked on the map. That's down the road by the church. The same road leads to St. Peter's Chapel. We'll try the pub next, and then we'll go back to the Green Man for lunch and talk to any local customers. If that doesn't yield anything then the hard work starts. I'll explain that after lunch.'

It was half a mile to the pub, the Cricketers. It looked like it was once a large house and had a conservatory extension that was used as a dining area.

Considering it was geographically remote, it was quite busy. With a number of people to question, they decided to have a drink this time, a gin and tonic for Natasha, but just an orange juice for Carl. They had to wait a few minutes, as the barman also seemed to be acting as cook and waiter. It transpired that he was the landlord too, a Scotsman aged about thirty, named Josh. When Carl showed him the photograph, he looked long and hard and was fairly confident he had seen her. Much to Carl's surprise, he even expressed his confidence mathematically, saying there was an eighty percent probability of being right, the terminology coming from the fact that he was a failed Maths undergraduate from Aberdeen University. He had not seen her in the pub, but on walks with his two dogs. Most interesting was that the walks were usually to and from the coast via St. Peter's Chapel. Josh thought he had last seen her about a month ago. Carl wanted to yelp for joy, but held back in case he gave the wrong impression to the patrons. He noticed that Natasha was not celebrating with him.

Natasha sat down at an empty table, while he circulated enthusiastically amongst the customers in the small bar, waving his photograph. Five minutes later he came to join Natasha.

'Shame. Nothing else to add to Josh's good news.' He noticed that she had already finished her drink.

'Something wrong?' he said, referring jointly to her mood and empty glass.

'No. Could I have another drink?'

Drinking his orange juice in one swallow he said, 'I think I'm the one who needs a strong drink. We're going now anyway. You can top-up at the Green Man.'

As they left he took a business card from his pocket, crossed out the MicaCom details, replaced them with his mobile telephone number and gave it to Josh, asking him to call if he encountered the blonde co-walker again.

The barman at the Green Man had been right in his forecast. Every table in the pub was occupied and many of the customers were eating an assortment of dishes from the menu. There was now two additional serving staff to cope with the peak period.

Carl and Natasha propped themselves against the bar and ordered a half of bitter and a gin and tonic. They studied the menu, spoilt for choice and were vigilant for a table to be vacated. When one was free Natasha went to sit down and he ordered the house special of fresh cod and chips for both of them after a recommendation from one of the bartenders, and *another* gin and tonic for Natasha. He had been warned that the meal might take up to half an hour, so he left Natasha on her own again, and started his enquiries.

The customers here were less co-operative, probably because I am interrupting their lunch he thought. He persisted nonetheless, putting on an authoritative air as though it was an official enquiry of some urgency. He returned to Natasha twenty minutes later just as their food was being delivered.

'I'm sorry to keep leaving you on your own,' he said sitting down.

'So am I. I've already had two men try to pick me up,' she replied moodily.

'It's your own fault. You shouldn't look so bloody gorgeous,' he said, expressing his true thoughts and trying to flatter Natasha out of her capriciousness. A weak smile in return told him his words were only partially effective.

While they ate, he related the results of his recent interviews. No new leads had been generated and he was beginning to wonder about the validity of Josh's statement at the Cricketers.

'Don't you think we ought to call it a day? Show me to the Chapel and take me for a walk along the coast,' Natasha said.

'I will, but not yet. We're going back to the village centre and then walk along East End road, that's the road we drove to the Cricketers. There are quite a few houses along that road and my guess is that if Sarah is here, that's where she'll be. Beyond the Cricketers, there are only a few more houses before the road dead-ends at a car park. Then there is a footpath to the Chapel and the coast.'

They finished eating and agreed that the meal had been delicious. They were both too full to consider a dessert and he vetoed Natasha's request for another drink before they left.

Carl estimated they had called at 50 houses when they arrived at the Rectory. Natasha was positively miserable with the exercise of following him from place to place like a well-trained dog. Every time he went through his standard "missing sister" dialogue, she grew visibly more impatient as though, he speculated, she was fearful that Sarah would suddenly emerge and a tearful reunion would ensue in which she would be cast aside. Even he was being worn down by the tediousness of the activity, but his resolve was undeterred and became revived after he had met the Rector's wife.

She apologized that the Reverend was visiting a neighbouring parish on some ecclesiastical matter and insisted they have some tea while she listened to Carl's dilemma. He readily capitulated to her wishes, wanting a break from the ennui and rest for his feet. He reverted to the true story of Sarah, needing to be candid to his gregarious, veracious and portly hostess, Ivy Broadstairs, and for simplicity introduced Natasha as a helpful friend.

Ivy recalled a time of eight or nine years ago, when her husband, Gerald, had encountered a young girl crying in St. Peter's Chapel; a girl strikingly similar to the one in the photograph that Carl had shown her. Gerald had seen her on several occasions before then, but approached her this time to ascertain if he could help. Then, for about six months, the girl had often spoken to Gerald to seek religious guidance to overcome a personal crisis in her life. She never made a formal appointment, merely took advantage of chance encounters with him at the Chapel. In fact during that period Gerald had remarked that she never mentioned her name nor had he discovered where she was from. She did recover apparently and thereafter Ivy had remembered seeing her occasionally in the grounds surrounding the Chapel, but could not recall a sighting in the last few years.

He questioned why Ivy could so vividly recollect an event from so long ago. She replied that the girl was an enigma to her and Gerald, stunningly beautiful except that she had never seen her smile.

Then how could Ivy be so sure when the photograph depicted a happy smiling girl?

Ivy admitted that she could not be positive, but was influenced by the setting of the photograph. Though barely discernible, she had observed that it had been taken at the Chapel, and she had always thought the girl had had an affinity with the place.

They thanked Ivy for her hospitality and the tea, and he left a modified business card in case Ivy recalled anything else that might help him.

Outside the Rectory, he was buoyant. 'Well Sarah definitely lived here but is she still here?'

Natasha seemed to want to dissuade him. 'I'm not convinced. I thought Ivy was a touch eccentric. I think she said what you wanted to hear. If the beautiful Sarah made such an impact with the rector's wife, why hasn't anyone else remembered her?'

'Josh did,' he countered.

'With 80% probability,' she reminded him.

'Listen to me Natasha. I know you think you have a personal stake in me not finding Sarah, but you are wrong, OK? I invited you along for your own safety and hoped that I might get your support and companionship. If you're going to be negative all the time then I'd prefer that you went back to the car and waited until I've finished.' He offered her the car key.

She looked hurt again and her refusal to take the key provided the answer to his question.

He resumed his enquiries with Natasha tagging behind reluctantly and silently. After they passed the Cricketers pub, flat cultivated land spread to the right and left of the road, interrupted only by the occasional cottage or farmhouse at the end of a drive.

He was disappointed and Natasha appeared relieved, when the road finally terminated at an area of waste ground that was the designated parking area for visitors to St. Peter's Chapel.

There was nowhere to sit comfortably, so they passed through a kissing-gate and started out on the gravel path, which led to the Chapel.

Natasha was inquisitive as to how a place of worship could be located in such a remote place. On the way, he told her the story.

'The Romans built the straight road we've been walking along towards the end of the third century. It led then to the Fort of Othona, which was a defensive outpost of the Saxon shore. I think someone called Carausius built it with stones brought by water from Kent and London. During the fall of the Roman Empire it was left to become the centre of a village called Ythancestrir. In 653, a missionary called Cedd from Lindisfarne in Northumbria was invited by King Sigbert to act as an Apostle to the East Saxons. Cedd built the Chapel dedicated to St. Peter from stones and tiles from the Roman fort. You'll see the main structure when we get there, but there also used to be an apse and two small rooms at one end. Cedd was consecrated as a Bishop in 654 and the Chapel became his Cathedral. St. Cedd is in fact the Saint of Essex.'

'And it's been used ever since?' Natasha asked.

'It was a centre of worship for the area to the fourteenth century until the building of St Thomas'. It was then used as a Chapel of ease until the seventeenth century when it became a barn. It was restored and rededicated in 1920. Now it's used for special Diocesan events and there is an annual Pilgrimage in July.'

'How do you so much about this place?'

'I'm not a great lover of history, but when I came here with Sarah, I fell in love with the place. I wanted to know its past so I picked up some literature.'

'And you still remember everything about it?'

'You never forget things that you love,' he said, wondering if Natasha had recognized the double meaning of Chapel and Sarah. Her thwarted look spoke volumes.

The Chapel was now in view and a few minutes later they sat down on a bench seat in the porch of a small wooden hut that was used as an administration office. It faced the stout wooden door of the Chapel. There was no one else there, and it was peacefully quiet, interrupted only by the song of birds in a nearby copse.

'Can we go inside?' Natasha asked.

'Yes, it should be open. First, I'd just like to sit here for a while.'

They sat there in silence for five minutes. He just stared into the distance as if in a trance. Natasha became restless and walked around the Chapel.

When she returned she said, 'Share them with me?'

'What?' he said.

'Your thoughts. You look so sad.'

'I can't really believe I'm here again after 11 years and 5 months. Where did the time go? What have I achieved?'

'By your own account you created a successful business; have had enormous job satisfaction; good health and now you are a millionaire.'

'But I haven't really lived.'

'I beg to disagree. If that wasn't living perhaps you'd like to relate it to the refugees around the world. I'm sure any one of them would like to trade places with you. What I think you meant to say was that you haven't loved, in other words, Sarah.'

'Yes, you're right. I'm being very ungrateful. It's been a waste of time, hasn't it?'

'I presume you mean the search for Sarah rather than your life.'

'Yes. I've clutched at every straw offered to me. It's so easy to do that when you have hope; her name on the Internet; the mystery about the letters; the manic behaviour of Oles; the wording of the suicide note; and the inconclusive revelations of Josh and Ivy. I still have hope. However, if she is alive, it would have been so much easier for her to trace me - assuming she wanted to. It's hard for me to accept that she might love someone else now.'

'Are you giving up?' Natasha asked.

'I'd still like to speak to Kate. After that, it will be the first day of the rest of my life. Let's look inside the Chapel now.'

The Chapel was the size of a tall detached-house. Structurally there were no storeys or partitions, just light grey stone walls and a marble floor. The walls were uneven and patched in places; elevated arched windows provided a passage for the daylight. There were low wooden benches for a congregation to sit and a stone altar supported by three stones. They read from a leaflet that the stones had been gifts from religious outposts of Lindisfarne, Iona and Lastingham. High on the back wall behind the altar was a large stone crucifix adorned in blue and red. It was cool inside.

'Peaceful, isn't it?' he said.

'Yes and very beautiful. It's no wonder that this was a special place for you. Not just because of Sarah. Just being here makes me feel ... content ... at peace with the World,' Natasha said with joy in her voice.

'Are you tired after all the trekking and walking that we've done?' he asked.

'I was earlier, but I think that was more from the boredom of following you from house to house without being able to contribute much. I feel fine now.'

'I'd quite like to walk along the sea wall. It's what Sarah and I did when we were here. I noticed from the map it's possible to walk along the coast past the power station then turn inland back to Bradwell village. It's about four miles though. It will probably take an hour and a half. It's still cloudy and cool outside but it doesn't look like it's going to rain.'

'OK. I'd love that too,' she said.

They left the Chapel and within 50 metres, they were standing on the elevated sea defence wall. In front of them were rough marshlands.

'This is the Saltings. We can't go through there; it's a nature reserve for shore nesting birds,' he explained.

They walked northwards past an observation tower. Inland - behind trees, there were a number of deserted single storey buildings, some old, some new.

'What's that?' Natasha asked.

'It's the Christian community of Othona. It's a sort of quasi-religious holiday camp and teaching centre. I think it's only used at certain times of the year.'

Clear of the trees they could see for miles across the sea and flat landscape. In the distance, almost two miles away, he pointed out the huge buildings of Bradwell nuclear power station.

'It doesn't seem right somehow that such a place should be here,' she said.

'It's not that bad. It doesn't spoil the tranquillity of the place. Listen,' he said, 'All you can hear are birds and the sea.'

The Saltings narrowed until they got to sharp curve in the sea wall called Sales Point. Thereafter, a white sandy beach with shell and shingle ridges stretched beyond them.

'Let's walk along the beach now,' he suggested. 'Take your shoes and socks off.'

'Why?'

'I thought … it might be fun,' he said hesitantly. 'No, that's not true. Well, it is true, but I had another motive. It doesn't matter.'

He walked on then noticed Natasha had not joined him. He stopped and looked back; her look suggested she wanted an explanation.

'Tell me,' Natasha insisted.

'Sarah loved walking barefoot whenever she could. She did that when we were here,' he said, hanging his head slightly with guilt. He realized it was an inappropriate thing to say; he was trying to relive a fantasy using Natasha as a substitute. If she stormed off he would understand.

'I don't have very hardy feet and the beach is stony in places, but I will if you do the same,' she replied.

He was pleased with the response but felt guilt again knowing that in her current mood she would probably do anything to please him.

'OK,' he said, and smiled as if to say *thank you for humouring me*.

Natasha was struggled with her balance as she removed her shoes and pop socks, so he offered his shoulder for support. She held on to him and he registered that this was the first time he had touched her.

They continued along the beach walking side by side clutching their footwear; progress was slowed by the inertia of the sand and the vigilance required to avoid treading upon beach debris.

'Where will we stay tonight?' she asked.

'I'm not sure. I didn't notice any accommodation in Bradwell. We'll find something on the way back. Maldon might be a possibility.'

'And what will we do tomorrow?'

'Damn. I left my phone in the car. I meant to bring it with me in case Kate called. I'd earmarked tomorrow to visit Kate, if she calls, will speak to me and hasn't moved to some distant place like Aberdeen,' he said. 'Otherwise I'll find some other highlights of Essex to show you while you are on holiday,' he added sarcastically.

For the next mile, they talked about shoreline trivia like seashells, boats and sandy beaches. Only twice did they encounter other people, a young couple walking along the seawall whom they waved to, and an elderly man scanning the beach with a metal detector. His haul for the day being a pound coin, several flattened drink cans - which he said he was going to place in the local recycling bin, and a metal comb.

They were nearing the power station and had begun to make their way back to the path along the seawall, when Natasha stumbled attempting to avoid a patch of seaweed. With her free left hand, she clutched his right hand to steady herself.

'Are you OK?' he asked.

'I think so. I turned my ankle slightly, but I think I'll live,' she replied, looking longingly into his eyes as though he'd just rescued her from a far more serious fate.

He cast his eye to their joined hands, enjoying the experience, but Natasha seemed to take this as a sign of disapproval and removed her hand, not catching his look of disappointment.

They came to steps to leave the beach and sat down to brush the sand from their damp feet.

'Make sure you get all the sand off,' he advised, 'otherwise it will be abrasive on your feet. We still have some way to go.'

Passing the power station, they remarked on the size of the buildings now they were barely 100 metres from them. The car park was almost full, but there were no signs of activity, noise or polluting emissions. Shortly after they left the coastal path and turned inland onto a tree-lined track to head towards Bradwell Village.

'We'll be back to civilisation in about 15 minutes,' he called, noticing that Natasha was tiring and slipping behind.

'I'm not really tired, just sad to leave the sea behind,' she called back.

He waited until she was alongside and then took her hand in his. Perhaps I'll bring you back here one day,' he said, squeezing her hand gently, this time not letting go.

Natasha stopped and looked at him. There were tears in her eyes. 'I think you know that I'm in love with you Carl,' she said.

He bent forward slightly and kissed each of her wet eyes. 'I know,' he said.

She looked at him for a more forthcoming reply then said, 'Whatever happens, will you *promise* to bring me back here one day?'

He thought for a moment. 'I promise,' he said, squeezing her hand again.

They held hands, but said nothing, for the remainder of their walk back to the village. He was unsure how and if he should react further to what Natasha had said. He could not, yet, make any further commitments; the promise he had made was sufficient for now.

They stopped briefly at the general store for cans of soft drinks to slake the thirst accumulated during their hike. The woman tending the store greeted them like old friends and to their joint embarrassment remarked what a happy couple they looked.

In the car, they were both relieved to be able to rest their legs and take a drink. He reached across to the back seat for his mobile phone that had been tucked under his jacket. On the display there was a message "Call Missed." 'Maybe it was Kate,' he said, pressing the button sequence to return the call. He noticed it was the same area code as the Cambridge University number that he had dialled that morning.

'Hammond Residence,' said a very young voice, which was then interrupted by an older female. 'Hello, sorry about that,' she said.

'Hello. I hope I have the right number. I wanted to speak to Kate, Kate Robins?'

'Well you've reached Kate Hammond. Robins was my maiden name. Oh, wait a second that must be Carl Denham?' she said.

'Yes, Kate. I'm so pleased you got my message, *and* that you phoned.'

'I must say I did think twice about it. Curiosity got the better of me. Why did you want to speak to me?'

Reacting to Kate's cold response, he kept his explanation short, concentrating on aspects of his conversation with Marion.

More conciliatory, Kate said, 'It was a long while ago, Carl. I'm not sure I could tell you anything useful.'

'Can I make a suggestion? Would you mind if I came to see you tomorrow? There's a good reason for my haste. You're the only person now who might be able to help me.'

It took some persuasion but eventually Kate agreed to his request; exceeding his expectations by inviting him and his "friend" to lunch, so long as they could tolerate the mischief of two fatherless young children. That begged some questions, which he would leave until tomorrow. She gave him the address and some rough directions.

He related his conversation with Kate to Natasha as they drove away from Bradwell.

'I think you had better be Natasha Minski tomorrow. I can't very well introduce you as Sarah Zurek. In fact, that's going to be a common problem whenever you meet any of my friends.'

'I don't think so. The problem will disappear whenever I go back to Portsmouth,' Natasha said, intoning the statement like a question.

A question he could not answer yet, instead he said, 'I have an idea. As we have to be in the Cambridge area tomorrow, why don't we head there now and find a hotel. We could be there within a couple of hours. If we get up early in the morning, I'd have time to show you some of Cambridge; we aren't expected at Kate's until twelve thirty.'

As he expected, Natasha thought it was a wonderful idea.

On the way to Cambridge, their conversations visited much of each other's pasts. Natasha's story started with her arrival in England. He prompted her a few times about Poland but she seemed unwilling to go that far back, so he let the subject drop.

She spoke enthusiastically about her job in Portsmouth and was clearly trying to impress him with her knowledge of computer software and hardware. He wondered if this had anything to do with his casual remark from yesterday about opening a computer shop.

He gained the impression that she was a lonely person from the description of her social life, which was oriented around her help for various charitable organisations. She liked helping people less fortunate than herself, but had not forged any strong relationships with her working or charity colleagues; Veronica had been the exception. Veronica was a girl permanently on heat looking for the ideal male companion and they had often gone out together to pubs, clubs and cinemas.

Despite Natasha being considerably more attractive, in his opinion, fifty percent of the time Veronica succeeded in attracting someone by her sheer persistence and bravado. Veronica had literally been out with dozens of men, but the longest she had held on to one was a month; she was insatiable but selective. Sometimes Veronica's surplus was hoisted on to Natasha and selflessly Natasha never complained since she wanted Veronica to be happy. Other than kissing and some tame touching, Natasha said she had never got close to anyone. Although she was fearful of relationships, she maintained she had never met anyone she could love, until yesterday. At which point he felt he might get involved in a conversation he could not handle right now, so he took the opportunity to tell his own story.

His allegory was strictly post-Sarah. He spent a long time telling Natasha about his year in America. It was a part of his life that he had never told anyone before, so it was fun remembering all the things he had done.

Then he went on to the formation of MicaCom and the two stressful, penniless years he had spent to establish the company; followed by the eight stressful, but financially comfortable years keeping it going.

Natasha quizzed him about his marriage to Janice, and he became loud and animated about what a mistake that had been. He went on to be quite open about her evil schemes and the way she had plagued him ever since. He laughed when Natasha repeated the telephone call she had taken from Janice last night. It was a joy to his ears that Janice had been so put out by a woman answering his phone.

The journey to Cambridge took about two hours and he headed for the town centre. He remembered a comfortable hotel facing the River Cam that he had visited once before on a seminar. Finding a hotel parking place was more difficult than he had expected; Cambridge was always a popular city but it was not the busiest time of year. At reception, he discovered the problem.

'Good evening,' he said to the receptionist. 'Would you have two single rooms for tonight?'

The look on the receptionist's face already showed this might be difficult. 'I'll check for you, but we are quite busy this weekend. There's been an open day at the colleges today for new students,' she explained, and tapped some keys on a computer terminal. 'I'm sorry, but we only have one luxury twin room available.'

Natasha nudged him and motioned him to one side. 'Look, I'm not trying to be forward but it's quite late already and I'd really like to relax for a while instead of trying to find somewhere else. Let's take the room, I'm sure we can manage.'

Manage what? He thought, but she seemed sincere. 'I may be a rich man now, but I suppose there's no point in wasting money with two rooms,' he replied, realizing it was rather a lame excuse. He turned back to reception, 'OK, we'll take it.'

He fetched the luggage from the car and as instructed they took the lift to the third floor. He noted that the suite was not much smaller than the size of his complete flat. The bedroom was large with an en-suite bathroom and modest television, and there was an entrance hall and separate lounge with a wide-screen television.

'Wow,' Natasha said, 'I've never stayed in such a posh place' as she dashed around the room opening cupboards and inspecting the facilities. 'In fact, I've never stayed in an hotel before, overnight that is'.

He raised his eyebrows in disbelief.

Natasha began unpacking and storing her clothes and toiletries, which he thought was unnecessary for a single night, but did not comment as she was obviously enjoying herself. He went to sit in the lounge and clicked on the TV, scanning the channels until he found the Sky News broadcast.

Natasha joined him in the lounge a few minutes later. 'Have I got time for a shower? I'll feel grubby after all the walking and travelling.'

'That depends. How hungry are you?' he asked.

'Not especially. Surprisingly I'm still quite full from the fish lunch.'

'OK. We'll pop out later and just get a snack somewhere, so there's plenty of time. I'll take a shower after you.'

His concentration on the news kept wavering as he wondered whether Natasha would repeat her morning dressing routine in front of him. He was guiltily disappointed when she appeared twenty minutes later fully clothed. She looked stunning in a fresh white blouse, long-sleeved this time, and a knee-length red skirt, which accentuated her curvy hips and shapely legs. Stylish short-heeled black shoes had added an inch to her height. She sat snugly next to him on the sofa and her skirt rode up, exposing a generous amount of bare thigh. He was ashamed at what was going through his mind, so took the easy option and went for his shower.

They strolled directly to main shopping area and eventually selected a Wimpy Bar for their snack. They both chose a regular cheeseburger and vanilla milkshake and shared a small portion of fries.

They started to eat and he said, 'It's strange. I've only known you for three days and in that time I've told you so much about my life including some very private things. I know very little about you though. Your Polish past I mean.'

'For obvious reasons, I've had to get used to keeping most of my early life a secret. I think I can trust you by now, so we'll play a game. I'll let you ask ten questions about me and I'll give you full and honest answers.'

'Now there's a challenge. OK, the first relates to something you said earlier. You mentioned you'd never stayed in a hotel. Why?'

'Overnight, no. I've been in hotels on one-day training courses and seminars sponsored by the Council. And once during the summer I attended a week long course in Southampton, but I stayed in a student hall of residence.'

'What about holidays?'

'In the eight years I've been in Portsmouth, I've only been away on holiday four times. Three times with Vi - once to Devon and once to Cornwall, where we stayed in a caravan. Last year we stayed in a Lake District holiday cottage which Vi's parents bought as an investment. In my second year in England, I stayed for a week in a cheap guesthouse in Brighton.'

'Holidays with your Parents?'

'My parents died in a train crash when I was six years old. I don't remember much about them. I lived with an aunt and uncle until I went to Warsaw University. They were quite poor and had a small farm. During my school holidays I worked on the farm.'

'No brothers or sisters?'

'That's the fourth. No.'

'What did you study at University? I'd guess at English.'

'You guessed right.'

'Hobbies?'

'Cooking, DIY, walking, English literature, children's charity work.'

'Date of birth?'

'June 12th, 1967.'

217

'Ever married or engaged?'

'No. You've only got two left.'

'Favourite sports?'

'I play a little tennis and go to aerobics classes. I like watching football and snooker. Last question.'

'Favourite pop group?'

'The Beach Boys.'

'Amazing. Me too, what a coincidence,' he said.

She laughed.

'Hey, now wait a minute. You said that because you saw the stack of their albums at my flat. Didn't you?'

Natasha just looked at him with a smirk on her face.

He then saw the joke. 'I've used up all my questions, haven't I?'

'I can't answer that, because it would be a breach of contract,' she said and they both burst out laughing.

'Joking apart,' he said, 'can I ask one more question? It's quite important to me.'

'With such a serious expression, I had better say yes.'

'Why are you in love with me?'

'Gosh, a question to end all questions. That's not as difficult as it seems. I've a prepared answer.'

He was amazed by her response and looked questioningly.

'During our long walk today I asked myself the same question. I think I was in love with you before we met. I used to read your letters to Sarah. I fantasized that you had written them to me. In my mind, I tried to be Sarah. My life hasn't been particularly exciting but generally I've no cause for complaint, except that I wanted to be loved and give love in return. When your first e-mail arrived, I was scared and excited at the same time. Scared that my identity might be uncovered and excited that I might actually meet you. When we did meet on Thursday morning at first my feelings changed. Suddenly I hated you. It was the horrible realisation that I couldn't be the real Sarah Zurek you wanted. I thought of nothing else for the rest of the day. Then the hate turned to sympathy. I was sad that you were so sad. When the parcel arrived, I hoped that it was a sign that you liked me. It never crossed my mind that it was a trick. Today I've been through a similar roller coaster of emotions. It was in St Peter's Chapel that I finally understood. All the turmoil in my mind was the process of making me accept that I wanted to spend the rest of my life with you. That's the best way I have of explaining *Why?* It would hurt not being with you.'

He had not banked upon such a rational answer. He had gone through a similar contradiction of emotions exacerbated by his search for Sarah. He now wished he had not asked the question. The answer had only served to make his future even more complicated.

They had finished their meal. 'Let's go,' he said, 'it doesn't seem right that a Wimpy Bar should be host to such a serious statement.'

It was noticeably cooler when they got outside. Despite wearing a matching red jacket to go with her skirt, Natasha shivered as they turned a corner and a chilling gust of wind caught them.

He put his arm around her waist and pulled her to him. 'Does that help?' he said.

'Yes. Thank you,' she replied.

Even with the chill, he took a longer route back to the hotel. He realized he liked having Natasha close to him.

It was eleven o'clock when they returned to their hotel room.

'I'm so tired,' Natasha said, removing her jacket and shoes and then collapsing on one of the beds.

'Yes, it has been a busy day, physically and emotionally.' He examined the self-service hot drinks tray. 'How about a nightcap? There are a couple of sachets of hot chocolate here.'

'That's a good idea. A perfect end to the day.'

He switched the TV on and tuned into the news. The Serbian invasion of Kosovo was still dominating the international headlines. While waiting for the kettle to boil, he went to the bathroom, where he undressed and slipped on one of the hotel supplied towelled dressing gowns.

'Dressing gowns too, I never spotted those,' she said when he returned robed in white. 'I must use the facilities too,' and she disappeared to the bathroom.

He made the drinks, gave them a thorough stir and placed the cups on the cabinets either side of the bed where Natasha had been laying.

Natasha returned similarly robed and resumed her position, albeit this time to one side of the bed. She patted the space she had left and said 'There's room for both of us.'

He stretched out beside her and they watched the news and sipped at their drinks for a few minutes.

Natasha adjusted a pillow behind her and when she was satisfied, she casually placed her hand on his towelled arm. During the movement, her loosely tied robe parted exposing one leg almost to the thigh.

He felt his heart beating faster than normal and found the television no longer held his attention. He kept looking at the exposed white flesh without trying to be too obvious. He made a small adjustment to his position and placed his hand on Natasha's leg, just above the knee. His heart was now pounding in overdrive, his mouth was dry and he was conscious of movement under his robe.

Natasha had not stirred or complained so he started to caress her leg, very gradually moving upwards. He tried to fight the urge he had. This was not right; he should be here with Sarah not Natasha. He reached the soft hairs on her inner thigh and her legs parted slightly. The photograph of Sarah and her smiling face came to mind but did not linger; Sarah would want him to be happy. He had been true to her memory for eleven years.

Natasha was breathing deeper and moaning quietly. He had to stop now. Concentrate on the television he told himself, the local news was coming on. Natasha was now gripping his arm and her body was beginning to gently rock from side to side.

His erect penis searching for release suddenly pushed through a gap in his robe and Natasha's hand moved towards it. Unable to hold back any longer, he moved the short, but irresistible distance to his target. When his hand met the slippery wetness of her lips, it was like an electric shock running through him. He leant over and released the cord on Natasha's robe, then drew it back revealing her smooth white body.

A fire broke out early this morning ...

Natasha sat forward slightly and quickly released her arms from the oversized garment. As she did so, he knelt between her legs and in a swift movement cast his robe onto the floor.

... on the Blue Stone industrial estate ...

He stared in admiration at Natasha's body and placed his hands on the outside of her thighs.

... in Sudbury. It took ...

He leaned towards her and delicately steered his tongue between her blonde curls, exhilarated by the taste and scent of her moistness.

... the fire services two hours ...

'Hurry,' she said holding out her arms to entice him onward.

... to bring the blaze under control.

He responded to her urgency, kissing her navel and then circling her engorged nipples with his lips. Natasha arched her legs so he could get closer.

... A police spokesman said that they were treating the ...

With his arms astride her shoulders, he moved his mouth towards hers. She drew him towards her, placing her hands behind his head.

... blaze as suspicious ...

Their lips touched and their tongues began to explore each other's mouths.

... The premises owned by ...

Independently they manoeuvred their bodies to achieve penetration.

... Travis Security were completely destroyed ...

He leapt up and stared in disbelief at the television as he saw the tail end of pictures depicting a fire-gutted building.

...and an adjoining building suffered fire damage. The company is seeking emergency accommodation to carry on its business. Now the local weather forecast for tomorrow ...

'Did you see that? Poor Don, what a thing to happen. I hope he's OK. They didn't mention that anybody was injured. The police believe that it was suspicious. Do you think Oles was involved?' he said in a rush; all thoughts of intercourse gone, evident from his waning penis.

He looked at Natasha and her face showed a cross between anger and disbelief, clearly speechless to reply. He turned away embarrassed by her stare and began to search in his travel bag for his organizer to get Don's home telephone number. It was late, but he had to call to find out what had happened. He turned the television off then dialled the number and waited patiently; eventually a sleepy Don answered.

'I am sorry to wake you, Don. I've just seen the news on TV.'

'Carl. I've been trying to ring you today between all the other calls I've had to make. I was wondering about that project on Friday,' Don said.

He was puzzled by his reply. Then it clicked. 'I'm assuming Wendy's nearby and you can't speak openly?'

'That's correct.'

'You think the fire was something to do with Oles?'

'I think that's quite feasible.'

'Have you said anything to the police?'

'No I haven't. I wanted to consult with you first. How have your investigations been going?'

'There have been quite a few developments. I think Oles is trying to find me. I'm hiding out in Cambridge at the moment. I'm visiting an old friend of Sarah's tomorrow. I'll call you after that so that we can arrange to meet. Is there anything I can do to help?'

'No. Most things are in hand, though tomorrow is going to be hectic. I'll hear from you then.'

He hung up the phone, and thought that perhaps it was fortunate that he had decided to stay away for a few days. Oles had struck at Don maybe he was next. Casting away the thoughts of Don and Oles, his nakedness reminded him of his present situation and he turned to Natasha to apologize for his behaviour. She was lying on her side with her back towards him. He walked around the bed to face her and she appeared to be asleep. Feigning or not, it was not the time to make excuses. Instead he leant down, kissed her gently on the forehead, and whispered, 'I might be falling in love with you, Natasha Minski. Sweet dreams.' She didn't stir.

Chapter 25

Sunday, March 14, 1999 – 7:00 a.m.

Natasha heard a short buzz as the electronic key triggered the door. Then a slight rattle as the door handle was turned. A shaft of light shone from the corridor outside the room and remained, as though the door had been wedged open. It was still relatively gloomy in the hotel room but sufficiently lit for the person that had just entered.

The first tinge of petrol smell was stimulating then the odour became suffocating as Natasha tried to take gulps of fresh air. The tall, dark shape was moving so quickly and quietly through the room, that she could not focus on it long enough to discern its form. She tried to move but her body seemed to be numb from the neck down. She could still tilt her head and moved it to the right seeing Carl asleep in the other bed. The dark shape was pouring petrol from a can over his bed but Carl was not stirring. She tried to call out and while her brain confirmed she was mouthing the words, her ears detected nothing.

Then the shape came towards her bed. As it came closer it took the form of a tall, well built man, dressed in a dark suit. He began to spill petrol over her bed, but the stream seemed endless, far greater than it should have been from such a small can. Her legs were still paralysed but she could feel the stinging of the petrol as it seeped through the bedclothes.

The man began to laugh; a soft snigger at first then it soared louder and louder until it was hurting her ears. Now he leaned towards her. The outline of his face was still unclear until he reached into a pocket and withdrew a cigarette lighter. His thumb played deftly over the knurled ignition wheel and then with downward pressure and a spark, a flame appeared. The flickering light illuminated his face. Natasha first noticed that his left cheek was covered in blood, which was oozing from a gash above his left ear. Then as her eyes adjusted she recognized the face. A face she knew, except the eyes were wide and menacing, and the mouth was distorted with the ongoing laughter – it was Oles.

He lowered the lighter towards the petrol soaked bed. She desperately tried to move her arms and legs. She tried to scream but the fumes were conspiring to make her want to vomit instead. Oles shook his head to indicate she was wasting her time. He stopped laughing and as he dropped the lighter he growled '*Do widzenia, Natasha*'

As the flames engulfed her, Natasha tried once more to scream.

'Natasha, Natasha, calm down. You've been dreaming'. Carl was cradling Natasha's head in his arms after she had sat bolt upright in her bed screaming. She was now sobbing and shaking. There were beads of perspiration on her forehead. He stroked her hair and held her tight to give reassurance.

'Oh Carl. It was Oles. He'd set fire to us in this room. It was … so real.' she looked up at him, wide-eyed. Her face still showed the fear she had experienced in the nightmare.

'Hey, I want you forget about Oles. Forget about the fire at Don's. We'll have breakfast then I'll take you on the tour of Cambridge that I promised.'

He did not admit it to Natasha, but their quick tour of the city was a nostalgia trip of the places he had frequented with Sarah. From the city centre, their favourite walk had been along the River Cam meandering in and out of the grounds and cloisters of Queens', King's, Trinity and St. John's colleges. As they walked holding hands he imagined again that it was Sarah with him instead of Natasha, remembering conversations of the happy times spent together. When they reached Magdalene Street, he headed for a pub on the edge of Jesus Green for a coffee break, but the diversion was planned as a means of passing the house in St. John's road where Sarah had lived. It was the place where they had passed most time as a couple.

They chatted idly about aspects of their pasts, carefully avoiding any references to, and implications of, the disaster that had befallen Don last night, and what the news of the event had controversially interrupted.

Back at the hotel by midday, they collected the car and drove straight to Kate's using the directions Carl had been given. Kate's house was semi-detached in a neat but otherwise ordinary estate road in the village of Isleham, north of Newmarket. An old Ford Fiesta was occupying the small front drive so they parked in the road outside. They were ten minutes late. A small girl in bright green dungarees and white blouse answered the front door.

'Hello. You must be Carl and Natasha. My name is Rebecca. Mummy's expecting you,' she said formally, sounding at least ten years older than she probably was. A small boy of about the same age came running down the passage complaining that it was his turn to answer the door. He broke into a walk as he neared the front door. 'Hello. I'm William. Please come in.

Mummy's busy in the kitchen'. William took charge and led Carl and Natasha into the front room lounge. Moments later, Kate appeared at the door.

He recognized her immediately. The striking reddish-brown hair was her strongest and most memorable feature. She was below average height, but having borne two children she was still slim, although bustier than he remembered. She wore blue jeans and a plain white T-shirt, covered with a kitchen-stained apron.

'Hello. You found us all right then. I see you've met Bill and Beccy,' Kate said.

It was a friendly greeting, better than he had expected, perhaps because the children were present. He was wondering whether he ought to peck Kate on the cheek, but she extended her hand formally and he shook it. 'Hello, Carl, long time, no see.'

He introduced Natasha as a friend; then Kate and Natasha smiled, nodded and said hello to each other.

'Will you excuse me, I'm a bit behind schedule with lunch. The children will look after you,' Kate said and immediately disappeared back to the kitchen.

Rebecca now took over as hostess and took the orders for drinks. On offer was sherry, orange juice or lemonade. Carl and Natasha both selected sherry and Rebecca sent William to the kitchen to satisfy the requests. He returned walking very slowly and steadily carrying two glasses, desperate not to spill any of the contents.

He was unfamiliar how to mix socially with children, but the problem did not arise because they instantly formed a bond with Natasha. Initially they sat at her feet innocently asking personal questions about what she did, if she was married, what kind of car she had, and Natasha answered them as diplomatically as she could. They were impressed that she knew about computers so steered her towards a PC resting on a small table in the corner. All three quickly became engrossed in a falling numbers mental arithmetic game. He felt shut out and went to find Kate.

Kate was busy mixing a salad concoction in a huge bowl. 'You have two wonderful children,' he said. 'How old are they?'

'William is eight and Rebecca is seven,' she said, stirring the salad vigorously with her right hand and adding dressing with her left.

'Your husband?' he asked awkwardly.

'Long gone. We don't need him,' she said nonchalantly.

He was unsure whether Kate was being stiff with him or just preoccupied with preparing lunch. 'Can I help with something?' he said expecting her independence to be compromised.

'There's a huge dish of pasta in the oven. Could you take it out and serve it on the plates for me.' She indicated three large and two smaller plates ready on a worktop. 'Use these oven gloves, the dish will be heavy and hot.'

He did as he was instructed and said, 'I'm glad you responded to the e-mail so quickly. There are so many things I need to ask you.'

'It was lucky really. I don't use the computer much, but I needed to check whether there was a message from my sister in Australia. Could you pop the plates back in the oven for me to keep warm? I'll be a few minutes yet.'

Kate had finished mixing the salad and he helped her take sauces, condiments and bread into the dining room.

'I think we're ready now. Bill. Beccy. Lunch is ready,' she shouted along the passage to the front room.

All that could be heard in response were squeals of excitement. He joined Kate to see what was happening. Natasha, William and Rebecca were huddled around the computer screen each awkwardly taking turns to press keys on the keyboard. The noise of the game and the boisterous laughter had made them oblivious to the summoning for lunch.

'Come on you lot, it'll get cold,' Kate shouted.

Adult conversation during lunch was at a premium, the excited children taking the lead to display their junior conversational skills to the guests. When they had finished eating, Kate rose and started to clear dishes from the table. Without offering, Carl joined in the exercise. Led by his example, Natasha was about to do the same when the children, no longer distracted by food, began to yell about going to the park. Kate explained that it was a Sunday afternoon ritual to take them to the children's playground in the village and she urged William and Rebecca to wait until later.

'I'd be happy to take them. If that's OK,' Natasha offered. 'It will give you two a chance to catch up on old times.'

Kate looked at Carl as if he could attest to Natasha's child-minding abilities, but her uncertainty was dismissed when the children bounced and voiced their consent.

After giving Natasha directions to the playground and advice on aspects of her children's behaviour, she packed the threesome on their way. In the kitchen Carl had finished the washing and wiping up and was trying to decide where the crockery should be stored.

'Where did you find *her*?' Kate asked.

He could not determine from her question whether it registered approval or disapproval.

'I *found* her just three days ago. She's one of the reasons I'm here. It's a long story, which is best not elaborated on now.'

'Well she's a real charmer and wonderful with kids. And you're not an item?'

'No. I said we only met … on Thursday,' he said with some guilt and uncertainty.

'That may be, but she's soft on you. I can tell the way she looks at you. Oops, I didn't think to ask. Are you married?'

'I was once, for a short while, many years ago.'

'Your fault I presume?' Kate said. It was not, but it was easier for him to nod an affirmative.

'It usually is – the man I mean. Coffee?'

They went to sit out on the rear lawn on white chairs around a white table. Kate refused to call it a garden since it was just grass. 'Plants need looking after and are not child-proof,' she philosophized.

'What have you been doing since 1988 then?' she asked, getting on to the reason for his visit.

He covered ten years in as many minutes, the last five devoted to his recent visit to Marion Zurek.

When he had finished Kate said, 'You really didn't know she was dead? My God, that must have been a shock.'

'The biggest shock was that everyone thinks it's my fault. I'm here to clear my name. You seemed to turn against me just after we met at the hospital when Sarah was first admitted. What happened?'

Kate looked up to the sky as if to gain inspiration.

'When you dropped me off at the student house I went into Sarah's room and reminded myself of the mess it was in. Books and papers were strewn everywhere and several ornaments had been smashed into tiny pieces. I couldn't leave it like that, Sarah was my best friend and I felt protective towards her. I decided to do the best I could to restore the room to its former state.

'Sarah was not a particularly tidy person, but I was, so it took time to get everything into logical order. I picked up a short letter, which had been signed by an Eliza Zurek. Initially that was a surprise to me, since Sarah had often mentioned her family, but never someone called Eliza.

'To be able to categorise this letter into one of the many neat piles I had created - rather than to be nosy, I scanned the first part of the letter. It was from her stepmother expressing regret about the death of her father. That explained a lot. She had been upset and touchy for a few days since she received a phone call. I guessed it had been a call saying her father had died.'

Kate paused to drink some coffee then continued.

'I carried on my tidying then I found the anonymous letter on the bed. I read that too and was shocked and disgusted by its explicit content. It referred to some photographs and these were in pieces on the floor. I reassembled the pieces and made two photographs. I immediately realized what had initiated the breakdown.

'From that point onwards I hated you more than anyone in the world. After Sarah's love and devotion to you I couldn't comprehend how someone could be so cruel. It affected everyone in the house. For weeks we conducted an *all men are bastards* campaign. We even stuck up a picture of you in the kitchen and regularly verbally and physically abused it. When Sarah committed suicide we ceremonially burnt your photograph.'

He was finding it ever more difficult to look Kate in the eye and was fidgeting in his chair. With the mention of the suicide he prayed that the ground would open and swallow him.

'I don't think any of us ever got over that episode. It was a year before I dated another guy. Even then I made sure I never became emotionally involved.

'Then two years later, after I got my post-graduate degree, I fell for one of the senior lecturers. We married in 1990. He fucked off to live with one of his students twenty-two months later, just after Rebecca was born. Oddly, his name was Carl too. I should have known better.' Kate was speaking with venom and bitterness in her voice.

'I am blessed with two wonderful children though. It's such a shame that we have to involve a man in the reproduction process.'

'How do you manage? Financially, I mean,' he asked.

'I stung the bastard for everything he had. This house is paid for and I get regular blood money for his sins. And I have a teaching job at my children's school. We get by.'

'Are you still in contact with your old housemates? Caroline, Kyoko and …'

'…Vanessa,' prompted Kate. 'Caroline's running an environmental research mission in Africa. Kyoko went back to Japan and is working for Hitachi. They've never married. Vanessa is living happily ever after in Manchester, she's just had her second daughter.'

'I'm feeling very queasy. Did you poison my lunch? I wouldn't blame you if you had,' he said trying to inject some humour into her verbal tirade.

Kate did not laugh.

He was becoming weighed down with the direction of the conversation and wanted to get to the crucial point he had come to resolve. 'Can you remember the details of the photographs,' he asked.

'There were two. The first looked like it may have been taken in a club or disco perhaps. The background was dark but you could just make out pinpoints of light and moving bodies. In the foreground was a head and shoulders shot of you. A girl was passionately kissing you. She had her hands clasped around your face,' Kate said.

'She was kissing me rather than I was kissing her?' he asked.

'There's a difference?'

'Subtly, yes. Did it look as though I had initiated the kiss?'

'I recall there was a shocked look on your face, if that answers your question.'

'And did the photo look genuine. Not doctored in any way?'

'I couldn't say. It looked genuine enough to me.'

'Describe the girl.'

'You couldn't see her face. It was turned away from the camera. She had the same colour hair as me, but in tight curls,' Kate said. 'You couldn't see her clothes either ...' she added, anticipating his next question, '... though I remember she wore a thin black watch on her left wrist.'

Carl had a sudden adrenaline rush as though he had just avoided a car accident. He desperately wanted to kick or break something.

Kate was shocked by the evil look that appeared on his face. 'Are you OK?' she said. 'You suddenly went pale.'

Ignoring the concern he asked, 'How can you recall such detail?'

'The whole Sarah saga was one of the most worrisome in my life. Remember, I had laboriously reconstructed the photographs, and they became the centre of attention with the police for a while after she disappeared - until they accepted the suicide verdict.'

'And the second photograph?'

'*That* was the damning one. It was taken in a bedroom. You were lying naked on the bed. Crouched on all fours over you was the same girl. It was the hair that gave it away. Again you couldn't see her face. She was wearing just a black bra and panties,' Kate said slightly embarrassed.

'Could you say for sure that it was a bedroom? Or could it have been a hotel room?'

'It was impossible to tell from the angle of the photograph. You know this is very eerie, you're acting as though you know nothing about them,' Kate said accusingly.

'I know it sounds incredible, but it's true. Although from what you've described I can imagine where the first photograph was taken. I'm puzzled by the second. What was I doing on the bed? Enjoying it? Erect?'

Kate blushed. 'Not a lot. You looked asleep.'

'Drunk and passed out more like,' he said.

'And you know who the girl was?'

'I'm pretty sure it was my ex-wife, Janice'

229

'I don't understand. You were married *before* you met Sarah?'

'No, of course not. I met Janice at Oxitel. She knew I was spoken for but chased me anyway. We met up again a few years later. She wore me down eventually and proposed to me. I was still trying to get over Sarah at the time. I thought marriage might be the social tonic I needed. Sounds crazy I know. Suffice to say it never worked out. It was over in three months.'

'How did Janice know Sarah's address?'

'That's easy. Janice used to run errands for the staff when she went out at lunchtimes, including posting personal letters.'

'So Janice set you up?'

'If the repercussions were correct, I'd say it was a lot worse than that.'

'And the source of the photos?'

'There's only one possible source I can think of - my only Christmas party at Oxitel. They hired a function room at a local hotel and brought in a disco. I certainly got very drunk there and I don't remember how I got home. The first photo could have been one of many taken at the party. The second one must have been engineered. You don't get a photo like that taken by chance at a party. Do you recall anything about the accompanying letter?'

'Not especially, other than it was crude, defamatory, threatening and anonymous.'

'Oh. It didn't say anything interesting then,' he joked. 'Anything about the handwriting, type of paper or a postmark on the envelope?'

'I can't remember now.'

'When Sarah released herself from the hospital, how did she seem to you?'

'Edgy, withdrawn, not the old Sarah at all. We all rallied round her, but she just tried to bury herself in studies. Her father's death and your infidelity ...'

'Assumed infidelity,' he corrected.

'OK, assumed infidelity ... had crushed her. For a while she would only entertain her mother and sister's regular visits, then she turned against them.'

'What caused that?'

'I don't know. She had a kind of relapse. She stopped her studies and told me that she couldn't be bothered anymore. She had discovered from Marion that you had gone abroad and she had got it into her head that Marion and her mother were trying to take the seemingly large inheritance from her father. The only odd thing I recall is she said she had a visit from Marion's husband just before she disappeared.'

'A visit from Alex? Strange, Marion never mentioned that. What happened on the day she went missing?'

'All of us had lectures that morning. We assumed Sarah was still in bed. Kyoko was the first back that day and noticed that Sarah wasn't there. It wasn't until about nine o'clock that night that we started to worry. I went into Sarah's room. There was a large bloodstain on her pillow with the note resting on top of it.'

'Blood? Marion never mentioned the blood either.'

'The police took samples and it was the same blood group as Sarah's. There were also some blood soaked cotton swabs in the bathroom waste bin. They couldn't draw any conclusions from it. There was no blood anywhere else in the room or near the house.'

'Can you remember the *exact* words on the note?'

'Oh yes, vividly. *My life is over. I'll start again at the Nearest FarAway Place.* The last three words were capitalized.'

'Marion thought it said, *I'm going to the Nearest FarAway Place.*'

'No. It was definitely *I'll start again.*'

'Didn't that strike you as a strange thing to say?'

'I'm sorry Carl, but Sarah said some pretty strange things before she disappeared.'

'What made you think it was a suicide note?'

'We didn't at first. We were just worried that she'd gone out and not come back. She hadn't been out for days. We left it until midnight and then phoned the police. They said she would turn up and couldn't be classified as missing until she'd been gone for at least twenty-four hours. She didn't come back that night so I phoned her mother the following morning. That afternoon her mother arrived and she pestered the police until they came in the evening to take statements. The police weren't particularly tactful. When they heard what Sarah had been through and saw the note they immediately concluded she had killed herself. It was quite common apparently for suicides to leave obscure parting notes. The longer she was missing the more positive they became and when your letters were discovered by the river a few months later, they as good as closed the case.'

He then explained his own theory about *The Nearest FarAway Place* and what he had done the previous day.

'Oh Carl, if only your theory had been right and you had found Sarah – wouldn't that have been wonderful? And to think I've hated you all these years for something that never happened.'

'I think you ought to get in touch with Marion again and start a Carl Denham fan club,' he quipped.

'Maybe I will. I'll certainly get in touch with Caroline, Kyoko and Vanessa and tell them about your visit. Now tell me about Natasha's involvement in all this.'

He was afraid that this moment would arrive. He now thought it unwise to tell Kate the truth about Natasha and was forming a response when Natasha and the children appeared in the garden via the walkway beside the house.

'Hi kids. Have you had fun?' Kate asked.

'Oh yes,' William said. 'We played in a football match against some other children and I scored a goal. And Natasha is a brilliant goalkeeper.'

'And I scored a goal too,' Rebecca added quickly, not wanting to be left out of the role of honour.

Kate noticed that the footballers looked quite hot. 'Anyone thirsty?'

'Me,' shouted the two children.

They returned to the lounge and Kate made tea for the adults and lemonade for the children. While they drank, William gave a detailed commentary of the football match they had played.

When William had finished, Carl looked at Natasha and said, 'I think it's time we were going.'

Natasha looked reluctant and the children spoke their disappointments.

'It really has been good to see you Carl,' Kate said. 'And to meet you Natasha. You're both welcome back here anytime.'

They stood and headed for the front door, the children and Natasha leading the way. Carl held back to speak to Kate.

'You know I said earlier that I'd made quite a lot of money from selling my business. Well, I'd like to give …'

'I won't accept charity Carl,' Kate interrupted.

'I knew you wouldn't and that's not what I'm offering. I'd like to help your school. If you and the school can produce such exemplary children as William and Rebecca, I'd find that a worthy cause.'

'On one condition.'

'Which is?'

'You don't do anything stupid - as far as your ex-wife is concerned. I have a very uncomfortable feeling about your reaction to the photographs. Forget the past Carl. I think you might have a bright future - with Natasha.'

'I hear what you say,' he said avoiding a direct answer.

Kate looked at him, wishing he would say something more positive. Instead he put his arms around her in a hug, and she hugged him back. He kissed her on the forehead and said, 'Take care, see you sometime.'

Looking over his shoulder through the open front door she whispered back, 'You'd better be off Carl, Natasha is giving us a funny look.'

As they left in the car waving their good-byes Natasha said, 'Well, that was a turnaround. Arrive to a handshake, leave with a cuddle.'

'I do believe you're jealous,' he said.

'You've never cuddled me like that,' she said forcing a petulant look.

He laughed, pulled to the side of the road and stopped the car.

'What are you doing?'

He stepped out of the car and walked round to the passenger side and opened Natasha's door. 'OK, get out,' he said casually, struggling to keep a straight face. Down the road he could still see Kate and the children standing on the pavement.

Natasha nervously got out of the car and stood in front of him. He put his arms around her, drew her close, squeezing her gently and pressing his cheek against hers.

'You can't do this here, we're in a public place,' she said, feigning a complaint.

'How about this then?' He moved his head and kissed her mouth softly on one side and with teasing, delicate movements and kisses, gradually moved to the other side. Finally, he kissed her full on the lips, slowly caressing her teeth with his tongue. Natasha responded and held on tight. They clung to each for ten seconds then broke away when they heard clapping. Two houses away an elderly couple had interrupted their gardening and were applauding enthusiastically. Further along Kate, William and Rebecca were doing the same.

'You're crazy, do you know that?' Natasha said.

'Crazy, yes. But I can't abide jealous women,' he said. 'Come on, or shall we do an encore?'

They cut across country heading for the M11 and Carl relayed the information he had obtained from Kate about the photographs.

'Have you ever wanted to kill someone so badly, that the consequences of your action are immaterial? That's how I feel about Janice right now,' he said.

'You can't be serious. Sure, it was a despicable thing to do, but you have no right to take the law into your own hands.'

'I'm afraid law has nothing to do with it. Legally, I don't think Janice did anything wrong. Morally she has to face retribution. I'm taking a different way back to pay her a visit.'

'What are you going to do?'

'I don't know, but I'll think of something - fatal.'

'My God, you really are crazy. Stop the car now and let me out. I'm not having anything to do with this.'

He just stared ahead. He was about to join the M11.

'It's all in the past, Carl. You can't change anything now. You have a future. I want to be your future. Please don't do this,' Natasha pleaded.

Now on the motorway he increased his speed. He was in a hurry to get to Ongar.

'Carl, talk to me. I'm frightened. I'm in love with you. You ruined Sarah's life, don't ruin mine too.' Natasha was screaming.

'I never ruined Sarah's life. Janice did.' He looked in the rear view mirror and then at his speedometer. 'Oh, Shit. The police are behind us.'

Natasha looked over her shoulder and saw the blue flashing light of the following police car. He slowed and moved to the inside lane, praying that they were in pursuit of someone else, but they drew alongside and motioned him to pull over.

He stopped on the hard shoulder and the police car pulled in behind.

'Don't say anything unless you are asked,' he advised as he wound down the window.

'Good Afternoon, Sir. I am Sergeant Frewer. Is this your vehicle?'

'No, Sergeant, it's a loan vehicle from a dealership. My car is in for repair.'

'Can I see your driving licence please?'

Carl leaned across to his jacket on the back seat and pulled his licence from the inside pocket. He handed it to the Sergeant.

'Carl Denham, that's you is it?'

'Yes, Sergeant.'

Sergeant Frewer looked across to Natasha. 'And your name Miss?'

'Natas … Sarah Zurek,' Natasha stumbled.

'Natasarah Zurek?'

'No, Sarah Zurek.'

'Have you any ID?'

'Just my security pass for work.'

'May I see it?'

Natasha nervously searched inside her handbag, found the pass and showed it to the Sergeant.

'Thank you, Miss,' he said.

'Where are you headed Mr. Denham?' asked the Sergeant.

The truth was Ongar, thought Carl, but that might beg further questions he did not want to answer just now. 'On my way home to Chelmsford,' he said.

'Wait here a moment, Sir,' said the Sergeant and he walked back towards the passenger side of the police car. He leaned in and extracted the handset of a radio and began talking.

'What's this about?' Natasha said. 'Do you think the car's bugged?' referring to the conversation before they were stopped.

'No. Don't be silly. I was just a bit over the speed limit. They're probably going to book me. I expect they're checking my story about ownership of the car.'

'Why did they want to know who I was? God, I hope they are not checking my credentials. That's the last thing I need.'

'Don't worry we'll be on our way soon.'

'To Chelmsford. Not Ongar?' asked Natasha, but before Carl could answer Sergeant was leaning through the window again.

'You need to report immediately to Chelmsford Police Station. Ask for a Detective Inspector Bryant.'

'Look officer, I'm sure I couldn't have been doing more than eighty miles per hour. Is there any need for that.'

'Are you admitting to me that you were speeding, Sir? That's not the reason I stopped you.'

'Oh, well no. Then why do I need to go to the Police Station?'

'You're wanted for questioning in connection with an incident in Chelmsford this morning.'

'An incident? What sort of incident?'

'Something to do with your car exploding under suspicious circumstances. I don't have any further details,' said the Sergeant with an edge to his voice which implied to Carl the Sergeant knew more than he wanted to admit.

Carl swallowed hard.

'Oh God, no,' Natasha shrieked.

'I'm going to Chelmsford myself, I'll escort you, Sir.'

'That won't be necessary Sergeant, I know where the Police Station is,' Carl said, thinking he'd like to make a detour before he got to Chelmsford.

'I think it's best, Sir. For the safety of both of you,' said the Sergeant, his manner indicating there was not a choice. 'You lead the way. Exit at junction 8. A120 to Great Dunmow, then the A130 to Chelmsford.'

Carl pulled back onto the motorway and kept to a steady seventy miles per hour. The police car kept station behind.

'Are you thinking what I'm thinking?' he said.

'Oles?'

'Who else? I'm not aware I have any other enemies, unless you include Janice. Though I have reason enough to kill her, I don't think she would resort to blowing up or bombing my car. However, Oles found out very quickly where I live, but how did he know my car? I bet this was Janice again. She said she didn't give Oles my new address, I reckon she did together with a description of my car. Christ I'm going to get even with her,' he said, gripping the steering wheel so tight his knuckles were turning white.

'Do you think there's any connection with Don's place burning down yesterday?' Natasha asked.

'It is a bit of a coincidence. But I still can't fathom why Oles is so desperate to get rid of Don and me. We are missing something somewhere. There has to be some correlation with Sarah. The biggest problem I have now is what to tell the police.

'Do I act dumb and deny any knowledge of why my car could have been blown up and let them conclude it was perhaps a case of mistaken identity? I doubt whether they'd buy that. They'll want to know where I've been over the last few days and why. That would bring you into the equation. Plus, we'll then be on our own against Oles.

'If I'm honest about what's been going on, you will be in trouble, but at least we might get some protection while the police find Oles.

'What about the gun?'

'Christ. I had forgotten about that. The police are bound to find it. God knows how we will explain *that*.'

'Do you think the police will want to interview me?' Natasha asked.

'I don't know. It's possible if they think that I had anything to do with the bombing. They would treat you as a possible accomplice.'

They sat in silence for some time, both thinking about what they should do. They had turned off the M11 when Natasha eventually spoke.

'I have a rather leading question. The answer will dictate what I think we ought to do.' She waited for his acknowledgement.

'OK, go ahead.'

'Do we have a future together?'

He thought for a moment. 'I think I understand your reasoning. If we do, then we'll play dumb; if we get away with it we can start a new life together. If we don't, then we may as well tell the police everything we know, which would include declaring you are an illegal immigrant. Is that right?'

'Yes.'

'I'm sorry Natasha I can't give you a firm answer at the moment. But I believe the *act dumb* route is the best option for now. We'll need to get our distortion of the truth in line though,' he said.

So they colluded on their stories until they reached the outskirts of Chelmsford.

Despite the heavy traffic through the town, Sergeant Frewer's police car had always been close behind. Had it been delayed somewhere, Carl had still considered making a small detour to see Janice, but it was hardly going to be a short meeting with her, and he did not want to arouse any more police suspicion. The visit to Janice would have to wait for a while.

They pulled into Chelmsford Police Station at five fifteen and were directed to a visitor's car park nearby. Sergeant Frewer drove to the rear of the building, but hurried back as if he was afraid they might drive away.

'Not a bad journey,' said the Sergeant as all three went through the main entrance. Carl and Natasha were too nervous to reply.

Waiting for them was Inspector Bryant carrying a box file. He was a tall, thin man in a blue suit and wore thick-lens spectacles that seemed to be on the verge of toppling from his nose. Carl guessed he was about fifty years old. He directed him and Natasha down a corridor and stopped outside a door marked "Interview Room 5". He showed Natasha to a seat further along the corridor and said that an officer would be along shortly to offer her a drink. The Inspector led him into the interview room and closed the door.

'Thank you for dropping by Mr. Denham, it's most generous of you,' said the Inspector. As if I had a choice thought Carl. 'Please take a seat'.

They were in a mostly empty room about eight metres by four. The windows were frosted and barred. The table they sat at was at one end of the room with two chairs either side. On the table were a telephone, two used mugs and an overflowing ashtray. They sat down with Inspector Bryant facing the centre of the room. Behind him was some gadgetry, which included a tape recorder.

'I'm the SIO – Senior Investigating Officer, on this matter and have a few preliminary questions to ask you. A most unfortunate incident,' Bryant said, shaking his head and peering over his spectacles.

Carl looked blank. 'I don't know what happened other than some very brief details from Sergeant Frewer.'

There was a knock on the door and a man entered the room. Late twenties, unshaven, longish dark hair, togged in anorak, jeans and heavy shoes; facially he was like a young Bryant. Unemployed son crossed Carl's mind.

'Sorry I'm late, Sir,' he said and Bryant motioned him to sit next to him.

Bryant appeared vexed at the late arrival. 'Detective Sergeant Duckworth,' he said as introduction. He opened the box file and extracted some papers. He pushed his spectacles firmly onto his nose and read out in a formal voice. 'At approximately 09:06 this morning, Nicholas Lester a service mechanic and his driver Graham Weston from the local BMW dealers arrived in a breakdown truck outside Bishop's House in Springfield. They were to collect a red BMW 316 and take it back to the dealership for repair. Mr. Weston stood behind the truck while Mr. Lester, using the key you had deposited at the dealership earlier that morning, opened the door of the car, so that he might release the handbrake to facilitate towing. We believe he must have decided to try the ignition in case the vehicle would start. As he did so there was an explosion inside the car which killed Mr. Lester instantly.'

Carl uttered a moan and felt his stomach churn. His mouth felt like sandpaper.

Bryant looked up, 'Are you feeling unwell Mr. Denham?'

'Could I have something to drink?' Carl said and his wishes were answered instantly when there was a knock on the door and a uniformed woman PC delivered a battered tray laden with three mugs of tea, a sugar bowl and a spoon.

Carl helped himself to the tea and Bryant carried on reading.

'Mr. Weston suffered cuts to his face and arms from flying glass. There were no injuries to third parties. The BMW vehicle was rendered immobile and has been taken away by forensics to be examined. There was no other damage to property except for some slight body damage to the truck.'

Carl was surprised at the insensitive and matter of fact way that he said everything.

'I shall need your fingerprints Mr. Denham for the process of elimination and a list of recent occupants of the vehicle,' Bryant added.

'Yes, of course,' Carl said and reeled off a short list of names from the last month.

'According to our records you do not own the vehicle. It belongs to MicaCom Software.'

Carl explained that he was the keeper of the car and it was about to be transferred to him personally.

'Relate the events that led to the vehicle being immobilized,' Bryant said. The words came across as an order rather than a request.

Carl started with the visit to an old friend in Colchester on Friday afternoon, when his car broke down, and finished with being stopped on the M11. He concentrated on his movements by car leaving out the social details. He was mildly offended that he had to provide contact details for Marion and Kate so that his story could be verified. Throughout Inspector Bryant kept nodding, adjusting his spectacles and making copious jottings on his paper pad. Duckworth just stared vacantly around the room deferring to his superior. Carl could tell Bryant was bursting to ask questions.

'What was the reason for your visit to Marion on Friday? You didn't give me her surname.'

'Do you need this level of detail Inspector? Am I under suspicion?'

'I am merely trying to get a picture of events surrounding the bombing. If somebody wanted to kill you or booby-trap your car, such details might be very relevant.'

'Now that I have a lot of free time on my hands Inspector, I wanted to take the opportunity of visiting friends I haven't seen for years. I was catching up on old times with Marion. She'd married since I last saw her. Actually I didn't think to inquire what her married name was.'

Bryant raised his eyebrows. 'Did you visit the car or notice anyone near your car from Friday night to Saturday morning?'

'I collected some bits on Friday evening for the loan car. I never saw any activity near the car.'

'Can anyone confirm your activities in Bradwell on Saturday?'

'Lots of people I imagine.'

Bryant's pen visibly hovered over the pad ready to take names. Duckworth was making notes too now.

'Well, nobody specifically. Just people I met in the pubs and village.'

'You met a lot of people?'

'I have … an historical interest in the area. I chatted to pub landlords, customers, the village shop owner, and even the rector's wife.'

'Name?'

'I think it was … Ivy Broadstairs.'

'And you caught up on old times with Kate Hammond?'

'Yes, that's right.'

'Your passenger, Sarah Zurek. What's your relationship with her?'

'No relationship. She's just …'

'… an old friend?' completed the Inspector.

'No. A new friend actually.'

'Did she accompany you on all your trips?'

'No, I went alone to Marion's.'

'Think hard Mr. Denham. Is there anyone that bears you a serious grudge?'

Carl knew how to answer, but purposely delayed his response to satisfy the Inspector he was taking his question seriously.

'The only specific person that comes to mind is my ex-wife. She's plagued me since the divorce. As evil as she is, I don't think she would want me dead. I'm too convenient a source of income for her.'

'She's blackmailing you?'

Carl laughed. 'Only in the sense that an ex-wife tries to extort money from an ex-husband.' He gave Bryant her name and address and continued smiling at the thought of her being inconvenienced. 'Also, from a general point of view, I recently came into a lot of money. Not many people know about this, but I suppose there are some that could be jealous.'

'How did you acquire this money?'

'I've just sold my company for a large sum of money.'

'May I enquire how much?'

'About two million pounds.'

Eyebrows raised again, Bryant said, 'There are people that kill for a lot less. Who would benefit from your death?'

'Nobody directly. I haven't made a Will yet.'

'Well I think that covers all the questions I have for now.' Bryant looked at Duckworth as though he was checking he was still awake.

Duckworth responded to the hint. 'There is just one other matter we need to bring to your attention. The area around your flat is sealed off and is being examined for evidence. In addition, we currently have a plain clothed officer outside your flat in case you have an unwelcome visitor. I would advise you to stay away at least for tonight, maybe a few days. The Press is also on the prowl, so it may be best to avoid them too.'

'I was hoping to go there now to make sure everything was OK.'

'That won't be necessary, I've already had it checked over,' Duckworth said.

'You broke into my flat?'

'When we found out the car was yours, we needed to make sure that you and your property were unharmed. We obtained a warrant to search your flat. It was a very simple lock to pick. No damage has been done, though I would advise you generally to improve the security of your flat.'

'Yes, I'll do that.'

Bryant took over. 'I am prepared to offer you some protection Mr. Denham - just to be safe.'

Carl considered the idea. He had not decided yet how to proceed with his own investigation. On balance, at the moment, he was prepared to take the risk and did not want the police shadowing him. 'No thank you, Inspector. I'll be very careful.'

'When you have settled on somewhere to stay could you ring to advise a contact address and phone number?' Bryant said, passing Carl a business card. 'We'll call you when we think it's safe to return to your flat.'

'I can give you my mobile phone number now and if I could use the phone then I may be able to arrange my accommodation for tonight.'

Bryant indicated the phone on the table, 'Dial 9 for an outside line. I'll leave you now. When you've finished, leave the information with Sergeant Duckworth. He'll take you and Ms. Zurek along for fingerprinting. Goodbye Mr. Denham.' With a final adjustment to his spectacles, Bryant gathered together his papers and box file and left the room.

Carl remembered Don Travis's home telephone number from his call last night. As he was dialling the number, Natasha came into the room.

'Is everything OK?' Natasha said.

'Fine. I'll tell you in a minute,' he said.

Don answered the phone. 'Hello, Don, it's Carl. How are things?'

'Bloody awful. I've been chasing around all day, organizing people and staff. I'm getting there but it's hard work,' Don said.

Carl lowered his voice, 'There's been a development at my end and I ... or rather Sarah and I,' looking at Natasha, 'need somewhere to stay for a few nights. I know it might not be the best time but can you help?'

'Yes of course. The house is fairly empty at the moment. I've packed the kids off to the mother-in-law's for a few days. So tell me what's happened.'

'I'm at Chelmsford Police Station at the moment.'

'Police Station! Do I take it you can't talk at the moment?'

'Yes, that's right,' Carl said smiling at the Sergeant.

'OK, but there's one minor problem at this end. The spare bedroom only has a double bed,' Don said.

Carl laughed. 'That may not be a problem anymore.'

Don laughed in return. 'You dirty bugger. That's the best bit of news I've had all day. What time will you be here?'

Carl glanced at his watch. 'It's six now, so about seven o'clock.'

'OK. Dinner at eight o'clock then?'

'Yes, thanks Don. Nothing elaborate though. We had quite a big lunch.'

Carl put the phone down still grinning. 'You probably gathered the gist of that.'

'Yes. What were you laughing at?' Natasha asked.

'Just men's talk,' he said.

Carl and Natasha travelled North via Braintree and Halstead to get to Don's home in Sudbury. He briefed Natasha in detail about his interview with Inspector Bryant.

'I am so relieved that he didn't interview me. I was so nervous, I'm sure I would have let something slip,' Natasha said.

'I doubt that's the end of it though. The police have a murder investigation to clear up, so they are not going to ease off. They will certainly be after us when they find the gun. And unless they get something positive from a forensic examination of the car, I'm their best lead to discovering the bomber. The police or Oles might even be following us.' He did not really believe that, but he checked in his rear view mirror just in case.

He added. 'When they *do* interview us again, you have to be *very* careful about what you say. You can't afford to let anything slip. Inspector Bryant is no dummy.'

As a consequence of his worry, he spent the remainder of the journey schooling Natasha again on what she should say.

For a reasonably wealthy man, Don lived in a modest detached house in the centre of Sudbury. The front garden was split into two, with a concrete drive alongside a front lawn. Don's Audi was parked in the drive. The garden area was a picture of colour and neatness even though it was Spring, and there was a very narrow path set in the lawn in the shape of the Brands Hatch racing circuit – a testimony to Don's hobby of gardening and fanaticism about motor racing. Wendy opened the door after Carl had rung the doorbell, which made a sound of a car revving rather than the usual ding.

'Hello, Carl and this must be Natasha. You found us then. Come in. Put your bags at the bottom of the stairs. Don's still on the phone. Can I get you a drink?' Wendy said all in one breath.

He remembered that about Wendy. She was always busy, in a rush, had lots to say and was a bit bossy. She led them into the lounge and rushed away to fetch two sherries. Don was sitting at a small bureau piled high with paperwork. He was just finishing a phone call.

'That's good timing. I think that was my last call. God, what a day. I didn't think I'd be seeing you so soon. Sit down,' Don said.

Carl and Natasha sat next to each other on the sofa.

'Don't say anything about the business with Oles in front of Wendy,' Don whispered, 'I don't want her worrying. We'll swap stories after dinner.'

'What have you managed to organise about your business?' Carl asked.

'I'm quite proud of myself really. My building was gutted and the insurance company says that it will have to be flattened and re-built. The building next door housed an electrical repair business. That can be reconstructed, but I've joined forces with the guys there to temporarily move into a small industrial unit two roads away. All kinds of people will be arriving early in the morning to connect the phones, electricity and water, and to deliver furniture and essential materials,' Don said.

Wendy delivered the drinks and stood in awe of her husband as he related his story.

'You've done all this yourself? In 24 hours?' Carl queried.

'Good Lord, no,' Don said. 'I masterminded the operation, but some of my key staff and the insurance company have been doing the goffering.'

'What about your stock, company records and staff?'

'My biggest ally has been Nigel Davenport. He's the Company Secretary and looks after the paperwork and computer systems. He had a tape backup of just about everything we needed information-wise. This morning he went to

ComputerStores and bought some PCs and printers and already has a mini computer network with our data running in his garage. He's already produced listings of the stock we had and has passed that to the insurance company to source for us. Then from the employee list, he has managed to get in touch with everyone to tell them what's happened. We've given most of them tomorrow off, but they should be able to install themselves in the temporary office the day after.'

'I am impressed and surprised. I thought you'd be really down about it.'

'I was, when the police woke me up at two o'clock yesterday morning with the news. Seeing my company going up in smoke is the worst thing I've ever experienced. But I've been amazed at the way the people have rallied round to help. It's restored my faith in human nature.'

'Any clues yet on how the fire started?'

'The fire department began its examination this morning. Their best guess so far is that the front window was smashed and then a petrol bomb was thrown in. The police are treating it as arson, they were here just before you arrived, asking if I had any enemies.'

'I know the feeling,' Carl said quietly.

Wendy obviously never heard him and was looking restless. 'I think we've heard enough about the disaster now. I'll show Carl and Natasha to their room. They may want to freshen up before dinner. Follow me.'

Wendy led them upstairs, indicated the bathroom and guided them to the bedroom. 'There are fresh towels on the bed,' she said. 'Fifteen minutes to dinner, don't be late.'

Carl noticed her wry smile – Don must have been stirring again.

Despite Carl's request about the meal, Wendy had gone to some trouble to lay on a lavish roast beef main course with a cream gateau for dessert. Most of dinner conversation was between Carl and Wendy, who was most intrigued in Carl's achievement of selling his business. It was clear that this was not an idle interest, and that sometime soon she would be cajoling Don into attempting to do the same. Natasha contributed when the subject changed to compliments about the meal and how it was prepared and cooked. Don spent most of the time answering the phone dealing with peripheral arrangements for the next day.

With relief that the meal was over, Don hustled Carl into the study and left the women to clear up after dinner. Don shut the door so they could not be overheard.

'Tell me what's been happening at your end,' Don asked eagerly.

Carl told him about the visit to Marion; the day at Bradwell; Cambridge; lunch with Kate; the bombing and police interview.

'I haven't seen the television for two days with everything else going on but Wendy mentioned earlier there had been a car bombing in Chelmsford. So that was your car!' Don said pausing for a moment then continued, 'Are you going to kill him or am I?'

'Oles you mean? We've no evidence that either of our incidents have anything to do with him. However, it is too much of a coincidence to reason otherwise. What did you say to the police - About your enemies?'

'I suppose I was a bit flippant saying that I could have lots of enemies being in the security business, but qualified that there was no one that specifically came to mind. I did think of Oles, but thought that as manic as he appeared, he wouldn't hunt me down to Sudbury just because I brained him with a mobile phone. Anyway, Wendy was around, and I didn't want to panic her. After what you've told me about Oles visiting your ex-wife and the bombing, there can be no other possibility. The thing is, what do we do now?' Don posed.

'Under normal circumstances I'd have no problem in telling the police everything. With Natasha central to the plot I'm fearful of what would happen to her,' Carl replied.

'Have you humped her then?' Don teased.

'You are a crude sod at times,' Carl said. 'The honest answer is, almost. The news of your fire put a dampener on that last night.' Don looked puzzled. 'I'll tell you about it some other time.'

'Being serious. Are you an item now?' Don asked.

'Early days yet. But I don't want to get her into trouble and risk losing her,' Carl confessed.

'You were joking about killing Oles I take it?' Carl asked.

Don did not answer he just smirked.

Carl added, 'After your stance in Portsmouth I thought you didn't want to get involved.'

'That was before the Polish bastard torched my business. You still have the gun I hope,' Don asked.

Carl was about to answer when Wendy opened the door and presented two cups of coffee. 'What are you two scheming about?' she said noticing the guilty looks on their faces.

'Just a little security business I'm hoping to put Don's way, we won't be long,' Carl said as a cover up to their collusion.

'There's no rush. Natasha's telling me some interesting stories,' Wendy said coyly.

Don glanced at Carl suspiciously. Carl just shrugged his shoulders.

When Wendy had closed the door, Carl said, 'Natasha seems to have the knack of getting on with everybody.'

'The gun?' Don said in case Carl had forgotten the question.

'John McEnroe,' Carl said.

'What?'

'I thought that might be one of your euphemisms. *You cannot be serious?*' Carl explained.

'No, that's a new one on me.'

'Anyway, the gun was in my car when it was blown up.'

'Shame. You could have pointed it at Oles while I kicked the shit out of him,' Don said pumping his foot to illustrate how he would do it.

'Only one problem. We don't know where to find him. He could be anywhere.'

'What's his surname?' asked Don.

'Good question. I don't know.'

'Find out from Natasha. If it's as Polish as Zurek, he won't be that difficult to track down.'

'Assuming he hasn't got a false name. Then what?'

'I have a police contact in London who can find an address and telephone number for anyone in the U.K. within minutes. He's an old school mate of ours, Alan Higgins.'

'Alan, a copper?'

'In name only. He's a top systems man at Scotland Yard.'

'That's useful,' Carl said looking thoughtful. 'Could you ask him to look for the name Sarah Zurek too?'

Don looked disapprovingly. 'You still haven't given up have you?'

'I don't suppose I ever will. Not until I have definitive proof that she's dead,' Carl said.

'That will be double the fee.'

'Fee?'

'Alan charges £250 an enquiry.'

'Mercenary bugger.'

'Not really. He anonymously donates his search takings to the police benevolent fund. Right, I'll ring him in the morning.'

'That reminds me. Are you OK for money? Getting your business up and running again must be a cash drain.'

'No problem there. The insurance company has been quite responsive. They've underwritten most of the purchases and have given me a cash float,' Don said.

'Well, if you get stuck, just ask, OK?' Carl offered.

Don nodded.

'Let's get back to the ladies. I'm fascinated about Natasha's stories.'

Natasha and Wendy were in fits of laughter. The stories were from Natasha's experiences at work. Some were support stories from the strange situations that council computer users had got themselves into and others were observations of male behaviour, from a female point-of-view. Carl and Don laughed too at the former, but were rather nonplussed at the latter.

Their attentions turned to the plans for the following day.

'I need to get to a bank and a sex shop in the morning,' Carl announced knowing that Don would have a ribald remark to make.

'He needs some money for a very large blow-up doll,' Don joked.

Natasha and Wendy did not laugh.

'The bank's so that I can pay in my two million pound donation from BinaryByte, and the sex shop is so that I can buy some vaginal lip rings for Jacqui,' Carl said.

'Who's Jacqui?' Don and Natasha said together, Don with a glint in his eye and Natasha with a scowl.

'Jacqui is the receptionist at MicaCom that got me off the hook about disappearing to Portsmouth. She confided in me that she'd had her lips pierced. I thought some rings would be a suitable thank you present,' Carl clarified.

'If there's a sex shop in Sudbury, Don would know about it,' Wendy accused.

Don poked his tongue out in reply.

'You don't need a sex shop for them,' Natasha said, 'any jeweller will have a selection of simple earrings.'

'I also need to sort out the loan car. I'm supposed to take the BMW back in the morning, but I've grown quite attached to it, so I'm going to ask the dealer if I can buy it instead. Once that's all done then Natasha and I are going to help you with your relocation,' Carl said looking at Don.

'Yes, I'm sure there must be some computer work I could help with,' Natasha endorsed.

'There's no need. I think I've got everything sussed,' Don said.

'No. I insist. If I'm left to my freedom I'll probably go to Ongar and murder my ex-wife. Anyway, I might need to be around in case anything develops on the Portsmouth contract,' Carl said.

Wendy looked at Natasha for a possible explanation, but her expression was unknowing.

Don looked at the clock on the wall and stood up. 'I know it's only ten-thirty but I need to be out by six in the morning, so if you'll excuse me I'm going to bed,' he said.

Wendy prepared to join him. 'If you want anything before you go to bed just help yourself in the kitchen.'

'I'm quite tired too,' Natasha said, 'It's been another busy day'. She looked at Carl to gauge his intentions.

'Natasha and I *will* come to your new office when I've finished my errands tomorrow. How do I get there?' Carl asked.

Wendy left the room and Don found a piece of paper and a pen, and sketched a map. 'You can't miss it. It's just five minutes by car,' he said.

Don then kept his voice low. 'Oles's surname?'

Don and Carl fixed their attention on Natasha. 'What do you want that for?' she asked.

'I'll tell you in a minute,' Carl said.

'Gomulka,' Natasha said. Carl got another piece of paper and asked Natasha to write it down.

'I'm sure I've heard that name before,' Carl said.

'Probably because it's the same name as a famous Polish communist politician,' Natasha said.

'Have you any other information about him that might be useful to track him down?' Don asked.

Natasha looked anxiously at Carl and the back to Don. 'No. I only found out he was actually in the country two days ago.'

'What about your contact man, Ivan?' Carl suggested.

'He operates under cover from a shop in East London - Manor Park Bicycles. I have an emergency contact number for him, but that's in my flat in Portsmouth. I think his last name is Gorvan,' Natasha replied.

Don made some notes. 'Thanks. Goodnight. Be good you two,' Don said with a wink to Carl.

'Carl, what are you up to with Don?' Natasha said angrily when Don had left the room.

'Not so loud. Fancy a hot chocolate before we go to bed?' Carl said as a ploy to calm Natasha down before he answered the question.

'I'll make it. Then you'll tell me. Right?' Natasha said. It was an order not a request.

When she returned with the drinks, she sat close to Carl on the sofa.

'Don has a police contact that might be able to find out where Oles lives,' Carl said truthfully.

'And what will you do with that information?' Natasha asked accusingly.

Carl had prepared a deception while she was making the chocolate. 'Then I'm going to anonymously pass the information to Inspector Bryant,' he said.

'Why don't you just give him the information directly?'

'If I do, he'll ask lots of awkward questions, which I don't want to answer for fear of implicating you. This way, he'll get his man. End of story.'

Carl thought about what he had just said. Actually that was not such a bad idea. He didn't relish confronting the mad Oles even with Don's assistance. He'd discuss the idea with Don if he succeeded in locating Oles.

'As long as that's all you'll do, it sounds like a good idea,' Natasha said. She leaned across and kissed him lightly on the lips. 'Now take me to bed. You know what happens after hot chocolate.'

Chapter 26

Monday, March 15, 1999 – 8:00 a.m.

Carl was disorientated when he woke. The early morning erection he had was not unusual but the fact that it was nestling between the cheeks of a firm, smooth bottom was. Furthermore, his right hand was clearly clutching a soft breast. He opened his eyes and blinked them a few times to confirm he was awake. Facing him was golden blonde hair superficially ruffled. He moved slightly to sense his situation. He was on his left side almost in a foetal position; his body synchronized with the woman that he held. He recalled adopting that position when he came to bed and wondered whether he had preserved it all night. It was a position that was familiar from long ago. He knew it was not Sarah that he held - the scent was not right. Nonetheless, he fantasized it was her and managed the pretence for some time by remembering the places they had slept together.

When he came with Natasha to the bedroom last night, they had undressed, not knowing how to react after the *coitus interruptus* of the previous night. He had felt guilty about his earlier lust. As much as his body wanted to make love to Natasha, his mind was still preoccupied with thoughts of, and loyalty to, Sarah. It was a battle that his body had almost won in Cambridge. It was not a good analogy, but he drew comparisons with the business decisions he had had to resolve with Mike. If they could not agree on something *laisser-faire* prevailed - leave well enough alone. Mostly, the philosophy had worked to their advantage. They may have forsaken a few minor opportunities but they averted any major disasters. Until the Oles and Sarah matter was resolved, he had thought it best to adopt a laisser-faire approach and merely seek Natasha's companionship. He was not sure yet whether a committed relationship would be an opportunity or disaster.

His fear of disappointing Natasha had been unwarranted. After undressing, they had slipped into their double bed naked. Natasha had broken the awkward silence.

'I'm happy to wait,' she said. When he did not immediately reply, she added, 'To make love'.

'Natasha, I …' he began uncomfortably, but she interrupted.

'I think I know what's going through your mind, because I feel the same way. There are too many uncertainties now. Every day brings a new twist to this story and you've concluded that you don't want to commit to anything until it's over. Am I right?'

He turned to look at her. 'Not only are you beautiful, intelligent and good company, you're now a mind reader too,' he said.

'I've a lot more good attributes if you'll let me demonstrate them over the years to come. For now, just kiss me - softly, and then cuddle me to sleep,' she said.

He did kiss her, but there was more passion than he or she had intended. She eventually broke away and rolled over on to her left side. He had turned the light out and done the same.

He now raised himself a little to view the clock on the cabinet on Natasha's side of the bed. It was eight o'clock. He had been asleep for eight hours, the longest period he could remember for some time.

When they went downstairs, Wendy was using the phone. She was speaking to her mother to check that her children had been behaving themselves and made a sign to indicate that she would be with them shortly.

As forecast Don had made his early start two hours ago and Wendy had been busy ever since making sandwiches for the Travis Security staff that would be helping with the office relocation. Wendy broke off from the task to insist on preparing a cooked breakfast for Carl and Natasha, but under protest, they compromised instead on something simpler, boiled eggs. Wendy sat with them for a while talking about her children then excused herself to continue her catering assignment.

* * *

Detective Chief Inspector Bryant was sitting at his desk at half past eight, staring at some notes on his pad when Sergeant Duckworth knocked on the door and came into his office. Bryant did not look up.

'You're looking thoughtful Chief,' Duckworth said.

Bryant motioned him to sit down. 'What did you make of Denham yesterday?' he said.

'Seemed OK to me. A bit nervous perhaps. I would be if someone had just blown up my car,' Duckworth replied.

'I have a gut feeling he didn't tell me everything he should have. He answered all my questions, but there was certain sterility in his responses, as though he was afraid I was about to ask something awkward. I've been going through my notes and I'm convinced that there's a clue here somewhere. Let me have your opinion.'

Bryant went through yesterday's interview again.

'All sounds fairly routine stuff to me,' Duckworth said. 'Do you think he's shielding someone?'

'Duckworth, the only class of people that don't associate with crooks are sheepless shepherds,' Bryant quipped.

'That's very good Chief. Did you just think of that?'

'No. Just more words of wisdom from your Crime Minister of Essex.' Bryant smiled. 'So, I want you to do some checking around for me. Denham's activities are the only leads we have, so here's what I want you to do ….'

* * *

With breakfast over, Carl checked with Wendy that he could make some telephone calls and Natasha ventured to the kitchen to help with sandwich making.

He first called Beamers about the loan car and was put through to the pushy salesman named Barry that he had spoken on Saturday. They talked in subdued voices about the horror of the bombing and Barry explained how it had shocked all the staff. He was grateful that he was not asked any questions about his involvement in the incident or that any blame was apportioned to him.

Eventually the conversation got around to the purchase of the loan car and predictably Barry's demeanour changed with commission in the offing. After it had been established that the vehicle had no other immediate commitments, the price bargaining was quickly concluded. He promised to call in the next day and complete the purchase arrangements. Barry was keen to set a specific time, so they agreed on ten o'clock.

Next, he felt obliged to update Marion on his abortive trip to Bradwell. He dialled the number he had been given on Friday. She did not answer - a male voice spoke.

'Hello, that must be Alex. This is Carl Denham. Is Marion there?'

'Alexander actually. No, she always goes shopping early on Monday mornings. I heard about your visit. What did you find in Bradwell then?' Alexander said.

His voice seemed to be mocking him, but Carl dismissed his suspicion thinking it was perhaps the effect of his slight Polish accent.

'Nothing much,' Carl said.

'Nothing at all, more like,' Alexander retorted.

Carl changed his mind - Alexander *was* ridiculing him. He said, 'Strange that we should be speaking. I wanted to ask you a question anyway.'

'Go ahead. I have nothing to hide,' Alexander said.

This is a strange conversation thought Carl.

'I visited Kate, one of Sarah's University friends on Sunday. She said that you saw Sarah a couple of days before she died. I thought that was a bit odd since Marion never mentioned it.'

Alexander was quiet for a moment, too long for a spontaneous, honest reply.

'Quite a benign meeting. We were conducting some private business.'

'Care to tell me about it?'

'Yes, of course. I have a suggestion. I presume you wanted to update Marion on your trip to Bradwell. Why don't you come over for dinner this evening, and we'll swap stories. Bring a partner, we'll make it a foursome,' Alexander said.

'I can't this evening due to a prior engagement. I could make tomorrow though.'

'Yes, that will be acceptable. Shall we say seven thirty? Who will you be bringing?'

'I'll bring Natasha. She's just a friend.'

'Excellent. See you tomorrow night.'

Carl said goodbye and hung up the phone. It was the first time he had spoken to Alexander and he had taken an immediate dislike to him. Alexander seemed too sure of himself. Still he respected Marion's judgement. It would be interesting to see them behave as a couple. It was pity that Marion was out. He also wanted to warn her that Inspector Bryant might call and ask about him.

Carl thought he ought to ring Kate to tell her the same thing. He should have done it last night because she would probably be at work now and he did not have her work number. He tried nonetheless, but there was no answer. Just as well, he fancied, if Bryant got wind of the fact that he had been trying to influence his alibis, it could compromise him.

Natasha came in from the kitchen. 'Whom have you been phoning?' she asked.

'Well, I've bought the car, so I'll need to pop into Chelmsford tomorrow to pay for it. Then I tried to speak to Marion, but spoke to her husband instead. Alexander has invited us to dinner there tomorrow night.'

'Alexander?'

'Yes. He's sounds a pompous bastard. I called him Alex and he didn't like it. Still, it should be an interesting evening out,' Carl said. 'Are you OK?' he added, puzzled by the alarmed look on Natasha's face.

Natasha composed herself. 'Yes of course. Are you ready to go into town now?'

Sudbury town centre was only a short distance so Carl and Natasha decided to walk, as it was another clear spring morning. In the main street, Carl soon found a branch of the bank that he used and arranged to meet Natasha outside when he had completed his transaction. Natasha went off looking for a jeweller.

In the bank, he asked to speak to the manager to ensure that there was no delay or mistake in processing his banker's draft. The manager at first looked inconvenienced but became subservient when he saw the amount. Under the manager's advice, after the money had been credited to Carl's current account, all but £50,000 was then disbursed to a high interest deposit and various money-market accounts, until he had decided how he would more appropriately invest his fortune.

When he emerged from the bank there was no sign of Natasha so he strolled further down the high street until he came to a wine merchants where he bought two bottles of champagne to toast his wealth that evening. A few minutes later he met up with Natasha who was carrying an enormous bunch of flowers she had bought for Wendy as a gesture of thanks for accommodating them.

On their walk back, Natasha reported the tale of embarrassment she had suffered in the jewellers in explaining the nature of the rings she wished to buy. She had settled on plain gold rings, horseshoe shaped, terminating with two small gold balls one of which was threaded for ease of fastening. They joked crudely about the purchase, and were still laughing when Wendy opened the front door to them.

* * *

Carl and Natasha arrived at Don's new premises at eleven o'clock and there was a hive of activity. It was a small two-storey industrial unit, like a mini warehouse with six purpose built rooms for offices, two up two down. Electricians, telephone engineers and numerous builders were immersed in frantic activity with Don moving from place to place and person to person answering detailed questions about the refurbishment work.

Natasha was immediately put to work in one of the offices, which had become a makeshift computer room. Nigel Davenport had delivered his hastily built network from home and with Natasha they set about piecing everything together with temporary cables.

Carl felt surplus to requirements until a large truck arrived with some replacement stock. Then, except for a short lunch break when Wendy arrived with the huge quantity of sandwiches for the workforce, he worked solidly for the next five hours, unpacking, labelling and storing the new stock.

At half past four that afternoon Don and his key staff members on duty met to review their progress. Except for a delivery of some chairs and desks, all had gone according to plan and though the offices were by no means tidy, they were operational. Nigel and Natasha had the computer system running, so Nigel stayed on to start telephoning the staff to tell them that they could return to work tomorrow at the new premises. Don telephoned Wendy to give her an estimated arrival time for himself, Carl and Natasha for dinner, but the arrangements had to be cancelled when she gave him some news.

Don located Carl to relay the information from Wendy. 'Inspector Bryant called. He urgently wants you and Natasha to call him and then go to Chelmsford Police Station. Apparently there are some matters to resolve about the bombing. He's apparently tried you on your mobile but there was no answer,' Don said.

'I hope that means the police have a lead on Oles; which reminds me have you managed to contact Alan?' Carl asked.

'Yes, but not until about half an hour ago. He said he would do what he could and hoped to call me at home this evening.'

'If the police have drawn a blank, I have an alternative plan regarding Oles if Alan discovers anything, which I'll tell you tonight. I had better call Bryant now.'

Carl dialled Bryant's number and was connected to Sergeant Duckworth. The Sergeant refused to provide the reason for Carl's summoning and could not say how long the meeting might take. Carl committed to being in Chelmsford with Natasha around half past five.

'I think Natasha and I ought to make our own arrangements for dinner tonight rather than try to predict when we might be back. Perhaps we'll bring in a takeaway,' Carl said to Don when he had finished the call.

Sergeant Duckworth met Carl and Natasha when they arrived at the Police Station. Inspector Bryant was still detained on another matter, so Duckworth led them to the corridor outside the interview rooms to sit and wait. He disappeared for a few minutes then returned with mugs of tea before vanishing again.

On the way to the Headquarters Carl and Natasha had gone over the story they had prepared after their visit yesterday. Both sat in silence for a while sipping their tea and mentally rehearsed their responses to any awkward questions they might encounter.

'Do you think they've rung the council?' Natasha whispered.

'I doubt it. They only know you work there from a brief look at your security pass. I'm relying on the fact that they've just been investigating my friends and me,' Carl said, squeezing her hand for reassurance.

Bryant came bounding down the corridor with Duckworth in tow. He carried the same box file from yesterday and was dressed the same, just a bit more crumpled. Carl wondered if he had slept or been home in the last twenty-four hours.

'Ah, Mr. Denham and Ms. Zurek. I am sorry to have kept you waiting. *Crime and tide wait for no man*, as they say,' Bryant said.

Carl was not sure if his misquote was a joke, an excuse or a mistake.

'Let's get started then. I'll see you first Mr. Denham,' Bryant continued and led the way into the interview room.

It was the same room as yesterday. The ashtray was still overflowing and there were now four dirty mugs on the table. Bryant pushed them to one side to make space for his file and the notes that he extracted. Duckworth sat next to Bryant.

'You have some new transport then and very nice too,' Bryant said.

Carl presumed he was referring to his recently purchased loan BMW.

'We interviewed some of the Mr. Lester's work colleagues today. It came up in conversation,' Bryant added by way of explanation.

'You're being very thorough,' Carl said, feeling obliged to say something.

'As a potential murder victim, I'm sure you wouldn't expect anything less from the police force in trying to stop potential being converted to actual,' Bryant responded in a superior way. 'Well Mr. Denham, I think you have some explaining to do. Our investigative teams have discovered some interesting facts.'

Carl was irritated by Bryant's smug expression and that he was looking over the top of his spectacles at him. He guessed what was coming.

'Do you own a gun Mr. Denham?' Bryant asked.

'No, Inspector.'

'Can you explain why a gun was found in your car?'

Carl put on his best attempt at a surprised look, 'I've absolutely no idea.'

'You must be able to do better than that Mr. Denham. It's hardly likely that someone planting a bomb in your car would leave a gun in your glove box,' Bryant speculated.

'If someone has the mentality to put a bomb in a car, who really knows what other stupid things they might do,' Carl argued.

Bryant looked tempted to react to the contradictory response, but seemed to compose himself and continued calmly. 'We have managed to lift some fingerprints from the gun. Remember that we have yours to match, perhaps you might like to reconsider your response?'

Carl pretended to shift nervously in his seat and noticed Bryant's eyes widen. 'I don't own a gun, and never have done except perhaps toy ones when I was a little boy,' he said.

'I'm not looking for smart remarks,' Bryant said, continuing to remain calm. 'This is a very serious matter. On possessing the gun alone I could have you arrested. Just confine yourself to facts that might interest me.'

Carl finished drinking his tea and placed his mug next to the other dirty crockery.

'We've been checking some of the information you provided at our last meeting and have come up with some anomalies,' Bryant said.

'Are you implying I lied to you Inspector?'

'On the contrary, your story was impeccable. It's just that you apparently forgot to mention a few significant facts,' Bryant said, ordering his notes on the table.

'For example. On Friday afternoon, you visited your friend Marion in Colchester. First, you neglected to tell me that her maiden name was Zurek. Second, the majority of your conversation with her concerned your recent discovery that her sister Sarah had committed suicide eleven years ago. Of course, normally such matters would not be relevant to our enquiries except that your current companion also happens to be called Sarah Zurek,' Bryant said. As he mentioned Sarah's name, he leaned across the table towards Carl in an accusing manner.

'There is a very simple explanation, Inspector,' Carl said as innocuously as he could manage. He was about to continue when Bryant stood up holding his notes and began pacing up and down behind the table.

'Another anomaly. On Saturday you spent the day in Bradwell and called upon an Ivy Broadstairs, the rector's wife. Mrs. Broadstairs has stated that you were searching Bradwell looking for, of all people, Sarah Zurek. Now isn't that strange since one of them is dead and the other was with you all the time?' Bryant said, his voice becoming louder and more agitated.

'No Inspector. You see …'

'Not yet Mr. Denham, there's more. Yesterday you visited another old mutual friend of yours and Sarah Zurek's, Kate Hammond. Mrs. Hammond confirms your visit, but I'm puzzled since your companion there had adopted the name of Natasha,' Bryant said, now pacing behind Carl.

Carl looked over his shoulder to view the Inspector. 'That's because …'

Bryant ignored the interruption and bent towards Carl's right ear and said, 'And, almost finally, a most perplexing piece of the puzzle. You are currently staying with a Don Travis in Sudbury, whose business premises were set on fire under suspicious circumstances on Friday night.'

Bryant went back to his chair opposite Carl, sat down and folded his arms. He looked triumphant, as though he had just won the lottery. 'Quite a few things to clarify,' he prompted.

Carl began his prepared answer. 'Eleven years ago, Sarah Zurek was my girlfriend. Something went wrong between us and we separated. I was depressed by what had happened and went to America for a year to forget. When I came back to England, I started my own business. I've just sold that business as I told you yesterday and decided to try to find Sarah again. I found her, or *thought* I'd found her in Portsmouth by searching the Internet. Unfortunately it was just someone with the same name. That's the Sarah outside.

'I then spoke to Marion who told me that *my* Sarah had committed suicide after I had gone away. I visited Marion and Kate to find out the circumstances of her suicide. Mistakenly I read into the wording of the suicide note that Sarah wasn't really dead, but living in Bradwell. Hence the day I spent searching there. When I went to see Kate, I introduced the Portsmouth Sarah as Natasha, simply because I didn't want to complicate matters.

'As for the matter with Don Travis … that must be just a coincidence that we've both suffered some bad luck at the same time.'

'That's quite a remarkable story Mr. Denham. Did it take you long to think up?' Bryant charged.

'Now look Inspector, everything I've told you is the truth. I fail to see what you are trying to achieve by doubting what I've said.'

Sergeant Duckworth contributed for the first time. 'Mr. Denham, I'm sure Inspector Bryant's not doubting you, merely trying to establish if there is anything in your unusual story that might help us in our investigation.'

Carl had seen this type of interviewing on television police dramas. One officer takes a hard approach and the other acts as moderator. So it happens in real life, he thought.

There was a knock on the door and a middle-aged, white-coated woman peered into the room.

'Yes, Joyce,' Duckworth said. She motioned him outside.

Duckworth was outside for a few seconds then rejoined the interview.

Bryant looked inquisitively at Duckworth.

'Denham and Zurek's prints don't match those on the gun,' Duckworth said.

Carl noted Bryant's dumbstruck look. Clearly disappointed that his main accusation against Carl had just been shot down. He wanted to grin at the pun in his mind or say *I told you so*, but thought better of it after Bryant's earlier caution.

'Having only just met the Portsmouth Sarah, why does she now seem to be your companion?' Duckworth continued the interrogation.

'After we had resolved the confusion about mistaken identity we quickly became good friends and she wanted to accompany me in finding out the truth about Sarah,' Carl said now smiling. 'Plus the physical attraction, of course,' he added.

'What was in the suicide note that made you go to Bradwell,' Duckworth asked.

'Sarah had used the words *The Nearest FarAway Place*. It was a sort of nickname we had used for Bradwell. It wasn't just the note though. Her body was never found,' Carl commented.

Duckworth consulted his notes. 'According to Ivy Broadstairs she'd seen Sarah Zurek in Bradwell?'

'*Thought* she'd seen. Unfortunately, I had a few leads that day, which gave me some false hope. I've resigned myself to the fact that she's dead now.' Carl cast an eye to Bryant who seemed to have recovered after the disappointment about the gun and was now looking victorious again.

'Why would introducing the new Sarah as Natasha to Kate Hammond alleviate complicating matters?'

'Kate and Sarah were very close friends at University. I didn't want to upset her by saying I'd found another Sarah Zurek, so randomly I chose the name Natasha,' said Carl, feeling comfortable that he'd foreseen most of the interrogation so far.

Sergeant Duckworth sat back as though he had finished, but Bryant continued the questioning.

'When did you go to Portsmouth to find Sarah Zurek?' he said.

'On Thursday.'

'When did Don Travis join you there?' said Bryant, looking pleased when he recognized Carl's discomfort. 'I have a copy of Mr. Travis's statement to the Sudbury police,' he explained.

Carl was impressed and annoyed at the same time. He supposed that he ought to be thankful that the police could be so thorough in such a serious investigation. Yet he was unnerved that his deception might be uncovered. Maybe this was a trick question. Did Bryant actually know that Don had met him in Portsmouth? Why would Don travel all the way to Portsmouth that evening? It would be too much of a coincidence to be in the same place at the same time. Don's story to Wendy had been that Carl had given him an urgent sales lead. He had probably told the Sudbury police it was a routine business visit. Would Don have mentioned that he had met up with him? He doubted it. He had to think this through a bit more and decided on a stalling answer.

'I think you must already know the answer to that Inspector,' Carl said showing his annoyance more than this admiration.

'Just confirm it for me. Will you?' Bryant said with more than a hint of impatience.

Up to now Carl had been safe. He'd kept to an economical truth. Just answering the questions without elaborating. Once he departed from the facts it would be easy to make a mistake and he would open to an accusation of hampering police enquiries. He feared his first lie was not far away. He had to presume that Don had been truthful in his statement.

'Don joined me on Thursday evening,' he said.

'And why did he do that?' Bryant asked. Carl knew that was a mother of all questions and wanted to shift in his chair, but he knew that his body language would give away his disquiet with the question. Here comes the lie.

'Sarah works at the Portsmouth City Council offices. While I was waiting to see her on Thursday morning I got talking to one of the administrative staff in reception. Somehow we got on to the subject of security, particularly surveillance equipment. I mentioned I had a reputable contact in that line of business, and since they were eager to pursue the matter quickly, I immediately arranged an appointment for Don on Friday morning. He came down on the Thursday evening,' Carl said. He was pleased with his lie. It was a plausible answer, except if Natasha was asked the same question - they hadn't rehearsed any situations that might involve Don.

'Whom did Mr. Travis see on Friday morning?' Bryant pumped.

'I don't know,' said Carl, *but please don't ask him* was a thought he kept to himself.

'Where did you stay in Portsmouth and what did you do with Mr. Travis on Friday evening?' Bryant persisted.

'The Post House hotel. We just had dinner together there,' Carl said. He looked at his watch to demonstrate his frustration with the seemingly endless questioning. If he asks me what I had to eat, I will have to lie again mused Carl. He must have smiled.

'Something amusing Mr. Denham?' Bryant said.

'No. I just recalled a joke from the dinner.' Carl lied for a second time.

'And did you see Mr. Travis on Friday?'

'Only at breakfast.'

'I am convinced there is a Portsmouth connection with your respective disasters. Anything you would like to tell me to confirm my theory?'

'Perhaps we didn't tip the waitress at dinner?' Carl joked and then immediately regretted his flippant reply.

Bryant cheeks visibly puffed up and flushed. He clenched his fists. 'One more remark like that and I'll throw the book at you, Denham,' he said.

Attack is the best form of defence so Carl elected to go for it. 'I'm sorry, Inspector. I've come here voluntarily and I'm now getting rather tired of your theories and innuendoes. If I had any significant information to add to your investigation, I would have freely given it at the outset. Unless there is anything specific to go through I'd like to leave now,' he said.

Bryant laughed. 'Oh, very dramatic Mr. Denham. Your tactics will not work though. You don't know me very well. Such a trumped-up outburst just makes me more determined than ever to expose your concealment. Maybe I will not succeed today, but I *will* succeed. And when I do I shall do my utmost to make sure that your obstruction gets the punishment that it deserves.'

It was Carl's turn to fold his arms across his chest in defiance.

'In fact for now I have only one more line of enquiry. Whatever happened in Portsmouth you stirred somebody up, because your ex-wife has told one of our officers about the visit that she had on Friday afternoon. I suppose you're going to tell me that you've no idea who that visitor might have been,' Bryant said.

'If you want to believe the story of a murderess that's up to you,' Carl said, reminded now of what he learned from Kate.

'Are you suggesting that she killed Nicholas Lester?' Bryant exclaimed.

'No. No. She killed Sarah Zurek out of jealousy,' Carl accused.

Inspector Bryant looked totally bemused and exchanged glances with Sergeant Duckworth.

'I think we had better take this one step at a time. Answer my first question,' Bryant said.

'I've no idea what she's talking about. Why should someone supposedly looking for me call on Janice? I haven't lived at that address for eight years. I think this is probably another example of her on-going campaign at discrediting me,' Carl said.

He hoped that this was an adequate deflection from the subject. Yet the more this deception went on the more Carl really felt like revealing all he knew about Oles. The Inspector was winning in his tactics to wear him down. What would he and Don achieve if they found out the whereabouts of Oles? Maybe it was best to let the police do the hunting. All he had to do was construct a story to implicate Oles without getting Natasha involved.

'Despite what you say Mr. Denham we have circulated the description of Ms. Harding's caller. She is at least providing us with information. Now you are saying she is a murderer. Perhaps you could substantiate your accusation.

Or is this just further evidence of you wasting my time?' Bryant said clearly believing this was another diversionary tactic.

'Inspector, I have a horrible confession to make,' Carl said. He noticed a smile appear on Bryant's face. 'I don't regard myself as a violent man, but yesterday, had Sergeant Frewer not intercepted me on the M11, you might have had another murder investigation to conduct. I was on my way to see Janice after finding out from Kate that Janice was responsible for Sarah's death.' Carl went on to tell the story about the anonymous letter, photographs, and Sarah's subsequent suicide.

'Whilst I sympathise with the unfortunate events about your ex-girlfriend's suicide, I can't see the relevance to the bombing of your car.'

Carl saw his opportunity to point the finger at Janice.

'It gives Janice a motive, doesn't it? Maybe she wanted to stop me finding out about the photographs.'

'I don't think we'll be recruiting you as a detective Mr. Denham. Your argument is flawed in several respects. How did she know you might uncover the source of the photographs?'

'That's easy. There were a few people at MicaCom that knew I would go looking for Sarah. Maybe that information got to Paul Westdene. He is her current boyfriend and was an employee, until I arranged to have him sacked before I left. The bombing could have been a combination of her panic and Paul's revenge.'

Carl had only just thought of that connection. Maybe it had some substance. The way that Bryant was furiously writing indicated it had impressed him too.

'*You* didn't know that Sarah was dead. Did Ms. Harding?'

'Not to my knowledge. Whenever she's mentioned Sarah, it's always been in the present tense rather than past. Anyway, her guilt could have come from causing Sarah and I to separate, instead of influencing the suicide.'

'Why did you sack Mr. Westdene?'

'I didn't sack him personally. I got one of the new bosses to do it. Paul had been leaking the financial details of the sale to Janice. She was using her knowledge to stake a claim on some of my proceeds.'

'Would she have gained financially from your death?'

'I don't know. I believe I mentioned yesterday that I haven't made a Will, so I'm unsure whether she would be entitled to anything as an ex-wife.'

'Did your ex-wife or Mr. Westdene have any connection with Mr. Travis?'

'No. I don't believe they ever met.'

'That would destroy any link between the fire and the bombing,' Bryant said more to himself than Carl.

'As I said earlier, the two events must have been a coincidence.'

'Well, I think that's all, for now, Mr. Denham, but certainly not the end of the matter. I must say I remain sceptical about your stories. Because of the importance of this case, could you ensure you keep us up-to-date of your whereabouts? If you intend even leaving the County, I want to know about it.'

'Of course, Inspector. I intend staying with the Travis' again tonight, which you probably realize is in Suffolk not Essex - but I may move somewhere else tomorrow,' Carl said. He was just being factual but from Bryant's expression his geographical correctitude was taken as another sign of insolence. He knew he had put doubts in Bryant's mind and his own, particularly regarding the bombing. Could Janice have been behind the assassination attempt? After his discovery about the photographs, he conjectured that nothing would be beyond her. His attention now went to Natasha. Would she now have to suffer the pointed enquiries of the two policemen? The question was immediately answered.

'Sergeant, would you show Mr. Denham out and then ask Ms. Zurek to join us?'

Carl thought Natasha looked fatigued. She had been waiting for over half an hour and with nothing to do but stare at a wall, it was no wonder. He did not want to have to suffer the same frustration so he asked Sergeant Duckworth if he could find a magazine or newspaper he could read while he was waiting. His ploy to be alone with Natasha for a few moments to brief her regarding Don did not work, since the Sergeant led Natasha immediately to the interview room before vanishing down the corridor. Inspector Bryant came out of the room and did the same. It was ten minutes later they returned and rejoined Natasha, having left behind a well-thumbed copy of the *Sun* and a *News of the World* colour supplement – not exactly what Carl had in mind as reading material.

In the interview room, Bryant and Duckworth took their usual seats.

'I am sorry you have had to wait so long Ms. Zurek. I will not keep you much longer,' Bryant said. 'You have a very slight accent, where are you originally from?'

This would be the first time that she had to face questions from her past thought Natasha. It had been eight years since Ivan Gorvan had schooled her on what she should say and do in situations like this. Her original interview with Portsmouth council had concentrated on her experience and abilities, not on her background, such were the demands on employers these days to avoid any ethnic, sexual or age bias. The details of her past had been carefully constructed and rehearsed, and would resist any casual attempt at penetration. Carl had helped too, by providing some additional information about the real Zurek family background. The documents she possessed would also serve her well in benign situations. A golden rule from Ivan had been to behave as a model citizen - never get into trouble or conflict, particularly with the police. The coming interview would test how effective that long ago training had been.

'I am a British citizen but my father was originally from Poland. When I was young, he insisted I speak Polish at home. The accent comes from then,' she said.

'You're not related to the original Sarah Zurek?'

'No, I don't believe so.'

'Isn't it rather odd that you have the same name?'

'Not especially. Zurek is quite a common surname in Poland and there have been many Polish families in Britain since the last war.'

'Tell me how Mr. Denham contacted you and what happened afterwards.'

She had discussed this line of questioning with Carl and they had agreed to stick to the real story except for any events regarding Oles or Don, which is exactly what she told Bryant.

'I find it particularly strange that you became ...' Bryant paused while he sought an appropriate word, '... attached, to Mr. Denham so quickly.'

'His arrival happened to coincide with an empty period in my life. Work was hectic and I had not had a holiday for a while. Carl's sad story captivated me. I asked if he wanted a companion to accompany him on his search for the truth – he seemed so lonely. I was surprised and happy when he agreed, because ... I ... well I had fallen in love with him.' Natasha felt her cheeks flush as she admitted her feelings to someone other than Carl.

'Have you perhaps left a jealous boyfriend behind in Portsmouth?'

'No. I've been *unattached* for a while now.'

'From what you've learnt of Mr. Denham in the short time that you've know him, have you become aware of anyone that might want to harm him?'

'No ... well ... actually, yes. I did answer a telephone call from his ex-wife on Friday evening. The way she spoke to me indicated that she hated Carl.'

'And what will you do now Ms. Zurek?'

'I'm going back to Don Travis's home with Carl until you give the all clear on his flat.'

'I was thinking longer term,' Bryant clarified.

'I've two weeks holiday and then I'll be going back to Portsmouth.'

'That's all for now Ms. Zurek. I should caution you that it is a serious offence to withhold information that might be material to this case. Is there anything you can add to help us with our enquiries?'

'No, but if something does arise I'll inform you immediately.'

They all stood and Sergeant Duckworth led Natasha to the door. He thanked Carl and Natasha and hoped that they would not be bothered again, and then escorted them to the exit of the Police Station.

Sergeant Duckworth gave some instructions to the desk Sergeant before returning to the interview room.

'All sorted?' Bryant asked.

'Yes. Arkwright, Jensen and Fordham in Quebec Kilo one, and Prentis, Taylor and Bailey in Quebec Kilo two are on their tail. Two armed crews will catch up with them later and then the deployed QKs will return for their own arms,' Duckworth reported.

'OK,' Bryant said. 'Any comments from the interviews?'

'Nice girl,' Duckworth said.

'If you mean good-looking, I would agree. I reserve judgement on the rest,' Bryant said sceptically.

'She seemed innocent enough. Happy and in love.'

'*In love* is the problem. She's protecting Denham. You know my saying, *You can't judge a crook by her cover,*' Bryant said, practising his neologisms again.

'Denham is a cool character. Too cool do you think?' Duckworth asked.

'They are *both* hiding something, I am certain of that. We should have leaned on the Zurek girl more; I think she is less confident about her position. Next time maybe. The ex-wife link has merit though, if the two incidents are unconnected. We need to pay Janice Harding a visit. Plus there are still several lines of enquiry to pursue. Could you do what Denham did, search the Internet looking for references to Zurek?'

'Yes, Guv.'

'Also contact Cambridge. Check if they have still have anything on file about the Zurek suicide - probably not, as it was a long time ago, but there may be a clue there somewhere. Chase Forensics too. They must have some details about the bomb by now. And prepare a report about our interviews and update the rest of the investigative team.'

'Tonight?'

'Yes of course, tonight. The Super's getting edgy because we haven't uncovered anything yet.'

'Excuse me asking, but what are you going to do?'

'On my way home I am going to take another look around Denham's flat. Tomorrow, we will speak to Janice Harding and call in at MicaCom.'

Don had developed a phobia about the phone ringing and was ruffled when it rang at seven o'clock. 'Hello,' he said with a grumpy voice.

'What sort of welcome is that when I'm about to give you some good news,' said Alan Higgins.

'Alan. I'm sorry. I've had a bad few days. What do you have for me?'

'I have addresses for at least one of the people you asked about. Get your pen. Sarah Zurek, she works for Portsmouth City Council and lives at …'

Don interrupted 'I know where she lives. Was that the only Sarah Zurek you found?'

'Yes. I only located two Zureks. The other one was an Audrey.'

'OK, go on.'

'Not sure about the Gomulka. I found eight Gomulkas, but none of them has a first name of Oles or an initial of O,' Alan said.

'Read out the list anyway. It might help,' Don said.

Alan started to read the names and addresses, and the telephone numbers if he had them. He got to the fifth one when Don asked him to repeat it.

'That's interesting,' Don said.

'Is that the one you wanted?' Alan asked.

'I'm not sure. Maybe,' Don said. He then noted the last three.

'That's £500 you owe the Police Benevolent Fund,' Alan said.

'No problem. I'll have a cheque sent to you in the next few days. It will come from a Carl Denham.'

'Fine, nice doing business with you again.'

Don put the phone down and looked at what he had written down. He circled the fifth name on the list then scratched his beard with the pen. 'Well fuck a duck …' he said to himself, '… no wonder Oles has been a bit trigger-happy.'

* * *

Carl and Natasha drew up outside Don and Wendy's house at half past eight. As Carl was parking, he noticed the curtains in the front room pull to one side and by the time he got to the front door, Don was waiting for him.

'Come into the study, quickly. I've had some disturbing information from Alan,' Don said, grabbing Carl by the arm and pulling him inside. Natasha looked on hoping to be invited but Don specifically avoided her interest. Wendy looked at Natasha hoping for an explanation, but Natasha just shrugged.

Don and Carl went into the study and closed the door. Carl remained standing and looked inquisitively at Don.

'You had better sit down,' Don said, 'I think you've got a big surprise coming.'

Carl sat down, looking expectantly at Don. 'Have you found Sarah … *My* Sarah?'

'No, I'm sorry, but remember what you told me about your visit to Marion on Friday. You didn't mention where she lived. Right?' Don asked.

'I'm not sure. I may have said Colchester,' Carl said, wondering where the conversation was going.

'I think you said more than that. Does she live at Croftview in Lexden?' Don asked.

'Yes, how did you …'

'And is her husband's name Alexander?'

'Well, yes. I spoke to him this morning when I was trying to reach Marion.'

'You spoke to him?'

'He's invited Natasha and me round tomorrow evening. Get to the point Don, I've been answering questions all evening.'

'Marion and Alexander's surname is Gomulka.'

'Good Lord. I must have known that from when they got married. That's why the name rung a bell. It can't be a coincidence surely. Alan obviously didn't find an Oles Gomulka?'

'No. Eight Gomulkas, but no Oles.'

'Bloody Hell, I don't believe it,' Carl exclaimed and stood up abruptly.

'What? Is that too few or too many?' said a bewildered Don as Carl opened the door and dashed into the lounge. Don followed him through the lounge and into the kitchen where Natasha and Wendy were chatting. They were both startled at Carl's sudden appearance.

'Why did you react strangely this morning when I said I had spoken to Alexander?' Carl said angrily to Natasha.

Natasha stared back at him in dismay and cowered as though Carl was about to strike her.

'Steady on Carl. What's wrong?' Don said, standing behind Carl as if he might have to restrain him.

Carl ignored him and stepped closer to Natasha, 'Well?'

'It … It reminded me of Oles,' she stuttered in reply.

'Who's Oles?' Wendy said, but everyone ignored her.

'Why?' Carl shouted.

'His full name is Alexander Ludwik Gomulka. He hated me calling him Alex, just like Marion's husband.'

'Then why on earth have you been referring to him as Oles?'

'Oles is a nickname used by Poles for Alexander,' Natasha said, looking around as though she was expecting someone to acknowledge her statement.

'And we are supposed to know that are we?' Carl was shouting again. 'You've kept that a secret all this time!'

'It wasn't a secret. Why is it so important?' Natasha asked innocently.

'Because Alexander Gomulka *is* Marion's husband!'

Ten minutes later, the four of them were sitting on easy chairs around the coffee table. As her guests had not eaten and as a ploy to calm the tension, Wendy had hastily prepared plates of biscuits, cheese, fruit and a variety of finger treats for them.

Carl, Don and Natasha recounted various parts of their stories from the last few days, to remind themselves of Alex's involvement and to expose their collusion to Wendy. They had agreed to refer to him as Alex to avoid misunderstanding and with the knowledge that he would disapprove if he knew.

During the story telling, Wendy interrupted several times often to admonish Don about his clandestine behaviour. On other occasions, she raised critical points about inconsistencies in the assumptions being made. She quickly assimilated the situation and by the time the full story had unfolded, Wendy had emerged as the unlikely chairperson to guide them into a plan of action.

'I still think we should tell the police,' Wendy said for at least the fourth time. She looked at the gathering for support.

Carl had other possibilities going through his mind. 'It's the obvious solution, but not necessarily the best solution,' he said.

Wendy was undaunted. 'Then let's consider the alternatives and hypothesise the outcomes,' she continued. 'Perhaps we could involve the police, but anonymously. We could suggest that Alex was the bomber and arsonist. It's then up to them to get evidence and prove their case.'

Carl persisted. 'The police won't pursue the matter without a motive.'

'They will have to wring that out of Alex. When they find his fingerprints on the gun they will have to dig deeper,' Wendy said.

Don looked eager to contribute. 'The fingerprints don't prove he bombed Carl's car, just that he had touched the gun. He may well have an alibi.'

Wendy looked at Carl. 'Would Marion conjure an alibi for him?'

'Her character suggests no, but I remember noticing she had some nasty bruises. Maybe Alex is an evil bastard at home too,' Carl answered. 'Anyway, a fingerprint match would lead the police straight back to me for another round of questioning. I could bluff my way through it, but if they start to check on Natasha …'

'I'm willing to risk the consequences if it puts Alex behind bars,' Natasha said.

'Have I missed something?' Wendy asked. 'From your stories I don't remember Natasha having any additional information that would implicate Alex in either the bombing or the arson.'

Natasha gave the answer. 'You're right. By revealing my true identity I could expose the transient operation, maybe Alex's involvement in it, but that's all.'

Wendy summarized. 'So telling the police openly or secretly, won't necessarily get us anywhere. Is that the conclusion?'

The assembly went quiet and but for Carl who used the break to help themselves to the food.

Carl looked at his co-conspirators. 'And what about Sarah?' he demanded.

They paused in mid-munch.

Carl continued. 'I'm sorry, I know this sounds selfish, but my main objective is to uncover the truth about Sarah. I don't believe she committed suicide and I'm sure Alex had something to do with her death. For me, discovering the bomber and arsonist are incidental. Alex told me on the phone that at the dinner party tomorrow night he would tell me why he saw Sarah two days before she died. It could reveal the link I'm looking for.'

'Now that we've made the connection between Oles and Alex, you can't be serious about going through with that. It has to be a trap. I'll wager Marion won't even be there, unless she has been a willing partner for Alex,' Wendy suggested.

'But does he know that we've made the connection?' Carl posed.

Wendy thought for a moment. 'He must do. Don and Natasha have met him, and you've spoken to Marion about him. He must believe that's enough.'

Carl was getting frustrated with the progress of the discussion. He already had a plan in his mind and wanted to clear the objections before he made a proposal.

'Then why did I accept his invitation? The acceptance was in good faith. I didn't know at the time that Oles and Alex were the same person. I concede to the theory about a trap. But *why* set a trap? Not because of the bomb or the fire - we've agreed we don't have enough evidence to pin that on him. The trap must be related to Sarah. He invited me to dinner just after I mentioned his meeting with her before she died.'

'So, you are willing to risk your life to find out the truth about Sarah?' Natasha asked with sadness in her voice.

'Yes, however …' Carl started.

'Shit,' Don said suddenly. 'You called Alex from here didn't you?'

'Yes,' Carl said realizing Don's concern. 'If he has one of those special phones that displays the number of the caller, he could trace it to this address.'

'But we are ex-directory,' Wendy commented.

'Your number will still be transmitted unless you have specifically asked it to be blocked. If Alex has the right contacts or database access it would be easy for him to get an address from a telephone number,' Carl said.

'That could mean he's outside now,' Wendy said nervously.

'That's possible, but I shouldn't worry. The police will be keeping a watch over us,' Carl said.

'Police?' Wendy said.

'Didn't you notice? Two men in a red Ford Sierra followed us all the way here from Chelmsford Police Headquarters. If you don't believe me have a peek through the curtains,' Carl said smugly. 'A tail like that could work to our advantage, particularly if I keep the appointment with Alex tomorrow. I have a plan with an element of risk to it, but it needs everyone's help, particularly and hopefully, Don's electronics wizardry. Wendy, why don't you break out the champagne I bought this morning? Let's celebrate my wealth and I'll tell you what I have in mind.'

Chapter 27

Tuesday, March 16, 1999 – 8:30 a.m.

Carl had planned his morning around visits to MicaCom, the BMW dealer and his flat - if he could get in. Natasha wanted to join him, but he convinced her that they would be mundane activities and it might be more appropriate to repay some of the Travis hospitality by helping Don again with his relocation. Besides, having spent the last four days together, he viewed it was time to seek some space from each other.

Yet, as he drove towards Chelmsford, noting the red Sierra a few cars behind, he began to regret his decision. After being somewhat of a loner for the last ten years, he had become accustomed to and welcomed Natasha's presence at his side. He would feel proud walking into MicaCom with Natasha; it would be a revelation to the long established staff to see him with a woman at his side. Not that they thought he was gay - not to his knowledge anyway; rather that he was a man whose priorities were with *bits and bytes rather than tits and tights* he had heard someone once say. Would they be pleased that their old boss had moved happily on to pastures new? Probably not, he thought. Cynically he viewed that they were now sucking up to their new bosses to further their careers or at least make their current one as cosy as possible. The working relationship he had with the staff was generally business-like and arms-length and, with few exceptions, it had never gone beyond that.

His technical staff were a strange bunch, but that went with the territory of being employed in the dynamic, fast-flowing software industry. The other departments in the company had little contact with them in case they caught something contagious or addictive. Moreover, they were grossly jealous of the enormous salaries they earned and the working freedom they had.

They worked in a large room with a permanently shut door at the remotest end of the building. Whenever customers came to visit and wanted a guided tour, the asylum - as it was known, was strictly out of bounds. Not only was their environment an image problem, but also the vapours of possibly illegal substances would have stoned an average customer. Carl used to spend hours with them talking about software design and wondered whether the new bosses would succeed in getting the best out of them. A sacred rule was to address each of them by their nickname. His favourite was Fault, derived from a contraction of his real name of Sandy Andreas. Two of the original team, Richard Edmunds and Richard Edgeley were known as DickEd1 and DickEd2, to avoid the confusion of first names; the apostate Paul Westdene had been called Knave - from his middle name of Jack, but the literal meaning was more appropriate he thought.

When it came to outside interests there was a social gap that he found too great to span. In spite of being, on average, only five years older than them, he found conversation difficult when it came to giving opinions about the latest designer drugs, obscure rock bands, rave happenings, pizza toppings and acne ointments. Their work rate was exemplary, but their conventionality was zero. Nonetheless, he would miss them.

Naomi Tomson was a true friend, and had been since the early company days. She was always a diplomat, a good sounding board and had often extricated him and Mike from difficult situations. Why was it that angry customers or suppliers always became more moderate and understanding when they were dealing with a sexy-voiced woman?

Jacqui Boniface was a more recent recruit, but despite being a gossip, nosy, scatty and freaky, she was probably the most loyal employee he had come across. Nothing was ever too much trouble, and she was always quick to criticise any other employee, quite openly, if she thought their behaviour was in any way detrimental to the company. Her surname was most fitting thought Carl.

He smiled as he remembered an unwritten company rule he had agreed with Mike. The PPP rule. Don't *Put Penis in the Payroll*. In other words, never get sexually involved with any of the staff. He had not broken the rule, had never wanted to, but had got close when Jacqui arrived. She seemed to follow him everywhere and had gone out of her way to win his attention by flirting shamelessly. She even had the nerve to ask him out once. Had it not been for his obsession with the Sarah past and the recent developments with Natasha, now that he was no longer bound by the PPP rule, he might have asked Jacqui if the offer was still open. She was in her early twenties, petite, perhaps a touch skinny, but had lovely breasts from what he had observed when she wore low-cut T-shirts. She did seem to like him and was genuinely sad that he was leaving MicaCom.

If he ever decided to start a new venture, and wanted an office manager and receptionist, he would do his utmost to secure the services of Naomi and Jacqui.

It was only five days since he had walked out of MicaCom, yet it seemed an eternity as he drove into the car park. He had experienced more life outside of work in that period that he had done for a considerable time. So far, he was not regretting his decision.

He cursed when he saw there was a car in his parking place, and then realized that now he had to compete for one of the few visitors' spaces. As it was only just into the business day, that was not a problem.

Word must have got round quickly about his arrival. He had just locked the car and begun his walk to the main entrance when Jacqui, wearing a short blue-skirt and his favourite kind of T-shirt, came rushing out and flung her arms around him.

'Thank God, you're all right,' she said, refusing to let go.

'Hey, now steady on, I've only been gone a few days,' he said, looking down at her and prising her gently away, embarrassed that there was an audience at a window.

'But your car was blown up!' Jacqui whispered.

'How did you know that?' he asked. He was aware of the Press and TV coverage, but as far as he knew the details of the car and the owner had not been publicized.

'I *heard* the explosion,' she replied.

Then it dawned on him that she lived just a few roads away from his flat. He had occasionally given her lifts home from work when, like him, she had worked late at the office. Afraid of what she might have spread around the office, he said, 'I hope you haven't told anyone it was my car. I'm hoping to avoid any publicity.'

'As unbelievable as it might seem, the answer is no - except Naomi of course. She knew anyway because the police telephoned her yesterday morning to confirm who was using the car. What happened? Was it an accident? Is somebody trying to kill you?'

'It's a long story, which I can't really go into now. However, the police may be visiting you to take your fingerprints.' He noticed her troubled expression and added, 'It's nothing to worry about. They need them for the process of elimination, as you were a passenger in my car last week. Shall we go inside, I have a present for you.'

The reception area was busy with a few interested employees wanting to know how he was spending his new found freedom. Together they laughed and joked for a while and he was relieved that nobody mentioned the car bombing. Eventually he was left alone with Jacqui. He perched on the edge of the reception desk.

'Have you any gossip about the new bosses yet?' he asked.

'Not yet, but it shouldn't take me long. Pete Hayden seems pretty straight and they haven't replaced Tony Cookson yet, but it's rumoured to be someone called Chris Finchley. Can I have my present now?' Jacqui said, flicking her eyelids provocatively.

'There is one condition. I'll need to check that they fit OK,' he said, responding with the same gesture.

'Ooh. Is it something to wear then?'

He put his hand in his pocket, pulled out a small box covered in gold wrapping paper and passed it to her. 'With thanks for getting me out of a jam last Friday.'

She leaned forward to take the package and he felt self-conscious as he caught sight of her unveiled cleavage. She opened it excitedly and squealed when she realized what the gift was. A number of nearby inquisitive heads turned towards her. 'You saucy thing. Thank you very much; they're lovely. I'm free tonight for the fitting.'

He wondered briefly if she was serious and decided to change the subject. 'Is Naomi free? I ought to say hello as I'm here.'

'She was in a meeting with Pete just before you arrived. I'll try her phone.'

Jacqui dialled the number but he could hear the unanswered ringing tone. 'No doubt I'll be passing again, I'll see her then.'

'Did you find Sarah?' Jacqui said suddenly as Carl was preparing to leave.

Jacqui observed the shocked expression and silence from the question and added, 'I'm not prying, honestly. Naomi told me about your search following your disappearance last week. It was such a sad story. I *personally* wanted to know if you had been successful.'

He guessed that Mike had confided the story to Naomi in the pub last Wednesday. 'The honest answer is Yes and No. It's another long story. You'll have to wait until my book is published.'

'You're writing a book?'

'Not yet, but after the last week, I certainly have enough material for one. See you soon.'

'Carl.'

'Yes?'

'Be happy.'

He gave Jacqui a wink, said a few more goodbyes and headed towards the main entrance. Through the glass door, he saw his newly acquired adversaries, Bryant and Duckworth emerging from a Ford Mondeo. He doubled back to Jacqui and said, 'Let the asylum know that we have a police visit, just in case anyone is breaking the company no-smoking rule.'

Jacqui immediately understood his warning and hastened away to alert the technical miscreants.

'Small world, Inspector?' He said as the duo appeared at reception. 'Or are you still checking up on me?'

Bryant and Duckworth were momentarily stunned and then ignoring the question, Bryant said, 'I thought you did not work here anymore. We have an appointment with Mrs. Tomson.'

Clandestinely, Carl clutched Bryant's arm and took him on one side. He said quietly, 'Inspector, I think I may have a lead for you.' Bryant raised his eyebrows and adjusted his spectacles in acknowledgement. 'I think I'm being followed. There's a red Sierra parked in the road opposite this building containing two suspicious looking men. Could you check it out for me?'

He did not wait for the answer, if indeed there was going to be one. Instead he resumed his departure and waved to Jacqui as she returned to reception.

It was a short journey and he arrived ten minutes later than arranged. The eager Barry was waiting outside the showroom to greet him.

'Good morning, Mr. Denham. Lovely day. Everything OK with the car? I've prepared all the paperwork for you,' Barry said in an unusually loud voice. He led Carl to a comfortable seating area where various documents were laid out on a smoked glass coffee table. In a similar area close by, three casually dressed men, one with an expensive looking camera slung round his neck, were chatting quietly and looking in his direction.

Carl signed the papers, retained his copies and then tore two cheques from his chequebook. One he made payable to Beamers in full payment for his new car; on the second he wrote an amount of £5,000, signed, and dated it.

'I presume there is a collection being made for Nicholas Lester's next of kin?' he asked.

'Yes. For his wife Amanda,' Barry said.

He added a payee name of Mrs A Lester to the cheque and handed it to Barry. 'Would you make sure that this Mrs. Lester gets this?'

Barry studied the cheque. 'But Mr. Denham this is for £5,000.'

Carl confirmed with a nod and a smile that it was not a mistake.

They both stood and shook hands. Barry averted Carl's eyes and looked nervously over Carl's shoulder as though in two minds about something.

'Thank you again. For both cheques,' Barry said and rushed uncomfortably towards an office cubicle at the back of the showroom.

Carl looked after him, shrugged and then turned towards the exit when a light flashed in his face.

'Mr. Denham, is it true that someone tried to kill you on Saturday afternoon?' said a voice as Carl's eyes were recovering from the bright light.

'Are you under police protection?' Another voice and another flash.

Blocking Carl's way were the Tall, the Short and the Ugly. The tall man was to his left holding a portable tape recorder and a connected microphone that was being held level with his nose. The short man, aiming the camera, was in front of him. The ugly man, by virtue of the pock marked face and wen on his forehead, was poised with pen and notepad to his right.

'Who are you people?' Carl asked and then it dawned on him why he had been asked to attend at ten o'clock. The disappearing Barry had set him up with a Press reception.

'Have you any connection with Irish terrorist groups ... Did you know Nicholas Lester ... Was the incident something to do with MicaCom?' and so the questions went on with the camera flashing in unison. Carl ignored them. It was best to say nothing, not even a *No Comment*. He pushed his way past the threesome, gently and calmly, just in case they were seeking an angry young man photograph. They pursued him to his car, firing increasingly controversial questions to elicit a response or quote, but he resisted the taunting.

Carl got into his car and started the engine. He wondered if they would try to follow him. Probably not, he concluded. They were still hovering around like frightened bees outside. He stabbed the accelerator and sped away, hoping that his non-committal reaction would mean that Barry would have to forsake whatever introductory fee he had negotiated.

It was only a short journey to his flat, but Carl took a circuitous route and kept glancing in his rear-view mirror to ensure he was not followed. He at least expected a red Sierra. He stopped the car 50 metres before his flat and kept watch for a few minutes. Establishing that there was no Press or Police staked out or in pursuit, he got out of the car and hurried towards the entrance to the flat. He paused briefly in the residents' private parking area and shuddered when he saw the scorched tarmac and tree where his old car and an unknown mechanic had met their deaths.

At the door to his flat, he examined the lock before inserting the key. As Inspector Bryant had indicated, there was no sign of a forced entry. He ignored the stack of mail behind the front door and carried out a quick inspection of the rooms. As far as he could detect, nothing had been disturbed. Not wanting to linger, he swiftly collected a few sets of clean clothes for himself, put them into Natasha's suitcase and made ready to leave. He picked up the mail to inspect it and noticed some unusual items. There were two business cards. Both had notes scrawled on the back asking him to contact the owners. One was from a reporter of the leading local newspaper, the other from a tabloid daily - probably the Tall and the Ugly from earlier. A third item was a sheet of plain writing paper with a note from Janice, asking him to contact her urgently. Angrily he tossed the mail bundle onto the telephone table by the front door. The note had brought to the fore the vengeance he knew he would seek one day. 'Oh yes,' he said to himself, 'I'll contact you urgently.'

Carl thought he had his anger with Janice under control, but the closer he got to Ongar, the more the hatred swelled up inside him again, almost making him physically sick. He recalled the bombardment of letters he had received while in the States, her seduction of him when he returned, and the disastrous short engagement and even shorter marriage. All that time she must have known that her anonymous photograph scheme had successfully broken his bond with Sarah. Could she really be a suspect in the bombing of his car as he had suggested to inspector Bryant?

He had not planned to go to Ongar, particularly with a police red Sierra following him, but checking in his mirror he was satisfied that the shadowers had been removed, so Janice's enticement could be honoured. And what would he do exactly? He was not sure he knew. The extremes were physical injury and verbal abuse. The latter he could manage, but would there be any point to it? None except perhaps imparting to Janice that he knew about the photographs. Perhaps then she might stay out of his life.

As he drove into Wickham Gardens his mind was made up for him - Inspector Bryant's car was parked outside. After his confession to Bryant yesterday about wanting to visit Janice, he certainly did not want to be seen here. He stopped the car, executed a rapid U-turn and headed back towards Chelmsford. Yet again, any settlement or satisfaction with Janice would have to wait for another time.

* * *

'Ms. Harding you told one of our officers yesterday about the visit you had on Friday afternoon from someone looking for Carl Denham, your ex-husband. Could I indulge you to repeat the story for my benefit?' Bryant asked.

Janice repeated her account of the unexpected arrival of the big man in the Mercedes, then asked, 'What is this all about Inspector? The constable yesterday couldn't or wouldn't say. He merely asked when I had last seen or spoken to Carl and I happened to mention the foreigner that called.'

'Foreigner?' Bryant queried. 'I don't recall that from the report.'

'He had an accent. Russian probably.'

'Are you a linguistics expert Ms. Harding or are you guessing?'

'East European then. His voice sounded like Boris Yeltsin speaking English.'

'And you gave him Mr. Denham's address?'

'I had to; I was frightened. He acted very peculiarly about Carl not being here.'

'In what way?'

'He kept rubbing his forehead as though he had a headache. Then he got angry and Paul – he's my boyfriend, had to see him off.'

'Did you tell him anything else about Mr. Denham?'

Janice thought for a moment. 'Yes, I did. He wanted to know what make of car Carl had.'

'And did you tell him?'

'Yes, a red BMW and the registration number.'

Bryant looked knowingly at Duckworth. Duckworth made some notes.

'Did you also tell …' Bryant was interrupted by the ringing of Duckworth's phone. Duckworth apologized and went to the other side of the room to answer the call, speaking quietly into the receiver.

Bryant wanted to eavesdrop, but carried on. 'Did you also tell …Mr. Denham about the man?'

'Yes. He claimed he had no idea who it was.'

'And you didn't believe him?'

'I tend not to be believe anything Carl says - he has a habit of lying to me. You haven't answered my question Inspector. Why are you asking about Carl? Has something happened to him?'

'Not yet,' he lied, 'but we have reason to believe that his life is in danger. In fact he suggested that you might want to … harm him.'

'Me? That's ridiculous. He was a miserable husband, but that was a long while ago. I don't bear grudges.'

Duckworth had been brief and returned.

Bryant prompted, 'Something to do with the death of an old girlfriend?'

Janice looked shocked. 'Death? What girlfriend?'

'A Sarah Zurek that committed suicide.'

Bryant was watching her closely. He was convinced that she started a smile before she spoke.

'Sarah's dead? What's that got to do with me?'

'Mr. Denham believes you may … have influenced her suicide.'

Janice's expression changed rapidly to a severe hateful look. She jumped up screaming so suddenly that Bryant almost fell off his chair.

'That's fucking crazy. That bastard knows nothing. Sarah was bad for Carl. She twisted his mind. It was unhealthy the way he worshipped that bimbo.'

She sat down again, visibly shaking. There were beads of sweat on her forehead. The outburst seemed to be over.

'Ms Harding, are you all right?

'I will be. I'll just get myself some water. Can I get you anything?'

Bryant and Duckworth refused, and Janice came back a minute later appearing cool and calm as though nothing had happened.

Bryant wanted some rational statement from her before he dropped the subject. 'No more to add about the matter with Sarah Zurek?'

'No Inspector. I've never met or had anything to do with Sarah. Carl had finished with her a long while before I got together with him.'

'I think that is all for now Ms. Harding,' Bryant said, and he and Duckworth prepared to leave.

Duckworth decided to contribute, 'Where is your partner at the moment Ms. Harding?'

'Out … job hunting. Did you want to speak to him?'

'No, that won't be necessary at the moment.'

Back in their car, Duckworth spoke first.

'Christ, you touched a nerve there boss … about Sarah Zurek.'

'Denham was probably right. The outburst suggested that she did contribute to her death. There is nothing we can or should do about that – it's history. *There's no crime like the present.* We should keep a close eye on Denham though. He has a right to be an angry man. Maybe his new blonde consort will moderate or eradicate his hate. Who phoned?'

'The call was relevant to what you've just said. Quebec Lima Two followed Denham here. He arrived about five minutes after us. Presumably saw your car and executed a hasty retreat.'

'Well, well. Those guys better not lose him. I want to know immediately he comes anywhere near here.'

* * *

On his way to Colchester, Carl stopped at a Little Chef restaurant on the A12 for a cup of coffee and a toasted teacake. He needed something to quell the unease in his stomach, not caused by hunger, but by the events of the morning and the coming evening.

As he approached Lexden, the snack had perhaps deferred a developing hunger but had done nothing to dispel the qualms he still had. If he felt like this now, how would he feel tonight?

He drove around the roads adjacent to Alex and Marion's house looking for somewhere conveniently, but unobtrusively, to park. He settled at a kerbside location almost opposite the entrance to a pot-holed track. By his geographical calculations, this looked the most likely rear entrance to reach Croftview.

He viewed his disguise was adequate. His car was different from the last visit and he had been deliberate about wearing Don's distinct baggy combat trousers and Ford blue anorak; he now added sunglasses to aid his deception. If Don's theory was right perhaps Marion would not be there to recognize him and, at best, Alexander had only seen the old head and shoulders photograph from the Internet. Nonetheless, he would need to be cautious – he did not want to spoil the plan for tonight.

A black and white cat greeted him as he crossed the road. Normally he had time for animals, but he left the cat unstroked, eager to complete his mission.

The track sloped up for about thirty metres then reached a plateau. The main track went straight on; a narrower track to the left – at the rear of a line of houses and their gardens – ran parallel to the road where he had parked his car. Leading to each house from this track was a short driveway, some terminated at a garage, others at just a parking area. He began to walk along the track, keeping vigilant for any oncoming vehicles. A hundred metres further, a footpath veered left and the track turned gently right and stopped before an open-gated entrance, wide enough for almost two cars. From the gateway there was a bricked drive that led to the back of a large house. The summerhouse to the left confirmed it was Croftview. Parked near the house was a Mercedes and behind it, alongside the summerhouse, a new Skoda facing towards the gateway. No sign of Marion's car. There were two men in conversation standing by the open driver's door of the Skoda.

Fortunately, they were not looking in his direction as he continued walking on to the footpath. A high, dense, evergreen hedge stood as a boundary between the footpath and the back of the pavilion look-alike. There was a man-sized gap in the hedge, which gave access to the Gomulka property. That was all he needed to know for his reconnaissance, but he stopped and tried to listen to the conversation. It was clear, but unintelligible - he assumed they were speaking in Polish. By the intonation of voices and the structure of the pauses, he could establish that the men were referring to each other as Ivan and Oles. There was only one other word distinguishable from the foreign sounds, his own name *Denham*.

Peering covertly through the gap, he could observe a transaction taking place. The shorter man, presumably Ivan, passed a cloth bag to Oles. Oles looked inside and nodded. Then he was given a small box, which he opened and poked inside with a finger before closing it and dropping it into the bag. Oles reached into a trouser back pocket, withdrew a wad of notes and counted some into Ivan's outstretched hand. There was a final exchange of words before Ivan climbed into the Skoda and drove off.

Carl waited for a few minutes, then continued along the footpath and returned to his car.

* * *

Paul opened the front door and Janice was waiting for him with a glass in her hand. She was swaying from side to side.

'Where have you been … you shit? We've got slerious celevating to do,' Janice said slurring her words.

'You know where I've been. In London registering with agencies for a job while you've been at home getting smashed by the looks of it.'

'Ah, don't be a mirable sod. Let's dance.'

She grabbed Paul with her free hand and began to jig about singing. 'Ding Dong! The Witch is dead. Which old Witch? The Wicked Witch! Ding Dong! The Wicked Witch is dead.' Then she spilt her drink over his interview suit.

'You silly cow. What the hell's been going on here?'

'The pleece came here wiz some news.'

'What? About the car bomb?'

But the answer never came as Janice staggered towards the bathroom, threw up and then slid into a drunken oblivion next to the bath.

A cold flannel, a black coffee and twenty minutes later, Janice was conscious again.

'The bimbo is dead. She's really dead. I killed her. Carl is free again.'

'Are you out of your brains? Who's dead?'

'Sarah Zurek of course.'

She was sober now and seemed to have restored her manic ways too - it made no sense to Paul. He was more interested in what the police had to say about the bombing; he would find out who Sarah was later.

'Just tell me about the bombing.'

'As we gathered from the papers and the police interviews, it appears the explosion didn't hit Carl - he must be hiding somewhere. Now I'm sure the police are convinced that our foreign visitor is the bomber - I told them that I gave him Carl's address and car details.'

'Wonders will never cease. You did something sensible for once. Now who's Sarah?'

Chapter 28

Tuesday, March 16, 1999 – 6:00 p.m.

It was six o'clock and Carl stood close to Wendy as she dialled Alex and Marion's number. He watched her precede the number with 141 so that her own number was not transmitted.

'Hello, is Marion there?' Wendy said when a male voice answered.

'Who's that?' he said.

'It's Margaret Hampshire. Marion asked me to call her tonight about the hospital fete,' Wendy said, privately praying that her reason might be plausible.

'I'm sorry Margaret, but Marion is staying with her mother tonight. Can I take a message?'

'No. That won't be necessary. I'll call tomorrow night if that's OK.'

'It might be best to call on Thursday. I'm not certain she'll be back tomorrow night.'

Wendy had the information she wanted and finished the call.

'Well done, Wendy,' Carl said, 'It's as we expected.'

Don came into the lounge from the garden carrying a black plastic box about the size of a cigarette packet. It had a small antenna attached. 'Perfect,' he said. 'Crystal clear. Heard every word.' He was referring to the transmission check he had just carried out using the miniature microphone concealed under the lapel of Carl's jacket. He pressed some recessed buttons and played back the recording.

'Pretty good, eh? Latest model from my Japanese contact.' Don said proudly.

'Where's the tape?' Natasha asked, picking up the device and inspecting it.

'It doesn't have one. The signal is recorded digitally directly to non-volatile memory. It's not much good for music, but it will record up to an hour's worth of voice transmission,' Don explained.

'Will it have sufficient range? I estimate it's about 50 metres from the summerhouse to the front gate of the house,' Carl asked.

Don opened a small instruction book. 'Well, the English translation says, *Please to advice operation in building wok four 100 mieters.*' He used a Japanese accent and everyone laughed.

'So we are all set. Time to call Bryant, I think.' Carl said and reached for the telephone. He also prefixed the number with 141.

Bryant answered immediately.

'Inspector, Good Evening. This is Carl Denham. I hope I haven't called at an inconvenient time?'

'Not quite. I was just about to go home. Something important to tell me I hope?' Bryant snapped.

'I believe so. In ten minutes I will be leaving to go to the house of whom I believe to be your bomber and arsonist - that part is up to you to sort out. *I* intend to find out what role he had to play in Sarah's death.'

'Don't be a fool Denham. If what you say is true, it's too risky – the man must be a maniac. Anyway, I've now got a copy of the file on Sarah Zurek in front of me. The Cambridge police were satisfied that she committed suicide.'

'I think *satisfied* is a rather disrespectful adjective to use, *convinced* might be more appropriate. You see that's my problem. Unless *I* unearth some further evidence or a confession to make you re-open the case, the truth might never come out. All *you* want is a conviction for the bombing and fire.'

'That's not true. If there's substance to any evidence that you have, of course we'll consider it.'

'I'm sorry, Inspector; I can't take the risk that you won't. But I am prepared to share the spoils with you, because I need some back up.'

'How do you know that your man is the one I'm looking for?'

'The arson is guesswork, although I have some additional information about my Portsmouth trip, which may prove helpful. As for the bombing, I'm certain you will find his fingerprints on the gun that was found in my car.'

'I bloody knew you were holding back on me about Portsmouth and the gun. Look, just leave it to the police.' Bryant was shouting and then trying to be calm and convincing added, 'I *promise* to help you in anyway I can about Sarah Zurek. Now, please, where can I find this man?'

Carl ignored the question. 'You'll get a call later on your mobile phone of where to go. When you do get the call, make sure you get to the location quickly, I have reason to be believe our man will be armed.'

'You're crazy …'

'Just confirm you understand the instructions,' Carl interjected.

'Yes, but …'

Bryant could not continue because Carl had already replaced the receiver.

'Why do you think he will be armed?' Wendy asked.

'Don't worry. I just wanted to make sure that Bryant treats my request seriously,' Carl lied. 'Time that you set out Don. Are you clear about the location and procedures?'

'Give me a break. You've been through the plan half a dozen times.' Don replied, putting on the anorak over the trousers, both of which Carl had been wearing earlier.

Carl tossed his car keys to Don.

Wendy rushed up to him and kissed him. 'Take care and don't forget your promise. If things look like getting rough, you abort, OK?'

'OK.'

Don pulled the hood of his anorak over his head and went to the front door. He turned the porch light off and opened the door; Carl's already unlocked car faced him in the drive. Don quickly got into the car and sped off towards Sudbury town centre.

Carl was in the unlit upstairs front bedroom. He peered through the curtains and smiled with satisfaction as he saw two Ford Sierras each with three occupants give chase.

* * *

Alexander did not like the thought of being interrupted while he was preparing himself to solve Mamusia's problem. He went to the socket on the wall and unplugged the telephone.

* * *

DCI Bryant had spent the last five minutes apparently staring into space. It was his way of pondering a problem. His body had gone into hibernation but his mind was furious with activity. Despite being annoyed with himself, it did not show on his face. In hindsight, he should have leaned harder on Denham. He *knew* that Denham had not told him the complete story about his connection to the bombing, yet he had backed off in his interrogation. Perhaps he should have persisted with the blonde bitch - she would have been an easier target. He vowed it was the last time that he would let a pretty face get the better of him. Some self-analysis would be required soon to avoid these kinds of mistakes in the future, but that would have to wait for now, he had some important decisions to make.

Did he believe Denham now? There was surely a hint of desperation in his voice a moment ago. If his statement of action were true, it would warrant immediate mobilisation of a strike team. He could not afford to ignore his plea for help. But if Denham were conning him, he would find as many reasons as possible to put that bastard behind bars.

Bryant was emerging from his trance as a knock on his door announced the arrival of Sergeant Duckworth.

'I'm off now Guv.'

'A Morse! A Morse! My kingdom for a Morse,' Bryant bellowed, leaping from his chair to the great surprise of Duckworth.

'Are you OK, Sir,' Duckworth said, reverting to his politest form of address in case his oft-eccentric boss was about to foam at the mouth.

'You know that quote don't you?'

'I thought I did. Don't you mean horse, Sir?'

'Morse. Chief Inspector Endeavour Morse – my hero.'

'Does he work on our patch?'

'No, you illiterate; the television character. He often relies on instinct and first impressions. I should have done the same with Denham.'

Duckworth looked none the wiser. 'I don't watch police dramas on the television. I think it trivialises the work we do,' he said.

'Right Lewis … I mean Duckworth, we have to go out,' Bryant said. 'Who's currently on Denham surveillance?'

'It think it's Quebec Lima One, Two and Four.'

'You think? You should fucking know! You're supposed to be co-ordinating them.'

'I'm sorry Guv. I've been writing up the reports of our interviews this morning. I've heard nothing from them. Is something up?'

'Now how did you manage to work that out? What's been reported in their logs?'

'Nothing significant. Denham went to MicaCom; Beamers; his flat; the aborted trip to Janice Harding – as you know, and then he stopped at a Little Chef on the A12. That's as far as I know.'

'And where has Denham been since then, and particularly, WHERE IS HE NOW?'

Embarrassed, Duckworth said, 'I'll find out,' and ran off.

Bryant followed at a walking pace. Duckworth was speaking to Arkwright when he caught up with him in the operations room.

'Denham has just left Travis's house, heading towards Halstead. Quebec Limas are tailing,' Duckworth said.

'Where did Denham go after the Little Chef?' Bryant asked.

Duckworth spoke into the microphone.

Arkwright replied over the airwaves from Quebec Lima One. 'Denham visited a location in Lexden. He disappeared down a track that led to the back of some houses. He was gone for about ten minutes. We didn't have the opportunity to follow him. After that he went back to Sudbury,'

Bryant grabbed the microphone. 'Why the hell didn't you report that immediately? You're supposed to notify any suspicious movements. If that wasn't suspicious I don't know what is!'

Before Arkwright could offer his excuse, Bryant continued. 'Stay with Denham. If you lose him I'll put you on lollipop control.'

* * *

Don pulled up in front of a brightly-lit fish and chip shop in Halstead High Street. He sat there for a couple of minutes looking into his rear-view mirror and keeping vigilant of passing traffic. He was counting; one; two; three surveillance cars, they were not very good – he could spot them in a fog bound car park. He dropped his anorak hood, stepped out of the car and stood prominently under the shop's neon lights looking in both directions to make sure he was recognized.

His smile became broader as he envisaged the in-car panic as one, two, then three Ford Sierras disappeared rapidly in the Sudbury direction.

He took out his mobile phone and dialled home. When it was answered he simply said 'Scalded Cats,' and cut the line.

* * *

Bryant was fuming. It had been a diversion. He had contemplated directing one of the crews to pick up Travis and have the guy *dealt with*; but what was the point, he had just been out to buy fish and chips in Denham's car – no law against that. Besides, he knew now that Denham was deadly serious about his quest. Bryant was going to need all his resources for a more important matter.

* * *

Don waited five minutes to satisfy himself that the three cats were well on their way back to Sudbury then he phoned Bryant and was brief with his words again. 'Carl Denham says go to Stanway,' he said and jumped in his car and set off towards Colchester. Stanway was on the west side of Colchester, but he did not want to reveal his real target, yet.

* * *

The radio operator was looking on in anticipation; he knew instructions were imminent.

Bryant did not disappoint him. 'If the Quebec Limas can't locate Denham when they get to back Sudbury, direct them to Stanway. Notify Colchester station we have an operation in their area. We'll need some uniformed back-up on standby.'

To his Sergeant he said, 'Duckworth, follow me. *There is a crime and place for everything.*'

* * *

Carl was enjoying his high speed driving. He liked Don's Audi A4; it seemed to hold the road better than his new BMW. He and Natasha had not spoken a word since they left Sudbury ten minutes ago, following the message from Don. He was considering the possible outcomes of his encounter with Alex. He wondered if Natasha was equally pre-occupied.

'Having second thoughts?' he asked.

'I'm scared Carl. Are we doing the right thing?'

'I'm unsure about *We*. I am sure about *my* involvement. I feel this is the only way I will satisfy my selfish curiosity. The more I think about it, the more I'm convinced that Alex contributed to Sarah's death. He's proved he can be a ruthless bastard and indirectly he had a motive. His mother was furious about Sarah inheriting the bulk of Max's estate. Marion was the beneficiary of Sarah's will. Get rid of Sarah, Marion becomes rich. Then maybe get rid of Marion, Alex presumably becomes rich and gives the money to his mother. The plan went wrong though - Sarah disposed of the money before she died. QED.'

Natasha was silent.

He continued. 'If I'm right, I could be dead within the hour. This is the scariest thing I've done since ... I ran the London Marathon.'

Natasha laughed.

'You don't have to be with me. My plan to make Alex talk will work without you.'

'But we've rehearsed the meeting on the basis I would be with you. You said that would make your scheme more plausible.'

'That's still true, but I always had a contingency plan if you opted out.'

* * *

Duckworth was speeding along the A12 towards Marks Tey. Bryant had been speaking non-stop on the radio to the mobile units.

His phone rang. A longer message from Travis this time, 'Carl Denham says he will be in the Colchester area. Have your back-up crews positioned at the roundabout off the A12 at the beginning of Remembrance Avenue by seven o'clock.'

Bryant updated Duckworth and relayed the message to HQ; then he went into trance mode. A notion hit him suddenly. 'Where do the Gomulkas live?'

'Colchester,' Duckworth said.

'I know that. Where in Colchester?'

'I don't know exactly. It'll be in the DC's report back at the office … and I think it's in my folder on the back seat. What are you thinking?'

'I'm thinking there's a connection between the dead Sarah Zurek, the current Sarah Zurek, the bombing and the fire.'

'Denham, obviously.'

'No, more than just Denham.'

Bryant leant behind for the manila folder, found the details and forwarded them with some information requests to Steve Rapley who was co-ordinating the operation at HQ. A minute later he had the information he wanted.

'Well, well. Denham's rendezvous point is just north of Lexden; the Gomulkas live in Lexden; the location that Denham visited in Lexden is close to the Gomulka's house. That's where I reckon Denham is headed. I think we might have solved our case Duckworth, *Crook, Line and Sinker*. Did we obtain any information about Mr. Gomulka?'

'No. The only fact I remember is that Marion Gomulka did refer to her husband during the interview. I'm pretty sure his name was Alexander.'

Bryant checked with HQ and learnt that the three pursuit vehicles were now heading towards the rendezvous point, but they had not caught up with Denham. He redirected one to the location Denham had visited earlier in the day and another to wait out-of-sight near the Gomulka residence. Then he requested a search through police records for information on Alexander Gomulka. Finally he dialled the Gomulka residence.

'I think you had better step on it Duckworth. I feel a bit uneasy about this there's no answer from the Gomulka number.'

* * *

When Don got to the outskirts of Colchester, he purposely avoided the obvious route to Lexden. It would have taken him via the roundabout that Carl had suggested as the police rendezvous and he did not want to risk being seen.

He soon found the footpath that ran along the side of Croftview. The map Carl had drawn for him was faultless. He turned the car around and parked adjacent to the footpath exit. If he needed to get away quickly he wanted the car close by. He checked his watch, ten past seven - he was early. Ten minutes before he needed to be in position.

* * *

The information Bryant had just received from HQ was a surprise. Not the content, but the speed in which it had been obtained; the power of computers continued to amaze him.

Alexander and Marion Gomulka, nee Zurek, married in Poland in 1987. They came to England in 1993 and had lived in Lexden ever since. Alexander and Marion were both currently unemployed. There was only one suspicious reference to Alexander Gomulka; an illegal immigrant from Poland that had been apprehended in Dover in 1992 had mentioned his name.

* * *

Don got out of his car and entered the footpath. Twenty metres along he found the gap in the hedge Carl had described to him. He squeezed through and positioned himself behind the summerhouse. He peered around the corner. The ground floor rooms of the house were lit, but the curtains were drawn; Alex's Mercedes was parked in the drive. He reached to an inside pocket and took out his mobile phone. He pressed the power-on button and the beep that it made sounded loud in the stillness of the evening. Certain that the noise had not carried to the house, he nonetheless pressed another button to suppress any further beeps, then dialled Carl's mobile.

* * *

Natasha *was* having second thoughts. She should have opted out. The mission they were on was not strictly necessary. Carl was about to find out the truth about Sarah, but she could tell him now – she had known since Friday afternoon. Selfishly she had kept the information from him in the hope that he would give up his quest and direct his affection to her instead. It had taken her until now to realise that her wish could never be granted. All she was doing now was to endanger her own life and Carl's.

'Carl, I have a serious confession to make ...,' she started but the mobile phone in her lap had begun its annoying Gallic tune. She clicked the answer button and passed the phone to Carl.

'I'm in position. All clear,' came the whispered voice from Don.

'I'll be there in about five minutes,' Carl said and killed the connection. 'What were you about to say about a confession?'

'Oh, it doesn't matter. It can wait,' Natasha replied. She had missed her opportunity - passed the point of no return.

* * *

One of the squad cars had arrived in the road Carl Denham had visited earlier that day. Bryant was speaking to Mike Brooks in Quebec Lima Four.

'Look for a silver Audi A4 or a black BMW 320,' Bryant said, then quoted the registration numbers he had noted for the Travis and Denham cars. He waited for a reply.

'The BMW's here – no occupants. It's parked next to a footpath entrance. No sign of the Audi,' Brooks said.

'Park nearby. Notify me if anyone comes back to the car.' Bryant said looking at his watch. 19:22. 'I'll be with you in about ten minutes.'

* * *

Don took out the recording device and switched it on. The battery indicator showed it was fully charged. He plugged the earphones into a small socket at the side and listened. All he could hear was an ambient level of static noise. He rested the recorder on an upturned flowerpot at the corner of the summerhouse and aimed the small antenna in the direction of the house. Then he retreated out of sight behind the wooden building taking care not to snag the connecting cable.

* * *

'We are in position,' radioed Mitch Bailey from Quebec Lima Two. 'We are parked at the head of Jessup Road - the opposite side of a crossroads to Quebec Lima Four. We can see Croftview. There are lights on downstairs. No cars parked outside.'

* * *

Arkwright radioed from Quebec Lima One: 'Denham has just entered Croft Road. We are holding back in case he stops.'

* * *

Mar ... lit ... la ... eece ...no ... went ... go

There were some broken words coming through Don's earphones. He moved close to the recorder. The signal meter was flickering.

Mary ... ad ... ittle ... am ... s flee ... was wh ... as snow ... where that Ma ... ent the ... am ... was ... to go

Carl was getting closer.

... and everywhere that Mary went the lamb was sure to go. I hope you are getting this Don because I'm getting bored saying this over and over again. I've stopped about ten metres from the front entrance to Croftview.

'Fucking brilliant,' Don mouthed to himself excitedly. He dialled Carl again and let the phone purr three times – the code that meant he was receiving his transmission. He uttered silent profanities again to the wonders of modern science as he heard the French tune echo in his ears.

* * *

Bailey radioed from Quebec Lima Two: 'A light coloured Audi has stopped just before the gateway to Croftview. Two occupants.'

* * *

Natasha noticeably jumped as the mobile phone sounded its coded signal.

Carl placed his hand on top of Natasha's. 'It's time. Are you ready?'

Natasha leaned across to Carl and kissed his lips. 'Yes. I love you, remember that.'

* * *

Bailey radioed: 'Male and female occupants have alighted from the Audi and are walking up the path to Croftview.'

Bryant radioed: 'Quebec Lima One pull in behind the Audi. Quebec Lima One and Two cover the front of the house - but keep concealed. I'll be joining Quebec Lima Four at the rear shortly.'

* * *

It was exactly seven thirty. Before Carl had the opportunity to rap the brass knocker, the door opened and was filled by the large imposing figure of Alexander Gomulka. Carl noticed Alex had at least dressed for a dinner party even if his scheme was more sinister.

'People who have perfect timing always impress me. I am pleased to meet you at last Carl. And by the lack of surprise on Natasha's face I assume you've made the connection – small world isn't it.' Alex grinned inanely, stood aside and gestured for them to enter.

Carl was glad Alex had not extended his hand as a greeting; he felt sick being near this man let alone touching him.

Alex led them to the lounge where Carl had sat during his visit to Marion.

'Marion's had to pop out for some urgent hospital business. She shouldn't be long,' Alex said.

Natasha gave Carl a knowing nudge.

'Make yourselves comfortable. A beer for you Carl?'

Carl and Natasha sat next to each other on the couch.

'Yes, thank you Alex.' Despite promising himself he would be as uncontroversial as possible, Carl could not resist the name taunt.

'Alexander, *please*,' Alex said, opening the door of an oak cabinet to retrieve some glasses.

Bad move thought Carl. It was a very angry *please*.

'I'll get Natasha her favourite drink, a gin and tonic. It looks as though she needs one,' Alex said.

Carl was reminded of the intimacy that Natasha and Alex once shared. He winced at the thought.

Alex went to the kitchen and returned with a can of cold beer and a tumbler with ice. He prepared the drinks at a hostess trolley, which was laden with spirit bottles and decanters. He then extracted a small table from a nest and placed it in front of Carl and Natasha, and set the drinks on it.

'Aren't you joining us,' Carl said for want of something to say to distract the nervousness advertised by his stomach.

'I don't drink when I need to keep my senses sharp,' Alex replied and sat down in an easy chair facing them.

Carl wondered what he meant but was afraid to ask. He wanted to get to the point of being here. 'You were going to tell me about your meeting with Sarah before she committed suicide.' He sipped his beer quickly to lubricate his dry mouth.

'Was I?'

'She didn't commit suicide, did she?'

'What makes you so sure of that?'

'Several reasons. For a start it was totally out of character.'

'You weren't actually around at the time to judge her character. Too busy screwing your other girlfriend I seem to remember. Sarah was so mentally unstable, taking her own life would have come as a relief to her.'

Carl took another sip of his beer. 'Secondly, she is living in Bradwell.'

'Don't be ridiculous. You've met her, have you?'

'Not yet. But there is good evidence that she lives or lived there.'

'Wishful thinking on your part I believe. I *know* she is dead.'

'How can you say that when her body has never been found?'

'Such privileged information can only be obtained at a price. But of course that's not a problem for you now that you have sold MicaCom.'

'How did you know that?'

'Give me some credit. You told Marion, it's public information on the Internet and a financial friend of mine has calculated what you probably got for it. I estimate you're a millionaire now.'

'Why do you want money for the information about Sarah?'

'My mother lost a great deal of money when Sarah died. The money that Max left to Sarah should have gone to my mother. It's payback time. I've waited eleven years to reclaim what was due to her.'

'But nobody knows what happened to that money.'

'I think you have missed the point. It doesn't have to be *that* money. Yours would make an adequate substitute.'

'And why should I pay for such information?'

'Quite simply because you are desperate to find the truth, otherwise you would not have embarked upon your search for her after eleven years. You are obsessed with the enigma and won't be able to rest until you find out what happened, even if you have to pay for the information. I am the only person who can supply it.'

'It started out like that, but things have changed now. I have quite a different reason for wanting to know. Natasha and I want to get married.' Carl placed his hand lovingly on Natasha's. 'I can't commit myself until I know that my search for Sarah is a waste of time.'

'Well, what a surprise. And you expect me to believe that? Have you slept with her yet?'

'I don't think that's any of your business.'

'I expect that's a *no*, I wouldn't bother if I were you. She's not very good.'

'We do want to marry, Oles … Alexander. I love Carl. It was my idea that he should meet you to find out about Sarah. It was the only way I could get him to forget about the past and concentrate on his future with me.'

'Anyway I'm not interested in your excuses or love life – only the money. The original amount that erroneously went to Sarah was £200,000. So, with compound interest of say … 6% for 11 years … £400,000 should cover it. I'll take a cheque.'

'You expect me to pay you £400,000 …'

'Take it or leave it.'

Carl gave a shrug of resignation, reached into his inside pocket and took out his chequebook. 'Payable to A. Gomulka?'

'Yes. I hope it won't bounce.'

'Carl, that's crazy. The information can't be worth that much to you,' Natasha shrieked.

Carl ignored Natasha. 'No. The proceeds from my sale of MicaCom are still in my current account – in case of emergencies, like this,' he lied.

Natasha shrieked again, this time shaking Carl's arm. 'Carl. Are you listening to me!'

Carl was impressed with Natasha's acting. It was his turn now. 'Shut up Natasha! I know what I'm doing.'

'Oh, dear. Am I causing a lover's tiff?' Alex said, sniggering like a child.

'There,' Carl said waving the cheque in the air, 'I've kept my part of the deal. Now it's your turn.'

Natasha had slumped back in her chair with her arms folded, looking like she was sucking a lemon.

'You want the graphically detailed version?' Alex asked reaching for the cheque, but Carl snatched it away.

'Look Alex*ander*, I don't like you and I may not like what I'm about to hear, but as long as it's the truth, this valuable piece of paper is yours. Guaranteed. No strings. I don't know about Poles, but you should know that an Englishman's word is his bond.' Carl placed the cheque on the table next to his beer glass.

'Would you like a stronger drink before I start?'

'No. Just get on with it.'

Alex began to pace up and down.

'I did visit Sarah a couple of days before she died. It was to warn her that her mother and sister were scheming to have her declared insane, and committed to a mental institution. Fortunately, this stacked up in Sarah's disturbed mind because Audrey and Marion were already urging her to check back into the hospital for some more treatment for her depression. Then I said they planned to take control of her assets including her recent inheritance. Sarah was very impressionable at the time and I was a good actor – she accepted the story completely. I said I would do my best to help her by coming up with a plan and I would be in touch. She was to stay at home the following day.'

Alex paused and looked at Carl and Natasha as though he was expecting questions.

Carl had plenty of questions, but did not want to interrupt Alex's flow. He moved to the edge of his seat, conscious that his hidden microphone should be as close as possible.

Alex continued. 'You see I had already arranged for her to have a surprise visit. My *Mamusia* - Eliza, had given me the money she had inherited from Max. I was to use it to take out a contract on Sarah's life. I called in a favour from a colleague – Ivan, and gave him £6,000 as a deposit for the assassin with another £6,000 to be paid on proof of the kill. The next morning, Sarah had her surprise visit, but the plan unfortunately backfired. You see I phoned the house not long after the kill should have taken place and was most surprised that she answered. Somehow, she had fought off or panicked her attacker, and had survived with just a knife slash on her face. She was distraught and didn't know what to do - I had to think quickly. I convinced her that it had almost certainly been a plot hatched by her family to kill her. I told her to do nothing until the following day because I would arrange to take her away to a secret hiding place. I briefed her on my imaginary plan.'

Carl struggled to remain quiet; Natasha had been making small gasping sounds.

'Later I contacted Ivan who had assumed Sarah had been killed and asked me when he could have the remaining £6,000. The assassin said he had various documents of Sarah in his possession, which was proof that the contract had been completed. I had to put him right on what had really happened. I did think of insisting that Ivan's assassin completed his contract, but I knew that wasn't going to be possible. After a hit, successful or otherwise, these degenerates lie low in case they are recognized. Either Ivan would have to quickly find another executioner or I would have to complete the task myself – I chose the latter.'

Carl saw that Alex was smiling now. The bastard was enjoying this.

'I drove from my hotel and parked in the street adjacent to the park at the end of St. John's Road. Sarah's house was just in view. I called at the house but there was nobody at home, which bothered me after our earlier conversation; I decided on a stake out from the car. Eventually she arrived, looking quite well I thought for someone who had survived a murder attempt. I waited a few minutes and was about to go to the house, when someone else turned up - an Asian girl, and let herself in. It was getting dark and starting to drizzle, I'd thought I'd missed my opportunity.'

Alex sat on the edge of an armchair and ran his fingers through his hair, pushing hard on his scalp.

'I waited another hour and then my patience was rewarded, first the Asian came out and headed towards the city centre. A minute later, Sarah, or someone who had to be Sarah emerged. She was wearing a dark green anorak, with a hood tightly wrapped around her head, barely showing her face. On her feet were heavy walking shoes and she was carrying a bulbous shoulder bag. She looked like a hiker about to set out on a survival course, but it was clearly Sarah by her shape and gait. She turned right, crossed the road and entered the park area, hurrying into the distance. I wondered briefly what she was doing. Having, apparently, been house bound for so long, she was venturing out for at least the second time that day. But it didn't really matter - it was dark, wet with nobody about, conditions were ideal.'

Alex paused and stood up again. His smile seemed to be getting wider as he narrated his story. Carl took the opportunity to take a sip from his glass.

'I followed at a safe distance, though safety wasn't really a concern. Sarah was striding determinedly as if she was late for an appointment, and looking behind her seemed a remote possibility. Noise wasn't an issue either; the pounding of the rain now easily masked it. I was well equipped for my task. I had borrowed a gun from Ivan – just in case, and had added a sharp spring-loaded knife and a length of rope. I preferred to use the gun, but as it wasn't silenced, I was wary of using it even in the open space of the park. As it turned I out I ended up using all three weapons.'

It was getting close to confession time. Carl silently prayed that Don was still receiving loud and clear.

'Sarah's pace had brought her close to the edge of the park where the River Cam separates it from a main road. It looked as though she might be heading for a bridge over the river, so I selected my knife and broke into a run in pursuit. I'm sure she couldn't have heard me, but as I struck down with the knife she suddenly turned and instead of the blade spilling blood, it tore open the shoulder bag and spilled its contents onto the path. The force of the impact knocked Sarah forwards on to the ground and the knife flew off into the darkness. Out of character, I must have momentarily panicked and drew the gun, aiming at the centre of her back as she tried to stand. Then I realized my folly. Rather than fire the gun, I brought it down on the back of her head. She was unconscious, but I didn't think she was dead. I checked that there was nobody nearby and dragged her body a few feet to the riverbank, intending to tip her into river. Then I thought I had better make sure that she really was finished so I took the rope, looped it around her neck and pulled it tight. She never uttered a sound, didn't resist, and just died there in the wet grass and mud by the River Cam. I detected a movement on the other side of the bridge, so as a final act I gave her body a couple of kicks and she slid down the bank into the water.'

Alex beamed triumphantly and bowed forward slightly as if expecting applause from his audience.

Carl did not react in case there was more to come.

Alex looked disappointed and then his face distorted rapidly to show anger. His right hand seemed to shake and he pressed it hard against his creased forehead. His erstwhile calm voice degraded into a roar.

'And you know what? Getting my hands dirty like that was a complete waste of time. The following morning I flew back to Poland to tell Mamusia the good news. Then that evening I got a call from Marion – Sarah had gone missing and had left a suicide note. So you see I did her a favour; she was on her way to kill her herself – I saved her the trouble.'

Throughout Alex's murderous uncensored confession Carl had sat transfixed with his fists tightly clenched. He had achieved his objective; Alex's deranged admission was now on record. This had to be the nadir of his life – the final realization that Sarah was really dead. *Get me out of here* was his silent plea to those that were hopefully surrounding the house. His head felt tight, the grief welling up inside of him. Breathing became difficult and he could not hold back any longer, the first tear rolled down his left cheek. Now the bile rising from his stomach - he knew he was going to be sick.

As calmly as he could manage Carl said, 'I think I need a cigarette,' and felt in his pocket. 'Damn, they are in the car. I'll just pop out and get them.'

Alex moved in front of the lounge door. 'I think you should stay where you are. Smoking is bad for your health, but not as bad as this.' He put his hand inside his jacket, produced a gun and pointed it at Carl.

Carl and Natasha froze.

Alex stepped forward and picked up the cheque to examine it. Satisfied with the amount, date and signature he placed it in his pocket. 'You don't really believe I'm going to let you live after what I've just told you. I can't take the risk that you won't go to the police with it. You see, I don't trust the word of Englishmen. You have disappointed me though Denham. I wanted to see the hate and disgust on your face when you heard how I killed Sarah, but your look hardly changed – just one, forgivable tear. I don't know whether to compliment your composure or congratulate you on being a cold-hearted bastard. What should it be?'

'Alexander, don't be foolish. The police are surrounding the house,' Carl pleaded.

Alex giggled. 'Ha. Good try, Denham, an old trick that won't work. The police have nothing on me.'

'What about the bombing of my car?'

'Oh, yes. I read about that. It seems you have more than one enemy. Sadly I can't take the credit for that.'

'I don't believe you and neither do the police. Your gun, presumably with your fingerprints on it, was found in the car.'

Alex looked bewildered for a moment. He obviously had not foreseen this possibility.

Carl had no choice. His coded signal to Don about the cigarette must have been missed or his lapel transmitter had failed. In one swift movement he kicked the table over and lunged in an upward movement towards Alex, attempting to keep his body on the blind side of the gun. He never saw the look of surprise and panic on Alex's face, but Natasha did as she endeavoured to follow Carl's assault.

There was a sudden eruption of noise from several directions.

A beer glass smashed against a wall.

The kitchen door to the back garden opened with a crash.

Alex uttered a winded yelp as Carl barged into him.

There was a muffled boom from the gun.

Footsteps could be heard running through the kitchen.

Carl screamed as a bullet tore through the flesh of his arm.

Tinkling glass again, this time from the front of the house.

No more than a moan from Natasha as the bullet continued its inexorable progress into her chest.

And finally, a cacophony of voices as four additional bodies tumbled into the lounge, quickly assessed the situation, and two of them leapt upon the toppled Alex, pinning him to the floor.

There was a brief period of silence as incredulous eyes surveyed the scene.

Carl was crawling laboriously towards Natasha with blood spilling from his arm onto the pink carpet leaving dark patches. Natasha was lying on the floor with her head propped against the base of the couch. He looked at her through eyes blurred by the pain in his arm and then blurred by tears as he saw the growing blood stain on her white blouse. There was a slight flutter in her closed eyes and her lips parted to ooze a trickle of blood.

'No. No.' Carl attempted to scream, but his voice was barely a whisper. He was close enough now to stroke her hair. 'I'm sorry.'

Natasha's eyes opened to a slit and there must have been some recognition as the slightest crease appeared in her mouth and then her lips struggled to form some words.

'I … Sarah … alive … find,' she coughed and her eyes closed for the last time.

Chapter 29

Wednesday, June 16, 1999 – 10:00 a.m.

It was good to be home thought Mike, as he opened his front door. The absence of mail blocking the door and the sweet smell suggested that his generous neighbour Monica had been diligent in her care of the house in his absence, as well as picking them up from the airport. Lisa dashed to the toilet with Monica in pursuit. The journey from the Gatwick had made Lisa feel queasy. She had always been a good traveller, but her two-month-old pregnancy was already beginning to affect her in new ways, no doubt exacerbated by a dose of jetlag. The last week in America had been particularly uncomfortable for her and they had decided to cut short their grand tour by two weeks. Lisa wanted to be home to begin preparations for the event that would change their lives in seven months time.

Mike went to the lounge to check the answering machine. Only twenty messages according to the small display; not surprising really, he had notified all regular callers that he would be away for over three months. He let the tape run through while he examined the neat piles of mail that Monica had arranged for him. A few of the messages were from Janice trying to locate Carl; he ignored them - Carl must be in Utopia somewhere with Susan.

It was the fourteenth message that made him stop his mail scan. *Mike, please call me as soon as you get back. Carl's gone missing.* It was Susan's voice – she finished her message with a telephone number. Mike went to the machine and noted the date of the call – it was almost three weeks earlier. The seventeenth message was similar but two weeks old.

Lisa came in as the last message was playing - another, now more desperate plea, just a few days ago. They both stood listening.

'Still getting calls from your mistress?' Lisa said. He knew she was joking; he had told her the story about Carl and Susan while they had been away.

'You're feeling better?'

'Yes, I'm into a rhythm now. Be sick, then drink a glass of water and I'm fine.'

Monica looked in on them. 'I've brought the suitcases in, put the kettle on and taken some bread out of the freezer. I'll be off now to let you two get resettled - unless there's something else I can do?'

'Monica, you've been an absolute angel. You've done quite enough already. I'm so grateful for all your help. I'll pop in to see you tomorrow,' Lisa said and escorted her to the front door.

Lisa quickly returned. 'What has happened to Carl and Susan?'

'I've no idea. The day before we left for America the reunion was going to plan. George must have given Susan our number. I'd better call her back.' Mike said and dialled the number.

'Susan?'

'Mike, is that you? At last. I really need your help.'

'What happened while I was away? You said Carl's gone missing?'

'I presume you don't know about the car bombing, the murder, the trial?'

'What on earth are you on about? No, nothing. I'm rather out of touch with UK events. Who's been bombed? Who's been murdered? What has all this got to do with Carl?'

'I can't possibly explain everything over the phone. Can we meet?'

'When?'

'Now. Today?'

'Just a moment.'

Mike looked at Lisa. 'Will you be all right? I need to go out – urgently,' he said.

'Yes, of course. What's happened?' Lisa asked.

'I'll tell you in a minute,' he replied.

'OK. Where?' he said to Susan.

'Could you come here? I live in Bradwell. I don't have a car.'

Mike took down the details, although he knew the area quite well – he had installed a copy of Protean at the power station a few years ago. He told Susan he would leave as soon as possible and replaced the receiver.

He recited his conversation with Susan to Lisa. 'Phone around a few mutual friends of Carl and myself. See if you can find out anything. I'll call you later.'

An hour later Mike turned right into a narrow lane just before the Cricketers pub. It was signposted to Hockley, which according to the Ordnance Survey map he had, was the name given to a small collection of buildings on the edge of Bradwell Marshes. The further he travelled the narrower the road became, until beyond Hockley it degraded to an unsurfaced track. A little further and a white-boarded bungalow appeared on the left. A homemade wooden sign with the words *The Nearest FarAway Place* confirmed he was in the right location. It was a pretty building with a red pantiled roof and black skirting, set back from the road behind a six-foot high hedge. Mike pulled off the track on to a cobbled stone driveway. Three wide brick steps led to a half-windowed black door surrounded by a colourful display of hanging baskets. The door opened as he stepped out of his car.

Immediately one of Mike's theories was dispelled. Until recently, he had spoken to Susan almost every month for the last eight years. During that time he had painted a picture in his mind of what she would look like. As he climbed the steps, he never believed that his picture would be so accurate. She was medium height with shoulder length and straw-coloured blonde hair with a centre parting. Her complexion was smooth except for a long mark on her left cheek. The only obvious make-up was a hint of lipstick on a full mouth. Her figure was concealed behind a loose, blue, floral-patterned knee length dress, but she appeared slim with shapely legs. She had bright, happy blue eyes, although the remainder of her face seemed melancholy, strained even.

Mike instantly felt comfortable in her presence, so much so that he kissed her on the cheek as if greeting an old friend. The mark was a faded three-inch scar.

'We meet at last. It's good of you to come so quickly. Come in,' Susan said.

She led him into a large cosy lounge with brown wood panelled walls. Shades of brown were the dominant colour.

'When did you get back from America?' she asked.

Mike grinned. 'The three of us landed about four hours ago.'

'Three of you?'

'Me and Lisa with child.'

'Your wife is pregnant? I am happy for you Mike. You must be tired. I feel guilty dragging you here so soon.'

'In reality I think I'm the guilty one. Whatever has happened you will conclude it's been my fault. I know I have a penance to pay.'

'I can't deny that. If you hadn't lied to me over the years Carl and I would have been together now.'

Susan had made the accusation in a casual manner, but nonetheless Mike looked at his hands embarrassed to meet her eye to eye. Susan noticed the discomfort.

'Don't worry, I'm no longer angry at your deception. Your own guilt will be retribution enough. Can I console you with a cup of tea or coffee?'

'A strong mug of English tea would help me recover from all the American coffee I've drunk, thanks.'

Mike sat down on the chocolate brown sofa and Susan disappeared to the kitchen. A minute later, she returned with a small silver tray with mugs of tea, sugar and a plate of biscuits. Mike took a long drink of tea and slumped back in his seat. The comfortable surroundings and twelve-hour flight were conspiring to make him suddenly feel very tired.

Susan sat next to him. 'How much did George tell you about me?' she asked.

'The day before I left for America George would only tell me a small part of your history because that afternoon he wanted to tell Carl first. I know that your name is now Susan Fellgate and you own half of BinaryByte. Your original name was Sarah Zurek and you are Carl's long lost girlfriend. Two days earlier Carl had told me how you first met; how your relationship grew from study partners to companions then to lovers; your inexplicable breakdown at Cambridge; how distraught he was and his exile in San Francisco for a year. It's the time in between I'm eager to know about. But first tell me what happened to Carl. He's not bombed or murdered anyone, has he? Or in any danger?'

'No to the first question. I don't know to the second. However, without some of the background you won't begin to understand what's been going on in your absence. Before today, the last time that you and I spoke was the Thursday before you went to America. You said that Carl had gone to Portsmouth to see Sarah Zurek.'

'Yes, you reacted very strangely, and then slammed the phone down on me. I can appreciate why now.'

'I'm not sure you do. I thought you were making a sick joke, because as far as I knew, Carl believed I was dead.'

'Excuse me?' Mike said, sitting upright – the tiredness briefly forgotten.

'I disappeared from Cambridge while Carl was in San Francisco. It was thought I had killed myself because of my state of mind and the suicide note I left. A classic Mark Twain - *Reports of my death are greatly exaggerated.*'

'You faked your suicide?' Mike exclaimed.

'Not exactly, I'll explain that later.'

'Carl certainly didn't know that. He said he had no knowledge of you from the day that you parted until he thought he'd found you, or at least someone with the same name, on the Internet.'

'I still don't understand why he didn't know.'

'He wrapped himself up totally in MicaCom – except for a brief marriage to Janice. He was trying to purge you from his mind and purposely avoided contact with anybody and anything that would remind him of you. Who knew you were still alive?'

'Only George and Samantha Fellgate.'

'What about your family?'

'No. It was especially important that they didn't know,' Susan said.

Mike slumped back in his seat again, totally bewildered by what he was hearing.

Susan continued. 'I'm not meaning to be obtuse. Believe me, it will become clear eventually. I am trying to present facts in a logical order.'

'So what did you do when you heard Carl had gone to Portsmouth?'

'I assumed it had to be a lie, although I couldn't work out the reason behind it. I had to make sure that Carl came back, so I phoned George and asked him to put a stop on your banker's drafts. I thought that would spur you into action to locate Carl and get him back.'

'Hang on a minute; I've just realized something. Did *you* instigate BinaryByte's take-over of MicaCom?'

'Yes.'

'To give Carl his freedom?'

'Yes. I'd suspected for a while that you hadn't been straight with me. I asked George to start poking around MicaCom. We even planted a spy, Jacqui Boniface, in MicaCom to feed back information about Carl.'

'Jacqui. A spy?'

'*Only* to find out about Carl's personal life. There was no commercial consideration. It emerged that the only barrier to Carl being free was his commitment to MicaCom. Apparently, the information you fed me about girlfriends and affairs was total crap.'

Mike was quiet for a moment to let the effect of the admonishment dissipate. 'I always thought that Jacqui had a soft spot for Carl. We joked about it sometimes. Carl would be very disappointed to hear that.'

'I sincerely hope not,' Susan said in a mock stern voice.

'I suppose the price that BinaryByte paid for MicaCom was immaterial, so long as Carl became unemployed.'

'Within reason, yes. BinaryByte is a pretty wealthy company, its purse wasn't bottomless, but I wanted the offer to be one you couldn't refuse, or would spend ages thinking about.'

'As a fifty percent shareholder that makes you a rich lady.'

'On paper anyway. These days I don't contribute a lot to the company's development; I draw a minimal salary. Just enough to keep up my modest living requirements,' Susan said, waving her hand to indicate the area around them. 'Now that MicaCom has been acquired, George feels the time is right to float BinaryByte on the stock market. I'll be selling my shares as part of the plan.'

'How did you get involved with George and BinaryByte?'

'One thing at a time. I'll come back to that too. Let me finish the story about Carl.

'Yes, sorry. Carry on.'

'George came here on the Friday morning and I told him the complete story about my interest in Carl.'

'He didn't know before then?'

'George knew I had had a troubled past with a boyfriend, but he didn't know it was Carl.'

'Then how did you convince him to buy out MicaCom?'

'I started BinaryByte with George to forget about Carl. I funded the formation of the company, and I was responsible for the development of its first products. George was the front man and managed the day-to-day business, but I was always in control. If I wanted something to happen, George did as he was told. Don't read me wrong I wasn't a tyrant; it's just that George had ultimate faith in me. Although I had personal reasons for taking over MicaCom, it was still a commercially sound proposition.'

'The similarities between MicaCom and BinaryByte are uncanny. You and Carl each started a company to forget each other. You both bankrolled your companies and were both the technical wizards that made them successful. Such things only happen in books and films, don't they?'

'Obviously not.'

'If your plan to get me to drag Carl back from Portsmouth worked, why is he now missing.'

'The plan worked, but Carl did not go back to the MicaCom office that day; so George was unable to break the news gently to him about me. Jacqui phoned to tell me that because the money pressure was off, Carl had decided to deal with some other pressing problem and had gone straight home. I discovered later that he had found out that I was dead, and had in fact gone to visit my sister to talk to her about what had happened. I didn't know that at the time, so I tried to ring him at home and a woman answered:

'Hello?'

'Is Carl there please?'

'No. Not at the moment, can I take a message for him?'

'That's depends. Who are you?'

'Just a friend. Who are you?'

'Tell Carl that Sarah Zurek called - the real, alive Sarah Zurek. I'm calling myself Susan Fellgate now. Tell him I'm at the Nearest FarAway

Place. Call me back urgently on the following number ... Now, I'll ask again. Who are you?'

'My name is Natasha Minski. I'm Carl's fiancée.'

'Natasha Minski? I've never heard of her,' Mike said.

'Neither had I. I accepted that you had obviously been right about Carl's romances and that my spy's information had fallen short. Carl must have gone to Portsmouth to collect his fiancée. So that was it for me - I had left it too late. I'd set Carl up nicely with two million pounds so that he could spend it on a Natasha Minski.'

'But why did Carl invent a story about going to Portsmouth to find Sarah Zurek?'

'It wasn't an invention, it was the truth.'

'Pinch me,' Mike said and offered his arm to Susan.

She pinched him.

'No. Nothing's changed, I'm not dreaming.'

They both laughed.

'Confusing, isn't it? I'm afraid the story gets even more complex and it wasn't until the media reports that I began to understand what had happened. I'll make some more tea.'

When Susan returned with fresh mugs of tea, she related to the best of her knowledge the chronology of events from Carl's trip to Portsmouth up to the trial of Alex Gomulka. She produced newspaper cuttings that she had kept from reports of the story in the local and national press. Mike asked many questions and got Susan to repeat some of the details such was the disbelief in what he had heard.

'I'm not sure I can take all this in. It's like ... like I've been transported to a parallel universe. I've known Carl for eleven years, but never really knew anything about him. I need some fresh air to keep me sane and awake. Do you fancy a walk to the pub at the end of the road? It will give me the opportunity to try to absorb what you've told me.'

'Yes, OK. I don't know what it's like – I've lived here for nine years and I've never been there.'

'I should call Lisa before we go though.'

'OK, you call Lisa and I'll get ready.'

Mike had to try his home number a few times before he could get through. 'Hey, you've been busy on the phone.'

'I've been phoning around. Everyone's talking about Carl,' Lisa said.

'Yes. We go on holiday and all hell breaks loose. Never could trust Carl on his own,' Mike joked. 'There have been quite a few revelations this end too. Have you any clues where he might be?'

'Just one vague lead. I'll tell you when you get home.'

'Ah, I'm going to be delayed. Susan and I have still a great deal to get through. I'll phone with an update later.'

The leisurely walk to the pub took about ten minutes. A couple of times Susan spoke, but Mike politely dismissed her. He needed to think.

He could not get out of his mind that none of this would have happened if he had been honest with Carl from the outset. For eight years he had kept a crucial secret from his business partner, which had almost got him killed and had led to the death of an innocent woman. Carl and Susan used to be his friends – surely now he was their enemy. Susan had let him off lightly considering the way he had deceived her. Perhaps she was just being tolerant while he was still in a position to help her find Carl. If he could find Carl and get him back with Susan, perhaps he would be forgiven.

Goodness knows what had happened to Carl. He had found out that Sarah had apparently been killed, had almost been killed himself, and then a new friend had died too. He tried to put himself in Carl's situation. How would he react? Where would he go? Carl must be feeling low, lower than he ever felt after Sarah had rejected him. Carl's solution to all problems had been to bury himself with work. He was not the kind of guy to brood and do nothing. Carl would purge whatever feelings he had by indulging himself in a technical challenge – something that consumed him so much that he would not have time to dwell on anything else.

He had often discussed new product opportunities with Carl. However, the commercial scope for further development of Protean had always won the day. It was the safest strategy. Why take risks creating new software when there had been enough mileage in Protean to make them a great deal of money? The safe routes had paid off in the end but were they just lucky because of Susan's involvement in BinaryByte and her past with Carl? They would never know now. If they had been more adventurous in their policy, would they be even richer than they were today? He tried to recall the ideas he had discussed with Carl, perhaps they would give him a clue to what Carl might be doing now. He did not think Carl had already started work on anything new – he would have known. So, he would be starting from scratch, like he did in San Francisco. Beavering away until he was satisfied that he was close to having a product worthy of launching. If he was right, it pointed to several conclusions.

He was probably holed up somewhere - working alone, so contacting any of his technical colleagues would be a waste of time. He might well be out of the country to get away from things that would remind him of the trauma he had recently experienced. San Francisco, or at least California, would be a good bet. He made a mental note to contact Carl's parents as soon as possible. Carl would no doubt need some heavy-duty computer equipment. The computing power he had at home would be ideal. Carl hated the frustration of configuring new PCs to his exacting requirements - the machine at his flat would already be set-up and tuned to his needs. He had a key to Carl's flat; he could check whether his PC was still there and whether his passport had been taken. Indeed, there may be some clue to his current whereabouts. Finally, there was the Internet. Carl was a surf junkie and wherever he was there had to be an electronic signature of him somewhere.

He and Susan had arrived at the Cricketers pub. Midday on a Thursday was obviously not prime time at the Cricketers. The place was deserted and it took the rattling of an ashtray on the bar to attract the attention of the barman from a back room, where a television seemed to playing on full volume.

'Sorry folks, I was catching up with some paperwork. What can I get you?' said the Scotsman with sandy coloured hair.

Mike really wanted something like a triple scotch to quickly numb his brain, but chose a pint of beer, as he would be driving later. Susan selected a grapefruit juice. They were both conscious of their host paying close attention to Susan while he prepared the drinks. He presented the drinks and then retrieved a small white card from a shelf behind him, looked at it and placed it in front of Susan, waiting for a reaction.

It was Carl's business card. 'He was here looking for me?' Susan asked.

'Aye, about three months ago. Then someone came looking for him and now you're here. Shall I ring him?'

'Not on the mobile number he wrote down – it's unavailable.'

'Mind if I try? I did promise him I would call if I saw you.'

'No, but it will be a waste of time.'

The barman went to the back room again and the television was turned down.

Susan gave Mike an exasperated look. 'It's quite unbelievable. He was only a mile away when he came here.'

'You knew Carl had been here?'

'Not this particular pub. I wondered whether Carl had come to Bradwell so I hired a private detective to discreetly visit every house within a five-mile radius showing his photograph from press reports. He became quite a celebrity during the trial and had been seen in the village with Natasha supposedly looking for his *sister* on the day you went to America.'

The television volume returned and the barman came back. 'There was no answer. I let it ring for a minute.'

'It actually rang, rather than the unobtainable tone or a recorded message?' Susan asked.

'That's what I said. Do you want me try later?'

Susan reached into the small black handbag she had brought with her and pulled out a pen. She wrote her phone number underneath Carl's on the business card. 'Yes, and if he answers he *must* ring this number it's *very* important. I'd be most grateful …'

'Josh is the name,' added the barman.

'Is this significant?' Mike asked.

'It might be,' Susan said. 'Up to now, every time I've tried that number it's been unobtainable. Perhaps Carl's resurfaced.'

'Och, based on what came out at the murder trial, your brother's probably been assassinated by the Polish mafia,' Josh joked, but nobody laughed with him.

Susan held her tongue and said 'Let's sit down.' She chose a window table as distant from the bar as possible.

'What was all that about?' Mike asked.

Susan sipped her grapefruit juice. 'Sorry, get your brain ready there's still quite a lot of the story to come.'

'Obviously the trial's already taken place. The British justice system's been working overtime?'

'I don't know. The trial started about two months after the murder and only lasted a week. The evidence for the murder was pretty incontrovertible. Four policemen had after all witnessed it, though Alex was committed to trial on several counts.'

'He wasn't convicted of my murder. Despite the recording of his confession, he said in court that he had made up the story purely to extort money from Carl. There was no other evidence or witnesses to confirm his story and no dead body. I don't think the police were too bothered to dig any deeper. The jury realistically had no option but to acquit him of that crime. The original belief that I had committed suicide while mentally disturbed was accepted. I expect Carl was unhappy about that. The prosecution didn't pursue the lesser count of extortion.

'He was found guilty of causing the death of Nicholas Lester and attempted murder of Carl by the car bombing. He supposedly had an alibi for the time when the bomb had been planted, but finding a gun with his fingerprints on at the scene of the crime and the testimony of Janice Harding was sufficient to convict him.'

Mike took the first mouthful of his forgotten beer then asked, 'How was Janice involved?'

'In trying to track Carl down after the incident in Portsmouth, he had visited Janice in Ongar, believing that Carl still lived there. She stated that Alex had threatened her into giving him Carl's address and car details. Since the bomb was attached to Carl's car a few hours after that, it clinched the conviction.

'Then there was the arson on Don Travis's warehouse. Forensic evidence proved that some of the materials used to start the fire matched those contained in Alex's summerhouse.

'There was obviously no doubt about the wounding of Carl and the killing of Natasha Minski. He'll be in prison for the rest of his life, thank goodness.'

Josh had crept up on them and had been hovering behind Susan waiting for a gap in her monologue; he placed a large plate of sandwiches on their table. 'Compliments of the house ...', he said to Susan, '... and an atonement for my careless remark. I'm truly very sorry.'

Before she could voice her thanks, Josh hurriedly returned to the bar to serve some newly arrived customers.

Mike immediately dived hungrily for a sandwich. 'He must have read my mind. I'm starving. I couldn't face the plastic breakfast at the end of my long flight.'

Susan helped herself too, but more demurely.

Several new patrons had sat at an adjacent table, so Mike lowered his voice to a whisper. 'Why did Josh refer to the Polish mafia?'

'Natasha Minski was an illegal immigrant. She was a product of an undertaking run by an Ivan Gorvan. Alex was involved in that too when he lived in Poland. That's how he made most of his money to afford to come to England. The operation was exposed by Carl's testimony and a number of arrests have been made. The tabloid press referred to the operation as the Polish mafia.'

'So Josh's unthinking remark could be true?'

'No, I don't think so – mere journalistic licence. My sister knew what was going on in Poland. It was apparently a government supported operation; though no one could prove it or would admit to it.'

'Your sister?'

'Yes. As soon as I saw the transcript of Alex's confession, I contacted my mother and sister. That was quite a reunion. We made a pact to not reveal I was still alive in case Alex wriggled out of all the other accusations against him. We wanted him to go to prison. Even Marion had no guilt about that – she'd had a miserable time with Alex over the last few years. He'd been regularly unfaithful and had beaten her. She'd long suspected that Alex had killed me for his mother, but had been too afraid to pursue it.'

'Didn't you try to contact Carl while all this was going on?' Mike asked.

'I asked my sister to try to find out where he was, but he was under police protection somewhere. The police said that only family visits were allowed and they could not pass on messages. As soon as the trial finished, Carl disappeared. We've searched everywhere. You are now my best and only remaining hope of finding him. You've been closer to him than anyone in recent years. I'm hoping that you might have some insight to where he may have gone.'

'Is it public knowledge now that you are alive?'

'No. The Zurek women thought it would unnecessarily stir up the past and public interest. We've had quite enough of that recently. Let sleeping Sarahs lie.'

Subconsciously Mike and Susan had eaten all the sandwiches and their glasses were empty. With a natural break in the story, Susan took the opportunity to renew their drinks with Mike just opting for mineral water this time. It took a few minutes for her return.

'Sorry it took so long. I had to suffer another round of apologies from Josh. He's quite sweet really. He has offered to help in any way he can.'

Mike was more interested in the search for his ex-partner. 'Where have you looked for Carl so far?'

'I've hired two private detectives to do most of the legwork. There's no answer from his flat. His mobile number doesn't ring. Nobody at MicaCom has heard from him. Local running clubs have been contacted in case he's been seen jogging. Ads have been in the personal columns of all daily newspapers and in the computer magazines that he used to read. Jacqui has phoned everyone in his address book that he left behind at MicaCom. One of the boffins at BinaryByte has tapped the e-mail accounts he had at MicaCom, but there's been no out-going activity for two months now, and only trivial in-coming messages. He's listed with the police as a missing person and details of his car have been circulated - they've checked his flat in Chelmsford. Don Travis has searched in Spain and Canada so far.'

'What's the connection with Don, Spain and Canada?'

'My sister made friends with Don during the trial. He hasn't heard from Carl, but his bizarre idea was that he'd be touring the world following the Formula 1 Championship. So, I paid for him and Wendy to go the Spanish Grand Prix at the end of May and Montreal last weekend for the Canadian Grand Prix. They checked hotels, asked Carl's favourite race team - Jordan, to keep a look out for him, with the promise of some sponsorship if they found him, and generally scoured the circuits on practice and race days. Nothing.'

'I can't really believe that Carl is gadding around the World enjoying himself. I still reckon he's totally pre-occupied with a work project somewhere. So Don also knows you are alive?'

'No. Arrangements were made through my sister. Though Don is getting suspicious that the costly search is more than just my sister wanting to thank Carl for putting her husband behind bars.'

'My God, you've certainly been thorough. I've been thinking about where he could be,' Mike said and explained what his thought processes had been in the quiet journey to the pub. 'So California is a definite possibility. Carl loved it there. He told me he might visit his parents if he never found you. I called in to see them three weeks ago and they receive e-mails from him every other week. They knew about MicaCom being sold, but Carl hadn't told them how much for, his plan to find you or a possible visit. And of course I presume they don't know what's been going on here.'

'They know now. I eventually tracked down their phone number two weeks ago. The news came as a big shock to them. They now phone me every other day for an update. They haven't had an e-mail from Carl for four weeks. Oh, by the way, they send their regards to you and hoped that Lisa was feeling better. I now know why she was poorly.'

Mike smiled. 'Interestingly Lisa and I decided on names on the flight back. If it's a boy, he'll be called Carl. If it's a girl, she'll be called Sarah. It was the least I could do after buggering up your lives together. We like the name Susan too if you would prefer that?'

'Sarah would be fine. If I ever get Carl back, I intend to change my name back to Sarah anyway.'

'You said the police had checked Carl's flat, but presumably to only establish he wasn't there. Why don't we search it for clues? I have a key.'

'Really? It has to be worth a try.'

'My only other idea is the Internet. I can't imagine Carl in the World without having access to the Internet. He'll be out there in Cyberspace somewhere. We ought to search for him just like he searched for you. So, can you now fill in the missing bits of the story? Particularly your fictitious suicide and how you met George.' Mike asked.

'I'll tell you on the way to Carl's flat.'

'You want to go now?'

'Whenever I get the slightest lead to Carl's whereabouts I have to follow it up straightaway. I'm sorry. Am I being unreasonable? You must be shattered and want to get back to Lisa.'

'Yes, yes and yes, but I can't wait any longer to hear the rest of your story.'

The walk back to *The Nearest FarAway Place* was at a stiffer pace, led by Susan's eagerness to see Carl's flat for the first time. Susan was talked out for the moment and steered Mike into narrating a travelogue about his American tour.

Mike rang Lisa again to tell her he was going to Carl's flat with Susan. Lisa was disappointed by Mike's prolonged absence, but said she understood how important the investigation was. Every day while they had been in America, Mike had mentioned his hope that Carl and Susan had got back together. Lisa knew that Mike would not be able to settle into his new life until he had done everything that he could to re-unite them. Despite wanting to begin making her nest at home in private, Lisa suggested to Mike that after the visit to Carl's flat, Susan might want to come to stay with them. Mike made the offer and he was surprised that Susan accepted. The barrier that he thought might be raised - *I don't want to be away in case Carl calls* – never arose after Susan had swiftly reprogrammed her answer phone saying that she could temporarily be contacted at Mike's number.

Susan retried the mobile number that Josh had rung but found the number was unobtainable again. The disappointment showed; for a moment even her bright eyes looked sad.

Heading away from Bradwell in the car, Mike could not contain his curiosity any more and asked, 'What actually happened at Cambridge?'

'Do you want the short version or the long version?' Susan offered.

'Now there's another Carl and Susan coincidence. Carl asked me exactly the same question about his story. I said then I wanted the long version, the same still applies.'

Part Four

Susan's Story

Chapter 30

Monday, February 8, 1988 – 7:00 a.m.

The telephone was ringing. It was early on a Monday morning. My room in the house was downstairs and opened into the passageway where the telephone was situated. It wasn't a harsh ring, but loud enough for me to be bothered by it and quiet enough for my housemates not to hear it. I was already awake and trying to solve a course work problem in my head. The ringing was an intrusion on my thoughts; if I didn't answer the phone - nobody would. The call was for me; it was Marion, my sister, phoning from Poland – my father had died from a heart attack.

Monday morning was always the low point of the week. After two mornings of waking with Carl, the vacant space beside me was disquieting. That day I remember I was particularly troubled; final exams were just a few months away and the extra-curricular project work I was conducting for my professor had hit a flat spot. But worst of all – my father was dead.

I cried, mostly for my father, but also for all the other things that weighed heavy on me. Normally I would have rung Carl for support except that we had a pact that Monday morning to Friday night was for working, the rest of the time was for loving. Besides, he had never met my father and I rarely mentioned him. It was something I would need to handle alone – for the time being. I cried so long and hard that exhausted, I went back to sleep and didn't wake until midday. I was due at lectures and a project meeting, which I missed that morning, but the absence was trivial in comparison to the news I had received.

I did little for the next two days except walk a lot particularly alongside the River Cam; I had always found that the flow of water had a calming effect. My housemates, especially Kate rallied round me although I didn't reveal why I was sad. Marion phoned me regularly to check I was coping and to update me on events in Poland.

Late on Wednesday evening Marion told me that the funeral had been set for the following Tuesday in my father's birthplace, Radom near Warsaw; would I be going? The answer was yes, of course, but I'd never been abroad alone before and hoped that Carl would accompany me and make the arrangements for us. I think I was over the worst of my grief and planned that on the following morning I would ring Carl at work, and then restart my studies.

I slept well that night and rose late, around half past nine. I could hear someone moving about in the kitchen and I could smell toast. It reminded me that I hadn't eaten properly since Sunday, and the thought of a hearty breakfast lifted me. The post had already arrived and two letters had been pushed under my door.

The first was from my stepmother, Eliza, in Poland. My relationship with Eliza had never been more than adequate and I was always mistrustful of her and her motives. She seemed a very determined woman, but my father loved her, so that was good enough for me. The early part of her letter expressed sincere condolences about my father's death and how privileged she had been to spend two wonderful years with him. Then the tone of the letter changed; she added that throughout her marriage she had tended diligently to my father's needs - despite the neglect of his daughters, and hoped that his Will had justifiably recognized Eliza's superior contribution. If it hadn't, then she might have to take some appropriate action!

I cried again, not because of the implied threat, but for my father who had died apparently unaware of his wife's complicity. The anxiety of a few days earlier came surging back with a vengeance; my head was pounding and I felt dizzy. I sat down on my bed, fearful that I was going to faint, and I tried to concentrate on the second letter. It was postmarked Chelmsford, but the handwriting on the envelope wasn't Carl's, or one that I recognized. I was shaking so vigorously that as I opened the envelope, two photographs tumbled out face up, onto my lap. I remember glancing at them, and then browsing the accompanying letter – then the world went blank.

I don't remember too much of the coming weeks. Most of what I will tell you was sourced from other people.

Kate had found me having some sort of seizure in my room. I was screaming and smashing things, and eventually collapsed. She phoned for an ambulance, which took me to Addenbrooke's hospital. She also called Carl and they met later at the hospital. I slept mostly for the first two days. The few times I awoke, I mumbled incoherently except for damning words against Carl. Because of that, and with the intervention of various people, I never saw Carl again.

I had various tests and I was diagnosed as suffering from reactive depression and hysterical amnesia. The contributory factors were judged to be my father's death and Carl's infidelity.

The photographs were viewed to be the turning point; they were intimate pictures of him with another woman. The details have been purged from my brain; a fact that supposedly confirms the photographs were the major cause of my trauma. The anonymous letter that came with them had explained in graphic detail the affair that Carl had been having.

When I became more conscious, I just laid in bed, disassociated from my surroundings. I was vaguely aware that my mother, and later Marion - after she had attended to the details of my father's funeral, were at my side. They tried to engage me in conversation but I used to stare at them blankly. I lost a lot of weight, and mentally there was a void in my mind like floating in the darkness and silence of space. I knew that I had suffered a great loss though I couldn't grasp what it was, except when reliving the trauma during sleep, but never recalling the details when I woke. The frustration produced dark thoughts of wanting to give up - even suicide. Later it was explained to me that these experiences and feelings were part of the healing process. For a while, I was under constant surveillance either by my mother, Marion or hospital staff.

With the help of psychotherapists and counsellors, the cause of my depression was gradually made to surface. I began to understand what had happened to me and was taught ways of dealing with the memories. Even the local Priest visited me on several occasions and preached an acceptance of death and forgiveness.

After a month in hospital, I felt ready to try to resume a normal life. The hospital was in accord so long as I left University and stayed with my mother. That was unthinkable; I was determined to sit my finals, so had to discharge myself and I went back to my shared house in St. Johns Road.

Part of my rehabilitation schedule was to make contact with Carl and discover why he had been so deceitful. Marion told me that Carl had made a nuisance of himself while I was in hospital. He had phoned everyday asking to speak to me and the hospital had to introduce special procedures to stop his calls getting through. My mother and Marion had pleaded with me to ignore this rehabilitation advice, in case I went into regression. But Carl's persistence had led me to believe that he wanted to make amends and I needed his apology to complete my recovery. I phoned and phoned but there was no answer from his home and I found out he had been dismissed from his job. I eventually persuaded Marion to help find him while I re-immersed myself in my studies; but all she could find out was that he had probably gone abroad. This lack of news, and the recognition that preparation for my exams was going to be harder than I had appreciated, began to play on my mind. The doctors had been right - perhaps I wasn't ready yet to face up to the realities of the world. My concentration wasn't there and I became obsessed with the need to speak to Carl.

However, unbeknown to me an additional complication in my life had arisen while I was in hospital. As I was agonizing over Carl, Marion revealed that I had inherited the majority of my father's estate - just under £200,000. I hadn't told Marion about the threatening letter from Eliza, since Marion was married to Eliza's son, Alexander, so it was no surprise when Marion said that Eliza had been trying to contest the Will. That and the lack of news about Carl put me again on to a downward spiral. I abandoned my studies for a final time and reverted to my introverted and insecure state. My mother and sister pleaded with me to go back into hospital or at least to leave the University and stay with my mother. I didn't know what to do - I just stayed in my room praying that Carl would contact me.

Then quite suddenly I had a visit from Alexander. He said he had come to England because he had made a promise to my father that if ever I were in trouble, he would take care of me. He had discovered that my mother and sister were conspiring to have me committed to a mental institution and thereby take control of the inheritance from my father. I obviously didn't believe him at first and suggested that if anyone was trying to usurp the money, it was his mother – Marion had told me. He argued this lie was part of Marion's plot against me and I would be best advised to temporarily transfer the money to him for safekeeping, in case her committal plan succeeded. Some doubts were certainly seeded in my mentally disturbed mind but I dismissed his suggestion, despite his insistence that I might be in danger if I didn't comply. He said he would be contacting me the following day to establish whether I had changed my mind.

Around that time, I was left in the house on my own during the day; my housemates were usually at their colleges or the library going through the final preparations for their exams. I think it was on March 17 that my visitor must have been watching the house because within ten minutes of everyone leaving the house for the day, there was a knock at the front door. I opened the door to a smartly dressed man proclaiming to be a legal messenger from my sister; could he come in? He followed me into my room and said my sister had asked him to retrieve any identification papers or other personal documents I had which would verify who I was. They were supposedly required as evidence of my inheritance entitlement in the dispute with Eliza. Foolishly, I gathered together the necessary paperwork without asking at least one obvious question like: why hasn't my sister come? My gullibility only registered as I tendered the bundle of documents to my caller – but it was too late. He took the bundle, stuffed them in an inside pocket and as he withdrew his hand he was holding what looked like a kitchen chopping knife. In a flash, he rushed forward and brought the knife down towards my head.

Despite my mental lethargy, physically I was still sharp; the previous year I had attended a course on self-defence after a spate of attacks on female students. Sharp, but not sharp enough, because that initial assault was so unexpected that my feint was too slow and the knife slashed my left cheek. As my attacker readjusted his stance for a second hit, I'd thought that would be the end of me; I was frozen to the spot my hand resting on my wound and blood running down my fingers. Thank God, my room was in its usual mess and he stumbled on a pile of books on the floor. He went down hard on one knee and used the hand holding the knife to arrest his fall. His shriek of surprise roused me from my catalepsy and I stamped on his hand with the heeled shoe of my left foot. He held on to the knife, but his astonishment was sufficient to allow me to aim a more effective blow to his face with my right foot, and he fell backwards with blood running from his nose. He was still in control, but with my raised foot I brought my heel down as hard as I could between his legs. The scream confirmed that this time I'd struck a sensitive target. Had he recovered from that blow to his manhood, I would probably not be here today. I was spent and the sight of blood on my hand had shocked me rigid and speechless. Another onslaught would surely have been successful, but he simply crawled along the floor into the hall, managed to rise to a crouching position desperately clutching his groin with his left hand and the knife in his right, and vanished through the front door.

I slumped onto my bed shaking uncontrollably now that it registered what had just happened and then either by shock or exhaustion I passed out. When I came round - I guess an hour later, I was lying on my left side. As I raised my head, there was a sickly sound as the clotted blood on my tingling cheek came unstuck from the pillow. I jumped up eager to inspect the wound, and realized the greatest source of pain was in my right toes, the result of contact with my assailant's nose. I hobbled to a mirror. Like all facial cuts the bleeding had been exaggerated - the depth of the laceration was superficial but I knew then that it would leave a scar.

I replayed the earlier events in my mind. I shivered from the worry that my haunted mind had cruelly invented a perverted nightmare and that somehow the damage had been self-inflicted. I went to the telephone to phone the police still uncertain of the origin of my story, when it rang – it was Alexander. He was hesitant as though he hadn't expected me to answer, then I confided to him what had happened. He easily convinced me that his forecast had come true. My mother or sister had undoubtedly engineered the attack; I was in extreme danger and was not to contact the police. He outlined the plan for my escape and boasted that in the extreme he could arrange for me to take a new identity.

I bathed my wound and considered what to do. While in hospital I had often thought about a new future, away from the sad memories of Cambridge. With this latest event to add to my suffering, I conjured a solution and made a list. I phoned my professor, George Fellgate to arrange to visit him at Queens' College.

George had approached me at the beginning of my second year at Cambridge to help him with some software routines for one of his private research projects called MBridge. How the project got that name lies in some of George's forgotten history. It was always one of three possibilities; a shortened form of Cambridge, a truncation of ComBridge – since its original purpose was a bridge between various communication protocols, or it was named after the view of the Mathematical Bridge from George's rooms in Queens' College. Whatever, he liked the name and that's what it's always been.

George had selected me because of the apparent flair I had in system design. I was first attracted to the idea because he was going to pay me for the work. Not because I particularly needed money – I had a full grant, which covered my modest spending requirements, it was the sense of satisfaction that I would achieve by doing something useful, as opposed to the regurgitated standard lectures and project work for my degree. Initially I spent a few hours a week on the work, but as the studies for my degree became trivial by comparison, I became more involved in some of the mainstream activities of MBridge development. By the beginning of the third year, George and I were effectively equal partners in the project. We became very good friends. About once a fortnight George and his wife Samantha invited me to dinner at their modest house in Fulbourn. To me he was like the local father I hadn't had for a few years; and I think to him and his wife I was the daughter that they'd never had.

I had to be secretive about what we were doing - I never even told Carl. The work did not use University equipment or materials, nor was it a University funded project. Whenever I needed to use a computer, I used one of George's personal machines. The secretiveness came from George not wanting to be accused of diverting my attention from my studies, and the commercial possibilities of the end-product. There was never any concern on my part for the former, if anything this special interest had a positive effect on my Computer Studies course. As for the latter, George had three dilemmas – Conscience, Risk and Funding.

George had been at Cambridge since he graduated thirty years earlier. He had pioneered some major developments in computers and software and Cambridge had become a way of life. He loved teaching and academia, and it bothered his conscience about venturing into the commercial world. It was a risk too. At the age of fifty-one, could he give up the comfort and security of a senior post at a renowned seat of learning, and plunge into an uncertain business venture? He only had a gut feel about the likely success of MBridge - there was no marketing intelligence to quantify its potential. And where would the money come from to fund such an opportunity? He had plenty of industry contacts that he believed would gladly buy the rights to MBridge - but his ideal was to pursue the project himself. This latter point was one of the things I wanted to discuss with him.

I prepared a folder containing the things I needed to discuss with George and I took my favourite walk from the house alongside the River Cam crossing the Mathematical Bridge to the President's Lodge of Queens' College. It was longer than the direct route through the city centre, but I did not want to draw attention to myself by the prominent dressing on my face. I hurried and kept vigilant in case I was being followed.

The professor had rooms on the first floor overlooking the river and he welcomed me like a long lost friend. 'Sarah, it is so good to see you up and about. Samantha and I have been so worried about you.'

He put his arms out towards me - I think he wanted to hug me, but his reserve took over and he dropped his left hand, leaving his right one extended for an embarrassed handshake. I tried a smile but the creasing of my face made my cheek sting.

'Kate said you were still poorly. Please sit down. And your face, what has happened to you now?'

The room had that characteristic musty smell that pervades every ancient building at Cambridge and the President's Lodge was one of the oldest. I sat down in an equally ancient leather easy chair. He sat facing me perched on a modern looking swivel chair, which like the computer on his desk was completely out of character with the surroundings.

'I didn't know that you had spoken to Kate, she never mentioned it.'

'I told her to say nothing in case you got the impression I was trying to expedite your return. I was very worried about your health. I wondered if I had been putting too much work pressure on you, but Kate assured me the cause was related to some personal tragedy. Is there something I can help with?'

'Yes, there is actually. Could you make me a mug of hot sweet tea? I think I'm suffering from shock at the moment and I have some bad news and good news to tell you.'

'Yes of course, my dear, except you will have to suffer a bone china cup and saucer. Mugs are frowned upon when one is a Cambridge professor.' He laughed - I tried not to, and he got up and went to what looked like a wardrobe built into an alcove. Hidden behind the door were a small sink and some shelves containing crockery, an electric kettle and various brewing components. 'How many sugars?'

'Two please.'

While he was rattling about in the cupboard, he said, 'For the offer of help I was really referring to your personal circumstances.'

'Yes, I know. You can help there too. The tragedy and knife wound on my face are part of the story you need to know.'

I realized I should have chosen my words more carefully as a freshly washed china cup bounced across the shiny wooden floorboards towards me.

'Knife wound!' George exclaimed, the tea making forgotten. 'Goodness, what are you saying?'

'I'm sorry, sir. I didn't mean to alarm you. I will explain, but I'm desperate for that cup of tea,' I said reaching for the stray cup and passing it to him.

He still looked bewildered with his mouth hanging open, so I posed a diversionary question.

'Would you mind if I called you George? I think what I'm about to say will be easier if I wasn't hindered by the formal teacher student relationship.'

Such a request was probably an even bigger shock, as his mouth hung lower, but he quickly recovered his normal composure, 'Um … well … yes, if the circumstances dictate it.'

I sat down again and clearly baffled, he resumed his charring. A minute later he cleared a pile of books from a small table, positioned it in front of me and placed the cup of tea.

I took a few sips for courage. 'I'm leaving Cambridge. I've thought about it long and hard, but the result was inevitable really. My mind's …'

Unusually he interjected and said animatedly, 'But surely, there is time enough for healing before your finals. You have probably enough marks from your project work already to get a pass. You could muddle through your final exams and still get a first class degree. Besides, there would be extenuating circumstances that could be taken into consideration when marking. Don't give up now Sarah. At the moment you appear to be … well … quite like your old self.'

'I'm not so sure. I'm excelling myself today being able to talk to you like this. Believe me, this is the longest, most lucid conversation I've had for over a month. I thought I would be able to tough it out, but in reality my mind's a foggy mess. I can't concentrate for long periods. I'd probably forget to turn up for the exams. I need a break from Cambridge, away from the academic pressures. I simply want to disappear to a quiet place for a period of rehabilitation. I don't know how long that will take. A month, two months, six months, a year, perhaps even longer.'

'You could take a year's sabbatical and then finish your third year. I could sanction that.' He was beginning to sound desperate.

'I wish the decision were that easy. The sad memories of Cambridge might prevent me from doing that.'

'I suppose there is nothing I can say or do that could dissuade you from your conclusion.'

'No George, I'm sorry.'

'I would like to understand your reasoning though. Do you feel you can tell me what you have been through?'

I finished my tea then told George briefly about my father's death, the deceit of my (unnamed) boyfriend, the ensuing breakdown and the time in hospital. He listened patiently and prompted me kindly when I paused at the parts that I found painful to recall.

'What's the current prognosis of your condition?'

'As I said earlier; I need rest, quiet, and a comfortable and stress-free environment, for as long as it takes to restore my mental constitution.'

He thought for a moment. 'You could work for me full-time on MBridge. That change could be as good as a rest,' he said triumphantly.

'The answer to that is yes.' He smiled. 'But not yet; I'll come to that.' The smile waned.

'So, you *really* want to drop out?'

'My heart says "no", but my mind and body say "yes" – and so do all the doctors and consultants that have seen me. I have to bow to their superior knowledge.'

George went into thought mode again, for longer this time, presumably searching for another approach. He must have given up when he continued, 'I presume that was the bad news?'

'The good and the bad are from your perspective not mine. There might be good news for me, it depends how you react to the good news I have for you.'

'I could use some good news after what you have told me. More hot sweet tea?'

I readily accepted and there was a gap of several minutes while he made the tea. I quenched my thirst again before I went on.

'As a result of my father's death, I inherited the major part of his estate - about £200,000 in cash. I have reason to believe that members of my family are so malcontent that they have been conspiring to take control of the money, either by having me committed to a mental institution or having me killed.'

I paused to let my statement take effect. It was clear that I would have to substantiate my accusation and for the first time George looked at me as though I really was a crackpot.

'Sarah, that can't possibly be true.'

'I know it sounds like a crazy woman talking, but there is evidence. Certainly my mother and sister are pushing me very hard to go back into hospital, and according to my brother-in-law this is their first step to having me declared insane. The cut on my face is the result of a failed attempt at my murder less than two hours ago.'

I went on to justify my conclusions and relate the knife attack on me in the house. George made sucking sounds of disbelief as I purposely described the scene in detail to convince him of the truth.

'Why haven't you contacted the police?' George posed the question and then immediately knew the answer. 'They would not believe you. No witnesses, no weapon and you currently suffering mental distress. Plus, if your theory is correct, you do not want to accuse your family, nor do you want to be drawn into an attempted murder inquiry. Am I right?'

'Perfectly. It's another reason for disappearing to a quiet place, where nobody can find me ... or perhaps dying so that nobody even bothers to try to find me.'

'What on earth are you suggesting?'

'Suicide,' I said, 'or rather an assumed suicide,' I hastily qualified.

'Really Sarah, I think you are going too far now. Frankly, I am beginning to form the same opinion as your mother and sister. Perhaps you should go back into hospital.' He had been on the edge of his seat up to then, now he leant back in his chair in a defiant manner.

'George, please believe me I'm as sane as you at the moment. I've come to you because you are the only person that I can still fully trust. So many people have let me down. As much as I value Kate's friendship, if I confided my plan to her, I think she would be too sensible to hang on to a dark secret. At least you are remote from my family and friends and would not be dragged into an investigation of our conspiracy.'

'There has to be a better way of handling this problem. I am puzzled anyway. Is this supposed to be the good news you had for me?' he queried.

'The beginning of it, yes. Let's come back to the suicide plan and instead, talk about making us rich and at least you famous.'

I reached into the folder I had brought with me, took out a piece of paper and a biro, and laid them on the table.

'This is a list showing my plan of action. You may need to make some additional notes as I go along. The first item is the details of my solicitors. I'll telephone them shortly with instructions of where to transfer the proceeds of my inheritance. I want to give them the details of your bank account ...'

George interrupted, 'Now just a minute, I ...'

I interrupted back. 'George, please hear me out. I have a lot to get through. Please save your questions for when I've finished.' If I'd still been calling him *sir* I'm sure my admonishment would have been repelled. Instead, he just blinked a few times in surprise.

'I want you to invest the money on my behalf in a short notice interest bearing account for probably about three months.

'With your help I am going to *commit suicide* tonight and disappear. I want you to take me to a hotel outside of Cambridge – but not too far away. Until the story of my suicide quietens down, I'll expect to swap hotels every week. I'll need to borrow some cash from you for living expenses, since I don't want to expose my name via cheques or credit card. Just withdraw from the new account the same amount as payback.

'I'll check into each hotel under an assumed name. The name I choose will eventually become my new name once I have changed it formally by Deed Poll or Statutory Declaration. I'll disguise my appearance as best I can so that if my photograph gets circulated I won't be recognized.

'I'll stay in hotels until I've found a place to live. I want to purchase a small property in the Bradwell area in Essex. After I've moved into the new place, I'll need a decent computer so that I can work full time on MBridge. I reckon that it will then take less than six months to knock it into shape as a marketable product.

'While I'm doing that, I want you to form a company jointly owned by you and me. Whatever is left of the inheritance - after purchasing and furnishing my home, buying the computer and giving me, say, a modest allowance for a year's living expenses – I want to invest in the company.'

As instructed, George had been making notes - lots of notes, so I expected a barrage of questions.

'I suppose I will have to change my opinion. I do not believe a mad woman could come up with such a detailed and imaginative plan. When did you decide this course of action?'

So far, so good. He hadn't said no - yet.

'While I was in hospital I thought a lot about the development of MBridge. It was something to focus my mind instead of the issues of my father and boyfriend. I resolved that if the chances of finishing my degree were mucked up, then to work full-time on MBridge was what I wanted to do. I wasn't sure whether you would be able to fund it, but that barrier was removed when I heard about the inheritance. I thought *I* would fund it instead. The suicide, disappearance and name change was conceived in my walk here.'

'Why can you not hang on to the money yourself?'

'If I die, my Will passes the proceeds of my estate to my sister. I obviously don't want that to happen if my sister is involved in my death. The money is in the family solicitor's bank account now. If I get it transferred to my own account, then transactions on the account might be traced when I disappear. Better to dispose of the money now since I don't have time to change my Will.'

'If someone finds out the money has been transferred to me, I might be implicated in your vanishing act.'

George was exploring possible flaws in the plan. I began to feel confident that I'd won him over. 'Nobody will find out. I've been assured of absolute discretion by my solicitors.'

'Why Bradwell?'

I must be home and dry. We were down to the trivia.

I was purposely vague. 'It's a personal thing. The area reminds me of happy times.'

'It seems you have thought of everything bar one point. Suppose I do not want to join the business rat race with MBridge. I had thought of placing the final product in the public domain because of the difficulties in commercializing it.'

'The difficulties won't exist anymore if you accept my plan. You'll have money and me. The risk will still be there but I'm determined that we will be successful - I have so many new ideas for MBridge and for complimentary products. The only barrier I imagine will be your intellectual conscience. Think of the challenge and excitement of it all. With respect, it would make a big change from the stuffy constraints of academia.'

George stood up and stretched his legs as though he had cramp. He began to pace up and down in front of me, stroking his chin and running his fingers through his grey hair. He paused a few times and looked at me as though he was about to ask a question, then resumed pacing. I slumped back in my chair - I was so tired. The morning's trauma and the effort to confront George were taking their toll on me. I didn't want to prompt George for an answer. He was a deep thinking man and was taking his time to weigh the pros and cons of what I had proposed. I think I had covered all the angles of my escape, which seemed to be confirmed by George's lack of questions. I knew that my future was in his hands. When he had come to his decision whatever he said could determine the outcome of the rest of my life. I closed my eyes.

'Sarah. Sarah. Are you all right?'

I was shivering and sweating at the same time. It was a mammoth struggle to open my eyes - George was shaking my arm gently.

'You had me worried for a moment. I couldn't wake you up. In fact I am *still* worried - you look totally exhausted.'

I sat up and raised my head. 'I'm sorry George, I must have dozed off.'

'I let you sleep for an hour. You looked as though you needed the rest.'

'And now I need a painkiller, my head is thumping. Have you got something I could take?'

He moved to his desk and opened a drawer. Shook a couple of pills from a box and fetched a glass of water.

As I swallowed the pills he said, 'When you feel you are ready, perhaps you could tell me about your suicide, we have a busy evening ahead of us.'

I walked back to the house. George had offered to give me a lift but I needed the fresh air and I didn't want him to be seen with me. I had phoned the solicitors and the inheritance money would be transferred to George's bank account in the morning. I had booked into the Bedford Court hotel in Newmarket for a couple of nights under the name of Susan Fellgate. George and I had spent at least twenty minutes deliberating on my new identity. We must have ranged from Abigail Aardvark to Zena Zodiac but in deference to George's wishes we chose the name he intended for the daughter he never had. I questioned whether it was wise to use his surname, but he was right - it didn't matter. If someone suspected that I had faked my suicide and changed my name, there was no obvious starting point for the name that I would choose.

In my room, I packed a small rucksack with a couple of changes of clothes and a few minor personal possessions - someone about to commit suicide would obviously not depart with their belongings. I'd soon have plenty of time and money to shop for replacements. I had gambled on my departure time - seven o'clock should be about right. The day had been cloudy and dull and it would be dark enough then to slip out of the house. It was no more than a few steps from the house to the quiet expanse of Jesus Green so the chance of being observed would be small. It should also be early enough to avoid bumping into my housemates. Their current routine was to work in the libraries until about eight, then go for a quick drink or party until late, before coming home. I felt guilty deserting my friends in such an inglorious way; particularly Kate who had been the most supportive friend anyone could wish for. When this was over, I would have to make amends to her.

The scheme almost went wrong. Not long after I arrived, Kyoko came home. She knocked lightly on my bedroom door and called out to me. I kept quiet, hoping that she would assume I was sleeping. I couldn't risk her seeing me. I listened to her movements – kitchen, bathroom and then creaking floorboards from the bedroom she had above mine.

It was still an hour before I was due to leave. I had planned everything meticulously except for one item - what the suicide note would say. It would have to be short and maybe a little obscure. I didn't think it was an offence to fake a suicide, so long as it didn't have an ulterior motive like an insurance fraud. Nonetheless, saying something like *Goodbye cruel world, I am going to kill myself* was a bit definitive, besides, if and when Carl heard the news I wanted him to know that I was still on earth and not in heaven (or should it be hell?). I wanted to imply I had committed suicide and pass Carl a message at the same time. Something only he and I would truly understand – and then it came to me: *My life is over. I'll start again at the Nearest FarAway Place.*

I wrote the note and placed it on my pillow. It seemed ironic seeing the bloodstains there and I wondered if anyone would try to make the connection between them and the note. I sat looking around the room, reminiscing and hoping that Kyoko would be going soon. My hope was rewarded five minutes after I needed to leave to meet George.

I had arranged to meet George on the Chesterton Road where the footbridge across the River Cam joins Jesus Green. I obviously didn't want him to come to the house so the meeting place was set to be a quiet location and only a short walk away. It had begun to rain so I wrapped myself in a cagoule to keep dry and conceal my appearance. The next thing I remembered was waking up in a strange room with George and Samantha leaning over me.

Chapter 31

Monday, March 17, 1988 – 7:30 p.m.

I've never recalled what happened to me that night, except in the uncertainty of a recurring nightmare. Until the trial, I didn't even know that Alex had ambushed me, but the nightmare must be fairly accurate because it correlates well with the recording made of Alex's confession that appeared in the newspapers.

He attacked me with a knife, knocked me out with a gun, strangled me with a rope and then threw me in the river. How did I survive that vicious onslaught? George had some plausible explanations. The knife had only penetrated my rucksack spilling the contents - including Carl's letters, onto the ground. The blow to my head was superficial, but just hard enough to render me unconscious. I had a bloody lump for a while, but that quickly healed without the aid of stitches. Apparently, it's quite difficult to strangle someone with a rope with your hands. I was wearing a flesh coloured polo-necked sweater and George surmised that in the darkness the sweater and the hood of my cagoule provided the marginal protection that was needed against the rope asphyxiating me. There was a feint red mark around my neck for a while and then it disappeared. Of course, an unconscious body dumped into a river will soon drown, but I had George to thank for saving my life. Remember I was late for the rendezvous. George had been worried and was about to cross the bridge when Alex jumped me. He saw the shapes of the attack and then heard the splash as I was thrown in the river. George may have been on the wrong side of fifty, but he was a fit man and, thank God, an excellent swimmer. He simply jumped into the water and dragged me to the bank. The cold water had a reviving effect and mostly with George's help, I made the short journey to his car.

He guessed what had happened, so rather than compromise our plan and rush me to hospital, he took me to the house of a close doctor friend of his just a few minutes away. The doctor tended to my surface injuries and treated me for shock. Much later George said that he had told his friend I was a niece who'd had an unfortunate accident and fallen into the river. George assumed the friend had remained discreet, thinking perhaps that he was having an affair with a young student.

Obviously, I never made it to the Newmarket hotel that night. Amazingly, I felt relatively fine within two days but I stayed secluded in his house for three weeks. The local papers reported my disappearance and supposed suicide and George had police visits at Queens' and at home. Within two weeks, it was old news. The press and police had written off the case as another overworked, and probably drug induced student, that had decided to end it all. The story briefly resurfaced a few months later when some sodden letters from Carl to me were found close to the river and the police dragged the immediate stretch of water. The police believed it was a lost cause. If my body had been in the river, it would have been eaten or decomposed by then and that was the last time it was reported, until the trial of course.

One night in mid-April, George smuggled me to a hotel in Maldon. By then, I had changed my appearance. I'd cut my hair short and begun to wear spectacles with clear lenses, plus I had now assumed the name of Susan Fellgate. I stayed in the Maldon area for about four months, changing hotels a couple of times. My main priority was to find somewhere permanent to live. I registered with the local estate agents for a property in the Bradwell area. Few appeared on the market, but I was patient, above all I wanted somewhere within walking distance of St. Peter's Chapel.

During the weeks, I was fully occupied during waking hours, which for a time was little more than half a day. I slept at least ten hours each night, sometimes over twelve. Often I thought there was perhaps something wrong with me, but was afraid to register with a local doctor until I'd formally changed my identity. Looking back I now realize it must have been my body's way of saying *Take it easy, you have a busy time ahead*, because once I had begun to look to the future rather than dwell on the past, my sleeping patterns returned to their pre-traumatic norm of seven hours.

My days were spent mostly reading, cycling and shopping. Until then I wasn't an avid fiction reader, but I found an enjoyable balance between novels, technical publications and magazines about house maintenance. I read on average about two novels a week, but subsequently avoided romantic stories when the first sad one brought me to tears comparing the protagonist's loss with my own.

With the comforting warmth of the late spring and summer months, I decided to purchase a bicycle. At first, I just used it for riding around the town, but as my confidence and strength grew, I became more adventurous. By early June, I considered myself rather an expert and the thirty-mile round trips with a packed lunch to St. Peter's Chapel and its surrounding lanes and footpaths became a weekly, then twice-weekly treat.

Shopping was fun too. Gradually I began to replace the clothes that I had left behind in Cambridge and I had window-shopped exactly the furniture and fittings I wanted for my new home.

George and Samantha came to visit me every weekend, bar two when George had unavoidable lecturing assignments in Scotland and Sweden. We talked at length about our proposed business venture. It was going to be a venture - George was resigned to the fact that he would quit Cambridge as soon as I had completed my side of the bargain. As time went on, he questioned me more frequently about when I would be able to resume my work on MBridge. I had to reassure him every time that my technical lobe was ready and able, but my emotional lobe was not quite ready to commit to the intensity of work required. On one occasion, presumably to test my resolve, he had brought a computer system in his car and offered to set it up in my hotel room. To George's great disappointment I declined the offer and it was then he confessed to me how frustrated he was feeling about the lack of new progress on MBridge. He had purposely not involved anyone else in the project so far and was personally getting to a make or break point regarding his commitment to its future.

I was beginning to have doubts myself too, overcoming the Carl effect was taking longer than I thought. The turning point came in early July when I found what was to become *The Nearest FarAway Place*. I'd been on one of my cycling excursions to St. Peter's Chapel and was returning to Maldon via the Bradwell Marshes. I knew the status of every dwelling in the area and in Hockley Road, just before the gravel track becomes metalled, there was a white-boarded bungalow. When I'd last passed it, it had been distinctly occupied – curtains at the windows and often a car parked at the front. This time it looked deserted so I stopped to take a look. I peered through the grimy windows and but for a few fragments of carpet and neat piles of rubbish the place was empty. I walked the perimeter and established it had a large lounge stretching from front to back, a dining room, kitchen, bathroom and a double and single bedroom. The garden was wild and overgrown – cleared, the plot would be quite large. The bungalow - then called *Honeydew*, was at least a quarter of a mile from the next dwelling and backed on to farmland. I fell in love with the place immediately. I'd not received any details from the estate agents so either it was newly available or currently between owners.

That day I must have cycled back in record time to Maldon and began my tour of the estate agents – and bingo, yes it had just become available, the nominated agent hadn't even had time to print and distribute the details. The owner was an elderly lady, who had been uprooted by her family and placed in a pensioner's home since she was now too infirm to risk remaining in such a poorly maintained and remote property. It was the agent's lucky day because his cost of sale so far had been virtually zero and I was an over eager potential buyer. £50,000 was the asking price, and after a quick review of the specification, I made an offer of £48,000, much to the spotty young salesman's amazement. A telephone call to the owner's son and my offer was accepted, subject to a deposit and the legal processes. The salesman, who introduced himself as Tom, understandably still looked doubtful. It wasn't every day that an excitable young girl walked into his office and without viewing the inside of a property, promptly decided to buy it. So to allay his suspicion and confirm I was serious, I rushed back to my hotel to retrieve £1,000 in cash for the deposit from the secret lining in one of my suitcases. The look on his face as I counted out a bundle of £10 and £20 notes in front of him was a joy to behold. Back at the hotel, I called George and he was probably more relieved than me. At last, his partner-in-waiting would be free to put her three-month old plan into effect.

The following day I went back to *Honeydew* with a notepad and tape measure to make a list of things to be done. Transport was not a problem because spotty Tom had the keys and offered to show me round. It was obvious from his ogles and sexual innuendoes that he had an ulterior motive, but on the way to Bradwell, I hinted that I was buying the bungalow as a betrothal present for my *girlfriend*. Surprise, surprise - he stopped asking about me, and bored me instead with tales of gazumping and loft conversions.

It set me back slightly seeing the interior of the bungalow. I couldn't work out whether it had been ill maintained or gorillas with boxing gloves had conducted the clearance. Still, I would be able to test my new found DIY skills and with MBridge to complete, my days at *The Nearest FarAway Place* were going to be very busy.

I had to stall with Tom regarding certain purchasing details – first I had to get my name legally changed, a bank account set up, a solicitor recruited. Fortunately, most of the groundwork had already been accomplished weeks earlier. The starting point was getting a copy of my birth certificate since the original had been stolen or lost when I was attacked on Jesus Green. I hoped it was now safe to emerge again as Sarah Zurek without attracting any attention. With the copy certificate in my hand, the rest was easy and with a solicitor appointed to handle the purchase of the bungalow and to arrange the name change Deed Poll, ten days later I was officially Susan Fellgate.

The weekend after I had paid my deposit, the Fellgate *family* of three spent the Saturday and Sunday making plans for the bungalow. George, who was a bit of a DIY enthusiast, reckoned it would need £10,000 of additional work - minimum, to make it comfortably habitable. We had great fun comparing notes between his practical knowledge and the theoretical knowledge I had acquired by my extensive reading, but I think I held my own on the subjects of electrical wiring, plumbing, replacement of rotten woodwork and general decorating. The major decision was where to start the refurbishment. I decided on the smaller bedroom first. It required the least work and as I wanted to take occupancy as soon as possible, I would need somewhere to sleep in comfort. The larger bedroom I had earmarked as an office – I needed space to work - not to sleep; besides it faced on to garden wilderness.

I became a property owner on August 26, 1988, but didn't move in for another two weeks. There were some essential repairs and major decorating to be completed, and I also needed to wait until George had finished his preparations for the start of the new academic year. After, he was available to help me with transport, lifting and carrying, and errand running - there was a limit to what I could do using a bicycle. In the third week of September, the procession of delivery vans was almost non-stop as new carpets; furniture and equipment arrived for unboxing and placement.

By the end of the month, I was well satisfied with my new home. It was clean, comfortable and warm now that the cooler autumn days had arrived. My study was a showcase of modern equipment, supplied and installed by a computer dealer friend of George's. Three brand new, high-spec IBM PCs – one configured as a network server for the other two, two printers, a fax machine, photocopier and a second telephone point with a modem connected, plus a host of development software, utilities and manuals. There seemed to be cables everywhere, but it was a picture of contemporary industry and it was all mine.

I remember the first morning that I awoke with no major domestic duties to attend to. I sat in the study and surveyed my technical domain, and a shiver went down my spine. It had been over six months since I had done anything productive on MBridge. I'd thought about it a lot, but after such a long break, I had an uncomfortable feeling about being able to apply my mind again to the abstract software world of bits and bytes. Everything was different now. In half a year I had gone from a broken down, relatively irresponsible, life-endangered undergraduate at Cambridge called Sarah Zurek, to a sound-minded, rather wealthy, property-owning lady of leisure in the outback of Essex, with the name Susan Fellgate – and I had only just turned twenty-one. My period of convalescence was clearly over. Suddenly I had new responsibilities. Above all, I had a University professor to repay for his kindness and trust. After his initial misgivings about giving up his secure academic life, he was now dependent upon my efforts to deliver us into a speculative commercial undertaking that he was now eager to pursue. I powered up the equipment and stared at a VDU screen through my dummy spectacles for a minute, recalling my MBridge knowledge. Discarding the masquerading spectacles, which I had habitually worn since my suicide, symbolically seemed to spell the end of my retreat, and but for liquid in and liquid out breaks, I worked solidly for the next fifteen hours. BinaryByte Software was underway.

Of course, it wasn't called that then. It was a name that had stuck in my mind thinking about bits and bytes, and when the company was formed two months later, George was happy to formally adopt the name.

After the first day's delirious activity, I settled into a more sensible routine, with each day roughly divided into three equal parts - sleep, work and leisure. Typically, it was midnight to eight for sleeping, then two sessions of four hours work and four hours leisure. The leisure hours comprised household chores, gardening, decorating, reading and television, with the leisure period from midday to four devoted to a walk or bicycle ride via St. Peter's Chapel to the coast. Domestic shopping was confined to the limited and expensive choices of the village store, but I soon got bored with the frequent load-carrying visits there – despite attaching a large basket to my bicycle, so I made a standard list of weekly requirements and arranged a delivery for every Saturday morning. I varied my diet by making occasional trips to the food shops of neighbouring villages and about once a month to Maldon.

On reflection, it was a lonely and repetitive existence, particularly as George was usually too busy at Cambridge to continue his regular weekend visits with Samantha, but I was too preoccupied with the work on MBridge to notice. I kept George up-to-date with progress by phone, fax and modem; and as my first Christmas in isolation approached, I was close to delivering the first commercial version of the product.

I spent Christmas in Fulbourn, nominally for two days, but extending to two weeks, as George and I made plans for formally unleashing MBridge and

BinaryByte to the outside world. For me there was no problem in going forward. All I had to do was to continue to develop the product, no longer in line with our requirements, but for the customers that would influence its future direction. George's decision was more complex. Should he resign from the University immediately, or wait until the company was better established?

The decision actually came back to me. From my original inheritance, I still had around £115,000 left. Was I still willing, as originally intended, to invest my money in establishing BinaryByte? The answer was an emphatic "Yes", so I kept £15,000 and the round sum balance was placed in BinaryByte's new bank account as working capital. With the funds, we inspected then purchased a two-year lease of a small office near Cambridge airport. That was the only time I ever saw a BinaryByte office. I've never seen the substantial offices in the Science Park that we acquired in 1991. We, or rather George, recruited a very efficient and discreet secretary/office manager (secretly head-hunted from the Physics department at the University) called Mary, a salesman, two support staff and a programmer, installed loads of equipment and were up and running by the end of the January.

George saw the academic year out, never neglecting his basic University duties, but directing all his extracurricular efforts and spare time to remotely directing the activities of BinaryByte. When George eventually left the University in July 1989, there was already a steady - albeit not profitable - level of income, generated mostly by sales deriving from industry contacts that he had cultivated during his years at Cambridge.

I stayed in Bradwell. The corporate reason was that the offices were, in both our opinions, a little to close to the scene of my recent *suicide*, and it should be a while yet before my revivification. *My* reason was a selfish one - I couldn't bear to be away from *The Nearest FarAway Place*. The fortnight away at Christmas had been harrowing; whilst I was at ease in George and Samantha's company, I was still suspicious of the outside world. Naturally, the absence of BinaryByte's co-founder from the day-to-day company operations was initially an oddity that generated all kinds of rumours about the grotesqueness of my shielded physical appearance, according to the circumspect Mary. Amongst working colleagues George simply and deliberately referred to me as "S". It served to confuse; the general belief becoming that S was for Samantha, his technically brilliant wife, closeted from the world, only able to communicate instructions and deliver software changes by out-going fax, phone or modem.

It's really quite amazing that we've continued to operate like that for over ten years. To BinaryByte it makes the current trend of teleworking seem rather dated.

Once George was permanently at the helm of BinaryByte, sales started to boom. The positive feedback from customers, led to an intensive period of enhancements to MBridge - which I undertook, and the start of some new subsidiary products - which were handled by the office programmers. For the next year, I was fully occupied, eight hours a day, seven days a week. Working like that was the best mental tonic I could possibly have had. More staff were recruited and BinaryByte started making a profit, even after deducting salaries for George and me.

You might conclude from what I've said so far that Carl was no longer in my thoughts. On the contrary, it would be truthful to say that he was with me every day. I've only told you about the working-third of my days - links to Carl were prominent in the sleeping and leisure thirds.

I never had any problem sleeping. The days were always so busy in mind and body that sleep came quickly from mental and physical exhaustion. It was the two nightmares that frequently reminded me of my troubled past. The one about the attack on Jesus Green I've already mentioned, the other was the scene in my bedroom opening the anonymous letter and the photographs dropping into my lap. I relived the panic of the moment, not from what they depicted - because I cannot remember their content, but that I could not focus upon the woman in the photographs. Abject fear came from unexpectedly meeting her somewhere and not recognizing that she was the source of Carl's unfaithfulness.

The daily visit to the coast by St. Peter's Chapel was compulsive, bringing a high like the occasional spliff I had had at Cambridge. I would cast my mind back to the happy day that we spent there, re-living the minute details of holding hands, walking along the paths, the sea wall and the beach, kissing and having fun, recalling conversations and christening the area *The Nearest FarAway Place*. On fine days I would take a book to read or some sewing, sit somewhere, and immerse myself in the sounds of the sea and birds - but the visits always ended in tears. After the rejoicing of a time past, the present always came back to haunt me. The despair and hate flowing back was still crushing. There was one small part missing from my rehabilitation – I still needed to understand why Carl had deceived me, so that I could finally forget how he had hurt me. My preference was that the truth would come from Carl personally; but that wasn't essential, I would accept the truth from anyone that might know.

In August 1990, there was a critical point in my personal life - I met someone who offered to help me. I was sitting on a pew in the Chapel staring up at the colourful crucifix high on the stone wall behind the altar.

'Is there something I can help you with?' said a soft-spoken voice.

I started because I hadn't heard anyone approach and through tears, I looked up into the kindly and chubby face of a clergyman standing beside me.

'I have seen you here many times. You always look sad. I've prayed that one day soon you will be happy.'

'No Father, I don't expect I will be truly happy ever again. It's a long story.'

That chance encounter led to a religious period in my life with the Reverend Broadstairs as my minister, and over the coming months, I did relate the basic reason for my sadness. I simplified the story to a tale of "boy meets girl, boy deceives girl", since even to a man of God I was nervous about revealing episodes of fake suicide and attempted murder.

Prior to my meetings with the Reverend Broadstairs, my objective had been merely to understand Carl's deception, so that I could cleanse the remnants of the deep-rooted trauma that still pervaded my brain. Forgiveness had not entered my thoughts, just a need to discover and forget.

The Reverend's teachings first helped me to question if my censure of Carl was right and just. Had *I* given him reason to act the way that he had? *Of course not* was my immediate reaction. Carl had been unilateral in his actions to have an affair with someone else and ecclesiastical preaching would not dissuade me otherwise. I had to concede though, that my mind could have conveniently dismissed something, which might have been a causal factor. Was this doubt not a justifiable reason to forgive, argued my teacher? He quoted from Luke, Chapter 6, Verse 37: *Judge not, and ye shall not be judged: condemn not, and ye shall not be condemned: forgive, and ye shall be forgiven.*

And irrespective of doubts, was not forgiveness a route to righteousness and peace of mind? The Reverend was not a supporter of the proverb *Forgive and Forget*, instead he felt that a saying of a noted American psychiatrist Thomas Szasz was more appropriate: *The stupid neither forgive nor forget; the naive forgive and forget; the wise forgive but do not forget.*

Within a few months, he had not succeeded in converting me totally to a Christian life, but he *had* convinced me that for my future happiness I would have to subscribe to the doctrine of "forgive and remember".

Now my daily leisure trips ended tearless in St. Peter's Chapel, with a prayer from the Christian part of me, to give me guidance to find Carl; so I could forgive him and then remember and recreate the good times we had together.

Six months after my first meeting with the Reverend Broadstairs my prayers were answered - I received a package postmarked from BinaryByte. Inside were six floppy disks, a technical manual, a glossy sales brochure and a note from George. The note referred to some competitor intelligence gathering that had been conducted by his trustworthy aide Mary. Apparently, the BinaryByte salesmen had been complaining that they now had to work harder to secure sales because a competitive offering called Protean was eroding their product monopoly. Although not functionally identical to MBridge, there was some overlap and in these areas, Protean was viewed to be considerably better. Mary's husband was the IT manager for a company in Huntingdon who had obtained, through Mary's duplicity, a fully working copy of Protean for a thirty-day evaluation. It was enclosed herewith for my dissection and comment.

I cast aside the documentation. I am a great believer in that a reputable software product should be operable purely from what you see on screen, what I called the WYSIWYD (What You See Is What You Do) test. I loaded Protean onto my computer network and began putting it through its paces. When I chose the configuration program, I began to get a strange feeling. The prompts describing the inputs used a terminology that was familiar to me. In fact, some of the words used I felt certain I had coined or had heard sometime in the past. When I clicked on the help button, the text that popped-up was also familiar. At first I thought that maybe parts of MBridge had been plagiarized so I began to check my own software - No, I had never used those words. The only people I had ever discussed such technology with were George and Carl.

I picked up the technical manual and flicked through it looking for an author name – there was none. Then I looked at the brochure; there was a short history of the company - MicaCom, based in Chelmsford, but with no mention of individuals. However, tucked inside the brochure there was the covering letter that had been sent with the product; the directors' names were printed at the bottom – M. A. Stanford and C. D. Denham. Carl David Denham – it had to be. My hand began to visibly shake. I went back to the company history – formed in 1989. Carl disappeared in 1988 and re-emerged in 1989? It was possible. And he had been running a competitive company for two years just twenty miles from here!

I immediately picked up the phone and dialled MicaCom; then put the receiver down before there was an answer. I had to think this through. I had no idea of Carl's status; by now, he could be married with ... one ... two ... maybe even three children. Irrespective of the forgiveness I wanted to offer, my resurrection from death, if he were aware of my suicide, would be unbelievable and possibly unwanted. I formed a plan in my head then redialled MicaCom.

Do you remember the first time I rang you Mike? I expect not, but I was so nervous that day, I can recall it well. It was only after the sixth attempt I eventually got through to you.

'Good Morning. May I speak to Mr. Stanford please?'

'Who shall I say is calling?'

'It's Susan again. I have called several times today already, and it is really very important that I speak to Mr. Stanford on a delicate personal matter.'

'Please hold. I'll try him again for you.'

During the delay, I was imagining the dialogue going on between boss and reception to dispose of my persistent calls. Then much to my surprise I was put through.

'Mike Stanford here, and before you say anything, if you are trying to sell me any computer equipment, software, double glazing, pensions, insurance, time-share holiday homes or anything else I am not interested in, I reserve the right to put the phone down. OK?'

I gathered my resolve and started my pre-prepared script. 'Mr. Stanford, I'm calling regarding Carl Denham. May I assume that we are speaking privately?'

'The implication is that we need to?'

'That's correct.'

'Just a moment, I'll close my office door.'

I heard you get up and click the door shut.

'Now, what's this about, and I don't believe I caught your name.'

'My name is Susan and I would be grateful if I could leave it at that for now, as I hope you'll appreciate shortly.'

'Continue.'

'Also, at the moment it's very important that what I say to you is kept between us. In other words, do not say anything to Carl.'

'I may not be able to adhere to that request. Carl and I have no secrets between each other.'

'Oh. Then all I can ask is that when I've finished you could let me know if you will say anything to Carl.'

'Agreed.' A busy man with few words I thought.

'I am an old friend of Carl. We met in 1983 and ... um ... lost contact three years ago. In fact, he probably thinks I am dead. I would like to contact him again, but, I know this sounds strange, I wanted to find out first what his current status is.'

'Why might he *think* you were dead and what do you mean by "status".'

'He may have read or heard that I had committed suicide. By status I meant is he married, engaged, or with someone?'

There was a noticeable delay before you replied.

'Is this some kind of wind-up or ruse to get information from me? If you are from the Inland Revenue, or another official or unofficial organisation, I think you should declare it now, before I consider replying.

'I assure you Mr. Stanford I am telling you the truth and this is a strictly personal matter.'

'Then give me your phone number and I'll call you back to verify who you are. Hang on ... I've just realized ... you must be a friend of Janice's.'

'Janice? Janice who?'

'Don't play games with me. This must be something related to his wife.'

'Wife? Carl's married?'

'Who are you exactly? An old girlfriend of Carl's?'

'I suppose that would be an accurate description, yes.'

'Then I don't think it would be very appropriate that you appeared in his life at the moment.'

'Could you tell me why?'

'I don't think that's any of your business.'

'Could you tell me *when* he got married?'

'That's on public record - December 1989.'

'And is Carl happy?'

'Yes, of course. He's happy in love and work, and to reiterate, I don't believe it would be a good idea for old girlfriends to turn up unexpectedly. So perhaps we ought to curtail this nonsense and forget it ever happened. Goodbye ...'

'No. Wait. Will you tell him about this call?'

'No, I don't think that would be appropriate.'

'Can I just ask you one more question - a small favour?'

'Try me.'

'If ever Carl is unhappy, unattached or gets into trouble in any way, could you promise to let me know?'

'I don't see how if I haven't got your phone number.'

'That's not a problem - I'll be calling you, about once a month.'

And I did. The more I called, the more you became well disposed to me and soon I was calling you Mike. Prior to each phone call to you, I said a little prayer at St. Peter's. I was careful with my words, not wishing Carl sudden harm or lost love, but pleading for a gradual change in his circumstances so that I could come to his rescue. But the situation never changed – Carl was always happy and always busy, getting on with his life.

I got on with my life too, convincing myself that some time in the future Carl would need me again.

My life did change a little over the next seven years. My work for BinaryByte tapered off as the day-to-day maintenance of MBridge was taken over by the company's programmers. For a few years, I still pioneered major developments, but these too eventually became the provinces of the new breed of technical wizards recruited for head office. I know it sounds bigheaded but I think MBridge suffered technically without my efforts during those years; Protean always seemed to be one step ahead.

I commuted my spare work time to quasi-leisure and became an occasional volunteer worker at the nearby ecumenical Christian community of Othona; a place that the Reverend Broadstairs had introduced me to.

By 1997, I was only used in a consultative capacity for guidance on new features and old code still being used in MBridge. At times, I felt I was no longer pulling my weight in BinaryByte, but George didn't feel the same way. He was enjoying the kudos of being the top man in a top company, and in his opinion, all thanks to me.

I began to get restless – I was now thirty, and all I could see in my future was an emotional vacuum. At the beginning of 1998, I received a copy of a report from BinaryByte's marketing department assessing competitive products and companies. The major competitor was still MicaCom and part of the report included information from their newly created Internet web-site. One of the pages gave personal profiles of the key personnel at MicaCom. Education, experience and employment histories were covered, including some family details, like married with so many children. The entry for Carl never mentioned family at all which I thought was strangely inconsistent, so the next time I called you I raised the subject.

At first you were suitably vague, so I persisted as usual and eventually you confessed that Carl had been divorced a "few" years ago (which turned out to be six – around the time I first called!), but had quickly formed a new relationship with someone else. You argued that the event had not satisfied my criteria of unhappy, unattached or in trouble – pedantic sod that you were, so there had been no need to tell me. I was bloody fuming that I had apparently missed a window of opportunity in my arrogation of Carl. I knew from that conversation that I could no longer rely on you as my only source of information.

So, I contacted George. I asked him if we employed any bright young girls that were unattached, trustworthy, and happy to relocate to Chelmsford and who wanted a big pay rise. George knew my quirky ways by now and avoided asking the reason, he just recommended Jacqui Boniface, and brought her to see me on one of his infrequent visits. I could tell that she was overawed by the secrecy required of her and by the fact that she was privileged to meet the mysterious "S". I briefed her on the objective – apply for a job at MicaCom, tell them you are relocating to Chelmsford and want a job in a similar company. I gambled on her being an irresistible recruit as a current BinaryByte employee with a glowing reference. Her clandestine, discreet duties were simple – keep close to Carl, find out what she could about his private life, report all findings to me – only me. I discovered that one of Jacqui's key attributes was her inquisitiveness, which would be an advantage for her new job, but was awkward when she kept asking me why she had to spy on Carl. I avoided answering and I refused to confirm her supposition that she was party to industrial espionage.

Six weeks later she was employed as a reserve receptionist come marketing assistant, living in a rent-free, furnished flat close to Carl (I had got someone to search the electoral register for his address) earning a good wage from MicaCom and a generous tax-free supplement from my bank account.

It took a couple of months before Jacqui was integrated enough in MicaCom to start forwarding intelligence reports. As far as she could determine Carl was an incurable workaholic. He attended the office seven days a week, typically arriving mid-morning and not leaving until late evening. Saturday afternoons and evenings were sometimes an exception but Jacqui concluded that this was probably to go shopping, having bumped into him a few times at the local supermarket. Sometimes she observed his flat after a shopping trip but there were never any female arrivals or departures and lights often stayed on until three o'clock in the morning. Periodically he disappeared for a few days, but this often coincided with you being away from the office, so it was assumed that these were business meetings.

Discreet enquiries among the MicaCom staff yielded little useful information. Carl was a likeable boss with no known partner, although a few employees speculated that he was gay. Jacqui commented that he was amiable enough (to her), and not outwardly unhappy or troubled by anything - other than the performance of his programmers.

So evidence pointed to him being at least unattached, so I decided to confront you during my next call, taking care not to reveal that I had inside knowledge. You refuted my accusation of Carl being partnerless, saying that he was emotionally involved with someone, but pressure of his work and her work meant that they only saw each other infrequently – and by the way, how did I come to my contrary conclusion? Fortunately, you accepted my answer of meeting someone who knew Carl quite well.

I put Jacqui back on the case, but short of breaking into his flat or tapping his phone, it seemed impossible to go much further. Then Jacqui had the idea to offer herself as bait to see what happened. I was not too impressed with the notion, being jealous and worried that such a plan might backfire on me, particularly as Jacqui had obviously developed a disturbing attraction to Carl. Nonetheless, I couldn't think of a better way forward other than to contact Carl myself and I wasn't ready, yet, to take the risk of complicating his life.

Jacqui began to flirt with Carl and to my chagrin, he flirted back, but that was the limit of his dalliance. So Jacqui, who had absolutely no inhibitions, forced the issue and asked Carl out. Jacqui reported back that at first Carl had been confused and had assumed that she perhaps wanted some career advice or counselling. When she had declared her real intentions, Carl had been flattered, but politely advised her that he was already committed to someone else. So, I was back to square one.

I decided to try you one more time. It was the call in early December last year that triggered a major change in the approach to my problem. You told me that there was a new love in Carl's life - a girl at the office called Jacqui. Predictably, I didn't quite know how to react to that statement. Had Jacqui been lying to me? Were you lying to me? Or was Carl lying to you? I'd never called Jacqui at the MicaCom office before, but this time I had to make an exception. Jacqui was deeply upset by my doubt of her honesty and because of her sincerity, I had to conclude that again you had lied to me to protect Carl in some way. The only way forward now was to remove you, in fact, remove the whole of MicaCom from the barrier that separated me from Carl.

I knew that George had been desperate to take BinaryByte to a new level of success. From his staid professor ways at Cambridge, he had transformed to a commercially hungry captain of industry. At the age of sixty-two his final ambition before retiring was to get BinaryByte listed on the stock market. Organic growth had proved difficult, so acquisition of a competitor was the best route to expansion and the most obvious company to purchase was MicaCom. This idea had indeed crossed George's mind and when I insisted that this was to happen, even under my own terms, George had no hesitation in acceding to my wishes.

Jacqui found out that you and Carl were attending a conference a week before Christmas and George booked a place too. Over Christmas, George and I plotted the take-over - I think you know the rest.

Part Five

New Life

Chapter 32

Wednesday, June 16, 1999 – 1:00 p.m.

'Lisa? Hi, it's Janice. How was your trip?'

'OK, thanks,' Lisa said sheepishly. She had not spoken to Janice for several years. They had been very close around the time that they both married. Even after her rapid divorce from Carl, they had kept in touch telephonically and socially for a while. Then Mike had warned her about the nuisance factor with Carl and she had stopped making contact. That did not stop Janice though. Janice had continued to call her, supposedly for a chat, but she had always steered the conversation eventually to statements and questions about Carl. *Carl is a bastard. Carl had broken her heart. Who is Carl seeing now? Is he making lots of money?* As a woman, she initially had some empathy with Janice's situation, but as time passed, Lisa began to think that there was something unnatural going on inside Janice's head. Janice was still obsessed with Carl, no longer as a lover it seemed, more as a form of hate. When Mike had told her the real reason for the divorce while on holiday, she had never wanted to see or speak to Janice again. Now she was on the phone.

'I guess you've heard about the business with Carl?'

Presumably, she meant the murder trial thought Lisa. 'Yes, a little.'

'Did Carl tell you?' Janice asked.

'No, one of my neighbours.'

'Have you heard from Carl?'

'Not yet. Mike and I only got back a couple of hours ago.'

'Oh. He hasn't moved, has he? It's just that I haven't been able to get hold of him since the trial. I have some important information for him.'

'Look Janice, I don't know where he is; and even if I did, I wouldn't tell you. By all accounts he's had a pretty rough time while I've been away and I imagine you would be the last person he would want to speak to.'

'But he needs me more than ever now that his childhood bimbo is dead.'

'On the contrary, he probably needs you about as much as you need a pregnancy testing kit.' Lisa waited a moment for the opprobrium to register. 'Goodbye ...' Lisa said, wanting the satisfaction of slamming the phoned down, but Janice had beaten her to it.

* * *

'... and I think you know the rest,' Susan finished.

The timing had been perfect; Mike had just stopped outside Carl's flat in Springfield. Yes, he did know the rest. He had been party to the takeover discussions with BinaryByte but still found it difficult to believe that Carl and Susan's abortive love story had been the primary influence over what had happened. Presumably, Carl was in the world somewhere, still oblivious to who the secret, rich admirer had been.

'It must be two years since I've been here,' Mike said as he opened the front door.

He held the door ajar for Susan to enter.

'This is weird,' Susan said. 'I can't believe I'm in the private domain of the only man I've ever loved. Do you think we could make a drink before we start the search? I'm so thirsty after telling you my life, and death, story.'

'I'm quite sure Carl wouldn't mind.' Mike went to the kitchen and searched the cupboards and the fridge. 'Well, I can offer you water, orange juice, and tea or coffee, but no milk - predictably it's gone off.'

'Orange juice will be fine,' Susan said joining Mike in the kitchen as he was rinsing the yellow coagulated mass from the milk carton down the sink. 'There are no photographs of me on display?' she queried.

'Janice destroyed them apparently. He had one left, taken at St. Peter's Chapel. It was his favourite.'

Mike opened a window to relieve the sour smell of the rotten milk and took two glasses of orange juice to the lounge. He sat on the settee. Susan was inspecting Carl's collection of music CDs.

Mike sipped his juice and said, 'Only man?'

'Sorry?' Susan said, looking puzzled at what she was examining.

'You said Carl was the only man you ever loved.'

'Yes, really. Sure, I've been physically attracted to other men, particularly to some of the hunky undergrads at Cambridge, but I've never *loved* anybody else. Isn't it strange? Of the last fifteen years, we were only together for the first five; I haven't seen him for the last ten, yet I still love him. I've never told him this, but I fell in love with him when he first asked me out. In his story did he tell you how he phoned from a cinema?' Susan said, joining Mike on the settee.

'Yes. It was the happiest I'd ever seen Carl when he was relating that part. Can you honestly say you still love him? It's been a long time. Perhaps the fire's gone out?'

'Why do you think I pestered you for years about his welfare if I didn't love him?'

'When Carl decided to try to find you, he was scared of failure. Not about finding you, but how you might react. Remember, he didn't know if you were married with kids, had become a nun or a lesbian, let alone that you were apparently dead. If you were single and available, and still loved him, he didn't know whether he could love you back. He knew he still loved the *memory* of Sarah of 1988, but didn't know if he would love the real Sarah of 1999. Doesn't the same apply to you?'

'I understand your concern. You don't want Carl to be hurt; but in those five years together a bond was formed that could never be broken.'

'But *you* broke it at Cambridge after his affair, and *he* also broke it with Janice and maybe Natasha,' Mike countered.

'They were merely transgressions in the relationship, the *bond* wasn't broken,' Susan replied, sounding hurt.

'I'm sorry; I didn't mean to be critical. I concede I am not an expert in such matters. Perhaps I would feel the same way if I had been parted from Lisa for ten years,' Mike said, and wanting to steer events back to the task in hand continued, 'Anyway, let's get busy. There's some basic detective work we can do before we start the search.'

'I'm not with you.'

Mike stood up and went to the pile of mail that had accumulated by the front door and started sifting through it.

Susan went to join him. 'What are you doing?'

'I'm looking for the earliest dated postmark on these envelopes. It will give an indication of the last time Carl was here. Look, this one is dated May 13 and has a first class stamp, so it probably got here on May 14. It suggests that Carl was perhaps last here on May 13.'

'That was the last day of Alex's trial.'

'So, after the trial he came here and then immediately went away again. That implies to me he probably hasn't gone abroad. He didn't know when the trial would end, so couldn't have booked a flight, say, to depart on May 13.'

'Brilliant, Mr Holmes. And why would he have taken his Beach Boys CDs with him?'

'How do you know he had Beach Boys CDs?'

'We were both huge Beach Boys fans. I've looked at his music collection; there are gaps in the rack and not a Beach Boys album in sight.'

'Well done, Doctor Watson. Now we can also find out two bits of information from his phone.' Mike picked up the receiver and dialled 1471. While listening he looked at his watch. 'Well, well. The last incoming call was an hour ago and if my memory serves me correctly, it was from Janice. That seems to eliminate him from being with Janice.'

'You didn't think he was with Janice?'

'After the way she's treated him over the years it was highly unlikely. Now let's find out who he last called.' Mike pressed the redial button and waited.

'Good Afternoon, Imperial College School of Medicine,' said the female voice.

'Er ... Hello. I wonder if you could help me with an odd request?' Mike said. 'I am calling on behalf of Carl Denham. Would you happen to know to whom Mr. Denham speaks when he calls this number?'

'I am sorry I can't help you; this is the main switchboard. Perhaps you have a department or a doctor's name?'

'Unfortunately no. Thanks anyway.' Mike said and replaced the receiver.

'Now there's a puzzle. Carl's last call was to the Imperial College School of Medicine.'

'In London? Why would he have called there? Are they a MicaCom customer? Was he having treatment for something?'

'Yes. I don't know. No. I don't think so,' Mike said making fun of her flood of questions. 'Let's have a look around now. You start in the bedroom. Make sure you search any jacket or trouser pockets. I'll take the lounge.'

Five minutes later Mike was flicking through hanging folders in a filing cabinet when a melancholy Susan returned from the bedroom.

'The look on your face says you found something.'

'Nothing that will help us find him.'

'What then?'

'His University scarf. I used to wear it ... I left it in his car the last time we were together; and some discarded ladies clothes.'

'Carl's a transvestite?'

'That's not funny,' Susan snapped, then added sadly, 'I presume they belong ... belonged ... to Natasha.'

Mike avoided commenting. 'My only discovery is an important one. I found his passport in the **Travel** section of the filing cabinet. So it shouldn't be difficult to find him somewhere in the U.K. or the EC.' The litotes chosen by Mike was meant to be jovial, but it passed Susan by, who was presumably dwelling on the previous topic.

'Do you think we should open his mail?' she eventually said.

'OK, it's no worse an intrusion than going through his underwear and personal files.'

He started to work his way through the pile he had examined earlier for postmarks, Susan through an older unopened stack on a table.

'There's nothing significant here, mostly circulars and bills,' he said.

'Bingo, this is maybe what we want.' Susan was brandishing a light blue business card. She showed it to Mike. Dr. **Maurice Patient, Research Director, UCSM.**

He immediately picked up the phone and dialled the number shown on the card. While he was waiting for an answer, he studied the card and said, 'I wonder what sort of doctor patient relationship Carl had with him?'

It took a moment before Susan understood the play on words, but then she laughed and gave him a playful nudge.

'Maurice Patient's office,' said the remote female secretarial voice.

Informal he thought, but using the Doctor form would have invited ridicule. 'Good Afternoon. May I speak to Maurice please?'

'I'm sorry the Doctor is lecturing at the moment. Who shall I say called?'

He put on his most formal voice. 'I am Detective Inspector Mike Stanford of the Chelmsford CID ...'

Susan was still giggling from the previous pun, and this latest invention had sent her running to the bathroom.

'... I am enquiring into the whereabouts of a Carl Denham. Can *you* help me?'

'Inspector, you will have to speak to the Doctor directly if it's about one of his students.'

'Ah, Mr. Denham is a student?'

'I did not say that Inspector. The truth is I don't know. I have heard the name mentioned - that's all.'

'Then, could you pass a message to the Doctor to call me at the earliest opportunity.'

'Yes, of course.'

He left his home phone number and replaced the receiver. Susan had returned.

'Sorry, I cracked up with your Inspector imitation and thought I was going to wet myself. Why did you do that?'

He was surprised, but comforted, by her uninhibited remark. It was the most relaxed he had seen Susan all day. Perhaps the tension of the quest was being relieved now that progress was being made. 'If you want confidential information or urgently need to get through to someone, pretend you are a policeman. I used that ploy many times at MicaCom.' He then told her about the call.

'I had a thought on the loo, I've decided to write Carl a letter and leave it here, in case he comes back before we find him.' Susan picked up the pad of paper and pen next to the telephone and went to sit at Carl's desk.

Mike picked up the phone again and called Lisa to tell her to expect a call from Maurice Patient. Lisa recounted her conversation with Janice and expressed her private thoughts about Janice's state of mind. He was careful in his responses – he did not want Susan to overhear any potentially bad news now that she was in higher spirits.

Susan showed him what she had written.

'What do you think? Is there a more considerate way of announcing my existence to him?'

'I don't know. It's difficult to imagine how Carl's mind might have been affected knowing that you were dead. Seeing is believing though. The words could only come from you and presumably he would recognize your handwriting?'

'Oh yes. He would know it's from me.'

Minutes later, having restored the flat as best they could to its unvisited state, they left for Mike and Lisa's to await Maurice's call.

* * *

'We have a problem,' Janice said as Paul dejectedly came through the front door.

'Yes, I know. I wasn't *suitable* for the Sencad Holdings job. I bet this is another contrivance of that ex-husband of yours,' Paul moaned.

'That wouldn't surprise me. He's been up to no good again. I spoke to Lisa earlier, I think Carl's surfaced and been stirring up trouble.'

'I had hoped he'd disappeared for good.'

'Well if he's just locked you out of another job and told Lisa a pack of lies about me, he must be around somewhere. I think we ought to shut him up – *properly* this time.'

Paul chose to ignore the latter remark. 'What's he been saying?'

'I don't know exactly, but I think he's said something to Lisa about my pregnancy hoax. I'm sure he didn't know.'

'What are you talking about?'

'I conned Carl into marrying me by saying I was pregnant.'

'Bloody hell, you kept that quiet. No wonder your marriage didn't last long.'

'We had better find him quickly before he stirs up any more trouble.'

'And how you intend to do that?'

'Well, he's not at his flat, because I've been ringing for days now and there's never an answer. He may have left something behind which will lead us to him.'

'Why didn't you ask Lisa?'

'I did. She *says* she doesn't know and I don't think she would tell me anyway. So, get on that computer of yours and take a crash course on the Internet about housebreaking. I've got a little job for you to do tomorrow.'

'No, Janice. I'm not getting involved in your anti-Carl schemes again.'

'If you ever want to fuck me again Paul, I think you had better do what is asked of you.'

Chapter 33

Thursday, June 17, 1999 – 11:55 a.m.

'Yes', Carl said out loud, although there was no one other than himself to hear the yelp of joy. He saved the work he had completed on his computer and sat back staring at the screen. For the first time since he arrived he could justify some daydreaming about past events.

To an onlooker the display showed nothing special, just several highlighted words and phrases, yet it was the culmination of an intense period of one month's work. To complete the work in such a short period, he had needed peace and seclusion, away from the people and events that had plagued his life from the moment he chose to drive to Portsmouth. It would have been an impossible target for any normal person to achieve, but currently he did not regard himself as being in a normal state. He had been focused - totally focused, on the project at the exclusion of all other activities, except those for his general well being such as eating, drinking, jogging and sleeping. Jogging was the only non-essential activity for his bodily survival, but it was the one luxury he had afforded himself for mental conditioning.

Maurice had portrayed the holiday cottage that he had made available to him as basic; lacking in most modern day comforts, Carl thought prehistoric was a better description. It was devoid of intrinsic electronic sounds; there was no radio, television or hi-fi system and the telephone was temporarily disconnected. He still had his old mobile phone with its irksome *Frère Jacques* tune, but he still had not figured out how to program something more cordial to his ears, nor had he found the time to purchase a modern version. He kept it fully charged but permanently switched off - it was there for infrequent outgoing calls only. Air-conditioning would have been a bonus, especially during the current hot weather spell, but he conceded that the Norfolk climate, global warming excluded, would rarely need to be moderated by such tropical apparatus. Besides, it would have been totally out of character in the ancient wood and stone building that surrounded him. To avoid the heat he had taken over the larger of the two tiny bedrooms to serve as his workplace. North facing, the room was shielded from the worst of the sun's rays and had the additional advantage of a vista of grazing land currently occupied by a few cattle and sheep living in sun drenched harmony.

It was quiet - very quiet. The cottage was a quarter of a mile along a gravel track from a minor road, which seemed to have no purpose other than to join two other minor roads, whose source was in the hamlet of North Creake two miles away. The surrounding land was either uncultivated or meadow, so there were no visits from noisy tractors or farm equipment. There were few trees or hedgerows so the birds had to find other places to squawk or coo, and the nearby four-legged creatures must have been too hot for their ululations. The only noticeable aural disturbance was the infrequent low-pass of a fighter jet plane from the RAF base twenty miles away. At least such interruptions were over quickly.

He appreciated the silence when he was in design or thinking mode. Once he was into production mode - cranking code or data, musical noise of his choosing was motivating. At short notice, Maurice had supplied the computer equipment surrounding him according to his specification, so it was the fastest available, with enormous disk storage and plenty of memory. His main work machine also had a CD drive, a top of the range sound card, and a speaker system that would have done justice to a heavy metal pop group playing at an open-air concert. So, while he worked, he regularly swapped audio CDs in and out of the drive, from the stock he had brought with him from Springfield. Beach Boys mostly, but the occasional Pink Floyd, Genesis or Status Quo at full volume was an indulgence that he had rarely experienced. At his flat such irresponsibility would have brought cries of protest from the neighbours and eventually a visit from the noise police; here the cows and sheep within audio range did not complain – perhaps they enjoyed 60's and 70's bands too?

The routine of the last month had been easy to fall into. Up at six o'clock for a simple breakfast of toast and tea. Work until twelve, with a couple of tea breaks. Something light and quick for lunch, fruit, cheese and crackers was the norm and then another six-hour shift, with coffee breaks and maybe a biscuit, or two. By then, it was usually cool enough for a jog to the coast and back. The shortest return trip was four miles but there were six and eight mile variants, which he tackled every other day. Once when he had a particularly thought provoking problem to mull over, he just ran in loops until he had cracked it – that day he must have covered ten miles. After a run, it was bath time; sadly there was no fixed shower - only a rubbery substitute appendage to the hot and cold taps, which was well past its plumbing date. A hot meal followed - often pasta or a boil-in-the-bag amalgam with boiled vegetables and more fruit, before the last work session to midnight or later, depending upon brain stamina. There were no such things as Saturdays or Sundays in his life then - every day was the same, except when he was low on food or household consumables, and then the daily routine was broken by a hasty visit to the nearest supermarket in Fakenham.

The chance meeting with Maurice Patient in March had certainly been fortuitous; otherwise, he supposed he would have taken exile in San Francisco again. He was glad of the peace of the Norfolk countryside rather than the hustle and bustle of an American city, in spite of needing some short-term comfort from his parents.

After the shooting, he had been rushed to Colchester General hospital to have his arm patched up. It was a clean wound - a neat hole drilled in the fleshy part of his arm below the left shoulder and beside his biceps. There was no damage to nerves, muscle or bone, just a lot of blood and pain. The resistance presented to the bullet was minimal; another few millimetres and some structural element of the arm would have arrested or deflected the speeding metal lump away from Natasha's chest. The *if only* scenarios had been debated in his head at length, and he would have had no compunction in trading a dysfunctional arm for Natasha's life.

At the hospital, he had spent two days in police-guarded recovery, and was arrested on impulse by DCI Bryant for obstructing a police enquiry. However, the charge was dismissed after giving a detailed statement of his activities for the previous week to a more conciliatory DS Duckworth. On release from hospital he had been escorted to his flat to collect a few essential belongings and then under the witness protection programme deposited in a police house in Colchester. He believed Bryant had instigated the move, not to protect him, more to restrain him in retaliation for the embarrassment he had caused the Inspector. The house was notionally for passing police cadets attending training courses or awaiting permanent accommodation, and of course, a perfect location to hide someone risky or at risk. At least his food and lodgings were free and one of the cadets insisted on acting as resident chef, though an unvarying diet of Italian spaghetti dishes became boring after a while.

Without a computer to occupy his time, he choose this as the opportunity in his life to catch up on some reading, particularly *Techniques of Internet Commerce* interspersed with some books on law and police procedures which were communal reference books in the house.

While confined, he spoke a few times with Maurice to check that he could still act as the technical guru that he required for his project. Time was pressing but as long as he could demonstrate a working solution by the middle of June the job was his. Maurice had asked once what was causing the delay in starting the project and he had simply replied, some personal matters, which were left over from the sale of MicaCom. Not strictly true, but sensitive enough that Maurice did not pursue the matter, and to this day he was uncertain whether Maurice had connected him with the Alex Gomulka trial.

The timing of the trial and his involvement had been critical and when he eventually walked from the court, his evidence presented, he had just one month to complete his task for Maurice. The escape from court had to be precisely planned. Reporters had pestered him for statements and exclusive rights to his story, but he wanted none of that. He wanted the guilt and misery about the whole proceedings to stay private. He was helped in his getaway by one of the police cadets, who arrived at a side entrance to the court shortly after he had made a phone call that he was free. His few belongings were already in the cadet's car and he was rushed away to collect his own car that had been parked in a remote side street. On reaching his flat he had offloaded his dirty washing, replenished his travel bag with toiletries and casual clothes, packed a selection of music CDs and added the unopened incoming mail to the ever-increasing pile next to the telephone; then he had phoned Maurice to advise that he was now available. Three hours later, they had met up at Maurice's holiday retreat in Norfolk. By the following afternoon the equipment that he had wanted for the project was delivered in a courier van, whose driver had spent over an hour trying to find what must have been one of the remotest dwellings in the County.

From his first meeting with Maurice he had been excited by the proposed project. Maurice was a Research Director at the Imperial College School of Medicine in London. From his early days as a humble GP, he had accumulated a mass of data relating patient symptoms with candidate diseases. Initially held on filing cards the data had been transferred to a simple computer database. Colleagues had added contributions, and a small team of researchers had digested the contents of medical journals worldwide to relate the cause and effect of illnesses. The volume of data was now vast and quite beyond the processing capabilities of the existing software and Maurice via his sponsors - an equally vast pharmaceuticals company, had wanted to go public with the impressive results of his work. The work itself was nothing revolutionary; it was the organisation of the data that provided the amazing results. From a few basic facts about an infirm individual, the symptoms (in its simplest form, point to the part of the body on a diagram and choose one of these words to describe the pain), Maurice's database could provide an 80% accurate prognosis. Answer the additional questions automatically posed by the software (like blood test results or X-rays) and the accuracy could go as high as 99%.

The program was not perfect though. He sighed to himself when he recalled a frivolous test he had carried out last week. He had clicked on the heart of the human body graphic and then chosen the word **broken** to describe its condition. Seconds later the program responded - **Consult a cardiologist for an ECG examination.** For a moment he had been tempted to alter the database logic so that it responded **Time warp back eleven years and kill Janice Harding.**

The key objective of the program was to guide any medic through a rigorous and formal consultation of their patient to arrive at a prognosis. It was not intended that the software would replace the skill of a doctor, merely remind him or her of essential aspects of diagnosis and ailments, particularly new ones that they might not recall or have ever encountered.

The problem with such software was its ubiquity. It would be impossible to keep every doctor up-to-date with the underlying data that would make such software a valuable adjunct to their patient counselling. The data would require storage far in excess of a conventional desktop PC and new knowledge would become available on at least a daily basis. The solution was of course to make it available on the Internet. That way the data and knowledge could be held on a central computer and would be accessible by anyone with a permanent or dial-up connection to the Internet.

So who would pay for this? He had asked the question but knew the answer. The pharmaceuticals company of course. Not only would the program diagnose a bodily fault, it would also recommended a possible treatment. If the treatment would benefit from one of the company's products or a visit to one of its specialist clinics, the program would say so. The company itself was not ubiquitous - it did not have an answer to all the world's medical problems; but other companies or medical facilities did, and would be charged for the privilege to have their products or services advertised.

Maurice had a big budget courtesy of the company and had explained to him that the majority of it had been used for data capture and analysis. Only a small part of it was earmarked for the Internet, so Maurice had been looking for a cheap, confidential and reliable route for the solution. Whether this was the truth, or merely a reason to offer only a modest fee for the job did not bother him. It was work he wanted; the pay was incidental. In fact, he could not remember exactly what the amount was, something around £5,000 and he did not have a contract; so he could end up with nothing. He doubted it; Maurice seemed an honourable guy, and if he got his fee he had already planned to donate it to a deserving cause.

Satisfied with what he saw on the screen, he knew he could go no further with the project until he had demonstrated his efforts to Maurice. He clicked a small disk shaped icon on the screen and the Beach Boys CD that his computer had been playing stopped instantly. The only sound remaining was the gentle tick-tock of the ancient grandfather clock in the hall. He stood up, stretched and shook his legs like an athlete preparing to start a race, as he aimed for the hall. His legs were stiff - and no wonder, when he noticed the time on the granddaddy, it showed eleven thirty-eight. The old timer was about twenty minutes slow, so the last work session had lasted almost six hours – without a break. With revived legs, he turned towards satisfying his thirst and entered the long narrow primitive kitchen. There was a refrigerator and an electric cooker (they had to be at least thirty years old) - no microwave, toaster or kettle. If you wanted hot water, the only appropriate utensil was a saucepan. Primitive it may be, but he would not have it any other way; it reminded him of holidays when he was younger and his then poorer parents used to rent a similar cottage near Shoesbury. It took him back to trouble-free days and he got some absurd satisfaction from knowing that he was rich, yet had to cope with a life-style of a generation before.

He put some water on to boil. He would make tea and then call Maurice to proclaim his success. First, he went to check his mobile phone in the main bedroom. Yes, it was plugged-in and fully charged. He rescued the phone from its charging cradle and switched it on. He examined the signal meter on the display - never the best of signals here in the Norfolk wilderness, but it would do.

He took the phone with him, placed it on the rickety kitchen table and sat down on a similarly rickety chair facing the window, remembering yesterday's disturbance.

He had been through a similar exercise; preparing to phone Maurice for a penultimate update, when the phone had rung. He had stared in horror at the noisy plastic device vibrating on the table; his heart had beat a little faster and he had stood up and paced around the table like an animal circling his prey, peering at the display until the ringing had stopped. An intrusion from the outside world still troubled him. The truth was that he was still afraid of being reminded about events three months ago. His recent exile and work had diverted his mind, but soon he would have to rejoin the real world and that is when the questions would come and the memories would be forced to return.

Through the kitchen window, he studied the small garden or more appropriately, a rear lawn, as Kate would have called it. As a holiday cottage there was no point in attempting to breed plants that holidaymakers would have no interest in tending. There was a small shed in one corner, which housed a lawnmower and a couple of deckchairs. A three-foot high evergreen hedge marked the boundary, just high and strong enough to prevent invasion from the sheep and cattle in the field beyond. No holiday bookings had been taken this year; Maurice had intended to give the cottage to his brother and sister-in-law. Sadly, Maurice's brother had died from a heart attack, and the sister-in-law had gone to live with her own widowed sister, so the cottage had stayed empty for most of the year. Routine maintenance – dusting and grass cutting, was still carried out by a local agent. The man from the agency had arrived one day a couple of weeks ago to mow the lawn, but he had sent him away because the sudden noise had driven Carl crazy. He had promised the man that he would do it himself just to get rid of him, and looking at the length of grass now, he resolved that he would fulfil the promise after he had taken his mid-day refreshment.

The bubbling noise and rattling of the saucepan alerted him to the hot water being ready. He poured the water into a mug and tossed in a tea bag. While it was brewing, he called Maurice.

Maurice was ecstatic with the news. He wanted to set out straightaway but was booked for the rest of the day with meetings that he could not cancel – he would be with Carl the following morning.

So that was almost it, he thought. If Maurice was happy with the work, all that was left was some documentation to handover, and transfer of the work to the computer system that Maurice would connect to the Internet at Imperial College. The former he could complete tonight, but Maurice would have to advise when the latter could be arranged. Right now, he was going to drink his tea and then do some unusual physical work – mow the lawn.

* * *

'You might be good at making bombs, but you are piss useless at breaking a lock,' Janice said - a little too loud for Paul's liking.

'Keep your bloody voice down,' Paul whispered. 'In fact, just shut up. You're spoiling my concentration.'

In fact, I don't know why I'm here in the first place thought Paul. Janice had coerced him here. She made excessive demands and he always acceded to them. One day his servility was going to get him into trouble - it had been a close call with the bombing. He was sleeping with Janice but she was still obsessed with his ex-boss, and her ex-husband. She had never got her own way with Carl and she was determined to make Carl suffer, again, for one final time. As much as he also hated Carl for presumably getting him the sack from MicaCom, he could not help but feel sorry for the bloke. Carl's fate had been sealed the first time he had met Janice. Paul's divine hope had been that once they, or rather, she was rid of Carl, perhaps they could lead a *normal* life, with Janice becoming a normal person rather than the schizophrenic she was. One minute she could be kind, considerate, loving and sexy, and then it was as if someone had pressed a switch in her head; quite suddenly, she would become foul-mouthed, aggressive, domineering and full of nothing but putrid hate for Carl. Bizarrely, on one occasion her multiformity had emerged during their lovemaking. They were close to climax when Janice had thrown him off, and had screamed and shouted at him to get down on his knees and lick her while she stood over him. Nothing unusual in that, except she had kicked and punched him, and uttered obscenities directed at *Carl*.

Carl refusing to give her a handout from his MicaCom sale proceeds had initiated her last preternatural scheme. She had really flipped and decided that she literally wanted to blow Carl and his car from this earth. Paul had been pestered to scour the Internet to find a recipe for an explosive confection that would rid her of Carl forever. Having just lost his job, he was temporarily equally disturbed, and had willingly conducted the research and acquired the components - quite easily, it so happened. On the day of the visit from Alex looking for Carl, and when Janice had discovered a new female at Carl's flat, her grudge had gone into overdrive and she had wanted to execute her destructive plan immediately. In the early hours of the following morning, they had delivered and installed their fatal package. Getting into the car to set the booby trap had been easy, Janice had long ago stolen a key from Carl's pocket to cause him some minor stress, but she had hung on to it, in case it had a future use.

When the car blew taking the life of an innocent party, the Mephistophelean Janice had no remorse. For her it was a small sacrifice towards the ultimate destruction of her ex-husband. She lied without conscience in court to steer the jury to convict Alex of the bombing and that had been the turning point for him. He had not openly displayed his absolute regret for what had happened in the event that Janice taunted him for a weakness. The vendetta had gone too far now, he needed to break from the spell that Janice had over him. He viewed that at least demotion from a car-bomber to a flat-breaker was a step in the right direction.

'Get a move on,' Janice said as she shuffled backwards and forwards making disapproving sighs.

'Keep still for Christ's sake. I'm almost there,' Paul said, dispensing with the piece of bent wire and extracting a miniature crowbar from the inside pocket of his leather jacket.

Soon there was the sound of breaking wood and a metallic clank as Paul toppled through the opened door almost losing his balance. Janice looked around for signs of other inhabitants hearing the racket and then followed him into Carl's flat. She had to lean against the door to close it.

'You stupid prick, you broke the door jamb.'

'I had to - the lock wouldn't budge. You can get the theory of house breaking from the Internet, but putting it into practice seems a completely different story.' Paul mitigated.

'That looks interesting,' Janice said, bending down and picking up some folded sheets of paper that had been placed in an obvious position in the middle of the floor just beyond the front door.

'Carl – Urgent,' Paul read from the facing sheet.

Janice unfolded the sheets. On the first page, there was a hand-written message.

Stop here!
The following sheet will be hard to believe. This is NOT a joke.

Please SIT DOWN before you turn over.
Think of The Nearest FarAway Place.

'What on earth is this all about?' Janice said, and turned to the next page.

My Dearest Carl,

This is from Sarah, YOUR Sarah.
I am NOT dead.
I did NOT commit suicide and I SURVIVED Alex's attempted murder.
I am ALIVE and living under the name of SUSAN FELLGATE.
Mike brought me here.
I miss you and I LOVE YOU.
Please phone me, visit me, anything!

Sarah

'Jesus, that's unbelievable. You said she was dead,' Paul said looking over Janice's shoulder.

'So unbelievable that it must be a wind-up,' Janice mocked.

'But who would do such a cruel thing if you didn't do it? Can it be real?'

'I don't know. Let me think.' She stared at the message. 'I suppose it's possible. Sarah's body was never found. But why did she leave it so long before returning from the dead? Then there's this strange reference to "The Nearest FarAway Place".'

'Perhaps it's some kind of code or phrase between them. Look - it's also in the address she's written at the bottom.'

'Where's Bradwell-on-Sea?'

'It's beyond Maldon – near Southminster. It's where they have the power station.'

'I wonder if she's always been there - probably not. Maybe she's been abroad and came here when she heard about the trial.'

'It would be a big coincidence though that she just happens to stay at a place, which has the same name as their code. There's another odd thing about the note. She said her surname is Fellgate.'

'What's so special about that?'

'It's the same name as the boss of BinaryByte, the company that bought out MicaCom.'

'That probably is a coincidence. Look, it says that Mike brought her here, that must have been yesterday or today, since Mike only got back yesterday. So obviously, Mike, Lisa and Sarah don't know where Carl is, so there seems to be little point in searching the flat. They must have done that already.' Janice tucked the letter into her skirt pocket. 'Never mind, we have perhaps an even bigger discovery.'

'What's that?'

'We know where that bitch Sarah is living.'

* * *

Mike came in from the garden. Lisa and Susan were still chatting. It had been like that last night and all today. They had bonded like two compatible sisters, so well that he had elected to stay outside most of the day to catch up on some post-holiday house and garden maintenance. Initially he thought he should have played host to Susan. He felt it was his duty to do everything possible to help locate Carl; a small token towards making up for the years he had deceived her - but it had not been necessary. Susan was a determined and independent woman. She had made a nuisance of herself with Maurice Patient's secretary – like a dog (or was it a bitch?) with a bone, since they returned from Carl's flat yesterday. Approximately every half-hour she had phoned, pretending to be Sergeant Fellgate, asking if Mr. Patient had been given the message about Carl Denham. Each time she obtained the same response – the Doctor had been in meetings all day and she was assured he would be given the message as soon as possible.

Last night she had spent two hours on the Internet looking for evidence of Carl in Cyberspace. She had been amazed at the number of Carl Denhams she found scattered around the electronic world, but sadly not the particular one that she had sought.

At other times, she had conversed with Lisa on a variety of subjects. Mike's theory was that she had led a lonely existence in Bradwell with little human contact, and now that her exile was nearing its end, she was making up for lost time. She had already visibly changed in the very short time since he had met her in person. Her eyes had become brighter and the smile wider.

As he looked at her now he experienced an overwhelming guilt that he had been partly responsible for keeping this vibrant woman sheltered from the world and Carl for so many years.

'Who or what are you talking about now?'

'You actually,' Lisa said.

'Am I a worthwhile subject for discussion?' he said, still feeling the after effects of his guilt sensation.

'As you are the nominated breadwinner for this growing Stanford family,' Lisa said patting her stomach, 'I was wondering when you might get a job.'

'In fact I already have several jobs - garden maintenance, painting and decorating, car valeting and later I may graduate to baby bathing and nappy changing. Plus I have a few other ideas from our American trip.'

'I could get you a job at BinaryByte,' Susan teased.

'I think nappy changing has the edge,' he said. 'Seriously though, there's no hurry is there? I've quite enjoyed tinkering about outside today. I think I could keep that up for a few more weeks yet, particularly while it's summer. Besides, I want to find out what Carl has in mind.'

'Do you think he'll actually want to talk to you when he discovers the secret you kept from him for the last eight years.'

'*If* he discovers. I wanted to talk to you about that. He knows about the existence of *my* Susan and will surely want to link that with *his* Susan. So ....'

Susan interrupted. 'I don't like what you are about to suggest. It's no foundation to rebuild a relationship if there are secrets. I intend to tell Carl my full story when I see him. I'm sorry Mike - it can't be any other way. Something is bound to slip out, and then he'll never trust you or me again.'

'Susan is right. You'll have to risk losing Carl as a friend, hopefully only temporarily. Susan and I have already discussed this and, assuming Carl and Susan get back together, we think our own friendship will eventually overcome any barriers that Carl erects.' Lisa said.

'Besides,' Susan said, 'I have some ideas of how we can invest our individual or collective monies from BinaryByte, so that the baby Denhams and Stanfords that arrive next year will be well provided for.'

'I'm intrigued on both counts.'

'First Carl and I will have a lot of catching up to do, and that includes making babies - to keep up with the Stanfords. While that goes on you can keep busy in the garden and attend the prenatal courses Lisa has planned for you. When Lisa and I are mothers and you and Carl have proved you can be good fathers, we'll let you go back into the business community. Deal?'

'Don't count chickens,' Mike said, 'remember we still haven't found Carl.'

* * *

Paul was watching the evening news on Channel 4, Janice was sitting beside him, fidgeting, her mind absorbed elsewhere.

'I've been thinking. A knife, a gun and a piece of rope would be appropriate, don't you think?' Janice said casually, as though she was creating a shopping list.

Paul, more interested in the current unemployment statistics said, 'What are you on about now?'

Annoyed at his indifference Janice got up and stood between Paul and the television. 'Don't you think it would be appropriate if the blonde bitch died the way her brother-in-law described the way he killed her?'

Paul craned his neck to see past Janice. 'I've told you before that I'm not getting involved again with your anti-Carl schemes.'

'That's all right then, because this is an anti-Sarah scheme. The more I think about it, the more I'm convinced that this is the best way of getting at Carl. We can't lose since Sarah's dead already. Getting a gun by tomorrow may be difficult though. It's not important because it wasn't used as a gun, merely as a heavy object to knock her out. So, we cut her a bit, knock her out with a brick, say, and then strangle her. With a bit of luck her death might get pinned on Carl – that would be perfect. Are you listening to me?' Janice was jigging to and fro to block Paul's view.

'Drop it, will you?'

'Look, I can't do this on my bloody own. I'll need your help.'

'Well, you're not getting it.' Paul slumped back in the seat, troubled that the exchange, as usual, would not finish until Janice had got her own way.

'And you're not getting *it* unless I do.'

'You'll change your mind. More than two days without sex and you're climbing up the wall.'

'That's not a problem, I'll find someone else to satisfy me.'

'OK,' Paul said nonchalantly.

'I'd better call that nice Inspector Bryant then and tell him what you've been up to.' Janice strode confidently to the telephone.

'You're bluffing.'

Janice searched the telephone table looking for something. 'Here it is,' she said, picking up a white card and began dialling.

'You've got nothing on me that wouldn't implicate you too.' Paul's voice had a nervous resonance to it.

'Hello. Could you put me through to Inspector Bryant? Just say it's an informant calling.' Janice drummed her fingers on the table and smirked at Paul.

Paul leapt up, dashed to the telephone and terminated the call. 'I still think you are bluffing.'

Janice brushed his hand away from the telephone and began dialling again.

'All right, all right, but this has got to be last time, OK?'

'OK,' Janice said, her smirk developing into one her evil smiles.

Chapter 34

Friday, June 18, 1999 – 6:00 a.m.

New habits die hard thought Carl, when, without the setting of an alarm clock and despite the restful quiet of the cottage, he woke at six o'clock. The sun had won the race again to be first awake, and its early lukewarm rays, the country dew and gentle breeze had combined to waft the smell of the newly mown grass through the open window.

There was no urgency to get up - Maurice was travelling from London and would not be here until nine o'clock or after, but the attraction of the floral odours was overpowering and he needed to experience them close-up, one more time, before returning from his self-imposed exile. He dressed, skipped breakfast and from the shed took a deckchair, which he positioned in the centre of his gardening efforts. The morning coolness was invigorating as he lay down and closed his eyes. He thought about the people who had contributed to his recent past and who might influence his immediate future.

He had enjoyed his recent job for Maurice and asking him if there was any further project work for him was a possibility. The occasional once-off, short-term systems job, where he could see it through from beginning to end, was appealing. He liked Maurice and had enjoyed the challenge of creating something useful. Working *for* Maurice was not an option. Once you had been a boss with responsibility to nobody but yourself, it was impossible to consider reporting to someone else.

There were a few unexplored, undocumented ideas for Protean which were in his head, but undeclared to BinaryByte. He had signed an agreement with BinaryByte during the sale of MicaCom that he would not compete against them or their products in the next two years. However, if he went to see George Fellgate with his proposals, he was sure George could sanction some consultancy work.

Then there was Mike. Mike's business objective while in the States was to identify a market opportunity that he could exploit in the U.K. or Europe. Carl wondered if Mike had bothered with any research, or whether he had been too busy being an enthusiastic tourist. Mike would be back soon, and what a shock he would get when he learnt how his ex-partner's adventure had taken its ugly shape. He resolved to call him later to see if he was back yet.

He then thought of the three women, Marion, Kate and Natasha, who in different ways had suffered at the hands of their partners or ex-partners.

What would Marion do now? He had not seen her since his first visit to Croftview and she had been conspicuous by her absence at the trial. Would she be coping? He guessed that it was probably a relief that her moonstruck husband would never disrupt her life or the community again. Perhaps she was tending her mother now. He added Marion to his mental list of people to see - soon.

Kate - who had brought enlightenment of Janice's deception. Was he now Kate's friend rather than foe? He remembered that he had promised some money for her school and had not delivered – but he had an idea to remedy that. No doubt she had followed the trial's proceedings in the National press. He owed her an explanation.

Dear Natasha. He still blamed himself for her death. If he had not set out on his fruitless adventure, she would still be alive. They might have made it together, now that the Sarah story was finally closed. Maybe he had brought a tiny bit of excitement to her life after she had been closeted in Portsmouth for so long. He would visit Veronica and tell her of the good times he had with Natasha.

He had a debt of gratitude to Don, who had taken great risks on his behalf. Don had managed to get past the police barrier once while Carl was in hospital, and he had last seen him, briefly, while he was waiting to give evidence against Alex for the arson attack on his premises. Another person to visit.

And lastly, there was Janice. The rot had started when Janice had sent the photographs to Sarah. If he had not been stopped en-route from Kate's to Janice's it could so easily have been him in prison for murder. Had he known then that two pointless deaths would have resulted, there would have been no doubt about his continued resolve. It had been clear to him in the past and was even clearer now, that the trail of destruction of lives was not his or anyone else's fault – it was Janice's.

Now he was content, because he felt his final fate had been determined. He now understood the despair that Sarah had suffered that led her to believe that suicide was the answer. He too would commit suicide – not physically but socially. No more projects; he would not speak to George; he was not interested in any opportunities that Mike had uncovered. He had people to see just one more time – his parents, Marion, Kate, Don and Wendy, Mike and Lisa; and some monetary provisions to make for those in need. Then there would be a death; how, could be decided later. It would be a fair exchange, one unworthy life traded for three unnecessary deaths. He refused to consider the morality and ethics of his decision. In his own mind he would be removing a sinner from the world. Yes, there would be a death, not his - but Janice's.

He should have smiled with his ultimate decision, but suddenly he was too tired to even curl the corners of his mouth. The sun's increasing warmth, the solitude and the relief of knowing his course of action had relaxed his brain and body so totally that he drifted into sleep.

'So this is how my highly paid consultant lives? Hey Carl, are you in this world?' Maurice said, shaking Carl gently - he had found him asleep in the back garden.

Carl shook his head and glanced at his watch.

'It's a bit early and cool for sunbathing, isn't it?' Maurice continued.

'Oh, hello, Maurice. You're two minutes early. I was just about to wake up,' Carl teased. 'Journey OK?'

'Yes, no problem. I left at six-thirty and the traffic was light,' Maurice said. 'Are you awake enough to show me your efforts?' he added excitedly.

Carl eased himself from the deckchair. 'Of course. Now, or would you like some breakfast first?'

'No. I never eat breakfast, but a cup of coffee would be fine. Oh, and before I forget I've had an urgent message from someone trying to contact you.' Maurice reached into his jacket pocket and withdrew a note his secretary had passed him on Wednesday. 'A Detective Inspector Mike Stanford from Chelmsford CID?'

Carl looked blank and then grinned knowingly. 'You are winding me up. Right?'

'Not consciously,' Maurice said and passed the note to Carl.

Carl studied it. 'I don't understand.'

'I assumed it was perhaps something to do with the murder trial.'

'You know about that?'

'Apparently most of the world knew about it – except me. My wife made the connection. She reads the newspapers, I read the medical journals.'

'But this message is nonsense. Mike Stanford was my business partner at MicaCom. He's been touring America and is not due back in England for a couple of weeks, yet this is his home telephone number. I'm certain he hasn't joined the police force and absolutely certain he didn't know I was working for you.'

'I doubt my secretary made a mistake. Do you want me to phone her to check?'

'No. I'll log you into the computer, put the hot water on and think this through.'

They went to the larger bedroom and he gave Maurice a swift demonstration of the program and then left him alone. In the kitchen he watched the proverbial hot water boil. Mike had to be back in England, that bit was fairly obvious, but how did he know about Maurice? Could my phone at the flat be tapped? That was hard to believe - Mike must have been to the flat looking for him and found ... Maurice's business card. Then why has Mike been masquerading as a police inspector? That was beyond his reckoning.

Despite his pot watching, the water did boil and he took the coffee to Maurice who was muttering to himself over the PC. He looked up embarrassed.

'This is brilliant. If you had been to the tropics for a holiday and came back with a runny nose, conjunctivitis, joint pains, swollen glands and a berry-like rash, what would be the prognosis and what treatment would you suggest?'

Carl knew it was the program being tested, not himself, so he replied tongue-in-cheek. 'How about death and suicide?'

Maurice took it seriously. 'No, no. Dengue fever of course and just pain killers to curb the temperature.'

'Of course,' Carl said.

'This application is going to make us famous.'

'Us?'

'I'll give you the design credit when the work is published. You'll get headhunted for similar work. In fact, I have lots of contacts, I'll broadcast your name.'

'Thanks, but no thanks Maurice,' Carl said, 'I have a job lined-up already. By the way, here's the design specification, reference manual and a CD, which contains a copy of the program code and documentation. The documentation also tells your systems staff how to install the software on the Internet web server, so you won't need me to do that.'

Maurice looked disappointed. 'What job are you going to do?'

Sewing mailbags was the response that came to mind. Instead he said, 'I'll be employed in a high security government department. I can't say anymore than that.' Carl tapped his nose implying secrecy.

'Gosh. You do get around.' Maurice took a sip from his coffee. 'Have you got over the ... um ... murder thing. Or is it none of my business?'

'It's over and forgotten,' Carl lied and changed the subject, 'My fee?'

'Don't worry about that. As soon as I get back, I'll authorize a cheque. You'll have it within days.'

'I want you to do me a favour. Could you make it payable to a Kate Hammond at this address.' Carl wrote the details on the back of the secretary's note and passed it to Maurice.

'If that's what you want.' Maurice must have assumed he would be paying some secret amour of Carl's and tapped his nose conspiratorially. Carl did likewise.

* * *

'Now you are sure about this. You're quite welcome to stay longer,' Lisa said.

'Quite sure. I've imposed on you long enough. I can play Sergeant Fellgate from home. Anyway, I'm certain that I shall see Carl soon; then we'll all have some catching up to do. I'll get the loan clothes back to you as soon as possible,' Susan replied.

'There's no hurry. At best, it will be another twelve months before they'll fit me again.'

Susan stepped out into the bright sunshine and towards Mike's car. Mike was about to follow when Lisa grabbed his arm.

'Try to calm her down, she's rather hyper at the moment,' Lisa said.

'Yes, I will. If the reunion with Carl backfires, she'll be distraught. I'll preach the art of handling disappointments,' Mike said.

Mike joined Susan in the car and they set out for Bradwell.

* * *

'There's a garage, pull in,' Janice said.

'Why? We don't need fuel,' Paul replied.

'Just do it will you,' Janice yelled.

Paul turned his Ford Fiesta into the filling station and pulled up to one of the pumps.

Janice jumped out and went to a gossamer glove dispenser, took four pairs and returned to the car.

'What do you need those for,' Paul asked.

'Christ, you can be stupid at times. Get moving and I'll tell you.'

Paul rejoined the road heading towards Maldon.

'Fingerprints. We don't want to leave fingerprints. We'll wear these.'

'Oh,' Paul said resignedly.

Oh shit is what he thought - Janice really was serious about her scheme. He should have known better; once Janice had a notion in her head, a lobotomy was the only way it could be removed. He silently prayed that Sarah would still not be at home. Janice had been ringing Sarah's Bradwell number all morning, and had become more and more agitated with Sarah's voice on the answering machine saying that she could be temporarily be contacted at Mike's number. So they were going to *The Nearest FarAway Place* for a reconnaissance and possibly an execution, literally, of Janice's plan. The tools of destruction were in a carrier bag on the back seat. Perhaps he would have one last attempt to dissuade her.

'So what will we do if she's still not there?' Paul asked.

'We'll wait. She won't stay at Mike's forever.'

'How long for?'

'For as long as it takes.'

'Just sit in the car? It could be days.'

'Oh no, the warm feeling between my legs is telling me that I will be satisfied today,' Janice sniggered.

Paul shuddered inside. Janice was sometimes a big turn on; it's a shame that she was totally mad.

* * *

As he crossed the threshold of his flat, Carl realized he did not want to live there any longer. There was an air of violation about it, emphasized by the gouge in the door pillar and the clunky way that the door opened – it was not like that a month ago. He believed that Mike had been there - he had a key, so it was possible that someone else had intruded on his personal territory. The opened pile of mail next to the telephone confirmed his invasion suspicions. But there was something else unusual, a faint smell, or rather a scent he could detect. Although it was often difficult to distinguish between male and female cosmetic fragrances these days, his nose suggested it had feminine origins. Perhaps Lisa had accompanied Mike on his exploratory visit?

He took his travel bag to the bedroom and the food shopping that he had purchased on the way home to the kitchen, and embarked upon a meticulous search of his flat. It revealed only two other discrepancies. There were *two* washed glasses on the draining board in the kitchen - hardly residual evidence of a burglar, which gave credence to a Mike and Lisa visit. More puzzling was the displacement of his iconic University scarf - now on the same shelf as his shirts, rather than occupying it's private shelf. Despite the newly acquired misgivings about his flat, he was thankful that whoever had visited had not been malevolent or vandalous.

On his way back from Norfolk, he had decided to stay in Springfield for about a week. That should be long enough to honour the private commitments he had made about calling on his friends, then he would go to San Francisco to stay with his parents for a couple of weeks. After that it would be Janice that would *benefit* from his gregariousness. So, he would only have to tolerate living in his flat for perhaps another two weeks, then, unless he was *very* lucky, it would be Her Majesty's Pleasure to keep a roof over his head.

In the meantime, perhaps he should busy himself with his most hated bachelor task, washing and ironing. Eager for any excuse to defer that onerous task he changed his mind and went to the telephone table – he ought to look through his maculate mail first. He checked his watch, almost two o'clock. Even better he could ring Mike the Inspector first. If Mike and Lisa were free tomorrow that could be one of his goodbye sessions dealt with. He dialled the number and Lisa answered.

'Lisa. I guessed you were back.'

'Carl? Where have you been?'

'Where have *I* been? You've been away for three months. How was the trip?'

'Have you seen the note?'

'Note?'

'Are you calling from your flat?'

'Well, yes.'

'And wasn't there a note staring at you on the floor?'

'I'm looking now. There's nothing on the floor. In fact I've checked the flat thoroughly since I've been back, but I've not seen a note. I presume it was from you and Mike. You've both been here haven't you? That's how you found out about Maurice Patient?'

'Mike's been there.'

'Somebody else has too, unless Mike broke down my front door. What's this about Lisa?'

'It's about the murder.'

'Oh. You've caught up with the news while you were away? I was hoping you and Mike were free tomorrow so that we could swap stories from the last few months.'

'Something's happened that you don't know about.'

'Obviously. Care to enlighten me?'

'I can't. It's a bit difficult to explain.'

'Then put Mike on to explain.'

'He's not here at the moment.'

'Then perhaps you could tell me about America and get Mike to ring me later.'

'No Carl, this is serious. I'll phone him. Could you meet him somewhere?'

'Where? When?'

'Just a moment, I need to get some directions.' There was a rustling of paper then Lisa continued. 'Go to Bradwell-on-Sea and head towards St. Peter's Chapel. Just before the Cricketers pub, turn right towards Hockley. About a mile on the left is a bungalow – you'll see Mike's car. Do you know the area?'

'Reasonably well. But why is he there? You haven't split up have you?'

'No, of course not, I'm pregnant.'

'Pregnant! Congratulations. So the American trip was a complete success?'

Lisa laughed for the first time, 'Yes, you could say that. Now, will you leave straightaway so that I can phone Mike?'

'Are you sure there's nothing else you can tell me?'

There was a pause. 'Plenty, but it's best coming from Mike. It is *good* news though Carl. Please hurry. I'll talk to you later.'

* * *

Paul turned his white Ford Fiesta into the narrow lane, signposted as a no through road, but clearly pointing to Hockley. Butterflies had now taken control of his stomach and he felt a nervous tic begin to annoy him below his left eye and tried to rub it into submission. Janice was wriggling in her seat presumably with excitement rather than discomfort. He glanced at her with a loathing he did not think he was capable of. He edged the car slowly along the lane not wishing to draw attention to his arrival. There were few buildings until he passed the Hockley sign, then he cowered and slid down into his seat as if this movement would shield him from any onlookers. Clear of the tiny hamlet, Janice wound the passenger window down further and stuck her head out looking for the target.

'There it is. See the sign,' Janice said.

He slowed the car to a crawl and turned towards the entrance.

'Bloody hell, the bimbo has got a Porsche,' Janice said.

He steered back to the road and speeded up.

'What the fucking hell are you doing? Stop the car,' Janice yelled.

'I recognize that Porsche and the guy about to get in it. It's Mike Stanford,' he explained.

Janice looked back. 'Pull over, so we can watch.'

'I can't, there are ditches either side of the road, but there's an opening ahead I'll turn in there.' He steered the car into a gravel entranceway barred by a gate, which led to fields of corn.

Looking back, the plot of *The Nearest FarAway Place* was in view. They could not see the bungalow, which was protected by a high hedge, but the exit was visible along the straight stretch of road.

'The Porsche is leaving. Mike must have dropped Susan off, now's our chance,' Janice said.

'Don't be so hasty. Let's wait a few minutes. Make sure he doesn't come back,' Paul said.

* * *

Before she took her coat off, Susan checked the answer phone in case Carl had called. There had been ten calls but each message was empty. Surely it must be Carl for somebody to be that persistent. Then why had he not left a message or rung Mike?

She turned off the auto-answering and the phone rang immediately – she grabbed the receiver.

'Carl is that you?' Susan asked excitedly.

'It's Lisa, Susan. Can I have a quick word with Mike?'

'Is it about Carl?'

'No,' Lisa lied.

'You've just missed him. He didn't stop. No disrespect, but I'd had enough of his *don't build up your hopes* preaching, so I didn't invite him in.'

'Did the sermon work?'

'No. I'm so excited I don't know what to do with myself.'

'Then you had better sit down Susan, I have some news for you.'

'What's happened? Something to do with Carl?' Susan asked, now in a frenzy.

'I've had a call from Carl,' Lisa said and paused to let the statement sink in.

Susan swallowed and prayed for good news.

'He's on his way to the bungalow. He thinks he is meeting Mike, so take it easy; it's going to be a shock for you both.'

'Oh Lisa, I wish Mike was still here. I think my heart is going to burst out of my body. When will Carl arrive?'

'He should be leaving his flat about now, so it will take him about forty-five minutes to get to you.'

'What will I say? What should I do?'

'After all this time and what we discussed yesterday, you should be well prepared. Just don't rush into things and don't assume that you can simply turn the clock back eleven years. People change, Carl thinks you are dead and goodness knows how he has been affected by the events of the last few months. Treat the meeting like a first date. Be polite, considerate - almost formal; above all don't try to rush into his arms. You won't be ready for that.'

'I know what we said, it's ... well ... I ...' and Susan started to cry, with happiness.

* * *

Carl used to like driving fast. In recent years, he had not felt the need to get the most out of a car. He treated his previous BMW with care and attention, mainly because he valued getting it from A to B, speed was not important – reliability was. But times had changed. He did not have a death wish, but his outlook on life was now quite different. He had little to look forward to, so indulging himself in a carefree demonstration of how well his new car handled, was exhilarating and a rare treat. The roads from Maldon to Bradwell were twisting and challenging, and fortunately today lacking traffic, so he felt good as he skilfully went through the gears and balanced the car on the edge of adhesion through the bends.

He was not driving to his limits - twenty percent of his concentration was devoted to analysing why he was driving to Bradwell. Was it only three months ago that he had travelled the same route with Natasha? It seemed an eternity. He remembered the Cricketers pub, a Scottish landlord – Josh wasn't it? A road to Hockley though, he'd missed that; by then he'd probably been too focused on getting to St. Peter's Chapel to relive his happiest day. What was Mike doing at a bungalow in the middle of nowhere? Was there a connection with Sarah? Had there been a significant message in her suicide note after all? There had always been the mystery of what had happened to her inheritance money. Perhaps she had bought a bungalow? If that were true, why would Mike, just back from America, suddenly know about it and be waiting for him to arrive there? None of it made any sense. Then again, not much had since he left MicaCom. There was sure to be a rational explanation, the sooner he got there, the sooner he would understand. He diverted his surplus twenty percent of concentration to his driving, pressed harder on the accelerator pedal and focused on the road ahead.

* * *

Susan had spent the last ten minutes preening herself for Carl's arrival. She had freshened her face, slipped out of Lisa's slightly oversized clothes and donned her own grey slacks and pale lilac blouse.

She heard a noise outside and dashed to the window as a white car pulled into the crescent shaped driveway. At first, she thought it was driving through, and then it stopped at the exit back to the road. It could not be Carl, it was too soon; besides, the car had entered from the dead-end direction of the marshes and there were two occupants. Perhaps it was only someone asking directions. She did not want company now just when her whole life was about to change.

She went to the front door and watched as a man and woman got out of the car. Susan noticed a look of excitement on the woman's face, while the man hung back and leaned into the back of the car to retrieve something.

'Susan Fellgate, once Sarah Zurek?' asked the woman.

Susan's immediate thought was that some reporters had discovered her real identity. The only people that knew the truth were the Stanfords, and her sister and mother. Surely they had not been indiscreet. She decided to lie.

'You must have the wrong place,' Susan said, 'I'm sorry, I don't know either of those names.' The man now stood behind the woman carrying a strong carrier bag, which was apparently straining with the weight of its contents.

'We've come with a message from Carl Denham. Can we come in?' Janice said politely.

It could still be a trick thought Susan. She would have to stall a bit longer. 'Nor a Carl Denham,' she said.

Now Janice looked doubtful and cast a glance to Paul for his verbal or physical support. She scowled at him when he just shrugged his shoulders helplessly.

Janice turned back, 'I know you are Sarah Zurek, I recognize you from the photographs; and perhaps this will jog your memory.' Janice slipped her hand into the tiny pocket of the skirt she wore and showed the letter Susan had left at Carl's flat.

Susan wanted to query the origin of the photographs but noticed the flimsy see-through gloves that Janice wore. Panic gripped her. 'What's happened to Carl? Where is he?'

Janice just grinned inanely.

'You had better come in,' Susan said nervously and held the door open for them to enter. Her fear was heightened as the man looked defensively over his shoulder as he came through the door. He was wearing the same type of gloves. 'Are you from the police?' she asked.

Paul and Janice were looking around the lounge, which stretched from the front to the rear of the bungalow.

'Well?' Susan said, looking from the man to the woman.

Ignoring her Janice said, 'That should do,' as she walked to the dining room table and chairs that were positioned under a rear window. She picked up one of the wooden chairs and carried it to the centre of the room.

'What the hell are you doing?' Susan yelled.

Janice pointed to the chair. 'Just sit down and you won't be hurt - yet.'

Susan caught the movement of the man as he darted behind her and was about to scream when he planted his left hand over her mouth and grabbed her hair with the right. She struggled, flailing her arms and pumping her elbows as her opponent swiftly dragged her towards the chair.

Janice dived towards the carrier bag that Paul had dropped to the floor, and took out lengths of rope.

Paul squeezed harder over Susan's mouth distorting her face and moved his right hand to compress her windpipe. 'If you scream or struggle I'll break your neck,' he threatened.

As Susan relaxed, Paul hauled her into the chair and Janice threaded the rope through the upright slats. Gasping for air Susan's arms dropped limply to the side and Janice yanked the left and then the right, and wound the rope tightly around Susan's wrists, binding them in a knot to the chair back.

'Hurry up,' Paul urged.

With a second piece a rope, Janice bound Susan's ankles after wedging each one behind a chair leg.

'OK,' Janice said, and Paul slowly released his grips.

Susan's head slumped forward choking for air. Spittle seeped from her mouth into her lap; then she passed out.

* * *

Mike sat very still with his heart pounding, replaying in his mind the accident that had just happened.

He had been approaching a sharp right-hand bend and was about to brake and change down into second gear when he saw the black BMW approaching. It was going fast, very fast, but in-control and on the correct side of the road. Then as he saw the BMW in his rear-view mirror two thoughts struck him one immediately after the other. The first was that it was Carl driving the car, the second that he suddenly knew the white Fiesta. In that momentary lapse in attention the necessity to operate foot pedals had completely escaped him. Instead, sub-consciously he had turned the wheel slightly left, as the lesser of two evils. Attempting to take the bend would have surely slammed the car into the trees that bordered the outer apex. The less damaging alternative had merely launched the Porsche over a grassy knoll and glanced a tree on the driver's side before sliding to a halt in a gravel driveway. He was shaken, but not hurt - other than in pride, but he knew that the car would need an expensive rear wing, some panel bashing, and maybe something else – it would not start.

He had clearly recognized Carl's face, despite the contradictory evidence of the car he was driving. Then it struck him that of course he didn't know what car Carl currently had - Susan had told him that Carl's ageing red BMW has been blown up. Seeing Carl had triggered the recent image when leaving Susan's of two people in a white Fiesta – with distinctive red and blue side stripes. It had been regularly parked at the MicaCom office since it belonged to Paul Westdene - Janice's current partner and the employee that he had arranged to get sacked for Carl. Why were they visiting Susan? Suddenly the horror of the situation hit him - he had to get to a phone. He cursed that he had not unearthed his mobile phone since his return from America, but there was a house at the end of the driveway. He unbuckled his seat belt, scrambled out of the car – shit, the door was stiff he must have damaged that too - and began running to the house.

* * *

Carl slowed down as he reached the outskirts of Bradwell. He'd had his speed fix and his thoughts had returned to the reason for his visit. Why *is* Mike in Bradwell? It was just too much of a coincidence after his visit here three months ago.

He felt his jacket pocket. Yes, he did have his mobile phone with him. Lisa said she was going to ring Mike; he could have saved himself some of the worrying time by getting Mike's number and ringing him direct. Still, he was driving down the Hockley road now; he would be there soon.

He checked his odometer; almost a mile since he had taken the turning, but it looked as though there was a building coming up on the left.

He stopped the car just before the entrance; there were no more buildings he could see in the distance, so this must be the place. Yet, there was a white Ford facing the road and blocking the driveway - no sign of Mike's Porsche. And then he saw the wooden sign; he had found *The Nearest FarAway Place*.

* * *

It took a few minutes for Susan to recover and raise her head. A similar wooden chair was in front of her, seating Janice with her legs apart and skirt hitched up to her thighs. Janice's gloveless left hand was buried between her legs making small movements; her right hand held a long bladed kitchen knife with a black handle. She was panting lightly with glazed eyes transfixed on Susan.

Susan sensed movement behind her, but the pain in her throat prevented her turning her head.

Paul said to Janice, 'You're sick. Do you know that?'

Susan guessed it would be pointless but chose the distraction as the moment to gather her strength and yell for help. She took a deep breath and got as far as the 'H' before Janice leapt from the chair and struck her across the face with her masturbation hand.

'Don't you dare interrupt my pleasure, you bitch,' Janice growled and as Susan's head flopped back to its forward position, Janice brandished the knife under Susan's chin. 'Do that again and I'll give you a matching scar on the other cheek.'

Susan whimpered and still with her head down managed to say, 'Where's Carl? What do you want?'

Janice used the blunt edge of the knife to raise Susan's head, so that their faces were just a few inches apart.

'I want you to die, just like Alex intended years ago,' Janice spat.

Susan studied Janice's face, concentrating on the hair, which circled her face. 'Y – Y – Y - You're … the girl … in the photographs,' she stammered, recalling the panic of not being able to discern the features of the woman in her nightmares.

'Well, well. You're not such a bimbo after all.'

Photographs? Susan recalled Janice's earlier remark. 'Photographs. W – W - What photographs do you have of me?'

Janice sniggered. 'No. I was right the first time. You are a dim bitch after all. You don't know who I am - do you? I'm your lover's ex-wife.' Her snigger grew to a demonic cackle.

'Janice?'

'That bastard kept photos of you after we were married; I merely destroyed your images then, now I can destroy your body.'

Paul stepped out from behind Susan, 'That's enough Janice. I think we ought to stop now.' He reached for the knife and Janice slashed it viciously across the back of his hand. Blood wept from the two-inch gash that appeared beneath the glove film. Paul stared at the wound in disbelief.

'Don't fuck things up now Paul, otherwise you know you'll regret it,' Janice snapped.

Susan thought that must be the end of her imprisonment. This male accomplice would rescue the situation. With effort, she glanced up at him pleadingly.

Paul took a step backwards and took a handkerchief from his pocket and wrapped it around his hand, but said nothing.

Janice moved the pointed end of the knife to rest gently against the skin of Sarah's chin. 'Is Carl coming here?'

Susan said nothing and raised her head slightly to avoid the pricking of the knife, but Janice pressed harder and raised her eyebrows to hasten a response.

Susan thought quickly. Carl must have found out her location from Lisa. He could not have seen the letter - Janice must have taken it.

'I don't know. He doesn't know I'm here. You stole my letter,' Susan said carefully and slowly, trying to keep her head still.

Janice considered the reply. 'But Mike knows where you are, so presumably does Lisa. So if Carl has contacted either of them ...' She jerked the knife upwards and a small bead of blood rolled down the blade.

'Oh God, please don't hurt me,' Susan cried and tears rolled down her cheek. 'What are you trying to achieve?'

Janice stepped back and sat down. Susan's head slumped forward again. Paul looked away in disgust.

Janice licked the end of the knife. 'Isn't it strange, for years I wanted to destroy Carl, because I thought that was the only way that I could destroy his memory of you? Of course, my real problem was that deep down he secretly hoped he would see you again. Then he found out you were dead and the problem goes away - I can get Carl back again. Now his long lost fucking bimbo comes back from the dead to spoil the party. Luckily Carl doesn't know that, so if the bimbo dies again, Janice and Carl can live happily ever after.'

'What about *me*? You said you wanted Carl dead so that *we* could have a future together,' Paul exclaimed.

'Good God, the deaf and dumb boy has spoken. Didn't you hear what I said? My problem is about to die. Carl will be free again, so you become surplus to requirements.'

Susan raised her head and a trickle of blood rolled slowly from her chin and dripped onto her grey slacks. 'Your plan won't work. Other people know I am alive. My mother, sister, Mike, Lisa ...'

Janice laughed. 'Irrelevant and soon they will know you are dead. I can see the newspaper headline now. Mystery woman tortured to death in remote part of Essex.'

'Carl will be here any minute,' Susan said desperately.

Janice laughed again. 'Oh, so now he *is* coming? To rescue his maiden in distress? Shall I wait so that he can witness the death of his bimbo or shall we give him a nice surprise? The trouble is I'm feeling very horny and I can't wait any longer. It's time that you began your suffering. Where shall I start? I know. That pretty face of yours is rather asymmetrical – it annoys me. I think your right cheek needs a little balancing surgery.' She stood up and took a stride forward.

Paul looked away again and noticed the front door opening.

Janice raised the knife over her left shoulder and swung it in an arc towards Susan's face.

Susan screamed like she had never screamed before.

Epilogue

Friday, December 31, 1999 – 11:50 p.m.

There was no perceptible draught but the candle flame flickered excitedly. It barely illuminated the space around Carl. He was cold, but warmer than he had been on the snow-covered walk to St. Peter's Chapel. The enclosing stone walls provided coolness in the summer but added warmth in the winter. Seated on a wooden pew in front of the altar he held the candle aloft and looked up at the crucifix high on the wall in front of him. The eerie silence and shadows, and religious symbol brought a lump to his throat. He inserted the candle in the holder on the altar and checked his watch; then he stared into the dancing flame, reflecting.

Ten minutes to a new Millennium.

He would be glad to say goodbye to the old one. He had been alive through thirty-three years of the second Millennium, but how many had he lived? One third of the years had been spent in a workaholic vacuum, seventeen in growing up - leaving just five years during which he had lived and loved. The events of the last year warranted nine minutes deliberation.

Nine minutes.

Travis Security was thriving. The new premises had long been fully operational and Don and Wendy had continued their sponsored world tour of Formula 1 racing circuits, not seeking a missing school friend, but acquiring lucrative contracts with the security conscious British-based racing teams. They had missed only one event, the Italian Grand Prix, because Don was committed to be best man at a wedding. Their lives were full of optimism, helped considerably no doubt by the fact that Wendy was pregnant again.

Eight minutes.

George Fellgate had lost his *daughter* and partner, but was nonetheless content and fully occupied counting the profits from the success of Protean V and preparing BinaryByte for a stock market listing.

Maurice Patient had just won an International award for *The Most Innovative Internet Application*. Maurice had tried to get him to come to the prize-giving ceremony in Geneva at the beginning of September, but Carl had to decline since he had been busy collecting his own prize.

Seven minutes.

Kate was seeing a teacher – in the romantic sense, her faith in the male race now fully restored. She had been making plans for a *Cambridge House of 88* reunion and subject to Kyoko getting time off from work and Caroline recovering from a mild dose of malaria, the celebration would take place at *The Nearest FarAway Place* in February.

Six minutes.

The Zureks were a family again. Marion had to sell Croftview to pay off the debts that Alex had left behind, and was now living with her mother, who was recovering, thanks in no small part to the return of her youngest daughter. Marion was working again - only at a checkout in Tesco, but was training to teach Polish at the University of Essex.

Five minutes.

He thought of Mike, who never did develop any of the commercial ideas he had brought back from America. With approaching fatherhood, Mike chose not to become involved in pioneering work that would demand his full-time attention. Instead, he went back to a previous pastime, which he had practised in the less demanding days before MicaCom – fixing up cars. Mike had re-awakened his old hobby when he decided to repair his Porsche after his accident, and now that he had capital he was not tinkering with Ford Escorts and Minis anymore, but restoring a Bentley and an old Ferrari rescued from a farmer's barn. Mike already had a buyer committed for the Bentley and had forecast, according to Lisa, that he could make enough money in the restoration business to lead a reasonably comfortable life without intruding too much on his MicaCom windfall.

Four minutes.

He still accredited the blame for the bad times to Janice, but he had not forgiven Mike for his eight-year secret and wondered if he ever would. Lisa had acted as intermediary between him and Mike, and had worked hard to bring them together. In two week's time, Lisa would be giving birth to a baby girl who was to be called Sarah. After deaths, Carl longed to honour new life, and in doing so would meet Mike for the first time in six months. Carl there and then made his only New Millennium's resolution, he would thank Mike for the warning phone call that had magically saved a precious life and initiated the destruction of an unworthy one – it could be the start of their reconciliation.

Three minutes.

Soon he would finally be able to bury the ghosts of 1999. He prayed for an unfortunate Natasha Minski and an unknown Nicholas Lester; unwilling performers in a drama now earmarked for interment. And a departed Susan Fellgate, she served her purpose well, but for too long.

Two minutes.

He cursed the killers Alex Gomulka - hopefully rotting in prison, and Janice Harding - rotting in hell.

It seemed unjustified that Paul Westdene was in prison for ridding the world of evil. When *Frère Jacques* had momentarily interrupted Janice's attack on Susan, Paul's parrying of the knife and blow to Janice's head would have been sufficient to end the matter. But Paul's subsequent frenzied stabbing of a defenceless Janice had clearly been homicide, justifiable in his opinion. Paul could have claimed self-defence and got away with it – he would have happily perjured himself and given appropriate evidence in Paul's favour. Before the police arrived, he had calmly discussed the subject with Paul, and whilst Paul felt no guilt for Janice's death, he was remorseful for the car bombing and ended up confessing to both murders.

One minute.

It was almost over. Soon he would return to *The (new) Nearest FarAway Place*. It had been an expensive operation to demolish the bloodstained, small bungalow and replace it with a larger custom designed home, now with three bedrooms. He would sleep there for the first time tonight. It had been finished just before Christmas and that afternoon the last of his wanted possessions had been transferred from Springfield. Tomorrow in his new home he would continue to procrastinate about how he might spend the rest of his working days, he still had too much living and loving to catch up with.

His watch beeped.

The third Millennium had begun.

He moved his left hand to rest against the blue woollen dress that covered the slight swelling that would become part of his future - a new Nicholas or

Natasha to replace the one cruelly taken away. He smiled when her hand rested on his and they intertwined fingers; it was the signal to leave. They stood in synchrony and he stroked her soft golden hair. He drew her closer by pulling gently on the familiar scarf around her neck. In the subdued light, he discerned a single tear of happiness roll down her cheek. He let the tear reach the edge of her mouth and then he kissed it away. Their lips lingered with the pleasure until the New Year was a minute old. This time it really was a New Beginning, with the real Sarah - Sarah Denham.

THE END

The author hopes that you have enjoyed reading *The Nearest FarAway Place*. The following pages are the opening of his next book *Panglossian* which will be published at the end of 2001.

Indeed, history is nothing more than a tableau of crimes and misfortunes.
Voltaire, L'Ingénu, Chapter 10

Prologue

I still have flashbacks and dreams about those prefatory days.

The flashbacks can arrive at any time without consideration for my safety or peace of mind. What triggers them, I cannot say. I have been crossing the road, turning a steering wheel, showering, even making love, when a slight pressure inside my head announces a flow of memories is on its way. They come as a trickle - a brief opening of a tap - and show in real-time, a few seconds of my normally inaccessible life. There is no pain and thankfully only a short lapse in concentration while I separate the past and present. I have now grown used to, and can handle, such minor debilitations.

When the manifestations of memories come in a dream, the trickle develops into an uncontrollable flood, and I am swamped with minutes or hours of personal history. When I wake, I am exhausted and emotionally confused, but I have learnt to deal with that too.

The recollections have become repetitive and unstimulating, and rarely do I glean any new fragments of information. I have wondered recently whether my perceived decline in images is real, or just my mind automatically discarding redundant material.

However, it does seem cruel and strange that my innocent past is denied me, yet the traumatic few days that led to this story have been continuously exposed in unrelenting detail.

My school and university days seem to be lost forever and most of my early working life too. Of course, the knowledge gained from distant lessons continues to be employed sub-consciously in my daily routine. It's the when, where and who that are missing, not the how and what. Time, place and person evade me. For example, I know how a petrol engine works, but not when I acquired the facts, or from where or whom. Does it really matter if Mr. Johnson (the Physics master?) taught me the principles of internal combustion in the third year of my secondary school education? Not to me - I have adjusted to the vacuum of my first twenty-five years.

Friends and family are willing and able to fill some of the gaps but I choose not to enlist their help.

Like me, perhaps your present is dominated by thoughts of the future rather than the past. I know that in making decisions I could be disadvantaged, since I cannot consult experiences of old, yet I console myself that at least I approach each new problem with a mind that is clear of earlier prejudices.

The doctors hypothesize that the earlier memories are still there - since my brain is complete and physically undamaged - so there can only be subconscious reasons why they cannot or will not be accessed. I have allowed my mind to be manipulated by hypnosis and drugs in order to satisfy the medical profession's curiosity, but each attempt has failed, and the highly-rewarded consultants have worried for me, only - cynical person that I am - until the next fee-paying appointment.

However, there will be no more appointments. Whatever the residual psychological or physiological reasons, the past no longer matters; I have a future to look forward to.

Chapter 1

FIRST FRIDAY – 3:30 p.m.

After my six-hour drive back from convalescence, it is a spur of the moment decision to visit the local library. I had borrowed a stack of books on French political history - a particular passion of mine - two weeks earlier. I haven't read them all and there is still a week remaining on the loan period, but I am passing the library so I call in. I am eager to cram my head with more knowledge of 18th century Gallic constitutional thought in the remaining two days before I go back to work, so I browse the shelves for more reading material. I am attracted to two volumes on Voltaire so I settle at a table and go through my ritual of scanning random pages to ensure that my selections are relevant to my studies. Satisfied, I head for the checkout counter and noisily place two piles of books and my library card in front of the apparently comatose middle-aged female librarian.

'Two to take out and these to return,' I say loudly, pointing to the separate heaps.

She visibly starts, and without looking up, swipes the barcode on the card with an electronic wand. The connected terminal beeps with specious satisfaction. She is about to swipe the first book when her attention moves from the display screen to me. Her look is blank and as if to mind read my observation she says, 'It's blank.'

'What's blank?' I ask innocently.

'Your library record of course,' she replies in a sleep-disturbed patronizing way. 'There's no name or address!'

'This happens often, does it?' I say, trying to echo her disdainful tone.

She chooses not to respond to my question but instead asks in the manner of a police officer accosting a suspect, 'I need to know who you are. What ID do you have with you? Passport? Driving Licence?'

'No, No,' I say with certainty and thrust my hand in my trouser back pocket searching for something with my name on it. I offer my plastic Visa card. 'How about a credit card?' I say triumphantly.

'Has it got your address on it?' my inquisitress demands.

'No, of course not; but then neither would my passport.'

That seems to stall her aggression. She looks bewildered for a moment then she bounces back. 'You'll have to come back with proof of address. You can't take these books out.'

'Then presumably as I don't exist, I can't return these books to you either?' I say argumentatively, placing my hand on the larger pile.

She taps a few keys on her keyboard, harder than seems necessary. She regards the screen, me, the books and then the screen again.

'You don't...' she begins and then realizing she is about to donate some books to me, she snatches them away. Reflexively I withdraw my hand as though snapped at by a dog, although bitch would have been a better analogy.

'Aren't you going to log them back in again?'

'I can't since they aren't booked out to you.'

It is now my turn to be officious. 'I'll need a receipt for them.'

The receipt dilemma leads to the summoning of the chief librarian - a large, balding, ruddy faced, casually dressed gentleman who I assess could be the prototypal pub landlord. His nature is more forgiving and, courtesy of his customer relations training, he apologetically resolves the quandary in my favour - the scapegoat emerging temporarily as the defenceless, inanimate computer system without regard to its human programming or operation. I discern though, from the accusatory glance from male to female librarian, that the matter will receive further scrutiny once I have departed.

Unfazed by the time-wasting experience in the library I leave the building in high spirits. Suddenly the Voltairean adjective I had spied earlier, Panglossian - pertaining to a person who is optimistic regardless of the circumstances - appears unannounced in my head; like an omen. I consider its predictive nature and dismiss it. Despite my mysterious disappearance from the library records - I had no pessimism. Indeed, I believe I have much to look forward to: my scar is almost healed; I have two days of leisure ahead - one of which will be spent with Julie; and on Monday I return to a job that I enjoy and which has great prospects.